The Londoners

Margaret Pemberton

CORGI BOOKS

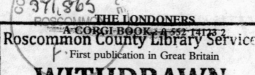

THE LONDONERS
A CORGI BOOK : 0 552 14123 2

First publication in Great Britain

PRINTING HISTORY
Corgi edition published 1995

Copyright © Margaret Pemberton 1995

Set in 10/11pt Monotype Plantin by Kestrel Data, Exeter

Corgi Books are published by Transworld Publishers Ltd,
61–63 Uxbridge Road, Ealing, London W5 5SA,
in Australia by Transworld Publishers (Australia) Pty Ltd,
15–25 Helles Avenue, Moorebank, NSW 2170,
and in New Zealand by Transworld Publishers (NZ) Ltd,
3 William Pickering Drive, Albany, Auckland.

Reproduced, printed and bound in Great Britain by
Cox & Wyman Ltd, Reading, Berks.

For my daughter, Rebecca May.
A South London girl.

Acknowledgements

I would like to thank Carol Smith, my agent and friend, for persuading me that the time had come to write about my own patch of south-east London.

I would also like to thank my editor, Diane Pearson, for all her unstinting help, support and expertise.

And last, but by no means least, I would like to thank the big-hearted family I married into so many years ago. Where *The Londoners* is concerned, they were truly inspirational.

Chapter One

July 1933

'Freedom!' Kate Voigt said exultantly, raising her face to the hot afternoon sun. 'Doesn't it feel wonderful?'

Carrie Jennings swung an empty, much-battered school-satchel round and round in a huge arc. 'It feels *blissful*,' she agreed in deep contentment, tempted to let go of the satchel and send it spinning into the stratosphere. 'No more boring old uniform, no more tedious lessons!'

Kate grinned. 'There may be no more lessons for you, but there's going to be lots more lessons for me. The principal at the secretarial school said that shorthand was almost as difficult as algebra.'

'Then why study it?' Carrie asked sensibly, shuddering at the memory of past maths lessons and deeply grateful that she would never have to sit through another one. 'Why don't you tell your dad you don't want to go to secretarial school? Why don't you tell him you want to work down the market with me?'

'Because I don't,' Kate said with the candour that was an honourable rule between them. 'I don't have the voice for it and besides, I couldn't stand the cold in winter. Do you remember your mum last December? She had so many layers of clothing on her that when she came home it took her an hour to struggle out of them and she was still half-perished.'

'There's the summer though,' Carrie said philosophically as they neared the end of the street in which Blackheath & Kidbrooke School was situated and stepped out on to the Heath. 'I'd much rather be down the market in summer than stuck in a stuffy office banging away on a typewriter.'

It was summer now and as Kate looked across the glory of the gorse-covered Heath towards the distant spire of All Saints' Church and the higgledy-piggledy grey and red roofs of Blackheath Village she couldn't help but agree that Carrie had a point. It was a very minor point though. Much as she enjoyed occasional Saturday work helping Carrie on her father's market stall, she didn't have the market in her blood and bones as Carrie did.

She knew, also, that the real work wasn't weighing out fruit and vegetables and exchanging light-hearted banter with customers. It was trawling up to Covent Garden before dawn to buy in produce and ferrying it back down the Old Kent Road to Lewisham Market by horse and cart hours before more conventional workers were even considering getting out of their beds. The very thought made her shudder in exactly the same way Carrie had shuddered at the memory of maths lessons.

'Even if I wanted to work in the market, Dad wouldn't let me,' she said truthfully as they walked over springy, coarse grass towards the south-west corner of the Heath. 'He still isn't happy about me doing Saturday work there and if it wasn't that I was working for your dad he wouldn't allow it at all.'

'That's 'cos he's a teacher,' Carrie said, unconcerned. 'All teachers think market trading common.'

A slight frown creased Kate's forehead. It was true that her father didn't have an overly high opinion of market trading as a profession, but he certainly didn't think Carrie's family common and she didn't want Carrie thinking that he did.

'My dad has a very high opinion of your family,' she said firmly. 'He was ever so pleased when your dad joined the pub's cricket team. He says he's the best bowler they've ever had.'

Carrie grinned. 'It comes of years of practice lobbing oranges and grapefruits. Are you going on the pub outing to Folkestone? It'll be fun. Especially if

10

the non-cricketers get up a side to play the cricket team on the beach like they did last year.'

'And especially if your gran takes her whippet with her again,' Kate said, giggling. 'He caught more balls than Dad did.'

They skirted an old gravel pit thick with gorse and Carrie said, 'Talking of Gran, why don't you celebrate school being finally over by staying for tea today? It'll be bean and barley soup,' she added temptingly. 'And fish.'

'I can't, Carrie. I've Dad's dinner to get ready.' There was genuine regret in her voice. Carrie's Jewish grandmother was an absolute whizz in the kitchen and the mere thought of her homemade soup was mouthwatering.

'He won't be home for another couple of hours,' Carrie persisted, 'You know he never leaves school till after six. You can eat with us and still be home in time to put his dinner on the table.'

The temptation was too great to resist and Kate no longer tried. 'I'll have to be home by six, though,' she warned as they crossed the road flanking the Heath, catching a distant glimpse of the Thames as they did.

'That's OK,' Carrie said easily. 'It'll give Gran plenty of time to find out what's happening in your life and to give an unasked opinion of it.'

Giggling, they turned, still arm in arm, into the short road leading into Magnolia Square. The spacious Square, named after the magnolia trees that grew in several of its gardens, had seen better days but its large Edwardian houses still retained an air of genteel dignity, a dignity that was enhanced by St Mark's Church, the small, eighteenth-century church the Square had been built around.

The short road leading into the Square from the Heath was Magnolia Terrace; the road leading out of it, Magnolia Hill. Lined with terrace houses it curved steeply down towards Lewisham and its busy High

Street, ensuring that the southern, less smart half of the Square was known as 'the Lewisham half' while the other half, with St Mark's Vicarage lording it on the north-east corner, was known more grandly as 'the Heath half'.

Kate and her widowed father lived on the west-hand side of 'the Heath half' and the Jennings family lived on the southern side of 'the Lewisham half' in a house abutting the west hand corner with Magnolia Hill.

As they walked towards it they walked past the bottom of Kate's garden and her elderly next-door-neighbour said to her, pausing in her task of trimming her hedge, 'Good afternoon, Katherine.'

'Good afternoon, Miss Godfrey,' Kate responded guardedly. Miss Godfrey, though now long retired, had been headmistress of their primary school and, in Kate's and Carrie's opinion, took far too much of an interest in their lives.

'Arternoon, Miss,' Carrie said with provocative carelessness.

Miss Godfrey paused in her task. 'The word is *after*-noon, Caroline. Sloppy speech leads to sloppy thinking.'

Carrie bridled. 'Not dahn the market it don't,' she said, allowing her speech to slip even further. 'And dahn the market any other kind o' speech 'ud be a right 'andicap.'

Miss Godfrey clicked her tongue in annoyance. Ever since she had been a little girl Carrie Jennings had enjoyed having the last word and it was a trait adolescence hadn't improved.

'The ability to speak good English is a great asset in life, Caroline,' she said reprovingly. 'And it is something we can all attain. When Katherine's father first found himself in England he couldn't speak a word of English. Now his English is perfect.'

She made it sound as if Kate's father were one of her ex-pupils and Kate suppressed a spurt of indignation, saying stiffly, 'There's no need to skirt the issue of how

Dad came to be resident in England. Everyone knows he was a prisoner-of-war. And his English isn't perfect. He speaks it with a German accent.'

'And my Dad speaks it with a Cockney accent,' Carrie added cheekily.

Miss Godfrey ignored her. 'I was not skirting the issue of how your father came to be resident in this country, Katherine,' she said, a slightly troubled expression entering her eyes. 'I was bearing in mind the revulsion the new German Chancellor's Nazi policies have aroused and the consequent tide of British ill-feeling against Germany and was merely being tactful.'

Kate stared at her, bewildered. 'I'm sorry, Miss Godfrey. I don't understand the connection. My father isn't a sympathizer of Mr Hitler. He never even visits Germany . . .'

Carrie, sensing that Kate and Miss Godfrey were on the verge of a discussion that would be as long as it would be tedious, tugged her arm, saying impatiently, 'Come on, Kate. If we don't get a move on you won't have time to stay to tea.'

Miss Godfrey, too, had no desire to continue the discussion. Through her own carelessness it had veered on to a subject too delicate to be pursued in the street, as if of no more importance than the latest Test Match score or the weather.

'We'll talk further another time, Katherine,' she said, for once grateful to Carrie for having interrupted a conversation that was nothing to do with her. 'Goodbye, Caroline. Give my regards to your mother.'

As Kate and Carrie walked away from her she stood for a long moment, her shears motionless over her privet, watching them. Even from the rear they made a handsomely distinctive pair. Both of them were tall and slender, though there was an underlying robustness about Carrie that indicated it was a slenderness she would soon outgrow. Where Carrie's untidy dark hair was held away from her face by combs, Kate's pale-gold hair was constrained in a single, thick, waist-length plait. It was a neat, sensible hairstyle and on any other girl Miss Godfrey would have approved of it. She didn't. however, approve of it on Kate. In her opinion, it made Kate look far too Teutonic.

Her frown deepened. Carl Voigt taught German at a local boys' Grammar School and was highly intelligent. Surely he was aware that in the present political climate it wasn't sensible to draw attention to his daughter's ancestry? Why, only that morning the *Daily Telegraph* had carried the most appalling report of the way Jews were being hounded in Germany, rounded up and sent to concentration camps on charges so flimsy they would be laughed out of any civilized court of law.

With a heavy sigh she once more began to clip her hedge. What with godlessness raging in a country that had been the cradle of Protestantism, anarchy spreading like a forest fire throughout Spain and Mussolini behaving like a madman in Italy, the world was becoming a very uncertain place. Almost as uncertain as it had been in the spring of 1914. Remembering how, when war had broken out in the summer of that year, many German traders in London had had their shop windows smashed by Kaiser-hating neighbours who had once been their friends and customers, Miss Godfrey resolved to have a tactful word with Carl Voigt. If he was blind to the ugliness inherent in human nature when arrant jingoism was let loose, she wasn't. And to be warned was to be forearmed.

'Silly old bat,' Carrie said dismissively the minute they were out of Miss Godfrey's hearing. 'Why does she make such a song and dance over everything? Do you think now I've left school Mum will let me have my hair permed and would you cut it for me and come with me to the hairdressers when I go?'

'I would, but not willingly,' Kate said, her mind still on Miss Godfrey's peculiar remarks, 'What if it makes your hair frizzy? Even worse, what if it falls out?'

Carrie giggled, 'Or turns my hair green? That would be a laugh, wouldn't it. Mum would have ten fits.'

All the houses in the Square had a short flight of broad, shallow stone steps leading up to their front doors and in the summer many residents sat out on them in order to enjoy the sun and to survey the comings and goings of their neighbours. As a consequence, Kate's and Carrie's conversation was punctuated every few yards by the necessity of returning greetings and answering questions about their general welfare.

'I'm very well thank you, Mr Nibbs,' Kate called out now in answer to a middle-aged, stocky man's enquiry. 'And you're right. Today was my last day at Blackheath & Kidbrooke. I'm starting secretarial school in September.'

Mr Nibbs, proprietor of Nibbs High Class Fruit and Vegetables, Blackheath Village, and enjoying his weekly half-closing day, grinned. 'When I want a secretary then I'll know where to come,' he said jovially.

As they continued to walk towards the bottom end of the Square, Carrie said in high amusement, 'You note he didn't speak to me? He regards my Dad as his arch enemy. Not surprising when you consider the amount of trade Dad manages to take away from him. Now about my hair. Do you think if . . .'

'You goin' to babysit for me tonight, Carrie?' A buxom young woman called as she sat shelling peas on the top step of a house on the Square's southern side, a house far shabbier than any of the previous houses. 'Ted's in the darts championship an' he wants me there to cheer 'im on.'

'An wot if I said I wasn't?' Carrie shouted back in like manner. 'Would it make any difference?'

Carrie's elder sister grinned, 'Not an 'a'porth. I'll see you seven, sharp.'

'Bloomin' cheek,' Carrie said crossly as they continued on their way. 'I hate babysitting for Mavis. She never has Billy in bed. When I babysat last Wednesday she hadn't even fed him.'

Kate, who had no family in the world apart from her father and was deeply envious of Carrie's warm-hearted, if slip-shod, extended family, said placatingly, 'I bet she left you money for fish and chips though.'

With bad grace Carrie admitted that Mavis had, indeed, left money for fish and chips and money for a bottle of ginger beer also.

'It's still a flippin' liberty,' she said as they turned in through the next gateway. 'Why should I be the one to go tramping down to the fish shop?'

'Why complain?' There was mischief in Kate's black-lashed blue eyes. 'It gives you a chance to look over the local talent, doesn't it?'

'If you mean the gang that hangs around the chippie you've got to be joking,' Carrie said without too much sincerity. 'Danny Collins was there last Wednesday, flaunting off his new army uniform. If that's the kind of reject the army are taking God help us if there's ever another war. We'll stand no chance!'

Her momentary flare of bad humour vanquished, she giggled as she opened a front door almost bare of paint. 'The Robson boys were there as well, full of how they're going to follow in Danny's footsteps only to hear them, they're going to be Marines!'

Jack and Jerry Robsons' widowed father, Charlie, was the acknowledged local villain and Kate said dryly, 'It'll be better than them following in their father's footsteps and ending up in prison!'

As Carrie hooted in laughter her gran called out from the kitchen, 'Carrie? Is that you already? Who do you have with you? Half the street?'

'No, Gran,' Carrie said, throwing her hated and now defunct school blazer over the first chair she came to. 'Only Kate. She's staying for tea.'

Leah Singer came barrelling out into the narrow hallway, a capacious apron tied around her ample waist, her blouse sleeves pushed high above her elbows, an uncommonly plump whippet at her heels. 'Kate! It's a *brocheh* to see you! How are you?'

'I'm fine thank you, Mrs Singer,' Kate said, sidestepping the dog and shrugging her arms out of her blazer and looking in vain for somewhere to hang it.

Carrie relieved her of the trouble by taking it from her and flinging it over a nearby clothes-horse full of airing ironing.

'Then come into the kitchen and get some good food inside you,' Leah said, beaming. 'I've got a *bissel* the best fried plaice you've ever tasted. Don't stand there like a *nebbish*, Carrie. Wash your hands and sit down at the table.'

They followed her back into the kitchen and Kate felt the rosy glow of well-being that always suffused her whenever she entered the large room that, thanks to Leah Singer's industry, was the heart of the Jennings' home. Exotic packets of dried foodstuffs crammed the open shelves beside the stone sink. A large smoked sausage hung enticingly from a hook in the ceiling. On the baking board covering the boiler was a pile of still oven-warm bagels with rich golden-brown crusts and on the kitchen-range the contents of a frying-pan sizzled, while beside it a pan of soup simmered, filling the room with a mouth-watering aroma.

'So, you're big girls now?' Leah asked rhetorically as she began ladling the soup into bowls and they washed their hands with hard pink soap. 'No more school? No more homework?'

'Kate will probably still have homework,' Carrie said, drying her hands on an off-cut of towelling hooked under the sink. 'She's going to secretarial school in September.'

Leah handed her the soup bowl and drew in an admiring breath. 'Secretarial school! That's what you should be doing Carrie, my girl. Better sitting in a fine office than shouting and touting like a fishwife in Lewisham High Street.'

'I'm like my dad,' Carrie said equably as she sat down at a deal table scrubbed almost white, 'I like shouting and touting.'

Leah, never reticent about voicing her disappointment in either Carrie's father's non-Jewishness or his occupation, merely clicked her tongue in exasperation much as Miss Godfrey had done only a little while earlier.

'You could do so much better for yourself, *bubbelah*,' she said, following Kate to the table and sitting down next to her. 'Typing, sewing, hairdressing. Anything but the market.'

'I don't have the patience to learn to type,' Carrie said truthfully, 'and besides, even if I did, nothing I ever typed would be spelt right. As for sewing and hairdressing, I'm a *klutz* in both departments, which is why Kate's going to come round at the weekend to cut my hair so that I can have it permed.'

Her announcement had the desired effect. The subject of her going to work in the market was immediately forgotten as Leah remonstrated long and loud on the insanity of putting chemicals onto perfectly healthy, God-given straight hair.

Conversations between Leah and Carrie were always lovingly volatile and Kate let the ensuing argument wash over her giving Bonzo, the whippet, an occasional pat as he nuzzled against her legs, hopeful of a tit-bit.

As Carrie protested that it was only sense to improve on nature whenever possible and Leah declared that if Carrie had been meant to have curly hair, she would have been born with curly hair, Kate thought back to her conversation with Miss Godfrey. It really had been most peculiar, not least because of the intensity of Miss Godfrey's manner. It had been almost as if she had been afraid of something, something she couldn't quite bring herself to put into words.

'. . . and then the next thing you'll be doing is peroxiding it like Gloria Swansong,' Leah was saying as she stacked the empty soup bowls and carried them across to the sink.

'It's Swanson, Gran. Not Swansong,' Carrie said with a giggle, adding teasingly, 'it's a good idea though. What do you think, Kate? Should I peroxide it before I have it permed, or after?'

Kate looked at Carrie's mane of almost blue-black hair and said in amusement, 'I doubt there's enough peroxide in the world to lift your hair to blonde.'

'We might be able to get it to go red, though,' Carrie said, enjoying herself hugely. 'Do you think it would make me look like Maureen O'Sullivan in *A Connecticut Yankee*? All wild and untameable?'

Leah snorted in disgust. 'A *nebbish* is what you would look,' she said, putting plates of fried plaice in front of them. 'Better you go bald than go red!'

Carrie shrieked in horror and Kate laughed, slipping Bonzo a surreptitious piece of fish.

Leah sat down again and this time it was her turn to do the teasing, 'And bald is what you'll go if you work down the market,' she said, giving Kate a wink Carrie didn't see. 'For why do you think all those market women wear headscarves, *bubbelah*? It's because all that fresh air makes them bald, that's for why.'

Kate and Carrie shouted in laughter and the laughter continued as the subject of home-perming and baldness gave way to a discussion as to whether Bonzo should be allowed on the Folkestone trip and, if he were, if he should go as an official member of the pub cricket team.

At last Kate said regretfully, 'It's nearly six. I have to go. Thank you for a marvellous tea, Mrs Singer.'

'I have to go as well, Gran,' Carrie said, pushing her chair away from the table. 'I'm babysitting for Mavis and I want to get round there early enough to make sure she's bathed Billy and fed him.'

As Kate followed Carrie out of the kitchen and down the hall towards the front door she picked her blazer up off the cluttered clothes-horse and said, 'Do you want me to call for you tomorrow at the usual time or are you going up to Covent Garden with your mum and dad?'

Carrie gave an exaggerated shudder. 'After a late night babysitting for Mavis? You must be joking! Eight o'clock will be quite early enough for me tomorrow, thank you very much.'

They stepped out into Magnolia Square and looked towards Mavis's top step. It was empty.

'Which could mean she's already getting Billy ready for bed,' Kate suggested optimistically.

'Or that she's resting with a cup of tea and a ciggie after shelling the peas,' Carrie said darkly. 'Honestly, how Ted puts up with her I don't know. Dad says the Pope should make him a saint.'

Albert Jennings's high opinion of his son-in-law was well-known to Kate. Mavis had always been what Albert described as 'a bit of a handful' and he had been vastly relieved when Mavis had married a level-headed, even-tempered young man who brought home an enviable pay-packet as a docker.

'See you tomorrow then,' Kate said to Carrie as they reached Mavis's front gate.

Carrie nodded, 'Dad says there's a glut of cherries at the moment so don't bother with breakfast, we'll be able to stuff ourselves all day.'

When they had been much younger, permission to help themselves to the produce had been one of the ways Albert Jennings had tempted them into spending long Saturdays helping out on the stall and even though he now gave them handsome wages for the hours they worked, it was a perk that still continued.

As Carrie walked up the Lomaxs' front path Kate hooked a thumb under the collar of her blazer and swung it over her shoulder. She liked the Square at this time of an evening. It possessed a mellow, friendly air. Men were coming home from work, the greater proportion of them walking into the Square from Magnolia Hill and the general direction of the river and the docks; children were making the most of the precious interim between teatime and bedtime, gathering around lampposts for games of chequers or hopscotch or long-rope skipping; women who had the leisure to do so, like Miss Godfrey, were trimming hedges and dead-heading flowers.

From the garden of the house tucked into the south-west corner of the Square a frail, apparently disembodied voice said pleasantly, 'Isn't it a lovely evening? The vibrations are perfect for contacting the dear departed.'

Kate stopped walking and faced a head-high bush of frilled white roses. 'It's a lovely evening, Miss Helliwell,' she agreed as two heavy trusses of blossom were parted by a pair of rheumatically afflicted, blue-veined hands.

Miss Emily Helliwell, Palm-Reader and Clairvoyant, beamed at her. 'I've been in touch with Chopin all afternoon. Such a dear, dear man and so sad there has never been a rose named after him. Something golden, I think, would be very suitable. A cross between *Star of Persia* and *Gloire de Dijon* perhaps?'

Well used to Miss Helliwell's eccentricities Kate replied gravely that she thought a rose on the lines of *Gloire de Dijon* would suit Chopin very well.

Miss Helliwell's cat, an enormous creature even more well fed than Bonzo, darted out of the garden and began to brush himself sinuously against her legs. Kate bent down and scratched him gently beneath the chin and Miss Helliwell said, 'I'm afraid Faust has been very naughty today. He will chase birds and it does so upset my sister.'

Kate made a murmur of sympathy. Miss Esther Helliwell was bedridden and her great pleasure in life was to look out at the garden and its masses of roses.

'Are you going to come in and have a few words with her?' Miss Helliwell asked, her bright-eyed, wrinkled face hopeful. 'Mr Nibbs called in this afternoon but I'm sure another visitor would be very welcome. I can make a pot of tea and . . .'

'I'm sorry, Miss Helliwell, I can't,' Kate said

apologetically. 'I'll call in tomorrow, on my way home from the market.'

'Evening, ladies,' Daniel Collins senior said, striding towards them wearing an oil-spattered boiler-suit, a newspaper tucked beneath his arm. 'Have you read what that bugger Hitler's doing now? Only rounding up everyone he doesn't like and flinging them into camps. Very odd race of people, the Germans. No sense of moderation.'

'Hitler isn't German, Mr Collins,' Kate said, her voice sounding a little odd even to herself. 'He's Austrian.'

'Whatever he is, he's a blighter,' Mr Collins said cheerfully. 'Don't you think it's about time you had those roses lopped down a bit, Miss Helliwell? They're beginning to look like a perishin' jungle.'

As Miss Helliwell protested strongly at the very idea of having her roses tampered with Kate walked away from them, continuing on her way home, wondering why everyone had Hitler on the brain.

'First it was Miss Godfrey,' she said to her father an hour later as she put a plate of sausage and mash on the table in front of him, 'and then it was Mr Collins.'

Carl Voigt smiled slightly and reached for a bottle of brown sauce. 'It's only to be expected,' he said in a voice betraying only the merest hint of an accent. 'Germany hasn't been out of the news all month. First it was the news that German citizenship had been declared conditional on Nazi membership and then there was the decree that the importing of banned books would be punishable by death. With Hitler instigating the passing into law of such obscenities, of course people are talking about him.'

Kate sat down opposite him and sipped at a mug of tea. 'It wasn't Hitler being mentioned, it was the *way* he was mentioned, or at least the way Miss Godfrey mentioned him, that was odd.' She hesitated and then said, troubled, 'She made it sound as if people would assume, because you're German, that you're an admirer of what is now going on in Germany.'

Carl Voigt's eyebrows rose slightly over the top of his rimless spectacles. 'Did she?' he queried mildly. 'Were those her exact words?'

'Not exactly,' Kate admitted, adding defensively, 'but that was definitely her implication.'

Carl speared the end of a crisply fried sausage. 'I think you misconstrued whatever it was she said to you,' he said at last, 'and I also think you're being over-sensitive, *Liebling*. No-one who knows me would ever, in a million years, imagine I was an admirer of the present German government.'

The idea was so preposterous that Kate's sensation of uneasiness immediately began to ebb. 'I know that,' she said with a grin, 'but all the same, her manner *was* odd.'

'If it will make you any happier I'll talk to her about it,' Carl said, keeping his own suspicions as to what Miss Godfrey had been trying to convey to Kate, to himself. There was no sense in anticipating unpleasantness, especially when it was unpleasantness that couldn't possibly affect his English-born daughter.

He speared the last piece of sausage with his fork and said appreciatively, 'That was a wonderful dinner, *Liebling*.'

She rose to her feet and picked up his plate, carrying it across to the sink. 'Are you going to The Swan this evening?' she asked, her thoughts no longer on her puzzling conversation with Miss Godfrey, but on the pub's annual outing to Folkestone which her father always helped to arrange.

He nodded. 'Yes, there's a meeting tonight to settle on the date of the trip. Daniel Collins thinks we should change it from August Bank Holiday weekend to an earlier date when Folkestone won't be so crowded.'

'It's a good idea, but it's a bit late to change this year's date, isn't it?' Kate asked, plunging her father's plate and knife and fork into a bowl of soapy hot water. 'It's July already.'

'We could go the week beforehand.' Carl pushed his chair away from the table. 'The only person it will inconvenience will be Nibbo. He doesn't mind closing shop on a Bank Holiday weekend but it's going to half-kill him to put up the shutters on a normal weekend.'

He picked up a large shabby briefcase and withdrew a pile of exercise-books from it, putting them on the table where he wouldn't be able to avoid seeing them when he came home from his meeting at The Swan.

'What on earth are those?' Kate asked, her eyebrows rising. 'School's over until September.'

'Not for teachers, it isn't,' Carl said dryly. He gave her a kiss on the cheek. 'Cheerio, *Liebling*. I'll be back by nine.'

When he had gone she dried her hands on a tea towel and went into the living-room. A library edition of J. B. Priestley's *The Good Companions* lay on the arm of a chair, a bookmark placed strategically at the end of chapter five. She picked it up and carried it outside, sitting on the scoured top step. Though it was now after seven the sun was still warm and the air was heavy with the fragrance of the flowers in her own, and her neighbours', gardens.

She read a few pages and was interrupted by Mr Nibbs calling out a greeting as he left his house intent on the same destination as her father and by Charlie Robson calling a greeting as he walked towards Magnolia Terrace, his alsatian, Queenie, at his heels.

Kate put her book face down on her knee and watched man and dog until they were out of sight. Charlie Robson was obviously going to take Queenie for a walk on the Heath. On such a lovely summer evening there couldn't be a nicer activity and she wished she had had the forethought to have asked Carrie's grandmother if she could take Bonzo for a walk. It was too late now and she closed her eyes, enjoying the heavy, sweet smell of Miss Godfrey's carnations and the rhythmic sound of a distant lawnmower.

'Lovely, isn't it?' Hettie Collins, Danny Collins's mother, called out cheerily. She was on her way to arrange the flowers at St Mark's Church and the shopping bag she was carrying was crammed with freshly cut sweet peas and lilies and columbines. 'On an evening like this you know that God's in his heaven and all's right with the world!'

'You certainly do, Mrs Collins,' Kate agreed, trying to remember where the quotation came from and flashing her a wide, sunny smile. 'I finished school today and I start secretarial school in September.'

'Good for you, dear. My Danny's joined the army. He doesn't half look a smasher in his uniform. I envy both of you. You've got your whole lives to look forward to. I must be getting on though, dear. I can't stay talking. There's a wedding tomorrow and there's a lot of flowers to arrange. Toodle-doo.'

'Toodle-doo,' Kate rejoined exuberantly, suffused with sheer animal good spirits. She had remembered where the quotation about God being in his heaven had come from. It was from a poem by Robert Browning. She knew also that Mrs Collins was right and that the whole of her adult life lay before her; a huge adventure she couldn't wait to begin.

She closed her eyes again, day-dreaming of the wonderful things to come. When her father came home she was still there, her book face down on her knee, asleep in the blue-spangled dusk.

Chapter Two

August 1936

'Don't you think it's a little beneath our dignity to go on the Folkestone trip this year?' Carrie asked, looking at herself critically in the full-length dressing-table mirror in Kate's bedroom. 'I mean, it isn't as if we can let our hair down, is it? Not when your dad is organizing it and my mum and dad and gran are going on it, not to mention Mavis and Ted and the kids.'

'Mrs Collins told me Danny is hoping to be home on leave that weekend and that, if he is, he wants to be counted in for the trip,' Kate said guilefully, continuing to paint her nails a devilish scarlet as Carrie surveyed the squared shoulders of the lavender crêpe dress Kate had helped her to make.

Carrie raised an eyebrow in mock offence. 'And just what is that remark supposed to mean?' she asked, knowing very well what it meant. 'If you'd said King Edward, I might have been tempted.'

'You're neither married or American so you stand no chance there,' Kate said dryly, painting her last nail with care.

Carrie returned her attention to her dress. 'I'm not at all sure about these puff sleeves,' she said doubtfully. 'They make me feel top-heavy.'

'You don't look top-heavy,' Kate said truthfully, 'and the skirt hangs wonderfully.'

Carrie did a pirouette, the cross-cut, mid-length skirt swirling around her legs. 'Do you think the rumours are true?' she asked, referring to King Edward. 'Do you think the King really does want to marry Mrs Simpson?'

Kate shook her head. 'He can't marry her, can he? I

26

expect he'll end up marrying Princess Frederica or Princess Alexandrine Louise.'

Carrie turned away from the mirror. 'And who are they, when they're at home?' she asked, flinging herself face down on the bed beside Kate.

Kate waved her wet fingernails in the air in order to dry them. Ever since she had left secretarial school two years ago and begun work as a junior typist in a City office, Carrie had treated her as the fount of all wisdom. 'Princess Frederica is the granddaughter of the Kaiser and Princess Alexandrine Louise is the third daughter of Prince Harald of Denmark,' she said obligingly.

'Blimey, we could do without a German queen at the moment. She might want Hitler to come to the wedding! And speaking of boring old Hitler, you'll never guess my latest news.'

She rolled over on to her side, propping herself up on her arm. 'We're taking a Jewish refugee in. She's the granddaughter of an old friend of Gran's who went to live in Dresden when she was a young girl. Gran kept in touch with her for a little while but hasn't heard from her for over forty years. Then, out of the blue, she received a letter via the Red Cross from something called an *Auffanglager* in Lucerne. Apparently it's a humanitarian camp for Jewish refugees who have managed to cross the lake that forms the border between Germany and Switzerland. Her friend's granddaughter is interned there and she'd given the Red Cross Gran's name in the hope Gran might be able to help her gain an entry visa into Britain.'

Kate stared at her round-eyed. 'And what did your gran do?'

Carrie grinned. 'She got Dad to write to the Home Office saying that if Christina Frank, her friend's granddaughter, was given an entry visa into Britain he would both give her a home and employment. It's taken quite a while to arrange and more letters than Dad's ever written in his life before, but she's finally been granted a visa.'

'I think that's . . .' Kate sought for a suitable word and couldn't find one that summed up her admiration sufficiently, '. . . *magnificent*,' she said at last.

'It ain't bad, is it?' Carrie agreed, enjoying the reflected glory. 'She'll have Mavis's old room and now he's going to have a third pair of hands helping down the market Dad's going to take on an extra stall. Mum says he's becoming quite a little empire-builder.'

Kate giggled. 'Mr Nibbs will have a pink fit. He was telling Dad last night that he thinks even Miss Helliwell is jaunting down to the market to do the bulk of her shopping.'

'She is,' Carrie said complacently. 'And as Dad always slips her some bruised fruit for free, she's likely to continue doing so.'

Through the open window Miss Godfrey could be heard discussing a forthcoming church fête with Mrs Collins and Kate said musingly, 'Miss Helliwell's going to be doing palm-readings at the fête. Don't you think it's about time we asked her to read ours?'

'Yes, but not at the fête. We don't want anyone listening in and you can bet your life that's what would happen. Why don't we call on her one evening next week? She's always glad of company and we can cross her palm with silver and discover our destinies. What does she charge? Do you know?'

'I haven't a clue. I think she just charges what she thinks people can afford.'

Carrie lay flat on her back and stretched a capable-looking hand high into the air, staring at the palm musingly. 'I wonder what she'll see there? Do you think she'll be able to tell me who I'm going to marry? Do you think he'll be tall, dark, handsome and rich?'

'I think he'll probably be five-foot-nine with a hint of red in his hair, more than passably good-looking and a private in the army,' Kate said dryly.

28

It was a fairly adequate description of Danny Collins and Carrie threw a pillow at her. 'I am *not* going to marry someone I've known since I was in nursery school,' she said firmly, sitting up and swinging her legs off the bed. 'I'm going to marry someone dangerously exciting, someone who will sweep me off my feet . . .'

'Someone who's taking a heck of a long time in appearing on the scene,' Kate finished for her.

Carrie grinned ruefully. 'He is, isn't he?' she said, standing up. 'Perhaps Miss Helliwell will be able to tell me what's keeping him. Shall we go and see her tomorrow night?'

Kate nodded, as eager as Carrie to have a glimpse into her future. 'Where are you going now?' she asked as Carrie picked up her clutch-bag. 'The dentist?'

Carrie shuddered. 'Yes, God help me. This is the third appointment I've made and if the last two are anything to go by my nerve is going to fail me again long before I reach the surgery!'

When Carrie had reluctantly gone on her way Kate went in search of her father. He was in the back garden, a battered straw hat shading his head from the sun as he sowed Brussels sprouts seeds in carefully prepared seed trays. She sat down on the low wall that separated the nursery garden from the rest of the garden and said, still hardly able to believe it, 'The Jennings family are taking in a German Jewish refugee. She's the granddaughter of an old friend of Carrie's gran's.'

'Are they indeed?' Carl leaned back on his heels and pushed his hat a little further back on his head. 'That is just the kind of generous, compassionate thing they would do. Are Mrs Singer's friend and daughter coming to England as well?'

Kate's waist-length braid had fallen forward over her shoulder and she flicked it back again, saying with surprise in her voice, 'I never thought to ask. Carrie didn't mention them and even if Mrs Singer's friend and daughter were also coming to England, they couldn't stay at Carrie's. There would be no room for them.' Her eyes met her father's and widened as a momentous thought occurred to her. 'They could stay here, though, couldn't they? They could stay with us!'

Her father stood up, dusting soil from the knees of his ancient corduroy trousers. 'They could most certainly stay with us,' he said slowly, 'if your mother were still alive she would certainly offer to give them a home. And even if Mrs Singer's friend and daughter are not in need of a home, there's no reason why we shouldn't contact the Home Office and make it known that we're willing to give a home to a German Jewish refugee family. That at least we can do.'

They were both silent for a few minutes, Kate thinking of the mother she could scarcely remember and Carl remembering in deep pain a much loved, much missed wife and friend.

They had met when he had been a POW working on the land in Kent. The farmer he was assigned to regularly offered accommodation and wages to Londoners in the hop-picking season and Anne had been one of the many East Enders who journeyed into the Kentish countryside for two weeks of hard hop-picking, thinking of the change of scene and routine not as labour but as a holiday.

She had been an only child and her parents had not been overly keen when they had discovered how things were between them. Carl smiled to himself at the memory. Anne had been uncaring of her parents' disapproval and, when it became obvious to them that she wasn't affecting love for a German POW merely to annoy them but was sincerely in love with him, they had adopted a practical live and let live attitude towards him and until their deaths, the year before Kate had been born, had been affectionate and supportive parents-in-law to him.

His smile faded. Anne had died in the winter of 1919,

30

when Kate was two years old, of pneumonia. Since then, apart from Kate, he had lived alone and he assumed now that he would always do so.

Kate, mistaking the bleak expression in his eyes for pain at the horrors now taking place in his homeland, stood up and impulsively crossed the distance between them, putting her arms around him and hugging tight. He very rarely spoke of Germany and he was so very English in so many ways, in his love of gardening, in his captaining of the local cricket team, in his enjoyment of a drink at the local pub with his friends, that she found it hard to believe that Germany *was* his homeland.

'I'm so glad you didn't want to return to Germany after you married Mum,' she said fervently, her head against the pullover she had knitted him for his birthday. 'I keep forgetting it might have been something you wanted to do; that I could have been born in Germany and that we could easily be living there now.'

He stroked the gleaming gold of her hair, saying tenderly, 'Why should I have taken your mother away from the country she loved, to a country whose inhabitants would have been hostile towards her? My parents were dead, I had no other family, there was no real reason for me to return home and there was every reason to remain here.'

Behind his spectacles his grey-blue eyes darkened. 'As things have worked out, I'm deeply relieved that I did so. Though I fought in the war, I didn't do so willingly. I'm a pacifist at heart and for many years now Germany has been no country for pacifists.'

She looked up into his gentle face, loving him with all her heart. 'And no country for Jews, either,' she said quietly. 'Let's find out how we can give a home to at least one refugee family. You've been happy in England. Perhaps they will be too.'

*   *   *

31

The next evening, in nervous anticipation of what Miss Helliwell might reveal to her, she strolled towards the bottom end of the Square with Carrie.

They had only gone a dozen yards or so when Carrie said in exasperation, 'Do you see what I see?'

Kate's heart sank. Ahead of them the tweed-suited figure of Miss Godfrey had just stepped out of St Mark's Church and was beginning to walk briskly across the grass towards them.

'We don't have to get involved in a long conversation with her,' she said firmly to Carrie. 'We simply have to say that we have an appointment and that . . .'

'Good evening, girls.' Miss Godfrey came to a halt full-square in front of them, physically preventing them from continuing on their way. 'I've just collected the fête raffle tickets. Would you like to buy one? The prize is a teddy bear. I did suggest to the vicar that a rose-bowl would be more suitable but . . .'

Resignedly Kate and Carrie sought in their clutch-bags for a suitable donation. As they did so Daniel Collins bore down on them from the Heath half of the Square and Charlie Robson's hulking figure ambled towards them from the Lewisham half of the Square.

'Raffle tickets?' Daniel beamed, fumbling in his boiler-suit pocket for loose change. 'What's the prize this year, Miss Godfrey? Not another perishin' teddy bear I hope.'

Charlie had also joined them. His criminal reputation was such that Miss Godfrey always tried to avoid him and she was so flurried at not having avoided him on this occasion that she fumbled in her attempts to tear off a raffle ticket for Daniel and dropped her handbag.

Charlie, who would never have dreamt of thieving on his home turf, bent down to retrieve it for her. Miss Godfrey, certain that he was about to abscond with it, snatched it from his grasp before he even had time to proffer it.

' 'ere, steady on,' Charlie protested mildly, his reactions blunted slightly by the pint of mild he had just downed in The Swan. 'I 'ain't going to do a runner wiv it!'

It was so obvious that this was exactly what Miss Godfrey had feared that even Daniel Collins looked disconcerted. As a diversionary tactic he thrust his copy of the evening paper into Charlie's now empty hands. 'I haven't my reading glasses with me, Charlie. Can you tell me what the latest news is on the cricket? Are Derbyshire really in with a chance?'

For some reason that Kate couldn't fathom it was now Charlie who looked disconcerted. He fumbled to the sports pages and after a little hesitation uncertainly read out the latest scores.

'And what does the sports commentator say about that?' Daniel asked. 'Does he reckon Derbyshire are going to win the country cricket championship?' While he waited for an answer he said helpfully to Kate and Carrie and Miss Godfrey, 'If they do, it'll be their first time in sixty-two years!'

Charlie scrutinized the paper for an inordinately long time and then said unhappily, 'It don't say.'

'Course it'll say! Have a look on the back page.'

Charlie did so and after another long pause said again, 'It don't say, Daniel.'

Daniel was just about to protest that there must be *some* comment on the back page when Miss Godfrey said slowly, 'You can't read, can you, Mr Robson?'

Kate sucked in her breath sharply. Daniel Collins leapt immediately to his friend's defence, saying scoffingly, 'Course Charlie can read!'

'No, I can't,' Charlie said with profound dignity. 'I don't know why, but I've never bin able to get the 'ang of it.'

It was Carrie who recovered from the shock first. 'I shouldn't worry about it, Mr Robson,' she said comfortingly. 'I could never get the hang of arithmetic.'

It was a blatant lie. Carrie could add up a string

of figures in her head with awe-inspiring accuracy as both Kate and Miss Godfrey were well aware.

'It don't matter,' Charlie said, aware that his revelation had caused a certain awkwardness. 'I'm used to it and it don't bother me.'

Daniel gave a sigh of relief, happy to let the embarrassing subject drop, but Miss Godfrey said, an odd note in her voice, 'But would you *like* to be able to read, Mr Robson?'

Kate held her breath as Charlie gave Miss Godfrey's question serious consideration. 'Yes,' he said at last, 'I reckon I would.'

'But how can you?' Daniel Collins asked practically. 'I mean, when all's said and done Charlie, if you didn't manage to learn at school you're not likely to learn now you're the wrong side of fifty, are you? Even if you were, who in their right mind would teach you?'

'I would,' Miss Godfrey said succinctly, the light of battle in her eyes. 'It's a sin and a shame that anyone not mentally handicapped should be unable to read and it's never too late to learn. I'm walking in the same direction as you, Mr Robson. Perhaps you'd like to walk with me as far as my gate and we can discuss times for lessons that will be convenient to us both.'

Daniel Collins gave a choking sound. Kate's jaw dropped open. Carrie gasped. Charlie blinked, bewildered by the speed of events and then, to his audience's stupefaction, amicably assented to Miss Godfrey's suggestion.

'Blimey,' Daniel Collins said in awed tones, as they walked away together. 'If that don't beat all!'

'It was pretty fast work, wasn't it?' Carrie said, grudging admiration in her voice. 'Do you think she fancies him?'

'She's sorry for him,' Kate said, watching as the two incongruous figures, Charlie's broad-shouldered and shambling, Miss Godfrey's tall and angular, walked away from them. 'To someone like Miss Godfrey, reading is the most important ability there is. If Charlie isn't careful, she's going to transform his life.'

'Which is all right if he wants it transforming, but a bit of a bugger if he doesn't,' Daniel Collins said, making no apology for his language.

Accustomed to the colourful language of the market, neither girl took offence.

'We've got to be on our way Mr Collins,' Kate said, mindful that they hadn't intended stopping to talk in the first place.

'And so have I.' Daniel tucked the newspaper that had caused all the kerfuffle once again under his arm. 'Hettie will have my dinner ready and she don't like to be kept waiting.'

He went on his way, a happy and uncomplicated man, and Kate said mischievously, 'He might one day be your father-in-law, Carrie. You could do a lot worse.'

'I could do a sight better!' Carrie said tartly. 'And with a bit of luck Miss Helliwell is going to tell me so *and* give me some details into the bargain.'

Without encountering any more of their neighbours they carried on down to Miss Helliwell's house and turned in at her gate. The garden beyond was turbulently overgrown. Though passionately fond of roses Miss Helliwell did not believe in restraining them nor did she favour new-fangled, prim and neat, hybrid-tea varieties. Her roses were the roses of medieval France and Persia. Damask roses and moss roses grew jungle-thick in great head-high bushes of white and crimson; gallicas and albas rampaged up trees, their scent intoxicating.

'Do you think she'll ask us to come back another time?' Carrie asked doubtfully as Faust appeared from beneath a thicket of sharply-pink *Empress Josephine* and began to stalk them up the pathway.

'I don't know. I hope not.' Now she had finally decided on having her palm read, Kate wanted the deed done as soon as possible. There was something she wanted to ask Miss Helliwell; something of a very practical nature. Though she enjoyed her job, she didn't particularly enjoy travelling to and from the City every day and a large local firm, Harvey's Construction Ltd, was advertising for a junior secretary. It would be quite an advancement from being a mere typist in a typing pool and an added advantage would be that she could walk to work instead of having to suffer a claustrophobic journey by train twice a day. The prospect was exceedingly tempting and she had made her mind up that if Miss Helliwell judged such a move wise, it was a move she was going to make.

'Well, well, this *is* a surprise,' Miss Helliwell said, opening the door to them and looking even more diminutive in her slippers than she did in outdoor shoes. 'Are you selling raffle tickets for the fête? I shall buy one of course but I do wish the Vicar would offer something a little more tempting as a prize than a teddy bear . . .'

'We're not selling raffle tickets,' Kate said, the breath tight in her chest. 'We've come to have our palms read.'

'*Have* you?' Miss Helliwell said, always happy to combine a little companionship with business. 'Then you'd better come inside.' She began to lead the way down a narrow hallway congested with piles of books and aspidistras. 'It takes quite a time, you know. I tried to explain that to dear Mr Collins when he came to me in the hope that I could tell him which horse would win the Derby.'

'And did you?' Kate asked curiously as Miss Helliwell led the way into a sitting-room crammed with yet more foliage.

'Not *exactly*,' Miss Helliwell said, mindful of dear Mr Collins's rather heavy losses on Derby day. 'I told him to back a Moslem and he thought I said muslin and put all his money on Summer Gauze. As it was, the Aga Khan's filly Mahmoud won by a head and Summer Gauze trailed in so far behind Mr Collins swore she wasn't in the same race.'

She seated herself at a large circular table covered in

fringed, rust-coloured moquette. 'Now,' she said in happy anticipation, 'Which of you is going to have their palm read first?'

'Kate will,' Carrie said quickly.

Shooting Carrie a look that indicated Carrie was going to have some apologizing to do when they left the house, Kate sat nervously down at the table opposite Miss Helliwell.

'Now dear, let me have a look at your hands,' Miss Helliwell instructed, adding, 'and if Caroline would like to go and have a chat with my sister, I'm sure Esther would appreciate it. She's in the conservatory and she does so like visitors.'

Aware that she was discreetly being asked to leave the room Carrie disappointedly turned her back on them and went in search of the wheelchair-bound Esther.

'Now dear,' Miss Helliwell said again as the door closed, leaving them in privacy. 'Let's see what we have here.'

She took Kate's hands in hers, examining them closely. 'Very nice,' she said at last. 'Very nice indeed. You have the long-fingered, well-shaped hand of a typical Water personality. Water hands are sometimes called sensitive hands because they indicate great sensitivity and emotional warmth.'

Kate felt some of her tension ease. If Miss Helliwell was going to say nice things about her there was no need for her to be apprehensive.

Miss Helliwell took hold of her right hand and cupped it, staring down intently into the palm. For a long moment she didn't speak and when she did her voice was oddly strained. 'Well, well,' she said, stalling for time in order to get over the shock she had just received. 'How very . . . unexpected.'

All Kate's apprehensions flooded back in full force. 'What is?' she demanded. 'What's wrong? Is it my life-line . . .'

'Oh no dear,' Miss Helliwell said swiftly. 'There's

nothing wrong with your life-line. Your life-line is so long it reaches your wrist! You're going to make old bones, dear. Very old bones.'

'Then what is it? What can you see that you didn't expect to see?'

Miss Helliwell squinted with renewed concentration at Kate's palm. 'It's rather difficult to explain dear,' she said at last, choosing her words with care. 'There is great happiness in your future. Very great happiness. It is, however, a happiness that comes only after heartache. You have an enviable capacity for love, and love is going to be central to your life, but where love is concerned you're going to have some very hard choices and decisions to make.'

'But can't you tell me what my choices and decisions should be?' Kate asked in rising anxiety.

Miss Helliwell shook her head. 'No, my dear. You will have to make up your own mind about the paths you will take. One thing you can take comfort from. You have a cross on your Mount of Jupiter which is very rare and very lucky. There, can you see it?' With a rheumatically afflicted finger she pointed to two small lines forming a cross on Kate's palm. 'That indicates that at some time in your life a great and lasting love will occur, a love from which nothing but good will come.' Gently she released Kate's hand.

'Is that it?' Kate asked in surprise. 'I thought you said that readings took a long time.'

'Some do and some don't,' Miss Helliwell said, carefully avoiding Kate's eyes so that Kate couldn't see the troubled expression she knew was there. 'Will you go and tell Caroline that I am ready to read her palm now?'

Reluctantly, wishing that Miss Helliwell had been a little more specific about the nature of the heartache she was apparently to suffer, Kate pushed her chair away from the table and went in search of the conservatory.

It was at the back of the house adjoining the kitchen and the instant she entered it Carrie leapt from the chair she had been sitting in. With a finger to her lips she indicated that Esther was asleep and then whispered urgently, 'What happened? What did she tell you?'

'She didn't say much at all.' For the first time in her life Kate was unwilling to share her experience with Carrie. Miss Helliwell's odd attitude had deeply disconcerted her and she wanted to think over what had been said to her, before trivializing it by gossiping about it.

Carrie's dark, well-defined eyebrows rose high. 'She must have said *something*!'

Aware that she was going to have to at least partially satisfy Carrie's curiosity Kate said, grateful that one part of her palm-reading had been uncomplicated, 'I have a Cross of Jupiter on my palm and it signifies great good fortune.'

'Golly!' There was envy in Carrie's voice. 'I wonder if I've got one as well?'

'You won't find out standing here, talking to me.' There was impatience as well as affection in Kate's voice.

'That's true,' Carrie said, ever-practical. 'I'd better be going, hadn't I? Wish me luck.'

'You're having your palm read, not swimming the Channel!'

Carrie gave an exaggerated shiver. 'It may not be a plunge into the Channel but it's a plunge into the future and I jolly well don't want any nasty surprises!'

With fingers crossed she left the conservatory and Kate sat down in a battered cane chair near to Esther's wheelchair. The younger Miss Helliwell, well into her seventies, was snoring gently, a worn tartan blanket covering her knees.

Kate stared out into a rear garden as dense with blossom as the rose-drowned front garden, wishing she had never broached the idea of palm-readings to Carrie. She was an intelligent girl and she was well aware that her palm-reading had been brief because Miss Helliwell had been too taken aback by what she had read in her palm to have talked to her truthfully and at length about what she had seen there. Instead she had taken refuge in generalities.

She looked down at her palm and at the faint web of lines forming a small cross below her forefinger. It hadn't all been generalities. There had been utter sincerity in Miss Helliwell's voice when she had told her that the cross signified great good luck and a lasting love. Some of the tension she had been feeling eased. Miss Helliwell had also been quite adamant that, beyond the heartache, happiness lay in wait for her. That being so, it was ridiculous of her to feel unnerved at being told she would have heartache and hard choices and decisions to make. Hard choices and decisions fête were, after all, something everyone had to cope with.

As Faust padded into the conservatory she gave a rueful smile. She had expected too much from the palm-reading, that was the trouble. And she had completely forgotten to ask Miss Helliwell whether or not she should apply for the job at Harvey's. Faust sprang up on to her knees and settled himself comfortably and she knew that her forgetfulness didn't matter. She didn't need advice where the new job was concerned. Of course she was going to apply for it. Her future would be what she would make of it. And she had stayed in the typing pool long enough.

On the following Saturday, as they walked towards the Heath where the church fête was being held, Carrie was still full of all the things Miss Helliwell had told her. 'She was quite adamant that I had already met my husband-to-be and that I would be married long before I was twenty-one,' she said, obviously highly delighted at the prediction.

'But that was precisely what you didn't want!' Kate protested. 'You didn't want to marry someone you'd known since nursery days! You wanted to be swept off your feet by a tall, dark stranger!'

Carrie grinned. 'I did, didn't I? However, I have

exercised a ladies prerogative and I've changed my mind.'

'But why on earth . . .' Kate began, exasperated.

'Because Miss Helliwell saw a uniform quite clearly and children with red in their hair. Danny Collins is quite obviously my *fate*. Don't you think that wonderfully romantic?'

'I think you're crackers,' Kate said starkly. 'You can't decide to marry someone just because of a palm-reading!'

'Oh, I've a little more reason than that,' Carrie said, a naughty sparkle in her eye. 'He's home on leave again and he's been promoted to sergeant. Stripes suit him. He looked *very* tasty when I ran into him at the chippie last night.'

Kate shook her head in mock despair and then began to laugh. Arm in arm, Kate in an ice-blue sundress that emphasized the blondeness of her hair, Carrie in her highly fashionable lavender crêpe dress, they walked out of Magnolia Terrace and across the main road and onto the Heath.

The tiny section of the Heath given over to the fête was resplendent with flags and bunting. There were white-naperied tables laden with homemade jams, cakes and pickles. A long trestle table groaned under the weight of entries for the most splendid basket of home-grown vegetables. A large crayoned notice pinned to a festively decorated tent, announced that Miss Helliwell, Palm-reader and Clairvoyant, was available for consultations.

Clumps of balloons flew from every available anchorage. Donkeys plodded contentedly around a roped-off circuit, small children on their backs. There were bagatelle tables and ping-pong tables. There was a section each for ninepins, quoits, skittles, darts and an impressive archery ground. A large bell-tent, the notice TEAS pinned to its entrance, was presided over by Hettie Collins. Nibbo was helping Kate's father to hammer cricket stumps into position ready for the obligatory cricket match. Mavis was sprucing up her little daughter ready for the Bonny Baby competition. Miss Godfrey, wearing her habitual tweed suit despite the brilliant sun and cloudless sky, was busy selling last minute raffle tickets. Ted Lomax, Carrie's quiet-spoken brother-in-law, was man-handling a barrel of sarsaparilla into place under a label proclaiming REFRESHMENTS.

'Well I haven't entered the home-grown vegetable competition and I don't have an entry for the Bonny Baby Competition,' Carrie said pragmatically, 'so we can give those a miss. How about a shot at archery. Are you game?'

Though she couldn't possibly have heard Carrie, Mavis shouted across to her, 'Don't go skiving off when it's time for the Bonny Baby competition, Carrie! I want you clapping your hands and stamping your feet on your niece's behalf!'

Carrie gave an exaggerated groan. 'You'd think she'd have enough support with Mum, Dad, Gran and Christina.'

'What is Christina like?' Kate asked curiously as they side-stepped members of St Mark's Boys' Brigade Band who were practising for the display they were to give later in the afternoon.

'Quiet. Though I think that's only temporary. She'd had a long and tiring journey and I reckon the nervous relief, when she realized she was actually in England, must have been enormous. She's here somewhere with Mum and Dad and Gran and she's dying to meet you and make friends.'

From behind them a piercing whistle stopped them dead in their tracks. 'It's Danny,' Carrie said without turning her head. 'With a whistle like that he could earn a living as a railway guard!'

The perm that had once made her hair look like a hottentot's had long since grown out and her hair now hung heavily and sleekly to her shoulders. As she pushed it away from her face and turned around, Kate

42

saw a tell-tale flush of colour in her cheeks. Wryly she acknowledged that where Carrie was concerned, Miss Helliwell's predictions had quite obviously been a hundred per cent accurate.

'Fancy a shot at the archery?' Danny asked, strolling towards them, Jerry and Jack Robson close behind him. 'After all the rifle practice I've done this past few months I reckon I should be able to hit the bull's-eye easily.'

Not overly tall but broad in the shoulders he had an engaging grin and the kind of pleasant, frank and open face, that would be boyish well into middle-age. The boyishness was enhanced by the hint of red in his hair and the freckles that peppered his rather snub nose. Until now Kate had been mystified as to why Carrie was so taken with him but seeing him in uniform she had to admit that the stripes on his shoulders did give him a certain allure. Or perhaps, she thought reflectively as Carrie teased him about being so confident of his chances, it wasn't the stripes but the self-assurance they had given him that was attractive.

'Archery?' Jack Robson asked as he and his brother joined them. 'Where the hell did the vicar get the idea for archery from? Lambeth Palace?'

Unlike Danny, there was nothing remotely homely about the Robson boys. Tall and hard-muscled, with thick shocks of unruly dark hair, they both possessed a reckless 'damn-your-eyes' quality that indicated they would be ugly customers in a fight and that they wouldn't need much excuse to join in any fight that was going.

'Archery is a very old and well respected sport,' Carrie said to him pertly. 'It isn't just for nobs. It was the bowmen of England that won the Battle of Agincourt for King Henry.'

'Well, isn't that nice to know?' Jack said affably, not remotely impressed by her show of knowledge. 'And leaving Henry out of it and talking about this afternoon, what prizes are being given for scoring bull's-eyes?'

'Knowing the vicar, it'll be teddy bears,' Jerry said glumly.

Kate giggled. Though the Robson boys had a reputation for being rough and ready they were also amusing company and she secretly had a soft spot for Jerry, whose swagger was marginally less blatant than his brother's. He said to her now: 'Have we to go over to the archery then? I don't want to hang around here. I might be asked to judge the Bonny Baby Competition!'

They all burst out laughing and Kate saw Danny take hold of Carrie's hand and tuck it proprietorially into the crook of his arm. 'I think your mum and dad are over at the archery ground,' he said to her. 'Shall we go?'

Carrie nodded, the sun glinting on the tortoiseshell combs holding her hair away from her face, the glow on her face radiant.

Kate felt her throat tighten. Carrie really *was* in love with Danny. A pang of wistfulness assailed her. She, too, would have liked to be in love, or at least to be on the verge of being in love. Certain that she was far from being so and with Jerry at her side, she followed Jack and Danny and Carrie to the far side of the fête where the archery target had been set up.

'This is the last time you'll be seeing me for a while,' Jerry said laconically, his hands deep in his trouser pockets. 'I'm off to Spain tomorrow.'

'Spain!' Kate forgot all about not being in love. Ever since civil war had erupted in Spain it had scarcely been out of the news. 'You're going out there to fight?'

She realized as soon as she said it that it was a stupid question and that of course he was going to Spain to fight. He nodded, saying with a lucidity and intensity of feeling that took her completely unawares, 'It's no use leaving things up to the League of Nations, is it? They didn't stop Mussolini marching into Abyssinia and it's quite obvious that where Spain is concerned they're going to be just as ineffectual. If we want to put an end

44

to fascism and to fascist bullies, we've got to stand up and be counted.'

It was so unexpected a speech that Kate felt momentarily robbed of breath. She looked across at him, her eyes wide, realizing in stunned surprise that there was a great deal more to Jerry Robson than met the eye. Regret shot through her. It was a realization that had come too late. If he was going to Spain there was no telling how long he might be away for. Hoping with passionate intensity that he would return home safe and uninjured and wanting to prolong the conversation, she said, 'Do you know that the Jennings family have taken in a German-Jewish refugee?'

He nodded. 'Jack was walking past the Jennings house the evening she arrived.' His face split into a sudden grin. 'He's been pretty smitten ever since and he's hoping she'll be here this afternoon.'

'She is,' Kate said, intrigued at the thought of Jack Robson falling for the Jennings's guest even before he had spoken to her. 'And I think his luck is in. I can see Carrie's mum and dad and a dark-haired girl over at the archery ground.'

Ahead of them, across a scenic stretch of green turf, the archery target had been set up well away from the stalls and donkey circuit. Albert Jennings, his shirt-sleeves rolled up to his elbows, his beer-belly protruding over the top of his trousers, was perspiringly pulling back the string of a large bow.

'Come on Albert, it's only a bow and arrow when all's said and done,' Carrie's mother was saying exasperatedly. 'I could do better with two broken arms.'

Beside her a dark-haired girl watched, a bemused expression on her face. She was ethereally slender, verging almost on the malnourished, and there was a disturbing air of frailty and vulnerability about her. Kate's first reaction was surprise that Jack should have been so drawn towards her and then, as they drew nearer, she understood. Christina Frank was beautiful.

Tiny, delicate features graced a face filled with enormous dark eyes and a gently curving mouth.

'Jack Robson,' Jack was saying to her without waiting for Carrie's mother to introduce him. 'I saw you in the street the night you arrived.'

A few feet away from them Albert Jennings let his arrow fly free. It soared, but not in the right direction.

'Lord help us, Albert!' Miriam protested. 'Another few yards and you'd have done for one of the donkeys!'

Albert took no notice of her. Wiping the perspiration from his forehead with a large handkerchief he said bluntly to Jack, 'I thought you'd buggered off to Spain.'

Well aware that it was his obvious interest in Christina that had put Albert's back up, Jack grinned. 'Not me, Albert. You're thinking of Jerry and he doesn't go till tomorrow.'

Sensing that her father was about to suggest to Jack that he accompany Jerry, Carrie said hastily, 'Christina hasn't been introduced to anyone.'

Without waiting for anyone else to do so, she proceeded to introduce Christina to Jerry and Danny, saying finally, 'And this is Kate, my best friend.'

Christina smiled a little shyly at Kate. 'I'm very pleased to meet with you,' she said in carefully rehearsed English and with a very heavy German accent. 'You are going on the trip to Folkestone, yes?'

'Yes,' Kate said, shaking her hand warmly. 'Welcome to England, Christina.'

'Thank you,' Christina said simply, 'It is good to be here. Very good.'

As their eyes held, Kate saw with a stab of shock that Christina's brave, shy smile was not reflected in her eyes. They were dark with grief and suffering – and stoic resignation. Immediately her thoughts flew to Christina's mother and grandmother. Only her father had wondered about their whereabouts. Was the reason they, also, had not requested help from the Jennings family because they were being held in a Nazi concentration camp? Were they perhaps dead?

With a heart full of compassion she squeezed Christina's hand wishing she could say something comforting, knowing that anything she said would be hopelessly trite and inadequate.

'Come on boys,' Miriam Jennings said robustly to Danny, Jack and Jerry. 'Show us what you're made of and try and get an arrow into the bull's-eye. The Vicar's already shot one in so it can't be that hard!'

Everyone laughed, even Christina, and for the next hour Danny, Jerry and Jack vied with each other for the highest score. It was Jerry who won and Jerry who, later on in the afternoon, won the official archery competition.

When the vicar's wife graciously presented him with the prize of a teddy bear he turned to Kate, handing it to her and saying with a grin she found quite heart-stopping, 'Look after him for me. I won't have much use for him in Spain.'

Later, still remaining together in a group that included Christina, they strolled over to the cricket pitch that Kate's father and Nibbo had marked out earlier in the day.

As they sat on the grass calling out encouragement to whoever was batting, Carrie's hand rested snugly in Danny's, Jack sat as close to Christina as was humanly possible and Jerry chatted almost exclusively to Kate.

Years later Kate had only to close her eyes and she could conjure up every detail of that sun-scorched, carefree afternoon. Her father, a panama shading his head from the sun, batted as if his life depended on it. Nibbo shouting, 'Well played, sir! Well played!'. Mavis's euphoria as she told them that Beryl had won the Bonny Baby Competition. The universal amusement when Charlie Robson won the raffle and was obliged to accept the teddy bear prize from the vicar. It had seemed as if the only cloud marring the day was Jerry's imminent departure for Spain. Then the cricket match had ended. They had all walked over to the tea-tent. And her father and the rest of the cricket team had joined them.

'You put up a good show out there, Carl,' Albert said, his shirt open almost to the navel, a pint pot of steaming tea in one hand, a buttered scone in the other. 'I thought the last ball you hit was going to reach Dover!'

'You haven't introduced Christina,' Carrie said to her father as Miss Helliwell squeezed past them, a flamboyant scarf worn exotically gypsy-fashion.

'Why all the fuss about introductions?' her father grumbled in mock exasperation. 'It ain't a Buckingham Palace garden-party!'

Carrie raised her eyes to heaven and took the honours on herself, 'Christina, allow me to introduce you to Mr Voigt. Mr Voigt is Kate's father and captain of the pub cricket team.'

Carl took hold of Christina's out-stretched hand. 'I'm very pleased to meet you,' he said in German. 'Welcome to England.'

Christina froze. 'You're German?' she said uncertainly. 'Jewish? You're a refugee also?'

'I'm not Jewish and not a refugee,' Carl said as Hettie Collins pushed through the throng towards them. 'But I am German. I was born in Heidelburg.'

Christina snatched her hand from his grasp as if from a fire and then, in front of all his neighbours and the entire pub cricket team, she spat full in his face.

Chapter Three

July 1938

'It's going to be a lovely sunny day for tomorrow's wedding,' Miss Pierce, Personnel Officer, said to Kate as they walked out of the forecourt of Harvey's head office.

Kate found Miss Pierce nearly as daunting as Miss Godfrey and in her eighteen months at Harvey's had never got beyond exchanging polite pleasantries with her. The only reason a hint of familiarity had now entered their conversation was that she had been obliged to make arrangements with Miss Pierce for a day's unpaid absence.

'I know it's a bloomin' nuisance,' Carrie had said to her when she had asked her to be her bridesmaid, 'but Danny's leave is from Wednesday to Friday and so we have to be married on a weekday. Dad's pleased, of course. It means he won't have to miss a Saturday's trading.'

Kate said now, as she and Miss Pierce stepped out into the steep street that ran up alongside Greenwich Park to the Heath, 'The long-term weather forecast has been a relief to Carrie. She was certain the heatwave was going to break on her wedding morning.'

'There's absolutely no chance of that,' Miss Pierce said confidently, pausing on the pavement before turning and making her way down the hill towards Greenwich. 'Enjoy your three day break. Next week is going to be *very* hectic. It's never easy having Mr Harvey in the office and with his grandson joining us next week he's bound to be calling in.'

'I'm not sure I've understood just why Mr Harvey's

grandson is going to be working in the office,' Kate said, genuinely puzzled. 'It obviously isn't because he needs a job.'

Miss Pierce's thin mouth twitched in amusement. 'Goodness me, no. Harvey's is a family firm and Mr Joss Harvey is obviously preparing his grandson for the day when the company will be his responsibility.'

'And so he wants him to spend some time in each department? Sales? Accounts? Marketing?'

'Exactly. It's becoming an old-fashioned concept that the head of a large company should be familiar with the mundane day-to-day running of that company, but then Mr Harvey *is* old-fashioned.'

It was the longest conversation that had ever taken place between them and both of them were rather surprised by it.

'Have a nice day tomorrow,' Miss Pierce said, realizing that she was on the verge of committing what was, in her eyes, the cardinal sin of gossiping about her employer. 'Give my best wishes to the bride.'

'I will. And thank you for arranging the day off for me.'

With a gratified smile Miss Pierce continued on her way down into Greenwich and Kate began to walk up the hill. She had known ever since the day of the fête, nearly two years ago, that Carrie intended marrying Danny but it still seemed incredible to her that the wedding was actually going to take place; that it was only hours away. She knew that she should be looking forward to it, but she couldn't help feeling a pang of regret. No matter how Carrie might deny it, their friendship would never be quite the same after she married Danny. There would be no more going to dances together; no more spending all their free time together.

As she neared the Heath she scolded herself for her selfishness. Carrie hadn't the faintest shadow of doubt that her future happiness lay in marriage to Danny.

Tomorrow was going to be a joyous occasion and there had been far too few such occasions of late. Reflecting back on the events of the last two years she shuddered. Ever since the traumatic scene between her father and Christina at the church fête, hideousness had followed hideousness.

A month after leaving England for Spain, Jerry Robson had been killed fighting for the Republican side against Franco's Nationalists in a small Spanish town no-one had even heard of.

'Badajoz,' a grief-stricken Charlie Robson had said, pronouncing the name with great difficulty. 'Jerry died in a place called Badajoz.'

His stunned incredulity had been heartrending. Even worse had been the knowledge, a month later and care of the Foreign Office, that Jerry had not died in battle but had been one of hundreds of disarmed militiamen who had been rounded up by the Nationalists and slaughtered in the city's bullring.

Kate had sat on her bed for a long time after hearing the news, her arms around the teddy bear he had given her. They had spent only one afternoon together and that had been in the company of his brother and Danny and Carrie and Christina. They had never kissed, never even held hands, yet she knew that in those few hours together at the fête he had become as suddenly aware of her as she had of him.

When she finally rose to her feet and put the teddy bear back on her dressing-table his orange-gold fabric fur was wet with her tears. She wouldn't forget Jerry. Not ever. And she wondered if Miss Helliwell had seen his death when she had read her palm and if that was the reason she had been so disconcerted and had brought her palm-reading to such an abrupt end.

The news continued to be as grim in the rest of the world as it was in Spain. In November, Hitler and Mussolini signed a formal pact agreeing that in future they would hunt as a pair.

In the New Year the international situation had become so perilous that the British government announced it was aiming to treble the strength of the air force via a massive recruiting drive. By the end of the year gas masks had been issued to all London schoolchildren and practice gas-mask drill had become compulsory.

'Do you think it's really going to come to a shindig with old Hitler?' Hettie Collins had asked her one day in the street. 'Mr Nibbs says it's bound to and he's digging an air raid shelter into his garden. Can't say I'd want to go down into one of 'em myself. It'd be like being buried alive.'

Kate didn't fancy the thought either but her father thought it was a precaution they should take and in the spring of 1939 she helped him dig an Anderson shelter into what had once been his prized back lawn.

It was hard physical work and by the time they had finished her father was exhausted.

'I'll make you a cup of tea,' she had said, disturbed by the extent of his weariness and knowing it was a weariness that went far deeper than temporary physical tiredness.

Ever since Christina had spat at him there had been a change in him. Always a quiet man, he had become even quieter and more withdrawn. Everyone had assured him, of course, that it was an incident he shouldn't take to heart; that Christina's action was understandable after the horrors she had endured at German hands.

'She wasn't to know that you're not like the Germans who carted her mother and grandmother off to a concentration camp,' Nibbo had said to him reasonably. '*We* know you're not like them, but she don't.'

Her father had said that he understood Christina's action utterly and that there wasn't the slightest iota of ill-feeling on his part. Kate had known he had been speaking the absolute truth and she had known also that the incident had shaken him far more than he was allowing people to believe.

'If it does come to war with Hitler, people will remember Christina's reaction to me,' he had said heavily. 'Though everyone in the Square knows I was born in Germany, very few people have ever thought of me as German. Now they will.'

His anxiety hadn't been eased when the Home Office had, on the grounds of his nationality, refused to allow him to act as sponser to a Jewish refugee family. Three months ago, on the day Hitler annexed Austria, the worst blow of all had fallen.

'I've been asked to resign my position at the school,' he had said to her in stunned tones when he had come home from work. 'From now on German is being dropped from the syllabus.'

He had sat down at the table she had laid ready for their evening meal and said unsteadily, 'The headmaster could hardly look me in the face when he told me. He said that the education authority had hinted to him that it would be better if no-one of German extraction was working in the school and that, very reluctantly of course, he was forced to agree with them.'

He passed a hand across his eyes and to her horror Kate saw that it was shaking. With an overpowering feeling of nausea she had sat down beside him and taken hold of his hand. 'You mustn't take it too much to heart Daddy,' she had said, so sick at heart herself she had found it hard to speak. 'Something else will turn up. Something much more enjoyable than teaching German.'

As she walked from the Heath into Magnolia Terrace she reflected that for once her optimism had been fully justified. Within days of the news of his forced resignation from the school becoming public knowledge Nibbo had told him that the elderly owner of the bookshop, next door to his own greengrocery shop in Blackheath Village, was looking for a manager. By the end of the month her father had exchanged teaching for book-selling and, to both his and her vast relief, was enjoying the novelty of his new occupation.

On the other side of the terrace Charlie Robson was walking in the opposite direction, Queenie at his heels. She gave him a wave which he cheerily reciprocated and it occurred to her that he hadn't been absent from the neighbourhood for quite some time. In the old days he was always dropping out of sight and it was common knowledge when he did that he wasn't on holiday or visiting friends but was serving time for petty theft in one of His Majesty's many prisons.

She began to cross the Square, wondering if Charlie's new way of life was in any way connected with Miss Godfrey and the reading lessons she had given him. Whether the reading lessons were still continuing or were now no longer necessary she didn't know, but she did know that Miss Godfrey and Charlie were still on friendly terms.

Smiling to herself at the oddness of some friendships she neared the Jennings' house. Ever since the incident between her father and Christina she hadn't been as regular a visitor there. It wasn't that Carrie's mum and dad and Gran had changed in their attitude towards her, but Christina was still living with them and her relationship with Christina was extremely strained.

In the aftermath of the horrendous incident in the tea-tent Albert Jennings had explained to his guest that the gentleman she had spat on had lived in England for nearly twenty years and that Kate's mother was English and that Kate had been born in England and had never ever left England. Christina had remained unimpressed.

'She says you have German Aryan blood and that all German Aryans are the same,' Carrie had said to her resignedly. 'Mind you, when you think of the Nazis dragging her family off to a concentration camp, you have to sympathize with her. Dad says he reckons her mum and gran will be dead by now. And her father and

54

brother are dead. The Nazis shot them in the street when they tried to prevent a mob burning their shop to the ground.'

Like everyone else in Magnolia Square, Kate did sympathize with Christina. She also felt resentful towards her. No matter what the horrors Christina had endured in Germany at the hands of the Nazis, it had been unfair of her to have publicly reacted towards one of her new neighbours as if he, too, were one of Hitler's National Socialists. It had caused her father deep distress and it was because of the distress he had suffered that Kate couldn't bring herself to totally forgive Christina.

'Nice to see you, *bubbelah*!' Leah called out from the hallway as Kate walked up to the already open front door. 'Carrie is upstairs trying her dress on.'

Her usual cheery face looked strained and Kate remembered that Leah, alone of everyone else in Magnolia Square, was not whole-heartedly looking forward to the wedding and, though she had promised to bake pies and tarts and bagels and blintz's for the reception, wasn't going to be in the church when Carrie became Danny's wife.

'She's never got over my mother marrying a *shaygets*,' Carrie had said in affectionate despair. 'Why she should have thought, after the rackety way Mum and Dad have brought me up, that I would have a *kosher* wedding I can't imagine.'

'But your gran doesn't *dislike* Danny, surely?' Kate had said, feeling rather out of her depth.

Carrie had shaken her head, her thick mane of hair tumbling around her face. 'No. If he was Jewish she would think he was the bee's knees. She just doesn't like the way Mum is so oblivious of what she sees as being Mum's religious and cultural heritage.' She gave a wry smile. 'If you ask me, I think it's one of the reasons Gran is so very Jewish in her speech. She does it in the hope that it annoys my Dad and as a constant reminder to Mum that she's let the side down.'

Now, as Kate entered Carrie's bedroom, Bonzo yapping at her heels, Carrie turned towards her saying anxiously, 'What do you think? Does the waist need letting out another half inch? I've been living on lettuce all week but I still seem to have put weight on since the last time we fitted it.'

Thankful that Christina was obviously not in the house Kate sat down on the edge of Carrie's bed and looked with critical eyes at the slipper-satin wedding dress the two of them had made from a McCalls paper pattern. 'You're imagining things,' she said to Carrie's vast relief. 'The fitting is perfect. You look wonderful.'

It was true. The design of the dress was simple and very elegant. The neckline was heart-shaped, the sleeves long and narrow, dipping to a medieval point over the backs of her hands. The bodice and skirt had been made in one piece, princess-fashion, the skirt merely skimming her toes in front and falling into a short train at the back. Although completely unadorned by ruffles or flounces it looked magnificent. Laid out on Christina's bed was a headdress of imitation orange-blossom and a thigh-length, lace-edged veil that Carrie's mother had worn on her wedding day. The bouquet of crimson roses and white carnations that would complete Carrie's ensemble was being made by a family friend who had a flower stall in the market.

'And I shall wear the pearl necklace Gran gave me for my birthday,' Carrie had said to Kate when they had first begun to discuss dress styles, 'that will make up for Gran not being there when I say my vows. I need to be wearing "something old, something new, something borrowed and something blue." My veil will be the something old, the necklace can be my something new. I'll wear Miss Helliwell's white net gloves for the borrowed bit and pin a blue ribbon to my underslip for the something blue.'

Kate said now: 'Do you think I should try my brides-maid dress on again?'

'What on earth for?' Carrie asked in mock exasperation. 'You're as likely to have put weight on as fly to the moon!'

Kate grinned. 'That's because I don't work down the market. If you didn't help yourself so liberally to whatever it is you're selling, you wouldn't have a weight problem either.'

'I only eat when there's a lull in customers and anyway, fruit isn't supposed to make you fat.'

'It depends how much you eat of it,' Kate said, amused. 'And isn't there a pie and mash stall near to your stall? Don't tell me you don't have a sneaky pie and mash every now and again because if you do, I won't believe you.'

'I haven't had a pie and mash since I knew the date of the wedding,' Carrie said grimly, breathing in and viewing her reflection sideways on. 'The prospect of lumbering down the aisle like a cart-horse with you sylph-like behind me has been nearly enough to make me stop eating altogether.'

'What about Beryl?' Kate asked, amused. Beryl, Mavis's two-and-a-half-year-old daughter was also to be a bridesmaid, though very much at Mavis's insistence, not Carrie's. 'Is she looking forward to tomorrow?'

'She's looking forward to it all right, but it's whether she's going to behave or not I'm worrying about,' Carrie said, beginning to carefully lift her wedding dress over her head.

Kate rose from the bed to help her and from beneath the sumptuous folds of material Carrie continued, her voice muffled, 'Thanks to Mavis she seems to think tomorrow is going to be a cross between a day trip to Folkestone and a church fête.'

Kate lifted the wedding dress free of Carrie's hair and laid it reverently on the bed.

'I told Mum I thought Beryl was too young to be a bridesmaid but Mum said Mavis would create murder if Beryl wasn't asked and so there you are, she's been asked and I have to worry about whether or not she's going to behave herself,' Carrie finished darkly, stepping into a cotton dress patterned with azure-blue cornflowers and scarlet poppies.

She pulled the dress up on to her shoulders and fastened the zip. 'Ted says I'm worrying unnecessarily. He says he's explained to her she's got to stand very quietly with you and Christina during the service but I have a vision of her saying she wants to wee-wee or have an ice-cream.'

'And what about Bonzo?' Kate asked, as Bonzo laid his head on her knee. 'Will he be at the wedding too?'

Carrie brushed her dishevelled hair away from her face, anchoring its heavy weight with tortoiseshell combs. 'He'd better not be in the church!' she said, overcome with horror at the thought, 'Though I wouldn't put it past Mum to try and take him in. She's already made a big blue satin bow for him to wear.'

Kate giggled and Carrie said in sudden solemnity, 'I can't believe it's really going to happen.' She stroked the heavy satin skirt of her wedding dress lovingly. 'I've looked forward to it for so long, ever since the day Miss Helliwell read our palms, and now it's actually going to happen. By this time tomorrow I'll be Mrs Danny Collins.'

Kate's giggles subsided. 'It is what you still want, isn't it?' she asked gently.

Carrie sat down on the bed beside her. 'Yes,' she said unhesitatingly. 'I can't describe it in clever words like you would be able to Kate, but when I'm with Danny I'm happy, it's as simple as that. We suit each other. He may be a bit of a rough diamond and I'm not so love-struck that I think he's the handsomest man in the world, or the brainiest, but he's the one person in the world right for me.' She took hold of Kate's hand and squeezed it tight. 'He knows what I want out of life and I know what he wants out of life, and what we want is the same thing. Someone to love and laugh with;

someone who'll be a friend as well as a lover; a home of our own; kids.'

Kate felt her throat tighten. It all sounded so simple and straightforward and, for Carrie, it was. 'I'm glad you're so happy,' she said thickly, 'I think Danny is very, very lucky.'

'His mother doesn't think he is,' Carrie said with dry humour, her moment of seriousness over. 'She seems to think that the minute he's married to me he's going to begin starving to death!'

Later, as she returned home, Miss Godfrey called out from her garden, 'Katherine! Could you do me a favour? Could you help me carry some boxes of crockery and cutlery down to the church hall?'

Kate nodded and opened Miss Godfrey's immaculately painted gate.

'Mrs Jennings has asked me to lend her whatever I have for tomorrow's wedding reception,' Miss Godfrey said in relief as Kate walked up the short front path, 'and if you gave me a hand it would mean my making only one trip, not two.'

She led the way into the house, saying as she did so, 'Is everything under control at Carrie's? I did offer to go down there and give Mrs Jennings any help she might need but she said she thought she could manage. Apparently her mother is doing all the catering and Mavis and her friends are setting out the tables in the hall.'

It had been a long time since Kate had been inside Miss Godfrey's home and she couldn't help being aware of how strikingly different the furnishings and decor were from the Jennings' house and even from her own home. A bordered red and brown patterned carpet runner graced the passageway leading towards the kitchen and Kate suspected it was no ordinary carpet but was probably Turkish or Indian. Through the open door leading into the sitting-room she glimpsed a highly polished glass-fronted bookcase and a walnut-framed easy-chair. Water-colours framed in gold hung on the cream papered walls and she remembered her father saying that Miss Godfrey possessed an exceptionally fine landscape by an English nineteenth-century artist he much admired, John Sell Cotman.

'Here we are,' Miss Godfrey said as she walked into her kitchen. 'Two cardboard boxes and a carrier-bag. Do you think we can manage them between us?'

'Is the crockery valuable?' Kate asked nervously. Everything Miss Godfrey owned seemed to be genuine this or genuine that and if the boxes contained precious china she knew it would be just her luck to trip and fall and smash the lot.

'No,' Miss Godfrey said, picking up one of the boxes and placing it in Kate's arms. 'I *do* have some good china, left to me by my mother, but I wouldn't dream of lending it out.' An edge of rare humour entered her voice. 'And *certainly* not for a wedding thrash in the church hall!'

She slipped the carrier-bag's string handles over her wrist and picked up the second box. 'I do enjoy weddings,' she said confidingly, 'especially summer weddings. I was so pleased when I received an invitation to this particular wedding and I was more than a little surprised. Caroline and I have had our differences of opinion in the past as I'm sure you must be aware.'

Kate made a polite, non-committal murmur and wondered whether, if Carrie's vowels were less than perfect when she made her wedding vows, Miss Godfrey would speak up from wherever she was sitting in the church and publicly correct her.

As Miss Godfrey led the way back down the hall to the front door Kate had a glimpse into the sitting-room from another angle. This time as well as the glass-fronted bookcase and the armchair she could see the corner of a distinguished-looking fireplace and, sitting by the corner of a highly-polished brass fender, a teddy bear.

Kate's eyes widened. It was a teddy bear she recognized. It was the teddy bear Charlie Robson had won in the church fête raffle two years ago.

Highly bemused and feeling a surge of empathy for Miss Godfrey, she followed her out of the house.

'I last loaned out my china when the vicar celebrated his twenty-fifth wedding anniversary,' Miss Godfrey said as they began to walk across the grass towards the church. 'That was a very decorous occasion. I have a feeling tomorrow's festivities might be a little more . . . lively.'

Kate thought of Mavis and her children and of Bonzo in his blue satin bow and of the many market traders who would be there and thought Miss Godfrey was probably underestimating things a little.

The minute they entered the hall adjoining the church Miriam Jennings, dressed in a flowered overall and with her hair in curlers and bound up in a headscarf tied turban-fashion, hurried towards them.

'Is that the china?' she asked. 'Lovely. We can make a start and get the tables laid.'

'I see you've got them set out already,' Miss Godfrey said, looking around at the dozen wooden trestle tables that served St Mark's for every event from fête to funeral wakes.

'Well, we couldn't 'ang about, could we?' Miriam said practically. 'It's goin' to be enough of a rush in the mornin'. 'ave you brought fruit bowls as well as plates? 'ettie's done enough fruit trifle to feed an army.'

'I've brought a dozen glass dessert dishes,' Miss Godfrey said, anxious to please. 'They won't go very far I'm afraid, but it's the best I can do.'

'They'll be a great help,' Miriam said, taking the box from Miss Godfrey's arms. 'Come and 'ave a look at the cake. 'ettie made it and it's a smasher.'

Deciding she might as well stay for a little while and help with the laying of the tables, Kate followed Miriam and Miss Godfrey to the far end of the hall where the cake stood in three-tiered magnificence on a table all to itself.

'Ain't it grand?' Miriam said proudly, adjusting the two little figures symbolizing the bride and groom on the top tier.

'It's beautiful,' Miss Godfrey said, wisely not commenting on Mrs Collins's rather disastrous efforts to stain the imitation groom's night-black hair to a dull red with cochineal.

'How are you doing, ladies?' Albert Jennings called out to them cheerily as he struggled past carrying several folding chairs, a similarly laden Charlie Robson in his wake. 'Have you got your glad-rags ready for tomorrer?'

'I have indeed, Mr Jennings,' Miss Godfrey said, guessing correctly that he was referring to the outfit she intended wearing.

The church hall doors were kicked open with such a clatter that Miriam nearly jumped out of her skin and Charlie dropped one of the chairs he was carrying.

It was Mavis, a heavy carrier-bag in either hand. 'You need to wedge this bloomin' door open so we can get in and out a bit easier,' she said to no-one in particular. Crossing the wood-boarded floor towards her mother and Miss Godfrey and Kate she dumped her cargo on the nearest table. ' 'as anyone seen our Billy? I 'ad a bobby at the door five minutes ago. 'e said Billy 'ad fired a broom handle from the roof of Nibbo's shed and it 'ad landed in a front garden in Magnolia 'ill.'

'Then 'e's talkin' out of the back of 'is 'ead,' Miriam said, opening one of the carrier-bags Mavis had put on the table. ' 'e'd 'ave 'ad to fire it over the flippin' rooftops for it to reach a front garden in Magnolia 'ill from Nibbo's tool shed.' She lifted a stack of crockery from the carrier-bag. 'These blue and white plates do look nice, don't they? They'll match the bridesmaids' dresses a treat.'

'Accordin' to the bobby it did go over the rooftops,' Mavis said, parental pride in her voice. 'Apparently Billy pinched a plank of wood from the shed and bent it into a giant-sized bow. With that and the 'elp of a clothes-line he could probably have fired the broom 'andle into the Thames. Only trouble was, 'e'd sharpened one end of it into a point and it nearly impaled a poor old codger doin' 'is garden.'

'Boys will be boys,' Miriam said philosophically, ' 'ave you brought any trifle dishes? We're runnin' low on trifle dishes.'

With laughter choking in her throat Kate said, 'I'm going now. I'll see you all tomorrow.'

'And I must be going too,' Miss Godfrey said hastily.

Very briskly she led the way to the door, efficiently propping it open with the nearest chair to hand and then, when they were safely some distance away, she said to a still laughing Kate, 'A broom handle over the rooftops for goodness sake! Billy Lomax is more of a death threat than Hitler's army! It could quite easily have killed someone and yet neither his mother nor his grandmother seemed to think it at all reprehensible.' She shook her head in disbelief. 'That family really is quite extraordinary. I wouldn't put it past them to have Bonzo in church tomorrow, a ribbon round his neck.'

Containing a fresh surge of laughter only with the greatest difficulty Kate said as demurely as possible, 'Neither would I, Miss Godfrey.'

Miss Godfrey looked across at her suspiciously, about to ask if she knew things about the wedding arrangements that she wasn't revealing and then, deciding she might sleep easier if she was left in ignorance, she said dryly, 'Life isn't dull in Magnolia Square, is it? I thought I'd heard everything when Miss Helliwell told me she'd asked Mr Nibbs to adapt a child's gas mask in order that it could be worn by her cat.'

'Did he succeed?' Kate asked, knowing that if he had done Mrs Singer would want a similarly adapted gas mask for Bonzo.

'I haven't the faintest idea,' Miss Godfrey said as they

reached her gate. 'I certainly haven't seen Faust rigged and accoutreed, nor do I particularly want to. In comparison, however, the Jennings' family's antics make Miss Helliwell's flights of fancy seem quite rational.'

Kate felt laughter again begin to bubble up in her throat. 'Goodbye Miss Godfrey,' she said, looking forward to seeing Miss Godfrey's face when she saw Bonzo in his bow, 'I'll see you tomorrow, in church.'

'Goodbye, Katherine,' Miss Godfrey said, looking forward to a little peace and quiet and a nice cup of tea. 'Sleep well.'

Later, freshly bathed and with her heavy waist-length hair shampooed and hanging loose, Kate sat dressed in a white terry dressing-gown near the open window of her bedroom. It was nearly nine o'clock and the hot summer evening was pleasantly cool as dusk approached. She rested her chin in her hands, her elbows on the windowsill, looking out over Magnolia Square.

Charlie Robson was walking Queenie across the grass surrounding the church. Miss Godfrey was watering her sweet peas, Mr Nibbs was sitting in a deck-chair, his head slumped a little to one side as if he had fallen asleep and Miss Helliwell was anxiously calling Faust in for his supper. In nearly every garden that she could see magnolia shrubs and trees were in flower. On the far side of the Square, the Collins's *magnolia grandiflora* was heavy with creamy-white blossom. Yards away from the church porch a *magnolia parviflora* was thick with pendants of white petals starred by wine-coloured stamens.

Smiling again at the thought of the gas mask Mr Nibbs had adapted for Faust, she wondered how Carrie would now be feeling. After tomorrow, the rest of her life would be irrevocably different. She wondered how she herself would feel if she were about to be married. Would she be nervous? Would she have any last minute doubts? And where, at this precise moment in time, was the man

64

she would one day marry? Was he half a world away or only a few miles away? Would she fall in love with him the instant she set eyes on him or would it be a long, slow, gradual process?

Her hair was dry now and she turned away from the window and began to brush it. Normally she would also have braided it but tomorrow she was going to wear it in an elegant Grecian knot and she wanted it to be smooth and kink-free. Twisting its long length as if it were a skein of heavy wool she secured the end with a piece of cotton and then took off her dressing-gown and climbed into bed.

There was a tap on her door and without opening it her father said, 'Goodnight, *Liebling*,' as he did every night.

She smiled lovingly. There were some advantages to not being in love and engaged. She wasn't having to face the prospect of moving far away from Magnolia Square as Carrie might have to do in order to remain near to Danny.

'Goodnight, Dad,' she said, nestling down against her pillows, unable to even imagine living anywhere else but the house in which she had been born. 'God Bless.'

Chapter Four

'And did everything go off without a hitch?' Miss Pierce asked Kate on Monday lunchtime as they sat together in the small canteen that catered for the needs of Harvey's office staff.

Kate thought of Carrie looking almost regal in her sumptuous satin wedding-gown, her face aglow with happiness as she walked down St Mark's aisle on her father's arm; of Miss Helliwell, draped in chiffon and triumphantly announcing to everyone that she had foreseen the wedding two years ago; of Miss Godfrey almost unrecognizable in a silk dress instead of her customary tweed suit; of the sentimental tears shed by Mrs Collins and Carrie's mother and of the gales of laughter that had rocked the church hall during the reception and the long evening of dancing that had followed.

There had been one incident that had marred the day, but only for herself, and she had no intention of discussing the incident with Miss Pierce.

'Everything went off beautifully,' she said, putting to the back of her mind the moment during the evening celebrations when Mr Nibbs and Daniel Collins and Charlie Robson had been grouped together nearby her, speculating as to the likelihood of war with Germany. Her father had approached them carrying a tray of drinks and as he did so the subject under discussion had abruptly swung from speculation about German intent to the latest cricket scores.

Her father had been happily unaware that the conversation had been doctored for his benefit but she had been acutely aware of it. She had also been uncertain as to how she felt about it. The most sensible way would have been to view it as being merely over-tactful, but the more she thought about her father's friends feeling that such tact was necessary, the less she liked it. It raised the suspicion that they were afraid of his taking Germany's part, of perhaps even speaking in Hitler's defence. It certainly meant they no longer thought of him as being one of themselves.

'And what about the little bridesmaid the bride was so worried about?' Miss Pierce asked with genuine interest. 'Did she behave herself?'

Kate grinned. 'At the precise moment Carrie was promising to love, honour and obey, Beryl asked the vicar if she could have an orange. Before she could be silenced she explained to him that she'd been promised one if she was a good little girl and that she'd been a good little girl and was now hungry. It threw the vicar off his stroke rather and I'm sure the bride could have murdered her, but it was the only time she put a foot wrong.'

'And did she get her orange?' Miss Pierce asked, highly entertained.

'Her grandad gave her one the minute we all left the church. Neither her mother or grandmother were very pleased as she insisted on sucking at it all the time the photographs were being taken.'

Miss Pierce's smile of amusement deepened. The stiff demeanour that her colleagues found so intimidating masked shyness and she had never before come so near to forming a friendship with another member of staff. That she was now doing so with a young woman twenty years her junior both surprised and pleased her.

'What a wonderful day you must all have had,' she said, carefully folding the greaseproof paper that had wrapped her homemade sandwiches and sliding it into the outer pocket of her capacious handbag. 'I almost feel as if I know some of your neighbours, especially Miss Helliwell, Miss Godfrey and Mrs Lomax.'

'Mrs Lomax?' For a brief second Kate didn't know to whom Miss Pierce was referring.

'The bride's elder sister. You did say her name was Lomax, didn't you? The young lady you described as looking rather like Betty Grable.'

'*Mavis?*' Kate asked incredulously, wondering what on earth she had said that could possibly have prompted Miss Pierce to think of Mavis in troika with Miss Helliwell and Miss Godfrey.

'Yes. Mavis. She sounds delightful.'

Kate was completely nonplussed, unable to think of anything she had said that could possibly warrant such an opinion. Certainly at the wedding Mavis had looked amazing. Her peroxide-blonde hair had been piled high on top of her head and over her forehead in sausage-thick curls. A wisp of turquoise net, the same colour as her figure-hugging two-piece costume, had served as a hat and been worn at a rakish angle. Her shoes had been high and peep-toed; her stockings silk; her nails scarlet.

Jack Robson, who had long since abandoned hope of making any headway with Christina, had given a wolf-whistle when he had seen her walking across the grass towards the church and Mavis had spent a large part of the subsequent evening flirting shamelessly with him.

'I've told her she's asking for trouble,' Carrie had said to Kate when there had been a lull in the dancing and they had managed to have a few quiet words together. 'Ted may be long-suffering, but he's not so long-suffering that he'll put up with her playing away from home.'

'Mavis wouldn't do anything so silly,' Kate had said, deeply shocked, adding uncertainly as she caught a sudden glimpse of Mavis and Jack laughing uproariously together, 'Would she?'

'Course I wouldn't,' Mavis had said five minutes later when she had breezed into their orbit and Carrie had grabbed her by the arm and again asked her what the hell she thought she was doing. 'It's only a bit of fun. If Ted doesn't mind I don't see why you should.'

Carrie had looked across to where Ted was talking to Danny, his youngest child asleep in his arms. He certainly didn't look overly concerned but then he was such a self-contained man that even if he were, she doubted if he would allow it to show. 'Never assume,' she had said, suddenly seriously worried about the problems her elder sister was making for herself. 'Ted isn't a fool. And quiet types are the worst, when roused.'

'Roused over what, for Christ's sake?' Mavis had said, her carefully pencilled eyebrows flying high. 'We've only been 'aving a laugh and a joke together. It isn't a crime, is it?'

'It isn't sense,' Carrie had retorted grimly. 'Jack Robson isn't a bloke you can lead on and then dump.'

Mavis had rolled her eyes to heaven. 'Just listen at her!' she'd said, presumably speaking to the Almighty, 'Four hours married and she's an expert on men!' Returning her attention to Carrie she had placed her hands on her hips and said with exaggerated patience, 'Listen, Carrie. When I want your advice I'll ask for it. Until then, do us both a favour an' keep it to yourself.'

Knowing there was no way she could recount this conversation to Miss Pierce, Kate said adroitly, 'I'm not sure I would describe Mavis as delightful but she is . . . lively.'

Miss Pierce smiled indulgently and glanced at her wristwatch. 'Time to be getting back to work,' she said regretfully. As they pushed their chairs away from the table and rose to their feet, she said hesitantly, 'Do you think your friend would allow you to bring some of the wedding photographs into the office? I would so like to see them, especially a photograph of the little bridesmaid and a photograph of Bonzo wearing his bow.'

'I'm sure she would,' Kate said, picking up her clutch-bag. For the first time it occurred to her that the older woman was lonely and as she made her way back to her office she wondered if there was a way in which she could introduce Miss Pierce to Miss Godfrey.

'Did you have a nice lunchbreak?' Mr Muff, the General Sales Manager asked her as she returned to her desk in the little room adjoining his. 'You should bring a packed lunch and take it into Greenwich Park. It's far pleasanter picnicking in the park than it is eating in the staff canteen.'

Kate liked Mr Muff. He was even older than Miss Pierce, and his manner towards her was kindly and avuncular. Right from the first he had made things easy for her. 'Voigt?' he had said musingly when she had told him her name. 'Voigt? I think that's perhaps originally a Tyneside name. Very nice people the Tynesiders. All heart.'

Kate hadn't disabused him and nothing more, by anyone at Harvey's, had ever been said about her name. He had made things equally easy where her work was concerned. 'Don't worry if you make a few mistakes,' he had said to her reassuringly. 'Everyone makes mistakes in a new job and they're nothing to be ashamed of. The most important thing to remember is this. When in doubt, ask. Do that, and you won't go far wrong.'

Kate hadn't gone wrong at all. Naturally quick-witted and conscientious she had soon become familiar with the building and contracting terminology Mr Muff used when dictating letters to her and within a week had gained enough self-confidence to embark on a complete overhaul of the office filing system.

'The lights are on the blink again,' Mr Muff said to her now, scooping up a sheaf of papers from his desk. 'If the electrician comes while I'm in my meeting with Mr Harvey and young Mr Harvey tell him the fuse-box is in the postroom.'

'I will,' Kate said, sitting at her desk and winding a piece of letter-headed stationery into her typewriter. 'How long do you think your meeting will take?'

70

'That's a difficult one.' Mr Muff's usually genial face was slightly harassed. 'Mr Harvey wants me to give young Mr Harvey an idea of my responsibilities. Quite what is going to happen after that I don't know. Mr Tutley of Planning and Design met with both Mr Harveys this morning and he found the experience quite unnerving.'

In the months she had been working at Harvey's Kate had never come into personal contact with Mr Harvey but she was well aware that members of staff who did so found him disconcertingly intimidating.

'You'll be all right, Mr Muff,' she said encouragingly, rather as if their positions were reversed and he was her age and she was his. 'Onwards and upwards.'

It was one of his many trite, favourite sayings and recognizing it, he grinned. 'You're a treasure,' he said, 'I don't know what I'd do without you,' and squaring his shoulders he marched resolutely from the room.

Kate grinned to herself, flicked open her shorthand pad and began to type. Without Mr Muff working away in the adjoining office it was relatively quiet. All the offices led off a linoleum-floored corridor and occasionally she was aware of footsteps passing up and down and distant doors opening and closing, but apart from that the only sound was the rapid click-click-click of her typewriter keys and the slam of the typewriter carriage each time it was returned.

When an unfamiliar male voice broke the comparative silence it was totally unexpected, for she had neither heard her visitor knock at the door nor open it.

'Excuse me,' he said pleasantly, 'I wonder if . . .'

Without looking up from her notepad she said, 'You'll find the fuse-box in the postroom. It's the second door down the corridor, on the left.'

'I wasn't actually in search of the fuse-box,' the voice said, bemused. 'I was in search of Mr Muff.'

It was an attractive voice, languid and educated.

Realizing she had made a grave error of identity she

71

looked up and said with an apologetic smile, 'I'm sorry. I thought you were the electrician. Mr Muff is in a meeting with Mr Harvey. Perhaps I could take a message for him?'

From the way he was dressed it was immediately obvious, not only that he wasn't an electrician, but that he wasn't any member of Harvey's large, manual workforce. Tall and loose-limbed he was dressed in beige flannel trousers and a tweed jacket. Though both garments were comfortably well-worn they bore the unmistakable imprint of having being made by a high-quality tailor. His shoes, too, looked suspiciously as though they had been hand-stitched.

'Which Mr Harvey would that be?' he asked, walking the few yards that separated him from Mr Muff's desk and perching on a corner of it, one leg swinging free, 'Mr Harvey senior or Mr Harvey junior?'

With the toe of her foot Kate nudged her revolving typing-chair around so that she was facing him. At Harvey's no-one sat on desks, not even their own desks, and for a stranger to do so was an effrontery that almost robbed her of breath.

'Both,' she said with uncharacteristic tartness. 'And I don't think Mr Muff would appreciate you sitting on his desk. If you intend waiting for him it would be preferable if you sat on a chair.'

His eyebrows shot high. 'Are you always so school-marmish?' he asked, not the least trace of offence in his voice. 'And if so, why do you wear your hair like a schoolgirl's?'

His own fair hair was well cut, growing thick and smooth. His eyes were grey and long-lashed and there was a faint hollow under his cheekbones that gave his features a classically sculptured look. It was an intelligent, forceful face. And its owner was being intensely annoying.

'My hairstyle is my own affair,' she said freezingly, 'and I am not being school-marmish. I just don't think it's good manners to sit on someone's desk. Especially when they're absent from it.'

'Oh?' he said, sounding mildly surprised, as if such a thought would not have occurred to him if she hadn't brought it to his attention, 'I see.' He stood up and said in easy familiarity, 'Your hair. I've never seen anyone other than a child wear it like that. At least not in England. Are you Swedish?'

'No,' Kate said shortly, wishing she knew who on earth he was. 'Why do you wish to see Mr Muff? Are you a site engineer?'

'Not exactly.'

With easy, well-knit movements he strolled across to the open doorway between the two offices. Leaning nonchalantly against the jamb, one foot crossing the other at the ankles and revealing socks of a startling shade of yellow, he said, 'I'm just an all-purpose dogs-body, though not likely to be so for long.'

It sounded the statement of a braggart but despite his annoying high-handedness he didn't look like a braggart. As she looked into his eyes she saw humour there. And admiration.

Swiftly she looked away, flicking over the page of her notepad, colour rising to her cheeks. 'Never assume,' she said archly, not wanting him to become aware of the unsettling effect he was having on her. 'No-one gains promotion quickly here because no-one ever leaves.'

It was a piece of information she was able to give with authority because Mr Muff had often complained to her of the 'dead mens' shoes' situation that balked his own hopes of promotion.

'You've misunderstood me,' he said, not the least rebuffed. 'I didn't mean I'm not going to be a dogsbody because I'm going to be something far more glorified. I meant I'm not going to be one because I'm not going to be here much longer. I'm joining the RAF.'

Kate wound a fresh piece of notepaper into her typewriter with unnecessary vigour. She would have liked to make a crushing reply but she could hardly be disparaging about such a worthy ambition. Certain that he was gaining a great deal of pleasure out of wrong-footing her and determined to give him no further opportunities of doing so, she said crisply, 'Mr Muff is likely to be some time. If you would like to leave your name and a message . . .'

She was interrupted by the door bursting open. 'Thank God!' Mr Muff said fervently, as he entered what at first glance appeared to be his empty office. 'I thought I wasn't going to get here before him!'

He hurried across to his desk, put the papers he was carrying down on it and in vast relief turned towards the permanently open door that led to the adjoining office and Kate.

'I'm sorry about the confusion,' the visitor said before Kate could even begin to explain his presence. 'I thought it would be more sensible for us to meet here, where you have your paperwork to hand. The message altering the arrangements obviously didn't reach you.'

'No . . .' Mr Muff looked quite shell-shocked and then, leaping gallantly to Kate's defence, he said, 'Though the fault for that wouldn't lie with my secretary. She's absolutely scrupulous where messages are concerned.'

'I'm sure she is,' Toby Harvey concurred, an underlying hint of amusement in his voice.

Kate kept her eyes firmly averted from him and on her shorthand pad. Having now guessed his identity she was furiously angry. Not for a moment did she believe there had been a message informing Mr Muff of the change in arrangements. Mr Harvey's grandson had merely wrong-footed Mr Muff just as he had tried to wrong-foot her.

Frozen-faced she began to type at speed, her back straight, her thick braid of hair skimming the seat of her typing-chair.

'Er . . . Perhaps it would be best if we closed the

inter-connecting door and allowed Miss Voigt to work undisturbed,' Mr Muff said unhappily, almost as disconcerted by her frigid coolness as he had been at finding Toby Harvey in his office.

Well aware that Toby Harvey's dark grey eyes had again turned in her direction, Kate continued to type. Only when the rarely used inter-connecting door creaked shut, leaving her in privacy, did some of the angry tension leave her shoulders. So that was Mr Harvey's grandson! No wonder Miss Pierce had forecast that his working his way from office to office would cause disruption. And what was the purpose of his doing so if he was about to join the RAF?

Gradually her excessive typing speed eased back to one of efficient normality. Perhaps his grandfather didn't yet know of his intentions. If he didn't, she wondered what his reaction would be when he found out. From everything she had heard about Mr Harvey he was not a man to take insubordination of any kind lightly.

Mr Muff's voice and Toby Harvey's voice were intermittently audible as she worked and she reminded herself that Mr Harvey's attitude towards his grandson would be very different to his attitude towards other members of his workforce. Perhaps, well aware of his grandson's intentions, Mr Harvey was hoping that if he could interest him in the running of the family firm, his grandson might change his plans and not join the RAF after all. Certainly with war with Germany looming so likely it would only be natural for Mr Harvey to be unhappy at the thought of his grandson joining the forces. Even Hettie Collins, once so proud of Danny's status as a sergeant, was beginning to express doubts as to the wisdom of his having chosen a military career. 'The army's all right in peacetime,' she had been heard to say on more than one occasion, 'but it ain't so much of a doddle in wartime. Bloody Hitler. His mother should have strangled him at birth!'

Having finished all her letters, Kate began to type the

relevant addresses on to envelopes. No doubt Mr Harvey felt very much as Hettie did. After all, if war did break out, no-one in their right mind would relish the idea of a child or grandchild being in the very forefront of the fighting. She remembered that her first impression of Toby Harvey had been one of athletic ability. Certainly the way he moved spoke of training and perfect physical fitness. As she began marrying the letters to the envelopes she did so convinced that if Mr Harvey was trying to deter his grandson from joining the RAF, he was destined to meet with disappointment.

From behind the closed inter-connecting door came the sound of mutual laughter and she raised her eyebrows slightly. No matter how inauspiciously the meeting had begun it was obviously now on a very amicable footing. Which was not too surprising, considering Toby Harvey's unorthodox manner.

Her flare of anger had now ebbed and as she put the pile of letters waiting for signature in a neat pile by the side of her typewriter it occurred to her that she might have gravely misjudged Toby Harvey. If his manner was merely unorthodox he might very well have had no deliberate intention of wrong-footing either her or Mr Muff. And if he hadn't, her manner towards him had been excessively impolite.

She gave a slight shrug of her shoulders. If she had been impolite, there was nothing that could be done about it now. He should have introduced himself properly and he shouldn't have made such over-familiar remarks about her hair. She remembered the expression of admiration in his eyes when he had looked at her and felt her cheeks warm. Though excessively annoying he was also excessively good-looking. She gave a wry smile. There was no use setting her sights in *that* direction. The grandson of Mr Harvey of Harvey Construction Ltd was nearly as far removed from her social orbit as King Edward VII had been from Carrie's.

*   *   *

76

'The Harveys?' Carrie asked as Kate walked with her down Magnolia Hill towards Lewisham market. 'Why on earth ask me? You're the one who works for them! All I know about old man Harvey is that he lives in a whopping great house facing the Heath and that he goes to all the nob events.'

'What events?' Kate asked curiously.

'Oh, you know,' Carrie said airily, 'racing at Ascot and sailing at Cowes.'

Kate's curiosity deepened. 'How on earth can you know that?'

'Cos I've seen photographs of him at Ascot and Cowes in the *Tatler*, and before you ask where the heck I read the *Tatler*, I read it at the hairdressers.'

Kate, who had never been to a hairdressers in her life, said, 'Are there ever any photographs of other members of his family in the *Tatler*?'

'He doesn't have any other family, does he?' Carrie said as they turned out of the bottom end of Magnolia Hill and into the busy High Street. 'He's widowed. His son was killed, fighting in Flanders and his daughter-in-law was killed in a motoring accident somewhere exotic. France or Italy, or was it Switzerland? I can't remember now, but I know there was an awful lot of fuss in the local papers when it happened. I'm surprised you don't remember it.'

Kate, who never read about accidents if she could avoid it, said persistently, 'How long ago was it?'

Carrie shrugged. 'Donkey's years ago. I must have been about twelve. I know I was impressed at the thought of someone local travelling as far as Italy or Switzerland. Why all the interest? Are you writing a family history for the work magazine?'

'No, I'm just curious that's all.'

'Seems a funny thing to be curious about. All I'm curious about is whether Hitler's going to invade Czechoslovakia and what the hell will happen if he does.'

Kate was silent. If Hitler occupied Czechoslovakia's

Sudetenland then Europe would most likely be plunged into full-scale war.

'Danny says all future leave has been cancelled,' Carrie said as the first of Lewisham's market stalls came into view, 'and he says there are rumours that the navy's about to be mobilized. It doesn't look very good, does it?'

'No,' Kate said soberly, wondering how her father would be affected if war were declared between Britain and Germany; wondering if Danny would be sent straight to the front; wondering how long it took for an RAF recruit to gain his wings.

'No war!' Mr Muff said to her with vast relief three weeks later. 'Mr Chamberlain has dealt with the matter and now we can all live in peace, thank God!'

'It isn't a very satisfactory peace, is it?' Kate asked from behind her typewriter. 'We haven't stood up to Hitler. We've given in to him. He now has the Sudetenland, which is what he wanted all along. What happens when he wants more of Czechoslovakia? When he turns his greedy eyes towards Bohemia and Moravia? What are we going to do then?'

'But he won't,' Mr Muff said patiently as he retrieved a letter from a filing cabinet. 'The Sudetan region of Czechoslovakia is inhabited mainly by Germans, which is why ceding it to Germany is, in a way, quite reasonable. And now he's got what he wants, Herr Hitler will settle down and we'll all be able to enjoy a little peace and quiet.'

'I'm not sure that the Sudetenland *is* inhabited mainly by Germans,' Kate said, mindful of her many conversations on the subject with her father. 'There are Czechs and Slovaks and Hungarians and Ruthenes living there as well.'

'Ruthenes?' Mr Muff asked with mild interest as he returned to his desk. 'What are Ruthenes? Are they members of a religious sect?'

'They're Slavs,' Kate said, trying to keep impatience from her voice and wondering if Mr Chamberlain was similarly ignorant. 'And no-one seems to have asked what will happen to *them* now the Sudetenland has been ceded to a fascist state.'

'I'm sure everything will work out quite satisfactorily,' Mr Muff said, too vastly relieved by the promise of peace for his own country to worry overmuch about the fate of a people he had, until that moment, been ignorant of.

'And there will be Jews in the Sudetenland,' Kate added, refusing to let him off the hook. 'What will happen to them now?'

Mr Muff didn't know, and if the answer was one which would keep him awake at night, neither did he want to know.

'There's a lot of post this morning,' he said, clinging determinedly to the cheerfulness he had felt ever since he had heard the BBC report of the Munich Peace Agreement. 'We'd better make a start on it. Onward and upward.'

Kate had brought a packed lunch to work and at lunchtime she walked down towards the river. Sitting on a conveniently sited bench a little down-river from Greenwich Pier she gazed out over the iron-grey surface of the Thames and wondered why it was that a man as essentially kind and decent as Mr Muff should be unable to see the Munich Peace Agreement for what it truly was; an obscene sell-out to Hitler.

The river was thick with shipping. Tugs and lighters, gunnel-deep with crates and bales destined for the wharves and warehouses of Bermondsey and Rother-hithe, vied for shipping space with barges and an occasional paddle-steamer.

Kate took her sandwiches out of her shoulder-bag and opened them, wondering where the larger ships had come from and where they were going; wondering if any of them were still trading with Germany.

'A penny for them,' a voice she would have recognized anywhere said, his shadow falling over her.

Her heart began to beat in sharp, slamming little strokes that she could feel even in her finger-tips. Ever since her initial meeting with him he had been working with Mr Tutley in Planning and Design and she had seen him only at a distance. From a distance she had, however, been acutely aware of him and she had become convinced that her revised opinion of him was correct. He hadn't intentionally meant to disconcert either her or Mr Muff. He was simply unorthodox in that he treated everyone, from senior management to cleaning staff, in the same direct and friendly manner.

As he sat down beside her she said truthfully, 'I was wondering where all the ships come from and go to and I was thinking that it must be very nice to be a sailor, especially if being a sailor means not having to endure newsreels of Mr Chamberlain waving his wretched piece of paper in the air and being congratulated for having achieved peace at Czechoslovakia's expense.'

'Do you think he has achieved peace?' Toby asked, helping himself, uninvited, to one of her cheese and tomato sandwiches.

To her amazement she felt her heartbeats steady and her tummy muscles relax. It was suddenly as if she was talking to someone she had known for a long time; someone with whom she was completely at ease.

'No,' she said with stark frankness. 'Do you?'

'No,' he said, as she had known he would. 'It's a cop-out. However loudly Hitler shouts that Czechoslovakia is his last territorial demand, no-one with any sense believes him.' He stretched his long legs out in front of him. 'Duff Cooper certainly doesn't believe him. It wouldn't surprise me if he didn't resign his position as First Lord of the Admiralty. And Anthony Eden and Winston Churchill certainly don't.'

'And I don't,' Kate said darkly as the *Laguna Belle* paddle-steamer hoved majestically into view.

'Well of course you don't,' he said with the easy confidence she found so attractive, 'we're always going to be in agreement about everything important. I knew it the moment I set eyes on you.'

It was so exactly her own feeling that she was robbed of breath, completely unable to make any kind of a reply.

He turned towards her, his eyes holding hers steadily. 'I want to know you better, Kate. It was hopeless my trying to do so while we were both working under the same roof. The speculation and gossip would have made life a misery for you.'

Her heart once more began to beat in painful, slamming strokes. He wasn't flirting with her. The depth of feeling in his voice and the expression in his dark grey eyes was heart-stoppingly serious.

'Today is my last day,' he said, taking hold of her hand. 'I leave for RAF training camp tomorrow. Will you write to me while I'm there? Will you go out with me when I have leave?'

Unnoticed by both of them the packet of sandwiches slid off her knee and onto the dusty ground.

'Yes,' she said, the blood drumming in her ears. 'Yes, of course I'll write to you. Of course I will go out with you.'

The paddle-steamer was now abreast of them and the many passengers en route to Southend were leaning against its deck-rails, regarding them with interest.

'Thank God,' he said with vast relief and, to the delight of their many onlookers and a cacophony of wolf-whistles and encouraging cheers, he leaned across and kissed her full on the mouth.

Chapter Five

When she left work at the end of the afternoon and walked out into the road leading up to the Heath he was sitting in a parked, open-topped sports car, waiting for her.

'Hop in,' he said with a wide grin, leaning over and opening the passenger-seat door. 'We may as well start the way we mean to go on.'

It wasn't the most romantic of invitations but it was a blatant affirmation of their new-found relationship and Kate's heart sang as she stepped into the tiny MG and settled herself into the low-slung seat.

'Which way?' he asked, switching on the ignition and gunning the engine into life. 'Uphill or downhill?'

'Up,' she said, acutely aware of how strong and sure his well-shaped hands were on the wheel. 'I live in Magnolia Square, just off the south-west corner of the Heath.'

'Then we're nearly neighbours,' he said, slipping the car into gear. 'My family home overlooks the Heath.'

She knew very well where his family home was because weeks ago, after Carrie had told her its location, she had walked past it when taking Bonzo for a walk. In comparison to her own middle-class home it was palatial. Built in the style of Robert Adams it had a columned portico and a front door decorated with a classical pediment. The windows were long and slender with delicately moulded architraves and the rear garden, enclosed by a high wall, had looked to be vast.

'Were you born in Blackheath?' she asked as they roared up the hill with Greenwich Park to the left of them.

'I was born in the house I still live in,' he said, slowing down as they neared the junction with the road skirting the Heath. 'What about you? You said you weren't Swedish, but were you born somewhere else in Scandinavia? Denmark or Norway or Finland?'

She shook her head, her heavy braid of hair flaxen-gold in the late afternoon sunlight. 'No, I was born in Magnolia Square.'

'Then you're English?' He drove across the old London to Dover road and on to one of the narrow roads that criss-crossed the Heath. 'I hope you won't take offence at my saying so, but you don't look it.' He flashed her a sudden, down-slanting smile. 'You look more like a goddess out of Norse mythology than a born and bred London girl.'

Her hands had been resting lightly clasped on her lap and now they tightened, the knuckles showing white. A few years ago it would never have occurred to her to be hesitant about admitting to her German ancestry, but that had been before the threat of war with Germany had loomed so large. She wondered what Toby's reaction would be when he learned that her father was German; she wondered if he would still want her to write to him; if he would still want to take her out when he came home on leave.

Taking the bull by the horns she said steadily, 'My father is German. He was a prisoner of war who married a London girl and never returned home.'

He looked towards her swiftly, his eyebrows rising slightly, 'German? Is that making things difficult for him? Or for you?'

Relief began to seep through her. From the tone of his voice it was obvious that he didn't find it a difficulty.

'Dad used to teach German at one of the local schools and when Hitler annexed Austria he was asked to resign,' she said hoping that he would realize how traumatic an experience it had been for her father without her having to say any more. 'And there was one more horrible incident.'

He had returned his attention to the road and remained silent, waiting for her to continue.

As unemotionally as she was able, she said, 'Neighbours of ours have taken a Jewish refugee in. Her brother and father were killed by the Nazis and her mother and sister are in a concentration camp. Dad knew that her English was minimal and when she was introduced to him he greeted her in German.'

He flashed her another quick glance and she said succinctly, 'It was a mistake.'

'I can imagine,' he said with so much feeling that she knew he wasn't being merely trite.

He turned off the road leading towards the south-west corner of the Heath, heading instead towards Blackheath Village. 'It's the "if some Germans are nasty bits of work, they're all nasty bits of work" school of thought. Unfortunately it's a school of thought my grandfather subscribes to with a vengeance.'

As they approached the Princess of Wales pub on the outskirts of the Village he said, 'Shall we continue this discussion over a couple of shandies? You're not in a hurry to go out anywhere, are you?'

She shook her head. Her father would no doubt be wondering where she was but he would think she was perhaps with Carrie and certainly wouldn't be worrying about her.

He slowed down, parking the car beside the pond across the road from the pub.

'One thing I'd better tell you now,' he said as he switched off the MG's engine, 'if my grandfather had known you were part German he would never have allowed Personnel to employ you.'

She sucked in her breath, her eyes flying wide.

He shot her a reassuring grin. 'Don't worry. It's never likely to come to his notice. It's something you have to know about though, especially if we're going to be seeing a lot of each other.'

He opened the door of the car and got out, saying nothing further until he had walked round the car and opened her door for her. 'The problem is,' he said, offering her a helping hand, 'my father was killed in Flanders in one of the last battles of the war. He was an only child and grandfather has never totally recovered from his grief, nor has he ever been able to bring himself to even speak the word "German".'

'Then he's not going to want you to be friends with me,' Kate said unsteadily, her face pale.

He kept hold of her hand and tucked it into the crook of his arm as he walked with her towards one of the many wood benches and tables set outside the front of the pub. 'He will do eventually, but it's going to take time.' His voice was infinitely reassuring, 'And time is something we have plenty of. What would you like to drink?'

'A shandy, please.'

He was so obviously uncaring himself of her German ancestry, so confident that even where his grandfather was concerned any difficulties would be eventually resolved, that the apprehension that had engulfed her only seconds before was already beginning to fade. Many people held his grandfather's prejudices, and for the same reason that his grandfather held them; and many more people held more recent prejudices and, considering the horrors now taking place in Germany, did so quite understandably.

She sat at one of the wooden tables whilst he went inside the pub for their drinks. His grandfather's attitude to Germany and Germans was nothing out of the ordinary and was unlikely to affect her in any profound way. As Mr Muff's secretary she held far too lowly a position at Harvey's for her German surname ever to come to Mr Harvey's notice and as to her friendship with Toby Harvey, that was their own affair and no-one else's.

London was enjoying an Indian summer and though it was now well after six o'clock and the beginning of October the early evening air was pleasantly warm. The pond lay across the narrow road from the Princess of Wales and, as always in daylight hours, a scattering of children were playing on its banks launching toy boats across its surface. Some were racing their boats against each other, others were trying to torpedo them with sticks and stones. Among the latter group Kate recognized Billy Lomax, Carrie's eldest nephew. At eight years old he was obviously leader of the small gang of boys happily torpedoing everything afloat.

Toby walked across to her carrying two glasses of shandy. 'Whenever I catch you unawares you always look as if you're contemplating the theory of relativity or the solution to the problems of the world,' he said, amusement once again in his voice. 'Which were you thinking about this time?'

'Neither,' she said, a feeling of heady happiness fizzing through her. 'I was just watching the children playing with their boats. The little boy in the torn short trousers and wellingtons, is my best friend's nephew.'

'He looks a little terror,' Toby said without the least trace of censure in his voice. 'Have you nieces and nephews?'

She took a sip of her shandy and then said a little regretfully, 'No. The only family I've got is my father.'

'And the only family I've got is my grandfather,' Toby said cheerfully. 'So lack of a large family is another thing we have in common.'

A large shambling figure was walking across the Heath and towards the pond, an alsatian at his heels. Kate had no difficulty at all in recognizing him and with a sinking heart she realized that Charlie was making a bee-line for the Princess of Wales.

'I think someone is trying to attract your attention,' Toby said as Queenie bounded across the road towards the pub and Charlie, ambling in her wake, waved genially in their direction.

Kate wasn't remotely a snob but she couldn't help wishing that Miss Godfrey or Mr Nibbs, not Charlie, had been the first of her neighbours to be introduced to Toby. Charlie, with a broad leather belt holding up trousers without belt-loops, a collarless shirt and a two-days growth of stubble on his chin, looked definitely disreputable.

'It's a neighbour,' Kate said resignedly as Queenie charged straight up to her and slammed two large heavy paws down on her lap. 'I'm sorry,' she added, not knowing quite what she was sorry for but certain that before the encounter was over, an apology of some sort would be in order.

'There's no need to apologize,' Toby said, moving their glasses of shandy out of the way of Queenie's powerful tail, 'but is that dog safe? A small dog licking your face is one thing, an alsatian licking your face seems a little risky.'

'She's perfectly safe with people she knows,' Kate said, fending Queenie off with as much firmness as she could muster. '*Down*, Queenie. There's a good dog.'

Queenie, her tail still wagging, did as she was told and, as Charlie approached them, transferred her attentions to Toby.

'Bit of a surprise seeing you 'ere, petal,' Charlie said as Queenie sniffed Toby's ankles and he obligingly scratched the top of her head. 'Does your Dad know you've started boozin'?'

'I'm not boozing,' Kate said wondering if, after this initial experience, Toby would ever ask her out again, 'I'm having a shandy, that's all.'

'And I'm goin' to 'ave a pint of mild,' Charlie said, his pleasure at the prospect obvious. 'Look after Queenie for me for a minute. The landlord doesn't like her going inside. Not after she peed on his floor.'

As Charlie pottered off into the pub Kate wished

fervently that the earth would open and swallow her up. Seeing her embarrassment Toby said comfortingly, 'Don't look so mortified. A bit of plain speaking never hurt anyone.'

Queenie was now sitting companionably at his feet and Kate prayed fervently that when Charlie re-emerged from the pub he would take his drink, and Queenie, and sit at a table some distance away from them.

He didn't. Instead, with a pint of mild ale in either hand and a shallow bowl tucked under one arm, he sat himself companionably down at their table.

'I've already got a drink, thanks very much,' Toby said pleasantly as Charlie set both glasses down on the table.

'I dare say you 'ave and it's a good job too 'cos this is for Queenie,' Charlie said equably, proceeding to pour a pint of mild into the bowl he had brought out of the pub with him. 'I used to let Queenie drink from the glass,' he added confidingly, 'but 'arriet said it weren't hygienic and so now the landlord keeps a bowl for 'er.'

'Harriet?' Kate asked, wondering for how long they were going to be saddled with Charlie's company and unsure whether Charlie was referring to Carrie's mother-in-law. 'Don't you mean Hettie?'

'No, I don't.' Charlie set the bowl and its frothing contents down on the ground for Queenie. 'I mean 'arriet.' He took a deep drink of his mild ale, wiped a line of foam from his top lip with the back of his hand and said to Toby, 'It's 'er 'avin' bin a teacher that makes 'er so particular. Still, it don't do no 'arm to 'umour 'er. I like keepin' people 'appy.'

'Are you referring to Miss Godfrey?' Kate asked, unable to even imagine Miss Godfrey in a public house, much less imagine her in one in Charlie's company.

'Well I 'ain't referring to the Pope,' Charlie replied reasonably. 'And when are you goin' to introduce me to your friend? 'arriet's very hot on introductions. She says it's a mark of good manners.'

'Toby Harvey,' Toby said, aware that Kate had been rendered temporarily speechless and stretching his hand across the table towards Charlie. 'I'm very pleased to meet you.'

'And I'm very pleased to meet you,' Charlie responded as Queenie settled herself comfortably at Toby's feet. 'The only Harvey I know of is old man Harvey who owns the construction company in Greenwich. You wouldn't be a relation by any chance, would you?'

There was a hair's breadth of hesitation and then Toby said, an edge of reluctance in his voice, 'I'm his grandson.'

Charlie's bushy eyebrows rose high and Kate understood why Toby had been reluctant to admit to the relationship. It was because, once he had done so, there was no knowing quite what reaction he would meet with.

Charlie was impressed but not overawed. 'Blimey!' he said graphically. 'I didn't know I was in such 'igh-flyin' company. What are you doin' boozin' 'ere? Why aren't you at the Ritz?'

Toby grinned. 'The beer's better here,' he said with the easy friendliness which Kate found so attractive.

Charlie chortled appreciatively. 'Is that a fact?' He took another deep drink of his pint of mild ale, wiped his mouth with the back of his hand again and said with an air of profound wisdom, 'You learn something new every day, don't you?' Another thought occurred to him and transferring his attention to Kate he said, 'Does your dad know the kind of company you're keepin'?'

Kate was just about to tell Charlie that whether her father knew or not was none of Charlie's business but as she drew in breath to do so Toby said quickly, 'We're going to Kate's home when we leave here so that she can introduce me to Mr Voigt.'

'Then that's all right then,' Charlie said, happy that the proprieties were being observed. He drained his glass of beer and to Kate's vast relief rose to his feet. 'Seein' you two are obviously courtin' I'll take meself off,' he

89

said, happily oblivious of the flush of embarrassed colour his words had brought to Kate's cheeks. He nudged the recumbent Queenie with a hob-nailed boot. 'Come on, Queenie girl. Two's company, three's a crowd and we're intrudin'. Let's pay a visit to The Three Tuns and see what the beer's like there.'

Queenie lumbered to her feet. Toby gave her a final affectionate pat and together, man and dog ambled off in the direction of the pub situated more centrally in the Village.

The moment Charlie was safely out of ear-shot Kate said awkwardly, still burning with embarrassment, 'I'm sorry. I don't know what gave him the idea that we were courting . . .'

'Probably because we are,' Toby said, taking hold of her hand and squeezing it tight. 'At least, I hope we are. And as Charlie so properly pointed out, under the circumstances it's about time I met your father.'

All her embarrassment fled. Happiness so deep she couldn't in a hundred years have found the words to describe it, suffused her.

As they rose from the table and began to walk back towards his car, their hands still tightly clasped, she wondered how Carrie could have been so prosaic about her feelings for Danny. The sensation Toby engendered in her was far more than one of his merely 'suiting' her. It was heart-stoppingly wonderful; utterly magical.

Although dusk was now fast approaching, Carl was taking advantage of the last hour of daylight and was dividing and re-planting large clumps of campanulas in the front garden when Toby's MG roared spectacularly into Magnolia Square and slowed to a halt only yards away from him. He looked up from his task, startled.

So, too, to Kate's chagrin, did Miss Godfrey, busy dead-heading the last of her roses; Mr Nibbs, who was trimming his hedge; and Jack Robson who was cleaning and polishing his motor cycle.

As Toby walked around the car to the passenger-seat door and opened it for Kate, Carl put down his gardening fork and with a slight frown of puzzlement walked down the short garden pathway to the gate.

Wishing he hadn't done so, wishing he hadn't been in the garden at all, Kate stepped out of the MG well aware that not only had she and Toby become a focus of interest for Miss Godfrey, Mr Nibbs and Jack Robson, but that Hettie Collins had twitched her net curtains back for a clearer view and that an avidly interested Mavis was fast approaching, Beryl skipping in her wake.

'Hello Dad,' Kate said, wishing her father would show some signs of turning away from the gate and leading the way into the house. 'I hope you haven't been worrying about me.'

'No,' Carl said truthfully, 'I thought perhaps you were with Carrie.'

With slightly troubled eyes he looked from her to Toby, to the sports car, and back to Toby again.

Aware that he was patiently waiting for both an introduction and an explanation and that he was not going to invite Toby into the garden, let alone the house, until he had received both, Kate resigned herself to performing the introductions in full view of her curious neighbours.

'I'd like you to meet Toby Harvey, Dad. He's been working at Harvey's but today was his last day. He's joined the RAF and leaves for training camp tomorrow.'

As Toby and Carl shook hands Mavis drew abreast of them.

'Nice weather we're 'aving for October 'ain't it, Mr Voigt?' she called out cheerfully, her magnificent bosoms straining against an excessively frilled and flounced blouse, her skirt tight across her hips.

Carl transferred his attention temporarily from Toby and replied with courtesy that it was indeed exceptional weather for early October.

Mavis had slowed down nearly to a standstill and

Kate, knowing very well that Mavis was hoping she would now be introduced to Toby, remained obstructively silent. Enough was enough. Toby had already been introduced to the least respectable resident of Magnolia Square without being introduced to its most flamboyant resident, all on the same day.

Cheated of her objective, Mavis continued hip-swingingly to where Jack Robson was making a show of applying polish to his motor cycle but was, in reality, watching the scene taking place at the Voigts' gate with just as much interest as Miss Godfrey and Hettie Collins.

'Would you like to join us for supper?' Carl asked Toby. 'I don't think the menu is going to be anything special. Ham and chips perhaps, but you're very welcome to join us.'

Toby shook his head regretfully. 'I'd love to accept the invitation Mr Voigt, but I can't. As it's my last night at home I'm dining out with my grandfather tonight.'

He didn't add that it had not been his intention to do so, that his intention had been to take Kate out to dinner and to embark on the delicious task of getting to know her better. His plan of action had been foiled at breakfast time when his grandfather had announced that, to mark his last night at home, he had arranged for them to dine in town that evening at Ketners in Soho.

'Have you time to come in for a cup of tea?' Carl asked, well aware that, as it was the first time Kate had ever brought a young man home, the young man in question was obviously of importance to her and that in meeting them at the gate he had made a grave tactical error. Mavis and Jack were now both lounging against Jack's motor cycle and regarding the three of them with prurient curiosity. Miss Godfrey was taking an unconscionable long time to dead-head the flowers nearest to their mutual garden fence. Nibbo was ostensibly trimming his hedge but was certainly not giving his full attention to the task and Daniel Collins had now joined Hettie at the window in order to share her grandstand view.

Well aware that his grandfather would already be wondering where the hell he was and that they were going to be horrendously late for their table reservation at Ketners, Toby again regretfully shook his head. 'No, I'm afraid I must be going.' He looked towards Kate. 'I'll write,' he said, 'I promise.'

As their eyes held, Kate knew that he would always keep his promises to her, the solemn as well as the not-so-solemn.

'Goodbye,' she said huskily, uncaring now of their rapt audience. 'Take care of yourself.'

'I will.' With immense effort he dragged his eyes away from hers. 'Goodbye, Mr Voigt,' he said to a deeply disconcerted Carl. 'It's been nice meeting you.'

'Goodbye,' Carl said, knowing that he had seriously underestimated the kind of relationship that existed between his daughter and Toby Harvey and wondering just when it had been formed and why, until now, Kate had given him not the faintest inkling of it.

Toby strode across the pavement to the MG and seconds later, watched by a growing number of Magnolia Square residents, gunned the engine into life. He gave one last look towards the Voigt garden gate, waved, and then put the car into gear and pressed his foot down on the accelerator, sweeping southwards out of the Square and into Magnolia Hill at a speed Jack Robson deeply envied.

'*Well!*' Carl said expressively as the sports car disappeared from view, 'it would seem there's been a lot going on in your life you haven't been telling me about, *Liebling.*'

'No,' Kate said as Miss Godfrey and Mr Nibbs put an end to their pretence of gardening in the deepening gloom and returned indoors and the Collins's net curtains fell once again into place. 'I first met Toby some weeks ago when he met with Mr Muff in Mr Muff's office, but we haven't talked together since. Not until today.'

Above his frameless spectacles Carl's eyebrows rose slightly. He didn't for one minute doubt what she was telling him but it didn't explain the depth of feeling he had sensed between them, instead it made that depth of feeling even odder.

'You can tell me more about Toby Harvey while we make something to eat,' he said, turning at last away from the gate and leading the way up the path towards the stone steps leading to their front door. 'What did he do at Harvey's? Was he an engineer? An architect? He must have had a responsible position if he can afford to drive a sports car.'

'He might be an engineer,' Kate said a little doubtfully, 'or he might even be a qualified architect. He wasn't actually working as either, though.'

'Then what was he working as?' Carl asked as they entered the house, his curiosity about Kate's new friend deepening even further.

Realizing that her father hadn't, unlike Charlie, immediately made a connection between Toby's surname and Harvey Construction Ltd and suddenly wondering what his reaction would be when she told him of it, she said a little hesitatingly, 'Toby was working his way through all the offices, Sales, Marketing, Export, spending a week or so in each so that he would have a grasp of the way they are run.'

'So he was a management trainee?' Carl asked, taking the chip-pan out of a cupboard beneath the sink and placing it on one of the oven's gas rings.

'Ye-ess.'

At the uncertainty in her voice Carl said patiently, 'Well either he was or he wasn't, *Liebling*.'

'It isn't quite so simple, Dad.' She lifted a couple of large potatoes from out of the vegetable rack and put them on a wooden chopping board next to the sink.

'Although I suppose you could describe what he was doing as trainee management it wasn't straightforward trainee management.' She took a potato peeler from out of the cutlery drawer. 'Mr Harvey who owns Harvey Construction Ltd, is Toby's grandfather and so he wants Toby to have a full understanding of what is involved in the day-to-day running of the company.'

As she began to peel the potatoes Carl's eyebrows rose once again above the edge of his spectacles, '*Wirklich?*' he said, unsure as to how he felt about Kate's first prospective boyfriend being from a world so far removed from their own world. 'Really?'

Kate paused in her task to turn and face him, understanding what it was that was troubling her father.

'He's very nice, Dad. In fact he's so nice that at first I thought he was a little odd! He has absolutely no side whatsoever.'

'Side?'

Kate's mouth tugged into a smile. Despite her father's many years of living in England there were still some informal English expressions which defeated him. 'By "side" I mean that he's not at all pretentious or snobbish or full of his own importance.'

'No,' Carl said as she again continued with her task of peeling the potatoes. 'Even though I only spoke to him for a few minutes, that much was obvious. It just seems a little strange, though, his not actually making time to get to know you until the day before he leaves London for what will obviously be many months.' He didn't add 'for good', though that was what he was thinking. As an RAF serviceman Toby Harvey was certainly not going to find himself stationed in the Blackheath vicinity.

Kate began to slice the peeled potatoes into chips. 'He told me that he wanted to get to know me better immediately after first meeting me, but that he knew the kind of gossip that would have begun to spread if he had done so and he didn't want to subject me to it. As it is,

95

we can now write to each other while he's at training camp.'

'And see each other when he has leave?'

'Yes,' Kate said, keeping her eyes very firmly on the potatoes she was slicing and acutely aware that a flush of colour was again warming her cheeks.

There were many more questions Carl would have liked to ask but he knew that to do so would be an invasion of Kate's privacy. She wasn't a child any more, she was a twenty-year-old woman and she was entitled to form friendships and emotional relationships without undue interference from him.

He scooped a handful of the sliced potatoes and dropped them into the, now, hot fat of the chip-pan. Toby Harvey had seemed to be an exceptionally pleasant young man and he had had the good manners to introduce himself to the father of the girl he intended corresponding with. Many young men would not have troubled to do so and the action indicated that Toby Harvey's intentions towards Kate were honourable.

Hoping fervently that his assumption would prove to be correct, and changing the subject, he said, 'I saw Miriam Jennings this evening as I was locking up the bookshop. She says Carrie has some news for you. When you were late home I thought you must have already got the message and gone straight down to see her.'

Kate passed the last of the chips over to him. 'I'll go down and see her after we've eaten. Perhaps Danny is being posted nearer to London. She's hardly seen him since he's been stationed at Catterick. Did I tell you that Toby took me for a drink to The Princess of Wales and that Charlie Robson joined us? He referred to Miss Godfrey as "Harriet" and they must sometimes go to The Princess of Wales for a drink together because Charlie says Miss Godfrey told him it was unhygienic for Queenie to drink from a glass and so he keeps a bowl there for her. I can't imagine the two of them out together, can you? They must look very odd.'

With a smile of amusement Carl agreed with her and for the next hour their conversation remained strictly on unimportant tit-bits of gossip. Nibbo's disguising of the roof of his Anderson shelter with gooseberry bushes; the gas mask Daniel Collins had adapted for Miss Helliwell's cat; the cricket team's decision to have a night out with wives and girlfriends in October and to go up town and see a show at the London Palladium. Toby Harvey wasn't mentioned again, nor was the current political situation.

'I'll do the washing-up tonight,' Carl said when they had finished their meal. 'You go and see Carrie and find out what her piece of news is.'

'Thanks, Dad.' She rose from the table, gave him a kiss on his forehead and pausing long enough to pick up her jacket, hurried from the house.

It was nearly dark now and apart from Billy Lomax and his mates, the Square was deserted. Billy had secured a piece of rope high up around the lamppost outside Miss Helliwell's and the length left dangling was now serving him and his friends as a makeshift swing.

' 'ello!' he called familiarly to her as he pushed his wellington-booted feet against the post to give himself more momentum for his next spin around it. 'Mum says she saw you with your boyfriend and his posh car this afternoon. She says if you're not careful you'll be gettin' so lad-di-dah we'll 'ave to pay tuppence to say 'ello to you!'

Kate could well imagine the tone of Mavis's remarks but was too well brought up to tell Billy her opinion of them. Instead she said with a tartness to her voice that wouldn't have discredited Miss Godfrey, 'You'll have that lamppost down Billie Lomax if you don't stop swinging round it like a dervish.'

'Like a wot?' Billy yelled out as he swung himself around the lamppost again, clutching tight hold of the end of the rope. 'A dervish? Wot the 'eck's a dervish? A German aeroplane?'

Giving Billy up as a lost cause and not deigning to reply Kate turned in at the Jennings's gateway, eager for a chat with Carrie. Her fear that the time they had always spent together would be severely curtailed once Carrie had married had proved groundless. With Danny stationed two hundred and fifty miles away in Yorkshire Carrie's lifestyle had changed very little. Nearly every evening they met up for an hour or two to chat and giggle together and every Saturday night, unless Danny was home on a forty-eight hour pass, they went to the local cinema together.

Leah opened the door to her and as she did so Carrie shouted down the stairs, 'Is that you, Kate? Come on up. I'm painting my nails.'

As Kate carried out Carrie's instructions and began to climb the stairs leading from the narrow hallway to the bedrooms, Leah returned to the kitchen and through the open kitchen door Kate caught a glimpse of Christina and Miriam and Albert sitting around the kitchen table in deep and grave discussion. A newspaper was spread open on the table and though Kate couldn't see its headlines or photographs she knew what their subject matter would be. The new peace accord that Prime Minister Chamberlain had signed in Munich with Hitler.

Well aware that no-one in the Jennings' household would have the slightest belief in Chamberlain's assertion that by signing the accord he had achieved 'peace in our time' she continued up the stairs wondering if it was her family's reaction to the news of the peace agreement that Carrie wanted to talk to her about.

' 'course it isn't,' Carrie said minutes later as she sat at her dressing-table, carefully continuing with her task of painting her nails a searing scarlet. 'I'm sick to death of hearing about Chamberlain and Munich. There's been no other subject of conversation in this house all day. Dad thinks Chamberlain should be certified and put in an asylum and Mum keeps asking why it is the

King doesn't intervene. She's such a royalist she believes one word of reprimand from the House of Windsor will bring Hitler to his knees.'

'Then what was it you wanted to tell me?' Kate asked, settling herself comfortably on Carrie's bed.

Being careful not to smudge her nails Carrie screwed the cap back on her nail varnish bottle and then turned to face her, her pretty, square-jawed face radiant. 'I'm having a baby,' she said jubilantly. 'Isn't it wonderful news? Isn't it absolutely blooming marvellous?'

Chapter Six

Kate could only agree with her that it was, indeed, marvellous news. Even as she said the words she was aware, however, of a very peculiar sensation. A baby. In some odd way she realized that she had only ever thought of mature women having babies, not girls of her own age. And even though Carrie was now married, her marriage had changed things between them so little that it had never seemed quite real. Carrie being pregnant would, however, change things quite a lot. It would mean her friend embarking on experiences and responsibilities that were still quite alien to herself; experiences and responsibilities she could scarcely imagine.

Immediately the thought occurred to her, her thoughts flew to Toby Harvey and the familiar sensation of heat that engulfed her whenever she allowed her thoughts to dwell on him again, suffused her. It would be easy to imagine herself married to Toby and bearing his child.

She said a little sheepishly, 'I have some news for you as well.'

Carrie's cat-green eyes widened in anticipation. 'What?' She began to giggle. 'You're not pregnant as well, are you?'

At the ludicrousness of the remark Kate grinned and threw a pillow at her. 'No, idiot,' she said as Carrie ducked adroitly. 'It's something I should have told you about weeks ago but I didn't want to put it into words because I was so sure nothing would come of it.'

'What's his name and where did you meet him?' Carrie asked, coming to the correct conclusion immediately and waving her scarlet-tipped nails in the air in order to dry them a little quicker.

Knowing very well the shock that Carrie was in for and experiencing a sense of fizzing excitement at the mere prospect of it, she said as casually as she was able, 'Toby Harvey and I met him at work.'

'Harvey?' Carrie was visibly bemused. 'That's a bit of a coincidence, isn't it? Meeting a bloke at Harvey's with the name Harvey.'

'Not really,' Kate said, keeping a straight face with difficulty. 'His grandfather is old man Harvey.'

Carrie's jaw dropped and as she stared goggle-eyed it was Kate's turn to giggle. 'I'm surprised Mavis hasn't already told you about what she terms my "posh" boyfriend. She saw us earlier and it would have been typical of her to have already broadcast the news far and wide.'

'I haven't spoken to Mavis for days. We had a row over the amount of time she spends talking to Jack Robson whenever she's coming back from shopping or taking the kids to and from school and he's messing about in the Square with his motor bike. I told her people would begin talking about it and that it would get back to Ted but she wouldn't have any of it. She says the idea of her being interested in Jack Robs[on] any way other than as someone to have a laugh a[nd] joke with is just plain daft and that she doesn't [care] a fig what the old biddies in the Square think abou[t.]

She rose from her dressing-table stool and crossed th[e] small room to sit next to Kate on the bed. 'So?' she asked, getting back to the real subject of interest, 'just how the hell did you manage to snare the grandson of the richest man in the neighbourhood?'

'I didn't snare him,' Kate replied with mock indignation. 'It just happened, that's all. He came into my office a few weeks ago for a meeting with Mr Muff. We exchanged a few words. Not very amicable words, actually. Then I kept seeing him in the canteen and I realized he was a much nicer a person than I had first thought . . .'

'Hang on a minute! What do you mean "we exchanged a few words not very amicably?"' Carrie's thick tangle of hair, which never fell into a sleek fall to her shoulders no matter how she coaxed and brushed it, tumbled hoydenishly around her rosy-cheeked face. 'How can you fall out with a bloke you've never set eyes on before within seconds of him walking into your office? Especially a bloke who is the boss's grandson?'

Kate curled her legs beneath her on the bed, knowing that the ensuing gossip was going to be a long one. 'I didn't know he was the boss's grandson when he swanned into Mr Muff's office as if he owned it.'

'Well if he doesn't own it right at this very moment, he will one day,' Carrie interrupted dryly.

Kate let the comment slide by. She wasn't interested in Toby Harvey because he would, in all likelihood, one day inherit his grandfather's company. She was interested in him because he was the most likeable man she had ever met; because they thought alike and instinctively understood one another; because he was kind and tolerant and because he made her laugh. Her cheeks warmed. And because she thought him unbelievably handsome and because he had the most dizzying physical effect on her.

'Are you going to let me continue or not?' she asked teasingly.

Carrie swung her legs up on to the bed and hugged her knees to her chest. 'I'm going to let you continue,' she said, her curiosity nearly a physical pain. 'Just get on with it, will you? What happened after you kept seeing him in the canteen? Did he ask you out? Did he take you somewhere really swish like the Café Royal? Has he got a flash car?'

'For God's sake, Carrie, one thing at a time! No, he didn't speak to me in the canteen. In fact he never spoke to me again until this lunchtime.'

'Then how do you know that he's seriously interested in you? And he must be seriously interested or you wouldn't be looking like a cat that's just swallowed the cream.'

'I know he's seriously interested in me because he told me so. We talked together at lunchtime and again earlier on this evening when he took me for a drink at The Princess of Wales. He's joined the RAF and leaves for training camp tomorrow and he's asked me if I'll write to him and go out with him when he has his first leave. As for your Mavis knowing about him. He brought me home from The Princess of Wales because he wanted to meet my dad and Mavis saw the three of us talking together by the gate.'

She didn't add that Mavis had viewed the proceedings leaning companionably with Jack Robson against his motor bike.

'Hell's bells and little fishes!' Carrie said graphically. 'Toby Harvey! Trust you to hook the most eligible bachelor Blackheath possesses! What on earth did your father say when he met him? Do you think anything will come of it? Do you think you might actually *marry* him and end up living in one of those posh houses overlooking the Heath?'

'Don't be ridiculous, Carrie,' Kate said, with n much conviction. 'We've had a drink together, tha He might never get in touch with me again.'

Carrie cocked her head to one side and rega Kate with sudden shrewdness. 'You don't really b lieve that, do you? You think this is the real thing, don't you?'

In all their years of being friends Kate could never remember lying to Carrie and she didn't do so now. 'Yes,' she said, unable to help herself from blushing slightly. 'I do.'

Carrie's grin nearly split her face from ear to ear. 'Blimey, Kate. That's just as marvellous news as my news. Why on earth didn't you bring him down here to meet me? How am I supposed to contain my impatience about what he looks like? Is he tall, dark and handsome? Is he anything like the man Miss Helliwell predicted you would marry?'

The answering grin on Kate's face faltered. It had been years since she had thought about her disquieting experience at Miss Helliwell's. What was it Miss Helliwell had said to her? That there was very great happiness in her future but that it would only come after heartache? That heartache had, surely, been Jerry Robson's terrible death in the bull-ring at Badajoz and was now over and done with.

'Miss Helliwell didn't give me a detailed description of my husband-to-be as she did to you,' she said, dismissing her momentary flash of uneasiness, 'And no, Toby isn't tall, dark and handsome. He's tall, fair-haired and handsome.'

'And rich,' Carrie said with satisfaction.

Kate frowned slightly. 'That's not why I'm interested in him, despite what Mavis might think and despite what other people might think in the future.'

'Well *I* don't think that!' Carrie said truthfully. 'I know you too well to ever think you would go out with anyone just for their money. It's just that it's *nice* he has money. I mean, it's such a blinkin' novelty, isn't it? Who else do I know who has a rich boyfriend or ever had a rich friend? Mavis certainly didn't, though God knows she tried hard enough! And I certainly didn't. If Danny took me out for a fish and chip supper I thought myself lucky.' She began to giggle again. 'Now we're married I don't even get taken out for fish and chips. All he does is bring them home and we eat them out of the paper in front of the fire while he listens to the football commentary on the wireless!'

Years later Kate was to remember that evening of girlish giggles and chatter very clearly. Not because of what was said between herself and Carrie but because of what he had considered himself as much at home in England as if he had been born there. Though it was probably true that his offer of providing a home for Jewish refugees had been turned down where Jewish children were concerned, surely the authorities could have accepted his offer on behalf of a Jewish family?

'Anyone would think I was a paid-up member of Hitler's National Socialists,' he said bitterly. 'Why on God's earth should the British Government assume I'm a Nazi just because I was born in Germany? And if they're going to take the same attitude to every German-born national living in Great Britain, what the devil are they planning to do with us all if and when war breaks out?'

She had had no answer for him then and she had no answer for him now. 'Don't fret about it,' she said lovingly, aware of how grossly inadequate her words were. 'Why don't you go down to The Swan and have a game of darts with Nibbo or Daniel Collins?'

His back straightened fractionally. 'I suppose you're right,' he said, forcing cheerfulness into his voice so as not to depress her as much as he, himself, was depressed. 'I shan't be long, only an hour or two. What will you do? Go down to Carrie's?'

She shook her head. 'No, Danny's home on leave. I've bought a copy of the new magazine Miss Pierce told me about. I'm going to make myself a cup of tea and sit comfortably in front of the fire with it.'

He kissed her on the cheek, took his winter jacket and scarf off the peg they were habitually hung on in the cupboard beneath the stairs, and let himself out of the house.

In a more subdued frame of mind than she had been in for weeks Kate did the washing-up and then made herself a cup of tea. Carrying it into the sitting-room she turned on the radio. The music of Reginald King and his Orchestra filled the room and with her cup of tea in one hand and a copy of *Picture Post* in the other, she settled herself down in an armchair in front of the glowing coal fire.

In early December she received a letter from Toby informing her that he would be home on leave from 23 December to the 27th. A week later she received another letter in which he told her that he would be arriving in London by train and that the train he intended travelling on was due in at Charing Cross Station on the 23 December at 6.15 p.m. Could she meet him there, beneath the clock inside the station?

Could she meet him? Did giraffes have long necks? Were there pyramids in Egypt? Of *course* she could meet him. No power on earth would prevent her from doing so. That evening, as she made the fruit and brandy soaked Christmas pudding that she and her father always shared on Christmas Day and that needed at least two weeks to mature, she sang happily as a lark, oblivious of her father's excessive quietness.

'What will you wear?' was the first question Carrie asked her when they had a girls' night out together after Danny had returned to Catterick.

'I don't know.' It was a dilemma that hadn't previously occurred to her and now that it had done it assumed astronomical proportions.

'Well where is he taking you?' Carrie asked, ever practical. 'Is he taking you dancing or to a show or to the cinema?'

'He didn't say.' Sudden doubt seized hold of her. 'He might not be taking me anywhere. He might just want me to be company for him on the last leg of his journey back to Blackheath.'

Carrie raised mascara-lashed eyes to heaven in despair. 'God help me, Kate Voigt. You aren't half an idiot at times! Of *course* he's going to take you out! He has five days leave. One of those days is Christmas and he'll most likely be obliged to spend all that day with his grandfather. He has to travel back to camp on the fifth day so that's another evening he won't be able to take you out anywhere. You don't think he's going to waste one of the precious remaining three nights hurrying home for a cup of hot cocoa, do you?'

Kate grinned. 'I sincerely hope not! I'm no nearer to solving my problem though, am I? What on earth shall I wear? I don't want to find myself looking ridiculous in too much finery in Lyons Corner House or wearing no finery at all and at the Ritz.'

'Wear something expensive looking but plain and take some jewellery with you,' Carrie advised as if the dilemma was one she had faced often and conquered with aplomb. 'If he ends up being an old meanie and taking you to a Corner House, keep the jewellery firmly in your handbag. If he takes you to the Ritz, whip out your rope of imitation pearls and a pair of matching earrings and you'll look as good as anyone else there.'

Kate doubted it but knew it was sensible advice. She would wear a very plain dress and the opal brooch and matching earrings that had been her mother's. As it was the middle of winter she would also have to wear her rather shabby coat, but she would give it a very careful brushing and pressing and she would wind her heavy plait of hair into an elegant chignon.

Two weeks later, standing beneath the huge clock in Charing Cross Station, Kate felt as if she needed to pinch herself to make sure she wasn't dreaming. Was she really waiting in love-sick fever for a man she had only spoken to on three occasions, one of which had been brief, impersonal and almost rude? The second occasion, when he had joined her as she ate her lunch-time sandwiches by the banks of the Thames, had been decidedly friendlier and had established a feeling of deep-seated rapport between them but that, too, had been relatively brief. The third occasion, when he had taken her for a drink at The Princess of Wales and then home, had been the only occasion that could remotely be classed as having been a date and even on that occasion their time alone together had been minimal, the first half of it having been spent in Charlie's company and the second half in her father's.

Self-consciously she stood directly beneath the clock. The station was crowded with London office and shop workers making their way home to the suburbs and into Kent. On her right-hand-side members of the Salvation Army stood in a small group singing Christmas Carols, collection tins conspicuously in their hands. On the left of her stood a Christmas tree decorated with baubles and tinsel and crowned by a glittering silver star.

Where was Toby? She knew the platform his train from Kent was due to arrive at because she had checked it when she had alighted from the Blackheath train fifteen minutes earlier. She had been tempted to wait at the barrier for him but the crush of home-going commuters was so thick that she decided there was a remote chance they would not see each other. Their pre-arranged meeting-place beneath the clock was a far safer bet and she stood there, her carefully brushed and pressed cherry-red wool coat buttoned up to her throat, her gleaming blonde hair coiled into a sleek knot in the nape of her neck, her black leather gloved hands clasped tightly together. What if his leave had been suddenly cancelled? What if he didn't come? What if she had mis-read his letter and the date was wrong? What if the time were wrong and he had arrived hours ago and, tired of waiting for her, travelled home to Blackheath alone?

'Kate!'

She swivelled around in the direction of his voice. He was forcing a way through the throng, stunningly handsome in his RAF uniform, his RAF cap crammed jauntily on to his thick shock of fair hair.

'Kate!' he said again, his face alight with joy at the sight of her and then, as if they had been lovers for years, he opened his arms to her and she ran into them like an arrow entering the gold.

His lips were hot and tender against her hair. 'Oh God, Kate,' he said hoarsely, 'I thought you might not be here. I thought you might have changed your mind.'

'No!' she said vehemently, her face pressed close against his chest as his arms held her tightly against him. 'Never!'

She felt loving laughter vibrate in his chest. 'Then that's all right then,' he said, his amusement that such a gentle-looking girl could be capable of such fighting fierceness, thick in his voice. Gently he tilted her face upwards with his forefinger so that he could look into her eyes. As their gaze deepened his amusement faded to be replaced by desire so strong he could barely contain it.

'I missed you,' he said thickly, the expression in his eyes telling her more clearly than words ever could, how very, very much.

'I missed you,' she said a little shyly and with utter sincerity.

Once again a smile touched the corners of his well-shaped, compassionate mouth and then, uncaring of the crowds milling around them, he lowered his head, his mouth meeting hers in sweet, unfumbled contact.

They went for a drink in the cocktail bar of the adjoining Charing Cross Hotel and then, hand in hand, walked the short distance into the West End to the Empire Cinema to see Walt Disney's much talked about first feature length cartoon, *Snow White and the Seven Dwarfs*.

Although Toby had made the choice only because the newly built cinema was within easy walking distance, it proved to be an inspired choice.

For two magical hours Kate sat in the lush Art Deco interior, revelling not only in Toby's nearness in the dark intimacy of the cinema, but also in the heady pleasure of being mentally transported from the harsh reality of grey, grim London to a magical fantasy world where good always triumphed over the forces of evil.

When the film ended they walked, still hand in hand, to a small friendly restaurant by the name of Bertorelli's where Toby was greeted as an old friend and where, when she removed her coat, she was grateful for the elegance of her mother's opal brooch pinned near the neckline of her dress.

'I want you to meet my grandfather sometime over the next four days,' he said to her as they were served with an hors d'oeuvres of delicious paté and hot toast.

She put her knife down, alarm flashing through her eyes. 'But you said he would want nothing to do with me because I'm German! You said that if he had known about it he wouldn't even have allowed Personnel to have employed me!'

'I know I did,' he said steadily, 'and, unfortunately, I was speaking the truth.'

'Then why . . . ?' she began bewilderedly.

He put his own knife down and reached across the table, taking her hands in his. 'Because we're going to have a very long and a very special relationship and the sooner my grandfather knows about it and is able to come to terms with it, the better it will be for all of us. Once he meets you, he won't be able to help himself from liking you. No-one could. For reasons I've already explained to you, he won't find the situation an easy one to adjust to, but he'll adjust to it eventually, especially when he realizes how important you are to me.'

Her fingers tightened on his. 'I'm glad I'm important to you,' she said huskily, emboldened by the gin and tonic she had drunk earlier in the cocktail bar at the Charing Cross Hotel and by the glass of wine she had just finished, 'You've become very important to me, too.'

The waitress came and removed their plates and re-filled their glasses. They were oblivious of her.

In the subdued romantic lighting of the restaurant his

classically sculpted features looked even more handsome than she had first thought them.

'How could we have lived so near to each other and been so unaware of each other for so long?' he asked wonderingly.

This time is was her turn to be amused. 'Because we might live geographically near to each other but socially we're worlds removed. Where did you go to Junior School? I bet it wasn't Sheriton Road Juniors?'

His quick easy smile made her heart feel as if it had turned over in her chest. 'Point taken. No, I most certainly did not go to Sheriton Road, I went to prep school when I was seven.'

Kate's eyes widened in dismay. '*Seven?* Wasn't that awful? Being taken away from your home and your parents when you were still such a small boy?'

Beneath his RAF jacket his broad shoulders gave an almost imperceptible shrug. 'It wasn't so bad. It's something you quickly adjust to.' He grinned suddenly, knowing instinctively how she was going to react to his next remark. 'The worst thing was the transition from being a seven-year-old to being an eight-year-old.'

'Why?' Mystified, she ignored the plate of grilled prawns that the waitress had just placed in front of her.

'Because although boys are allowed to take their teddy bears and to keep them with them for their first year, they're taken away from them when they move into the eight-year-old's dorm.'

The expression on Kate's face was a mixture of anguish and outraged indignation. 'I think that's appalling! In fact, I think it's even worse than appalling, I think it's downright criminal!'

A couple at a nearby table, overhearing only Kate's last two comments, cast comically quizzical looks towards her. Amusedly aware of them, and aware also that his main course of steak Béarnaise was rapidly going cold, he reluctantly released his hold of her hands.

'And what about you?' he asked, picking up his knife

and fork and continuing with his meal. 'Where did you go to school after leaving Sheriton Road Juniors?'

Kate began to give some attention to her grilled prawns, saying, 'I went to Blackheath and Kidbrooke.'

'And was that where you met the friend who was with you in the photograph you sent me?'

'Carrie?' Kate's generously full mouth curved in a deep smile. 'No, Carrie and I go back much further than that. We met even before we both went to Sheriton Road Juniors.'

'How?' he asked, wanting to know everything about her; everything about her past, no matter how trivial. 'Were you next-door neighbours?'

'Not quite. I live at the top, Blackheath end of Magnolia Square and Carrie lives nearer to the Lewisham end of the Square. We met at Blackheath Village Nursery School and we've been best friends ever since.'

Later, as he said a final goodnight to her outside her gate, he said, 'I want you to meet grandfather on Christmas Eve. We can all go for a meal together somewhere special. The Savoy Grill perhaps, or the Ritz.'

Held wonderfully close and secure in his arms she said slowly, 'I don't think I'm ready for such a meeting yet, Toby. It would be different if he wasn't my employer, but as it is . . . ' She left her sentence unfinished but he knew what it was she was worrying about. If his grandfather proved to be totally unreasonable she might lose her job and it was a risk she was not, as yet, prepared to take.

'All right,' he said tenderly, knowing that her reluctance was perfectly natural and knowing, deep in his heart, that it was sensible as well. The longer their relationship had endured by the time they spoke to his grandfather about it, the greater the chances that his grandfather, realizing the seriousness of their commitment to each other, would be tolerant and accepting of it. He knew also that his grandfather would now be waiting with exceeding impatience for him to arrive home.

'I have to go,' he said with deep reluctance. 'I'll see you tomorrow. You'll be finishing work early, won't you, as it's Christmas Eve? We could go for a meal in town and then to the midnight Carol Service in Trafalgar Square.'

'I'd love that,' she said, her arms lovingly around his waist, held so close against him that she could hear his heart beating beneath his airforce-blue jacket. 'It's something I've always wanted to go to but Dad would never let me.'

As his eyebrows rose quizzically she giggled. 'He wouldn't let me go because he was worried about my being out so late in town on my own. He's not going to worry about me if I'm with you.'

'I should hope not,' Toby said in dry amusement.

Dimly in the darkness the unmistakable figure of Charlie was approaching, Queenie at his heels.

Swiftly, before he could be cheated of the opportunity, Toby once more bent his head to Kate's, kissing her good night for the last time.

When at last he raised his head from hers he said huskily, 'I'll see you tomorrow, my love,' and then, uncaring of Charlie who was now rapidly drawing abreast of them, he said fiercely, 'I'm in love with you – you know that.'

'Evenin' both,' Charlie said pleasantly before Kate could even make an attempt at a reply. 'Long time since I've seen anyone kissin' and canoodlin' in Magnolia Square. Thought it was Mavis and Jack Robson for a moment. Thank Gawd I was wrong. Ted would have bloody killed the pair of 'em and then what sort of a Christmas would we 'ave 'ad?'

Kate had the best Christmas of her life. Apart from Christmas Day, which Toby dutifully spent with his grandfather and which she lovingly spent with her father, they were together every moment possible.

When he returned to camp on the twenty-seventh of December and she went with him to the railway station to say goodbye to him, it was in the knowledge that something utterly wonderful and magical had occurred in their lives. They were in love with each other and always would be.

In January, as letters flew fast and furious between them, Kate achieved a long term ambition by introducing Miss Pierce to Miss Godfrey at a St Mark's Church Sale of Work.

In February, world news reached an all-time low. Franco swept victoriously into a bomb-blasted Barcelona and Hitler began quite openly casting covetous eyes on what remained of Czechoslovakia.

In March, less than six months after he had declared that Germany had no more territorial demands in Europe, Hitler annexed the Czech provinces of Bohemia and Moravia and marched victoriously into Prague. Toby had a weekend leave at the end of the month and though he still couldn't persuade her to meet his grandfather, he and Kate and Carl spent a happy evening together in one of Blackheath Village's many restaurants. In April, when the thirty-foot-high, thirty-foot-wide *magnolia soulangiana* in the vicarage garden was in full, creamy, heart-stopping flower, Toby wrote to her with the news that he had received his 'wings' and was now a fully-fledged RAF officer.

In May, when Hitler had begun to eye Poland in the same way he had previously eyed Czechoslovakia and when it became obvious even to Chamberlain that no further compromise was possible, the House of Commons endorsed the British Government's decision to conscript men of twenty years of age for military service. Two days later Carrie gave birth to a daughter.

★   ★   ★

'We're going to call her Miriam Hester Margaret Rose,' Carrie said proudly, sitting up in bed, the baby in her arms. 'Miriam and Hester after my mother and Danny's mother and Margaret Rose after Princess Margaret.'

She looked down at the tiny, shawl-wrapped bundle in her arms with such fierce love that Kate's breath caught in her throat.

'I really like Princess Margaret's second name better than her first name,' Carrie confided, 'and Danny and I have already decided that we're not going to use the first three names, except officially, and that we're going to call her Rose.'

'I think Rose is a lovely name,' Kate said, her voice thick with emotion. 'She's a beautiful baby, Carrie. Can I hold her for a moment? I'll be really careful with her, I promise.'

It was at the beginning of June, as she was waiting in almost unbearable excitement for Toby to come home on his first leave as a fully-fledged officer, that it first dawned on her that although the cricket season was now in full swing, her father was still spending his weekends at home, pottering in the garden or reading.

'What's happened to the cricket team this year, Dad?' she asked curiously one Saturday morning as she pegged washing out on the clothes-line and he was stringing cotton between the branches of redcurrant bushes in order to protect them against birds. 'Haven't you been able to raise a team?'

He hesitated slightly and then said, without looking up from his task, 'It's no longer up to me to do so. There was a specially convened meeting of the Cricket Club Committee and the committee decided that I should be asked to resign my captaincy.'

Kate stopped what she was doing and stared at him. 'But why? If the committee thought it was time someone else had a shot at being captain why didn't they say so at the end of last season? And why have you stopped playing altogether? Haven't you been selected?'

Even as she said the words she realized how ridiculous they were. The Swan's Cricket Club was run on such an *ad hoc* basis that everyone who wanted to play was somehow incorporated on to the team and it had always been more a matter of scrambling around trying to make up a full quote of team members rather than having to disappoint people by not selecting them to play.

Her father straightened up from his task and reluctantly turned and faced her. 'No,' he said, his face strained and tired. 'I haven't been selected to play.'

She continued to stare at him, struggling for understanding. 'But why not? You've *always* played for the team!'

'Maybe,' he said, the pain in his usually gentle voice shocking her unutterably, 'but I haven't previously been seen as a potential enemy alien, have I?'

Kate's grief and fury on her father's behalf knew no bounds. It wasn't as if the men on the Cricket Club Committee were faceless strangers. They were men her father had always regarded as his friends: Nibbo and Albert and Daniel Collins.

'I'm sure my dad wouldn't have had anything to do with it,' Carrie said in utter sincerity as she suckled Rose. 'He's always regarded your dad as one of his best mates.'

'Mr Nibbs and Danny's father were his mates too, but *they* were on the committee as well and they obviously didn't speak out in Dad's defence. If they'd done so, he wouldn't have been excluded from the team,' Kate said, the rage which had streamed through her in a dark, dizzy tide when her father had first told her of the committee's decision still roaring through her veins.

'I'll speak to my dad,' Carrie said, deeply troubled. 'I'm sure there must be a mistake somewhere, Kate. Whatever the reason for your dad being dropped from the team it can't be for the reason he thinks. Perhaps your dad's eyesight is going a bit? They dropped Ted's brother a couple of years ago for the same reason. He couldn't see a ball coming at him from three yards, let alone twenty.'

Kate might have been slightly convinced by Carrie's argument if it hadn't been that Danny was home on leave and, as she left the house, called out to her unthinkingly, 'Have you seen the latest news, Kate? Hitler's being hailed as a bloody hero in Berlin! Bloody Germans! I'll be glad when war is finally declared and we can start shooting the buggers!'

In July, Danny's hopes came a step nearer to fruition. Government plans for the evacuation of London children to safe areas in the country, away from the dangers of German bombing, were made public.

'Then it is going to be war,' Miriam said agitatedly to Miss Godfrey in Kate's hearing. 'They wouldn't be plannin' to send the kids away otherwise, would they?'

'It's merely a precaution, Mrs Jennings,' Miss Godfrey said, not believing for one moment that it was but not wanting to add to Miriam's obvious panic.

In August, as the Polish crisis deepened and London schoolchildren were summarily issued with a list of essential clothing and articles to be packed in a single suitcase and to report to their various school playgrounds, Miriam's composure deserted her completely.

'Beryl's too young to be sent off into the country!' she protested hysterically. 'And what about Billy? 'e's never been away from 'ome before! 'e'll be cryin' 'imself to sleep every night, poor lamb.'

Knowing her son as she did, Mavis doubted it. Far from crying himself to sleep every night, Billy would most likely have the time of his life and she pitied the unknown and unsuspecting foster parents he was about to be foisted on.

'As long as he and Beryl stay together, they'll be right as rain,' she said firmly. 'Now for Gawd's 'sake stop bawlin' Mum and 'elp me pack this bloomin' case. Why the 'ell does this list say they need a toothbrush each? They're not goin' to the blinkin' Ritz, are they?'

When the children had gone to their temporary homes of refuge in the countryside, the London streets were dismally silent.

'When nasty Mr Hitler backs down and everything returns to normal I'll never again complain about Billy Lomax and his friends swinging around the lamp-post outside my gate,' Miss Helliwell said to Kate dolefully. 'It's so quiet my telepathic contact with the dear departed has been quite disrupted. I tried to contact Mr Nibbs's father for him but all I got was a Japanese gentleman from the twelfth century.'

Despite all the doom and gloom surrounding her, Kate's horror at what the political future held was mitigated by deep, personal joy. Toby had asked her to marry him and without a second's hesitation, without even the very faintest of fleeting doubts, she had said that she would do so.

A week later, little more than twenty-five years after her father had been conscripted into the Kaiser's Army at the commencement of the last war, Europe was again plunged into wholesale bloodshed. The Prime Minister's words as he broadcast to the nation were quite un-equivocal: 'This country is now at war with Germany,' he said in his thin, reedy voice. 'We are ready.'

Someone, somewhere in Blackheath, was more than ready to show what his emotions were for all Germans, no matter what their personal allegiances or political sympathies. At five o'clock that afternoon, just as Carl Voigt was beginning to think of closing the bookshop for the day, someone threw a brick through the window. Tied to it was a piece of card bearing a message printed in gory red ink, GET THE HELL OUT GERMAN PIG BEFORE WE CHASE YOU OUT!

Chapter Seven

'You must call the police!' Kate said to him as she faced him an hour later across their kitchen table, stunned disbelief, nausea and fury surging through her in such quick succession that she didn't know which emotion was uppermost. 'They'll find out who did it. They'll arrest them. They'll . . .'

'They'll do nothing of the kind,' Carl said with such weary passivity that Kate felt as if a fist had been slammed into her stomach. 'This country is now at war with Germany and I'm a German. However polite the local police might be about the incident to my face, deep down there's going to be empathy for whoever threw that brick, and for the message on it.'

'I don't believe that,' Kate said obstinately, staring across the table at him, sickeningly aware that her words held no ring of conviction.

Carl passed a hand across his eyes and then said, 'The time has come when you have to come down from that cloud you've been living on ever since you began your relationship with Toby and face facts, Kate. As far as the British Government is concerned I am now an enemy alien. And as an enemy alien I will, no doubt, be interned.'

'Interned?' Her eyes held his blankly. 'What do you mean "interned"? Internment means being confined, imprisoned!' There was rising hysteria in her voice. 'You've lived in this country for twenty years, Dad! You can't possibly imagine the British Government is going to imprison you!'

'Why not?' Carl said quietly, his eyes holding hers. 'They did once before.'

'But that was different!' She rose from the table in such agitation that she overturned a cup of tea. The cup rocked sideways in its saucer, the hot liquid streaming over the tablecloth and dripping onto the floor. Neither of them took the slightest notice of it. 'You were a prisoner of war then! You'd been a member of the German Army! You're not a member of the Germany Army now! England is your home! You've become as English as Mr Nibbs or Mr Collins or Charlie Robson!'

Despite the awfulness of what they were discussing a wry smile touched the corners of Carl's mouth. 'That might be how you see me, *Liebling*, but it isn't how our neighbours now see me or they wouldn't have asked me to resign as captain of the cricket team. And it certainly isn't how the government will see me.' The faint smile died. 'Reality has to be faced and we have to prepare for it. I've never interfered in your private life but I'm going to have to ask you a very personal question.'

She stood quite still, unable to even imagine what he was going to ask her.

With his eyes still holding hers unwaveringly, he said, 'Is there any chance of you and Toby getting married?'

The spilt tea continued to drip into a small pool by her feet. 'I . . . we . . .'

'I have to ask, *Liebling*. If the answer is yes, and if the two of you marry, then no matter how long the war continues, or how long I am interned, I won't have to worry about you. I will know you are being taken care of. Do you understand?'

'Yes.' She gripped hold of the edge of the table. She understood perfectly. He was going to be taken away from her. Sometime in the next few weeks, perhaps even the next few days, he was going to be classified by the government as an enemy alien and he was going to be placed in an internment camp. And he was worrying about her because when that moment came, she would be alone in the house; alone and without any other family member to call on for support.

'Toby has asked me to marry him,' she said, trying to relieve his terrible anxiety. She was about to say that the reason they were not already engaged was that she had, until now, felt unable to face the prospect of meeting his grandfather. To do so, however, would mean having to explain why such a meeting would be so traumatic.

As she saw her father's shoulders sag with visible relief she knew that she couldn't burden him with the knowledge of Mr Harvey's fervent prejudices. She was also faced with another realization that had not, until then, occurred to her. If, over the past few months, it would have been hard for Toby to have talked his grandfather into accepting her as a daughter-in-law, now it was going to be utterly impossible.

'Then perhaps you could talk to Toby,' her father was saying, rising from the table. 'Explain to him what the situation is.'

He picked up the upturned cup and its saucer and his own cup and saucer and began to carry them over to the sink. 'Once he realizes the very high chances of you being left to live on your own, he'll realize the sense of the two of you marrying sooner, rather than later.'

He placed the crockery into the sink, 'So that's one problem solved, isn't it?' he said, his relief so vast there was no way on earth she could even partially disillusion him. 'Now all we have to do is sit back and see what happens.' He turned away from the sink, forcing a smile and saying jokingly, 'With a bit of luck instead of the government interning me they might ask me to join the Home Guard!'

They didn't. On the same day that a buff envelope dropped through the Robsons' letter-box informing Jack Robson when and where he should report for conscripted military service, a very similar envelope dropped through the Voigt letter-box.

'I'm to go to Bow Street police station to register as an alien,' Carl said to her as she waited in an agony of suspense to learn its contents.

'Does it say anything about internment?' she asked fearfully, the slice of toast she had been eating for her breakfast still in her hand.

Carl shook his head. 'No. Simply that I have to register.' He looked up from the official letter. 'All aliens have to register, even refugees. It might not be as bad as it seems, *Liebling*. Try not to worry.'

All that day at work Kate worried herself sick. Mr Muff, under the mistaken assumption that her anxiety and tension were occasioned by fears of a German bombing raid on London or, even worse, imminent invasion, said with an unexpected show of bravado, 'No situation is ever as black as it's painted, Kate. In attacking the British Bulldog the Germans are going to find they've bitten off far more than they can chew! Onwards and upwards is the name of the game now!'

Even Miss Pierce displayed a quite unexpectedly aggressive truculence. 'Just let a German pilot bale out over *my* garden!' she said fiercely to Kate when she joined her in the canteen at lunchtime. 'I've got a pitch-fork at hand behind my front door and I'll soon give him a suitable reception!'

That evening, in her haste to be home and to find out what had happened to her father at Bow Street police station, Kate ran all the way across the Heath. When she burst into the house, her heart pumping as if it were going to give out any moment, the house was ominously empty.

Drawing in great gulps of air she turned around and hurried back outside. She needed to talk to someone and the only person she could possibly talk to was Carrie.

Mr Nibbs and Daniel Collins were engaged in close conversation outside Miss Godfrey's gate.

Neither of them paid her any attention and she didn't call out a greeting. Both of them had been members of the committee that had sat in such jingoistic judgement on her father and, ever since she had learned of the shameful way they had treated her father, she hadn't spoken to any of the committee members involved.

'Bloody war,' she heard Mr Nibbs say. 'It's completely spoilt the end of the cricket season.'

Savagely glad, she hurried down to the bottom end of the Square, passed Miss Helliwell's, where a Union Jack bought to celebrate George VI's coronation fluttered bravely from an upstairs window, and passed the Lomax's where Mavis was leaning out of her bedroom window, her folded arms resting on the sill, viewing the world with philosophic calm.

'*Cooee!*' she shouted out cheerfully to gain Kate's attention. 'Everything's a bit of a bugger, isn't it? Christina's had to register as an alien and Jack's got his conscription papers. He says the government needn't have bothered wasting money on a stamp because he volunteered for the Commandoes a week last Monday.'

Kate was still too out of breath after her marathon run across the Heath and in too much of a hurry to share her anxieties about her father with Carrie to stop and chat. With nothing more than an acknowledging wave she whirled in through the Jennings's open gateway and sprinted up the pathway.

'Mercy me, *bubbeleh*,' Leah said, so taken aback by Kate's obviously distressed state that she fell back into her old habit of greeting Kate with affection. 'What on earth has happened? Have the Germans invaded? Have . . .'

'No, Mrs Singer. Nothing like that. I need to see Carrie. Is she in?'

'She's upstairs, bathing Rose.'

'Thanks.' With no further ado Kate began to take the stairs two at a time.

'Arrested? Interned?' Carrie was kneeling by the side

of the peeling white-enamelled bath, supporting Rose's head with one hand, and splashing shallow water over her with the other. 'You're not making sense, Kate.'

Very gently she lifted a protesting Rose from the water and wrapped her kicking little body in a bath towel. Only then was she able to turn and face Kate and to give her her full attention. 'All non-British subjects have had to register. Christina's had to do so. It's a formality, that's all.'

'But Dad went early this morning and he hasn't come back! And it isn't the same for dad as it is for Christina! Christina's Jewish! She's a refugee! She's hardly going to be classed as being a danger to national security, is she?'

'But neither is your dad,' Carrie said in a voice of sweet reason, leading the way out of the bathroom and along the landing to her bedroom. 'How could he possibly be classed as being a threat to our national security? He's hardly Mata Hari, is he? No-one in their right mind could imagine he was a German Secret Service agent or a spy!'

At any other time Kate would have giggled in agreement at the very ludicrousness of the suggestion. Now she said, not remotely convinced by Carrie's argument, 'But people *aren't* in their right minds any longer! The war has unhinged them! Think of Dad being dropped from the cricket team! And by people who have been his friends for years! You can't tell me that was rational! And think of the brick someone threw through his shop window! That wasn't only irrational, it was criminal!'

Carrie laid Rose on the bed on the towel and began to sprinkle her with baby-powder, for once unable to think of a reply that would reassure and comfort.

Kate stood by her side, watching her as, with a piece of cotton-wool, Carrie patted powder into the tiny wrinkled crevices beneath Rose's arm-pits and into the little plump creases in her groin.

'I'm beginning to feel like Alice when she tumbled

down the rabbit-hole into Wonderland,' she said bleakly. 'Everything I've always accepted as being normal is normal no longer. The most unbelievable things are now real possibilities; that people Dad has always regarded as friends will now turn into enemies; that even though he is a law-abiding citizen and hates Hitler just as much as the most dyed-in-the-wool Englishman, he might be imprisoned.'

Under the force of the stress she was feeling her voice had a break in it as she said, 'Nothing is certain anymore. Nothing even feels the *same* anymore!'

'Nothing *is* the same anymore,' Carrie said practically as she folded a napkin into a triangle, 'not for anyone.' She laid Rose on the napkin and began to fold it neatly over her chubby thighs and between her legs. 'Danny's being shipped off to France as a member of the British Expeditionary Force. Ted's agonizing over whether to volunteer now or wait until conscription is extended to men of his age group – and he doesn't have the slightest doubt that it soon will be.' She pinned the neat muslin pleat she had made with a large safety pin. 'And Dad's joined the Home Guard. What use he's going to be I can't imagine. He hasn't been issued with a rifle or anything remotely resembling a rifle. If he ever comes face to face with a German all he'll be able to do is lob apples and oranges at him!'

Kate felt a wash of shame. Other people beside herself were mentally suffering over what the future might hold. 'I didn't know about Danny,' she said, wondering how she could have been so preoccupied with her own concerns not to have even thought to have asked Carrie where Danny had been posted. 'Do you know where he is going in France?'

'No,' Carrie said, the unusual brevity in her voice an indication of how very near she was to tears.

'I'm sorry, Carrie,' Kate said remorsefully, 'Truly. It was crass of me to come barging in here as if me and Dad are the only people whose lives are being disrupted.

It's just that he went to Bow Street police station to register as an alien this morning and he still isn't back . . .'

'He might be by now,' Carrie said sensibly, lifting a gurgling Rose from the bed and laying her in an expert manner against the comfort of her shoulder. 'I bet there were queues miles long at Bow Street. Just think of all the foreigners who will have had to register. The queue probably stretched as far as Buckingham Palace!'

She gave a giggle, suddenly the old Carrie again despite all her anxieties about Danny. 'Come to think of it, shouldn't King George be registering as an alien? His mother was German, wasn't she? And the Royal House of Windsor has only existed since the last war. Before that it was the very German House of Saxe-Coburg-Gotha!' The laughter in her voice was thick and rich. 'If the truth were known, I bet King George has more German blood in his veins than that trumped-up Austrian house-painter Hitler!'

'Carrie's probably right,' Carl said an hour later as Kate put a plate of sausage and mash down on the table in front of him. 'Puts things in perspective a little bit, doesn't it?'

'Not really,' Kate said, refusing to be comforted so easily. 'Even if King George were one hundred per cent German he wouldn't have to register as an alien. What happened at Bow Street? Why did it take so long? Did anyone mention the word internment to you?'

He poured brown sauce on his sausages and then said, 'It took so long because the queue seemed to stretch for miles. As for internment . . .' he paused and in the ensuing silence Kate could hear her heart slamming against her breast-bone. 'As for internment,' he said again, his voice calm and steady, 'aliens considered to be a threat to national security were told they were to be sent to an internment camp for the duration of the war. Those not considered to be potential enemy agents were told they would be required to report regularly to their local police station.'

He speared a sausage with his fork, looked up at her and smiled his slow, gentle smile. 'I fell into the latter category.'

She sat down weakly, overwhelmed by relief. 'Thank God! I've been imagining all sorts of things! That they had sent you away without allowing you to come home for your things and say goodbye to me! That . . .'

He laid down his fork and covered her hand with his. 'There's no need to worry any more, *Liebling*,' he said, praying that it was the truth, not telling her that his case would come under regular review and that his assessment could be altered at any time. 'Are you going to have some sausage and mash as well? Did Carrie say where Danny was being posted?'

All through the next few terrible months of the war, though Carrie never knew where on earth Danny was, Kate at least had the benefit of knowing that Toby was still in Great Britain.

'*My darling Kate,*
God, this posting is awful! I can't tell you where we are but it's cold enough to freeze hell over. Winter has already set in with a vengeance and winds are at hurricane force. Last night two of our aircraft were literally wrenched from their pickets by the strength of it. When it freezes we have to slice ice off the wings and when it thaws we have to scoop mud from the radiators! There's absolutely no winning!'

In all the ways that mattered, however, she knew that he was winning and, thank God, that he was still alive and uninjured.

In January he wrote to her with the news that he was hopeful of being transferred to 54 Squadron operating from Hornchurch in Essex. That was the good news. The bad news was that his grandfather had suffered a heart attack which, although their family doctor had described it as having been a relatively mild attack, excluded any immediate possibility of their visiting him together on his first leave after transferring to Hornchurch in order to inform him of their feelings for each other and of their intention of marrying.

Kate received the news with mixed feelings. After her conversation with her father, and knowing now how happy her father would be if she and Toby married, she had psyched herself up for the inevitable meeting with Mr Harvey. Now, because of his health, that meeting was indefinitely postponed and she couldn't help experiencing a feeling of relief. It wasn't as if the matter of her and Toby marrying was one of urgency. Her father was not going to be interned and so he wasn't going to be suffering untold anxieties at the thought of her living and managing on her own in a war-torn London.

She felt sorry for Toby, knowing how he would be worrying about his grandfather's health and she felt sorry for Mr Harvey whose health had, in all probability, been adversely affected by anxiety for Toby's safety. Over and above those feelings, however, she received the news with equanimity. Too much was happening in her own daily life in Magnolia Square for her to lay awake at night fretting over the health of a man she had never met.

Ever since the incident months earlier, when her father had been so summarily asked to resign as captain of The Swan's cricket team, she had ceased giving cheery greetings to any of the members of that committee and that included people she had always been on exceedingly friendly terms with, such as Mr Nibbs and Carrie's father-in-law, Daniel Collins.

It was with quite a shock that she realized that she had probably never snubbed them by not speaking to them because they had obviously decided, at the same point in time, not to exchange any more friendly greetings with her. Even though she didn't *want* to be on friendly terms with them any more, the realization was surprisingly unpleasant. Was she, too, to be classed by some of her neighbours as a German and an enemy? She dismissed the idea almost the minute it came to her as being too ridiculous to be true. It was Carrie who made her change her mind.

She stood on the doorstep in the weak February sunshine, Rose warmly wrapped and in a perambulator parked by the gate. 'I need to speak to you, Kate,' she said, her normally rose-cheeked face pale and strained, her shoulder-length tangle of dark curls constrained beneath a serviceable headscarf.

Kate's heart plummeted. 'What is it?' she asked as Carrie walked into the hallway. 'Is it Danny? Has something happened to Danny?'

Carrie unloosened the knot securing her headscarf and dragged it from her hair. 'No. It's not Danny. Though God knows where he is except that he's somewhere in France. It's something else, Kate. Something I've no idea how to say.'

Seeing Carrie's obvious distress Kate said, 'I'll put the kettle on. You can tell me over a cup of tea. Is Rose all right out there? I know it's sunny, but it's still cold.'

'She's fine,' Carrie said, following Kate unhappily into the kitchen. 'She's wrapped up snug as a bug in a rug and I've faced the pram out of the wind.'

Kate turned on the tap and filled the kettle. 'Tell me,' she said, lighting a gas ring on the stove and putting the kettle on top of it. 'If Danny's all right, your news can't be that bad, surely?'

Carrie sat down at the kitchen table, her square-jawed face so strained she looked almost middle-aged. 'It's Mum and Dad and Gran and Christina. There was a kind of family council last night and they've sent me up to see you to ask you not to call at the house any more.'

'Not call at the house?' For a moment Kate couldn't

imagine what on earth Carrie meant. She had been calling at Carrie's house and treating it as her second home ever since she had been able to walk. 'I'm sorry, Carrie. I don't understand. Is your gran ill? Is . . .'

Carrie shook her head. A tumble of smoke-dark hair fell across her eyes and she pushed it back with a hand red from the constant washing of Rose's nappies. 'No, Gran's fine. It's . . .' she hesitated, her cat-green eyes agonized. 'It's because of the war and because of all the hideous things the Germans are doing to Poles and Czechs and anyone else they feel like massacreing.'

Kate remained where she was, her back to the stove, waiting.

'Christina has made friends with a lot of fellow refugees,' Carrie said, her chocolate-brown coat still buttoned up to her throat, her headscarf in her hands. 'You wouldn't believe some of their stories. One Polish friend of Christina's told Mum and Dad how all the schoolteachers in her village were rounded up and locked inside the village school and how the Gestapo then set it on fire and watched, laughing and drinking, while the schoolteachers inside it were burnt to a cinder. It upset Mum so much she vomited in the sink and Dad said the entire German race were obviously sick and perverted and that he'd no intention of speaking to another German as long as he lived.'

'And that includes my dad?' Kate asked stiltedly, through frozen lips.

Carrie nodded. 'Apparently he saw your dad in the street yesterday and told him to his face how he felt. Didn't your dad tell you?'

'No,' Kate said, feeling almost as sick as Miriam had done when told of the atrocity that had taken place in Poland. The kettle had begun to steam but she ignored it. She wondered what else had been said to her father that he had never disclosed to her and she wondered which of their neighbours would be the next to follow the Jennings' example.

'What about you, Carrie?' she asked, when she could bring herself to speak again. 'Do you feel like your mum and dad and gran and Christina? Do you think my dad is sick and perverted and capable of burning people alive?'

Carrie flinched as though Kate had physically slapped her across the face. '*No!*' she protested vehemently, pushing her chair away from the table and stumbling to her feet, a strangled sob in her voice, 'Of course I don't think that! And neither do my mum and dad and gran! They just don't know how else to express their feelings about what is happening! Can't you see how difficult it is for them to be friends with someone who is German when they hear such first-hand reports of what Germans are capable of? They can't cope with it, Kate, and you can hardly blame them!'

The kettle began to puff great clouds of steam towards the kitchen ceiling. Numbly Kate turned her back on Carrie and picking up a kettle-holder she had made years ago in a junior school sewing-class, she removed the kettle from the stove.

'I hate the way people's attitudes to your dad are changing just as much as you do,' Carrie said, her passion spent, her voice weary. 'He's been everyone's friend and neighbour for twenty years and no-one seriously believes he's a Nazi or a spy but he *is* German and they don't know how to come to terms with it.'

Kate poured boiling water into a teapot. 'And I'm half-German,' she said tautly, 'and your family quite obviously can't come to terms with that either.'

Carrie pushed the thick fall of her hair away from her face. 'Forget the tea Kate,' she said, her voice drained of all emotion. 'I'd better be getting back to Rose.'

Kate nodded. She no longer felt in the mood for a cup of tea either. She felt more in the mood for a neat double whisky.

When Carrie had left the house, pushing the peram-bulator back down to the bottom end of the Square,

Kate put on her cherry-red coat and, with a scarf around her throat and a beret crammed on her hair, set off in the opposite direction, towards the Heath.

She was acutely aware of how much she missed being able to borrow Bonzo from Carrie's grandmother and have him trotting at her heels; of how much she would miss, if she met Mr Nibbs or Mr Collins, the cheerful repartee that had once existed between them; of how much she missed a friendly neighbourhood world that she had always taken for granted and which now was fast crumbling into oblivion.

Once on the Heath she headed across it diagonally, having no destination in mind, wanting only the release of energetic physical exercise. Britain had now been at war with Germany for six months. Millions of other lives had been disrupted out of all recognition; some destroyed for ever. Commonsense told her that by comparison with what millions of civilians and soldiers were suffering on mainland Europe, her own and her father's situation was so negligible as to be non-existent. The knowledge didn't stop the shock she was feeling, or the hurt.

Christina. If it hadn't been for Christina's arrival in the Jennings household none of this would have happened.

She strode savagely over the frost-tipped grass. The Cricket Club committee members hadn't behaved as they had because of Christina's influence. They had behaved as they had because of a common bond and that common bond was the primaeval, instinctive closing of ranks against a member of another tribe when danger from that tribe threatened.

She crossed one of the narrow roads bisecting the Heath, gravel scrunching beneath her feet. Despite having regarded Britain as his home for twenty years and of having lived for all that time in Magnolia Square, when the chips were down, as they were now between Britain and Germany, then her father was no longer perceived by their neighbours as being a member of their close-knit community. He was an outsider. A misfit.

She stepped once again on to frost-tipped turf, the church of All Saints', which sat squatly on the edge of the Heath at the upper end of Blackheath Village, only fifty yards or so distant. If her father was an outsider and a misfit, what did that make her? Was she, too, going to suffer the same kind of blinkered ostracism? Was she going to become a misfit amongst the community she had been born and brought up in?

She came to a halt, her hands deep in her coat pockets, staring up at All Saints' slender spire, her face pinched with cold, her eyes resolute. If that was what the future held then she would face it with the dignity that was so integral a part of her father's nature. To react in any other way would be to let him down and she would never do that. Not for anyone. Not even for Toby.

Chapter Eight

When she finally returned to Magnolia Square dusk was beginning to fall and as she crossed the road from the Heath she was at first uncertain of the identity of the two little figures trailing wearily towards it from the top end of the Park from the Old Dover Road direction.

The taller of the two was carrying a battered suitcase secured with string, his knee-high socks hanging in wrinkles around his ankles. Hanging on to his free hand was a small girl no more than three or four years old, her boxed gas mask hanging bulkily around her neck, her coat buttoned up lop-sidedly, her badly cut fringe so low across her eyes it was a miracle she could see where she was going.

'Come on,' she heard the taller figure say in an exhausted voice instantly recognizable. 'Yer can't lay dahn and cry again. We're nearly 'ome now.'

Kate sucked in her breath in disbelief and then broke into a run. '*Billy! What on earth has happened? How did you get here from Cornwall? Who is with you?*'

As she raced towards them she saw him totter slightly and as he did so Beryl's legs gave out on her completely and she fell down on her bottom, her tear-streaked face white with exhaustion.

'Who is with you?' Kate demanded, lifting Beryl up from the pavement and into her arms with difficulty. 'Where are they? Why have they brought you home?'

'No-one's wiv us,' Billy said, wiping his nose on his sleeve. 'We've run away. It were 'orrible in the country. We 'ad to sleep in a shed with smelly animals and Beryl were frightened and we didn't have enough to eat and . . .'

'Dear God in heaven!' Kate had only to look into his hollow-eyed face to know that he wasn't spinning her a story to excuse his running away and returning home, but was telling her the horrifying truth.

'The woman who said she'd 'ave us as evacuees only 'ad us 'cos she was forced to,' Billy continued, as if this was sufficient to explain the appalling treatment he and Beryl had been subjected to. 'She didn't want us in the 'ouse 'cos she said we'd make it dirty.' He shifted the cumbersome suitcase from one hand into the other, 'and when Beryl cried 'cos she was 'ungry she clouted her.'

'She hit her?' Kate asked, aghast. 'The woman you were billeted with hit Beryl for crying because she was hungry?'

Billy nodded, 'And she wouldn't let us 'ave a light in the shed and when Beryl wet herself 'cos she were scared she were clouted again.'

Over the last few weeks and months Kate had experienced roaring tides of rage over the way her father had been treated by his erstwhile friends. None of that previous emotion came remotely close to the ice-cold flood of fury that now enveloped her.

Hitching Beryl a little higher and holding her secure with one arm, she took hold of Billy's hand. 'Come along, Billy,' she said unsteadily, shaken to the core by the terrible knowledge that she was quite capable of murder. 'Let's get you and Beryl home, and warm and fed.'

With the suitcase still banging against Billy's legs and Beryl's frozen hands wrapped tightly around Kate's neck they trooped in the deepening gloom towards the bottom end of the Square, past Miss Godfrey's carefully blacked-out windows, past Kate's own home, past Mr Nibbs's house, past the carefully tended winter-sweet at Miss Helliwell's gate, its leafless branches heavy with fragrant flowers of waxy cream.

A sound suspiciously like a sob came from Billy's throat as they turned in the gateless entry of his home. With surprising regard for the strict black-out regulations no chink of light showed from behind Mavis's heavily curtained windows. There was no need for Kate to knock on the door. Billy let go of her hand and seized hold of the door-knob, turning it and nearly falling in his rush to be inside.

'*Mum!*' he cried, '*Mum!* Me and Beryl are 'ome and we ain't never goin' away again!'

'They walked from the house they had been billeted in to Truro and then hitched a lift with a lorry-driver from Truro to Southampton,' Miss Godfrey said an hour or so later.

They were drinking mugs of tea in the Lomax's tiny kitchen. Mavis's screams, initially of joy at seeing her children again, then horror when they told her their story and finally vows to send their billetor to an early grave had brought all her neighbours, even those who lived as distant from her as Miss Godfrey, hurrying out of their homes to discover what on earth was going on.

'I thought the Germans were here,' Miss Helliwell confided, one hand pressed against her still palpitating heart. 'I told Esther to feign dead. Even Germans wouldn't rape a dead woman, would they?'

Albert Jennings stared at her, momentarily diverted from the prospect of purloining Ted's motor bike and side-car and hurtling there and then down to Cornwall, to wreak revenge on his grandchildren's persecutor. It had never occurred to him that the aged Miss Helliwells were living in fear of being raped by the Hun. 'I wouldn't know,' he said truthfully, 'but I think they might have more on their minds when they first land. And if you'll excuse me for saying so, even if they didn't, I don't think you and your sister would be first in that particular queue.'

'What happened after they reached Southampton?'

Kate asked Miss Godfrey before the conversation became even more bizarre. She had been putting Beryl to bed while Billy had been telling his stupefied audience the details of his and Beryl's ordeal and was still in the dark about how the two of them had made the two-hundred-and-fifty-mile journey home.

'They couldn't get another lift and they slept on the street and then in the morning a naval officer, on his way home to Richmond from Southampton, on leave, took pity on them and gave them a lift in his car.'

'I'll bloody kill 'er if I get my 'ands on 'er,' Miriam sobbed, stumbling into the kitchen in search of a reviving mug of tea. 'If Ted had been 'ome she'd stand no chance! 'e'd be 'alfway to Cornwall by now and by the time 'e'd finished with 'er she'd be lucky if she could even open the door to 'er bloody shed, let alone keep children in it in the middle of winter!'

'What happened when they reached Richmond?' Mr Nibbs asked. Within days of war breaking out he had volunteered as an Air Raid Warden and his official Air Raid Warden's tin hat was strapped firmly beneath his chin lending him an air of authority.

'They got on a tube train to the Embankment without paying and nipped off it and underneath the barriers and then they tried to get on the overground train to Blackheath the same way, only a guard cottoned on to them and ejected them before the train left Charing Cross station,' Miss Godfrey said, contempt in her voice for the callous action of the guard in question. 'After that they simply walked.'

'All the way from Charing Cross?' Kate asked, stunned.

Miss Godfrey nodded grimly. 'The billetor in question won't get away with it, of course. I shall write immediately to Truro's Evacuation Committee chairman and inform him of the scandalous conditions Billy and Beryl endured. I shall certainly ensure that no other unfortunate children are billeted with her. As far as I'm concerned, the woman deserves a prison sentence.'

'*Prison!*' Mavis shrieked, hurtling into the small crowded kitchen in search of her headscarf and coat. '*Prison!* Prison's too good for her!' She yanked her coat from off a hook on the back of the kitchen door. 'Dad's borrowin' Ted's motor bike and side-car and he's takin' me down there now! Tonight!' She plunged her arms into her coat sleeves. 'How dare she treat my kids like that? How dare she make my little Beryl sleep in a smelly old shed?'

With hands shaking with fury she snatched up her headscarf from the kitchen table. 'Come on, Dad,' she said to Albert, flinging the scarf over her peroxided, Victory-roll hairstyle and knotting it beneath her chin. 'Mum's going to stay with Billy and Beryl. Let's be off!' And without waiting for a reply she whirled out of the kitchen into the narrow hallway beyond.

'I don't fancy her chances,' Mr Nibbs said from his position squeezed between the oven and the sink as Albert, clad in his Home Guard uniform, strode purposefully out of the kitchen in her wake.

'Whose chances?' Miss Helliwell asked, bewildered by the force of the passions surging around her.

'That bloody billetor's in Cornwall,' Mr Nibbs said grimly. 'She'd have an easier time facing Hitler and his entire army than Mavis in the mood she's in now!'

By the time Kate left the Lomax's, accompanied by Miss Godfrey, she was almost convinced she had severely overreacted in imagining that her neighbours were beginning to regard her as an outsider. The solidarity of high feeling about the way the Lomax children had been treated as evacuees, a solidarity in which she had been whole-heartedly included, made her feel once again an integral part of Magnolia Square's close-knit community.

*   *   *

Two days later the gossip over the garden fences was all about the Lomax children's billetor's near escape.

'Albert told Daniel that Mavis had her by the hair and was dragging her by it towards the shed,' Hettie said with relish to Miss Helliwell. 'She was going to lock her up in it and if she had done, she'd have thrown away the key!'

'And what happened?' Miss Helliwell asked, her eyes like saucers, wondering if her sister's heart would stand the strain of hearing this latest exciting instalment in the Lomax saga.

'Some silly sod of a neighbour called for the police,' Hettie said, her black hat tipped at a rakish angle, disappointment heavy in her voice. 'Mavis is back home now and she says she's never going to let the kids go away again. It's not as if all the bombs we thought would be dropped on London have been dropped. Daniel says old Hitler is biding his time in the hope that he's going to overrun France and that if he does, we'll get the jitters and come to an arrangement with him.' She snorted in derision at the very thought. 'As if we would!'

'As if Hitler will ever overrun France!' Miss Helliwell said, equally staunchly. 'How could he with your Danny fighting out there and Ted in France as well and Jack Robson in the Commandoes?'

'Now that Billy and Beryl are back home Mavis is findin' food rationin' a real 'eadache,' Miriam confided to Miss Godfrey. 'She never was what you would call a natural-born 'ousewife and this 'avin' to register with one grocer for everythin' is throwin' her somethin' shockin'.'

Miss Godfrey eased her wicker shopping basket from one arm to the other and made a murmur of sympathy. That Mavis was not a natural-born housewife came as not the remotest surprise. No-one who knew her would ever have come to any other conclusion.

'Course, Nibbo latched on to the advantages straight away,' Miriam said, a hint of bitterness in her voice. ' 'e no longer describes himself as a *green*-grocer, which is what 'e's been for as long as I can remember. Ever since 'e got a sniff of what the government intended 'e began stockin' sugar and tea and God knows what else and calling 'imself a grocer.'

Miss Godfrey frowned slightly, 'But that was quite sensible of him, surely?'

'Oh, *very* sensible,' Miriam said, her bitterness now blatantly apparent. 'It means 'e's not only cornered a captured market for rationed foods but that everyone who buys their food rations from 'im will also buy their unrationed greengroceries from 'im as well! After all, if you can buy everythin' under one roof, why tramp down to the market for your fruit and veg?'

Miss Godfrey, embarrassingly aware that three apples were nestling somewhere in her basket alongside her small supply of rationed tea, sugar and margarine, all of which had been purchased from Mr Nibbs, tried to adjust the basket so that its contents were not quite so visible.

'I'm sure none of your previous market customers will desert you,' she said, her conscience clear of hypocrisy because she had never shopped in the market but had always been one of Mr Nibbs's customers.

Miriam looked unconvinced and in an effort to move the conversation onto more neutral ground Miss Godfrey said, 'Personally, I'm far more worried about meat rationing than the rationing of groceries. I've always shopped around for my meat and I'm not looking forward to the prospect of having to use one butcher week in, week out.'

'Stockings!' Carrie said to Kate, highly disgruntled. 'How the hell are we going to manage if we can't buy silk stockings for special occasions?'

They were in Kate's bedroom and Kate, who was holding a sleeping Rose lovingly in her arms, was unable to proffer a suitable reply. Ever since war had been declared there had been shortages of all kinds of commodities but whereas neither she nor Carrie minded very much about food and petrol shortages, the near impossibility of obtaining silk stockings had hit hard.

'We could begin wearing lisle stockings, I suppose,' she said doubtfully.

'Lisle?' Carrie stared at her as if she had taken leave of her senses. '*Lisle?* We'd look like women of fifty! I might be married and a mum but I want to look like Betty Grable when I go out on the town! Not my mother or my mother-in-law or Miss Helliwell!'

Kate grinned. With her square-jawed face and heavy dark hair Carrie could never, in a million years, look like Betty Grable. She looked more like Katherine Hepburn or Claudette Colbert.

'Leave looking like Betty Grable to Mavis,' she said, easing Rose into a slightly more comfortable position in her arms. 'Why don't we follow the advice of the beauty article in last week's *Picture Post* and simply make-up our legs with foundation cream and draw a line down the middle of the backs of our legs so that it looks like a stocking seam?'

Carrie's eyes widened. 'Is that what it suggested?'

Kate nodded. 'According to the article there's leg make-up and pencils made specially for the purpose, but until we can buy them we can make do with foundation cream and an eyebrow pencil.'

Carrie had already reached for her handbag. 'It's an idea of genius!' she exulted, beginning to rummage through it for her make-up purse.

'Either genius or lunacy,' Kate said, giggling and laying the still-sleeping Rose carefully down on the bed. 'Have you found your foundation and a pencil? I'll make-up your legs first and then you can do mine. Do you think it will fool anyone?'

Carrie hitched her skirt up so that the pencil line could run from the back of her knee down to her ankle. 'If it fools Mavis, even for five minutes, it'll be worth it. I truly think Mavis would sell her soul for a pair of silk stockings!'

By early April the situation on mainland Europe was so dire even Mavis had more on her mind than silk stockings. Hitler invaded Denmark and Norway. Denmark fell almost immediately and though a Norwegian Nazi sympathizer, Major Vidkun Quisling, proclaimed himself head of the Norwegian Government and ordered all resistance to Germany to cease, Norwegian forces refused to do so. Aided by British and French troops they began a desperate battle to oust the invader from Norwegian soil.

'Let's 'ope they succeed,' Charlie Robson said to Kate as he crossed the Square, heading towards the Heath, Queenie at his heels, 'If they don't, Hitler will use all Norway's ports as naval bases for the German fleet and then his ships will be able to sweep down on us any time they like.'

Kate regarded him with a startled expression, taken aback by such a cogent explanation of the situation from a man usually inarticulate unless expressing an opinion on horse or greyhound racing.

'I know that for a fact,' he added, taking pity on her wonderment, ' 'cos Harriet told me.'

In Norway, as with doomed Poland and Denmark, nothing got better; events only grew worse. By the end of the month British and French troops had no option but to withdraw from their precarious Norwegian footholds. With all but nominal resistance in Norway crushed, Hitler turned his attention from northern Europe to western Europe.

Mavis, who had been listening to Reginald King and his Orchestra on the wireless, was the first person in Magnolia Square to hear the news. 'We are sorry to interrupt this programme . . .' a solemn voice began and seconds later Mavis was pushing up her sash window and yelling for the benefit of any of her neighbours who were within hearing distance, indoors or out, '*That bugger Hitler's just walked into France!*'

'*And* Belgium *and* Holland,' Carl said later to Kate, grim-faced. 'How much worse can things possibly get?'

He found out how much worse things could get for himself and for Kate next morning when it was officially announced that from now on, no matter what the mitigating circumstances, all male Germans and Austrians from the ages of sixteen to fifty were to be interned.

'But it can't apply to you, Dad!' Kate said in anguish as her father opened drawer after drawer in his bedroom, taking out underclothes, pullovers, belts and braces. 'Mum was *British*! She was a *Londoner*! *You're* a Londoner now! You've lived here for over half your life!'

'A policeman is waiting for me downstairs,' he said, his voice unsteady as he began placing underpants and socks into a small suitcase. 'All over Europe families are having to endure far worse partings, Kate. I'm not being taken into a German concentration camp, a Dachau or a Buchenwald, nor am I shortly going to be in battle in Belgium or Holland or France.'

She sat down on the bed, ashamed of her near hysterical outburst; sick at the thought of how long it might be before he was allowed to come home again.

Her father placed a copy of John Steinbeck's *The Grapes of Wrath*, lent to him by Toby, into the suitcase on top of his clothes. 'I'm sure we'll be allowed to write to each other, *Liebling*. And perhaps you will be able to send me parcels occasionally and keep me supplied with books.'

'Yes. Of course.' She could hardly speak she was so terrified of distressing him further by breaking down into tears. 'Where are you going? Will I be able to visit you?'

149

He closed the suitcase lid. 'I don't know where I'm to be interned. I imagine it will be somewhere remote; certainly somewhere far from London.'

The tears she had held in check with so much difficulty could be held in check no longer. They slid down her cheeks, falling on to her tightly clasped hands. 'I'm going to miss you, Daddy.' she said, as if she were a small child again. 'I love you.'

Very gently he reached down for her hands, taking them in his and drawing her to her feet. 'I love you too, *Liebling*,' he said, holding her close. 'And everything is going to be all right. The next few days and weeks of the war are going to be crucial but they're going to be crucial in the Allies' favour. Evil never triumphs for long and Hitler will be stopped in his tracks before he can overrun France and long before he can attempt an invasion of Britain. You'll see. Another few months and life will once again be normal.'

Her head was against his chest and she was glad that she couldn't see into his eyes for she knew that he was lying to her in the hope of comforting her. No matter what the outcome of the battles now being waged life would never be the same again, not for them and not for anyone else.

'Mr Voigt?' an unfamiliar voice called from the foot of the stairs. 'Are you ready, sir? Time's passing and we have to be on our way.'

'Goodbye, *Liebling*.' He kissed her tenderly on the top of her head. 'God Bless.'

As he reluctantly turned away from her and picked up his suitcase she said thickly, 'I'm coming downstairs with you.'

He merely nodded, the constriction in his throat too tight for speech. Silently he walked down the stairs towards the waiting policeman. The front door was open, as it had been ever since he had answered it to the unmistakably officious knock. As he stepped outside with his escort, Kate, a step or so behind him, could see a knot of curious onlookers standing on the pavement outside Miss Godfrey's.

Christina was there, her exquisitely boned face impassive, only the dark pools of her eyes betraying the deep pleasure she felt at the sight of an Aryan German being forcibly removed from his home and family. Miriam and Albert were with her, Albert having the grace to look slightly uncomfortable, Miriam displaying no such emotion. It was a warm day and she wore no cardigan over her sleeveless, flower-printed, cotton overall. Her plump arms were folded aggressively across her ample chest, her grim expression a clear announcement of her belief that the authorities wouldn't be interning Carl Voigt unless they were certain he was a secret Nazi.

Kate, remembering the long, happy years during which she had been made as welcome in Miriam's home as if it had been her own, stared at the hostile figure in sick disbelief. Miriam's eyes refused to meet hers.

'*Bloody Hun!*' a voice from the crowd that had gathered called out. '*Pity you're only being interned and not hung, drawn and quartered!*'

There was a shocked intake of breath from many members of the crowd but no-one spoke out in protest. Kate's eyes flew in the direction the voice had come from. Though there were many faces she recognized: Miss Helliwell's, Leah Singer's, Nibbo's, there were also many faces she didn't recognize. She wondered where they had come from; how they had come by the news that a German living locally was to be arrested and interned.

As her father stepped out on to the pavement he carefully closed the gate behind him, doing so before she could possibly follow him any further. Her hands tightened on its wrought-iron scrollwork. He didn't want her to follow him any further. He didn't want her to be witness to any more viciousness and hatred.

As he and his escort strode briskly out of Magnolia

Square and down Magnolia Terrace, the small crowd began to disperse. The faces she had been unable to recognize headed down towards Magnolia Hill and Lewisham. Albert put a work-gnarled hand beneath Miriam's elbow and steered her away in the direction of their home. Leah Singer followed them. Miss Helliwell looked at Kate in almost pathetic bewilderment and then, without speaking to her, turned her back, hurrying after the Jennings, not wanting to be the last to leave the scene.

That honour was Charlie's. He stood on the pavement, his shirt-sleeves rolled high, his shabby trousers held up around his paunch by a broad leather belt, Queenie at his heels.

Kate's knuckles were white as she tightened her hold on the gate. 'What about you, Charlie?' she demanded, her voice as taut as tightly strung wire. 'Do you think my father should be hung, drawn and quartered as well?'

Charlie, who had watched Carl Voigt's figure until it had walked out of sight, was still staring after him. Slowly he turned and faced her.

'I fink there's bin a mistake,' he said steadily. 'I fink the bloody authorities 'ave taken leave of their senses.' And in deep puzzlement he began to walk away from her and towards the Heath, Queenie trotting at his side.

For a fleeting moment a dark, dizzy tide engulfed her. She didn't know whether it was a supreme relief that at least Charlie had not metamorphosed into a hostile stranger or whether it was reaction to the knowledge that her father was no longer in sight, that he had gone and that she had no way of knowing when she would see him again.

As the threat of fainting receded she became aware of someone's presence by her side. 'You need a cup of tea, my dear,' Miss Godfrey said, her face nearly as white and strained as Kate's own. 'I've put the kettle on and I don't want any arguments. You need a breathing space in which to adjust to what has just happened and in which to recover from the shock you must feel. Where that dreadful man who shouted at your father came from I can't imagine. Lewisham, I suspect. Or possibly Catford.'

Kate didn't know, nor did she care. Wherever he came from the ugly sentiments he had expressed had not been shouted down by people her father had once regarded as friends; people who did not come from Lewisham or Catford but were his neighbours in Magnolia Square.

Very slowly she released her hold of the gate. 'Thank you very much for your offer, Miss Godfrey,' she said, deeply appreciative of Miss Godfrey's motivations, 'but I would prefer to be on my own for a little while.'

'I don't think that's at all wise, my dear,' Miss Godfrey began, deeply perturbed. 'I've put some Lapsang Souchong in the teapot and . . .'

Kate was no longer listening to her. With a heart that physically hurt her she was walking back down the short garden path towards a ringingly empty house.

Chapter Nine

The door closed behind her with a soft thud. Even when her father had been working at the bookshop his hours were such that he was invariably the first one of them home. After the brick incident, the owner of the bookshop had awkwardly suggested that it might be better, under the circumstances, if his employment there was terminated. Her father had had no option but to agree with him and since that date his days had been spent pottering about in the house, reading widely and following the war news avidly. Now his chair in the sitting-room was empty; in the kitchen, the atlas on the table, in which he did his best to plot the latest German and Allied troop movements, was closed.

She sat down and pressed her fingers to her aching temples. It had all been so sudden and unexpected. After the first scare about the internment of foreign enemy nationals when her father had registered as required, both of them had been happily convinced that he did not fall into the category of aliens to be interned and that as long as he reported regularly to his local police station, as had been demanded of him, all would be well. They had been wrong. With Hitler blitzkrieging his way across Europe in the direction of Britain, the British government was taking no chances where German-born aliens were concerned. Despite her father having been resident in the country for twenty years, having married an English girl and having a daughter who had been born in England and had never left it, he had been categorized as an enemy subversive. And there was nothing either of them could do about it.

Bleakly she rose to her feet and walked across to the bread bin, taking a loaf out of it for some toast. Even though there had been distressing reactions to his German nationality from some of their neighbours, his being dropped from the cricket team for instance and the Jennings' request that she no longer visit their home, the number of people who had gathered hostilely on the pavement to see her father being taken away to an internment camp had been just as unexpected. And deeply shocking.

As she put the bread she had sliced under the grill she struggled to remember just which of her neighbours had been part of the small crowd. Not Carrie, thank God. Nor Miss Godfrey. And Charlie Robson, though one of the onlookers, had been bewildered and disturbed by what was taking place and had not been hostile. Who else had been there? Carrie's mother and father had most certainly been there. And Carrie's grandmother. And Christina Frank.

She lifted a butter dish containing margarine out of a cupboard. With Christina as a long-term house-guest it was not surprising that the Jennings family, with the exception of Carrie, had reacted as they had. Living so closely with someone whose family had suffered so terribly at the hands of the Nazis it was no wonder that they now felt animosity towards all Germans.

She turned the bread over under the grill. Miss Helliwell had been there and her father's former closest friend, Mr Nibbs. What about the Collins'? She wasn't sure but she could almost swear she had seen Hettie's distinctive black hat amongst the crowd. And Mavis? Had Mavis been there as well?

Whoever had been there, no-one had called out a word of commiseration to her father; no-one had bade him a friendly goodbye; no-one had called out 'Shame!' when one of their number had shouted the desire that her father be hung, drawn and quartered.

She stared out through the kitchen window at the rear

garden her father had so lovingly tended. Which of her neighbours still bore neighbourly sentiments towards her? Miss Godfrey, obviously, and for that she was grateful. The knowledge eased the sense of isolation that was pressing in on her like a physical burden. She wanted, very badly, to see Carrie. Since Carrie's family had requested she no longer visit their home, and as she now wouldn't choose to visit it even if such a request had never been made, all she could do was wait until Carrie visited her.

With a heavy heart she removed the toast from beneath the grill and began to spread it with the margarine. She would visit Shooters Hill Police Station later in the day to find out where her father had been sent and then she would write to him. She poured scalding tea into the cup. And she would write to Toby. Though the world around her seemed to have taken leave of its senses two things at least remained constant. The deeply loving bond between herself and her father and the knowledge that Toby loved her just as much as she loved him.

'I couldn't believe it when Mavis told me,' Carrie said as Rose sat on a homemade rag-rug, playing with an assortment of teaspoons and a tin mug. 'I thought all that was going to happen to your father was that he would have to continue reporting regularly to the local nick. Where has he been sent? Do you know?'

'Not specifically,' Kate said, not trying to keep the bitterness she felt from her voice. 'The policeman who came to the house for him escorted him to the police station and from there he was taken to a collection point for enemy aliens in central London. According to the policeman who spoke to me at the station, they were then taken by coach to Kings Cross Railway Station, their destination "somewhere in the north of England".'

'Crikey,' Carrie said expressively as Rose tried to noisily ram every spoon that had been given her into the mug, 'it's a bit bloody grim, isn't it? I've known your dad ever since I can remember and until this war started it never occurred to me once to think of him as being German. I've never even heard him *speak* German!'

'He calls me *Liebling*,' Kate said, pain in her eyes. 'It's a term of affection. And sometimes, very rarely, he swears in German.' She managed a small smile. 'He says German is the best language in the world in which to swear.'

'Old Hitler obviously thinks so as well,' Carrie said with a grin. 'I went to the cinema with Mum last night and he was on the Pathé news, ranting and raving and looking like a bloomin' idiot.'

She bent down from where she was sitting and took the spoons out of Rose's tin mug, spilling them on to the rag-rug so that Rose could again embark on the enjoyable task of picking them all up and stowing them all away.

'It was Mum's idea we go to the cinema,' she continued chattily. 'Dad had called her a silly cow and she'd taken umbrage.'

Kate, remembering Albert and Miriam's hostile presence as her father had been led away, had not the slightest interest in their domestic squabbles but rather than risk a difficult situation between herself and Carrie by telling Carrie so, she said merely, 'Why? What had she done?'

'It wasn't over anything she'd done, it was over something she'd said.' Carrie began to giggle. 'As soon as the news was broadcast over the wireless that the Prime Minister had resigned and that Winston Churchill was to be the new Prime Minister, Mum said, "What? That old termagant? Why has he been made Prime Minister? He's nothing but a war-monger!" And Dad said, "Don't be such a silly cow! It's *because* he's a war-monger that he's been made Prime Minister! We are *at* war, or hadn't you noticed?" And from there on it was all downhill and in the end Mum grabbed her hat and coat and said she was off to the cinema. We went to see Spencer Tracy and Micky Rooney in *Boys Town*. I'd have preferred a musical or *Gone With The Wind* but beggars can't be choosers.'

Well aware at how deftly Carrie had steered the subject of conversation away from internment camps, Kate made no effort to return to it. Constant talking about it could do no good and no matter how sympathetic Carrie might be, she couldn't possibly understand the depth of hurt and disillusionment her father's internment had caused her; or him.

'I heard what had happened from Miss Godfrey,' Miss Pierce said to her a few days later as they sat together in the canteen at lunchtime. 'What a terrible experience for you, and for your father, too, of course. I remember the 1914–1918 war and the senselessly brutish anti-German feeling against Germans long resident in this country. Perhaps when you have an address at which to write to your father you would ask him if he would mind my writing to him occasionally. I should think letters, even from strangers, would be very welcome to him in the conditions in which he must be living.'

As she walked home from work that evening Kate mused on how odd it was that Miss Godfrey and Miss Pierce, two people she had never thought of as being anything other than in one instance a neighbour and in the other a work acquaintance, should prove to be two of her staunchest friends.

'*Cooee!*' a familiar voice shouted from the far side of the road. 'I knocked to see if you wanted me to take any of your pots and pans but as you weren't in, I couldn't. If you see what I mean.'

Kate stared in bemusement at the sight of Mavis, her peroxided-blonde hair no longer worn in a Victory roll but piled high on top of her head and over her forehead in thick, sausage-like curls. She was pushing a pram piled high with kettles, saucepans, frying-pans and aluminium baking-trays and roasting-trays.

'What on earth . . .' Kate began in mystification, starting to cross the road towards her. 'You don't have a child beneath that lot, do you?'

'Don't be daft,' Mavis said equably, her chiffon, heavily flounced blouse recklessly low-necked, her fingernails painted a roaring scarlet. 'I'm doin' my bit for king and country and answering Lord Beaverbrook's demand that the 'ousewives of Britain send 'im their pots and pans and aluminium so that 'e can melt 'em all down and make aeroplanes out of 'em.'

Kate regarded the contents of Mavis's pram with amusement intermingled with horror. 'I hope to God Toby doesn't end up flying any plane made out of that lot!'

Mavis regarded her cargo wryly, 'Can't say I'd fancy the thought myself. And God knows what I'm going to cook in from now on. We'll have to live on sandwiches.'

Rumour in Magnolia Square was that sandwiches, varied occasionally by fish and chips, had long been the Lomax family's staple diet and Kate tactfully refrained from making any comment to Mavis's last remark.

'I'm thinking of volunteering as an ambulance driver,' Mavis continued cheerfully. 'If that old bat Miss Godfrey can racket around London at night at the wheel of an ambulance I'm damned sure I can.'

'I didn't know Miss Godfrey was driving ambulances,' Kate said, wondering what on earth else was happening that she knew nothing about. 'And I didn't know that you could drive.'

'I can't, but I can ride Ted's motor bike and an ambulance can't be all that much different.' She grinned and, for the first time ever, Kate was aware of a family resemblance between Mavis and Carrie. 'Must be on my way,' Mavis said while she was still recovering from the surprise of the discovery. 'Ta-ra for now.'

In perilously high peep-toed shoes she continued on her way, proudly pushing her mountainous collection of pots and pans towards Greenwich and the advertised collection centre.

Cheered by the encounter and in better spirits than she had been for several days Kate continued on her way up the hill towards the Heath. She had read the news that Churchill had appointed the newspaper baron Lord Beaverbrook as Minister for Aircraft Production, but Beaverbrook's typically flamboyant request that the housewives of Britain help him build aircraft by donating their pots and pans and aluminium, had passed her by. In her misery since her father had been interned she had neither bought a newspaper nor listened to the BBC news. Resolving to mend her ways she began to cross the Heath, wondering if there would be a letter from Toby waiting for her on the mat when she arrived home; wondering if he would have news as to when he would next be home on leave.

As she turned into Magnolia Square the late afternoon sunshine was still hot. Hettie, her all-purpose black felt hat jauntily decorated with a bunch of imitation cherries and serving now as a rather bizarre sun-hat, was hurrying up the opposite side of the Square but she firmly avoided catching Kate's eye and Kate didn't force the issue by calling out a greeting. If Hettie no longer wished to acknowledge her then she most certainly had no intention of acknowledging Hettie.

Mr Nibbs, mowing his front lawn, ensured that as she drew near he was mowing it in the direction of his house and so had his back towards her. Kate deliberately slowed her pace, determined to cause him as much embarrassment as possible. Mr Nibbs also walked slower, so slowly that the blades of his lawn-mower barely revolved. When he reached the point where his small lawn finished beneath his front window he paused and, aware of his quandary, Kate felt a spasm of near-amusement. Resourcefully Mr Nibbs began to inspect the framework of his window, scrutinizing the putty work with close interest.

Wishing him joy of his task Kate tried hard not to remember previous summer evenings when every few yards one or other of her neighbours would have shouted out a cheery hello to her or engaged her in a few moments of friendly conversation. She opened her garden gate, wryly aware that if it wasn't for her continuing friendship with Carrie and the fierce support of Miss Godfrey and Miss Pierce, her disillusionment with the human race would have been total.

The instant she opened the front door her eyes flew to the mat and with a leap of joy she saw that there was a letter for her from Toby. She scooped it up eagerly, opening it with a singing heart.

Dearest love,

Thank you for forwarding me the address you received for your father. I've written him and sent him a parcel of books. Another Steinbeck, a J. B. Priestley, an Agatha Christie and Raymond Chandler's The Big Sleep. All pretty lightweight but then I imagine that is what he's in need of at the present moment. All the information I've been able to dig up indicates the conditions he's living under are pretty easy-going, which I hope will comfort you a little. The internment camp was actually built as a model housing estate and within its confines there is complete freedom of movement for everyone. No doubt you will have heard from your father by now and hopefully you will not be worrying quite so much about his welfare. Things could be a lot worse for him, but then you know that and don't need me pointing it out. I have a forty-eight hour pass this weekend coming. After that, it might be an age before I again have two days leave. Things are hotting up where Herr Hitler is concerned, God damn him. I love you like crazy and miss you like the very devil.

Be with you soonest. Toby.

She smoothed the letter lovingly and re-read it. He had made no mention of where they should meet because such arrangements were no longer necessary between them. As soon as he arrived home he spent a courteous and minimum amount of time with his grandfather and then drove immediately over to Magnolia Square where he usually spent an equally courteous amount of time chatting to her father before whizzing her off for a drink at the Princess of Wales and then up to the West End for a show and a meal, or perhaps to the Hammersmith Palais where they could dance the night away cheek-to-cheek.

She gazed through the kitchen window, deep in thought. She and Toby loved each other deeply but they were not yet lovers in the true, physical sense of the word. Though he had suggested on more than one occasion that they spend one of his leaves in the country or at the seaside together, she had always resisted the temptation. She knew that he wanted to marry her and that once his grandfather was recovered sufficiently from his heart attack for him to be told of their intentions, he *would* marry her. Until now it had never seriously occurred to her that when they did so she would be anything other than a virgin. Now, nursing her mug of freshly made tea, she wondered why such a notion had been so important to her and realized, with a stab of shock, that it was important no longer.

Hard on the heels of her momentous realization came another realization. Though she now had complete privacy in her home and there was nothing whatsoever to prevent the two of them from taking sexual advantage of that privacy, Toby would not wish to do so. He would see such an action as taking advantage of her father's enforced absence and the magic would be tarnished for them both.

A small smile touched her lips. It was because Toby was so innately honourable that she loved him so much. He would want the occasion when they first made love to be as perfect and as romantic as she wanted it to be and although when he arrived home on leave they could immediately drive down to Brighton or somewhere similar, and book into a hotel, precious hours of his leave would be wasted whilst they did so.

She mentally created a map of south-east England in her mind's eye. Toby's RAF camp was at Hornchurch, in Essex. Essex wasn't so far from London and there would no doubt be lots of pretty villages nearby. It would make far more sense for her to take the train and to meet him at the camp gates than for him to travel all the way into London and then for the two of them to travel out of it again.

Utterly sure of the decision she had just made she went hurriedly in search of pen and paper. If she wrote to him immediately and posted her letter that evening, he would receive it in time. The coming weekend would be the most wonderful weekend of their lives. A weekend they would never, ever forget.

As she packed a small overnight bag on Friday night someone knocked on the front door. Certain it must be Carrie, Kate hurried to open it, flinging it wide, only to find herself staring into the rather bemused face of St Mark's Church vicar, Bob Giles.

'Sorry to disturb you Katherine, only I have what I imagine is a rather important message for you,' he said kindly. 'A Flight Lieutenant Toby Harvey has just telephoned the vicarage and asked me if I would tell you that he has received your letter and that he will be at Hornchurch this weekend.' There was no surprise at being used as a glorified messenger-boy in Bob Giles' voice. The vicarage was the only house in Magnolia Square with a telephone and he was accustomed to taking emergency messages for his neighbours. 'He said you would understand and that there was no need for any reply.'

Kate's cheeks flushed scarlet. She could understand

that Toby had been anxious to let her know that he had received her letter and that their paths weren't going to cross by his travelling up to London as she was travelling out to Essex, but having the vicar act as unwitting intermediary for a rendezvous that he would, if he knew of its nature, undoubtedly disapprove of, embarrassed her deeply.

'Thank you,' she said, grateful that she hadn't already placed her overnight bag by the door, making the true meaning of the message he had just relayed glaringly apparent.

Bob Giles turned to leave and then hesitated, saying as an afterthought, 'The gentleman in question wouldn't be a relative of Mr Joss Harvey of Harvey Construction Ltd, would he?'

Kate felt the colour in her cheeks burn even deeper. 'Yes,' she said, certain that the true import of the message he had been asked to deliver would dawn on Mr Giles at any moment, 'Flight Lieutenant Harvey is his grandson.'

'Is he, indeed? Well, well. I'd heard he'd joined the RAF and was now a fighter pilot. Those boys are certainly in the thick of it at the moment, aren't they? Without them I'm afraid we'd be something of a walk-over for Herr Hitler. With them, we'll remain inviolate. Quite remarkable when you think about it, a mere handful of young boys defending our little island from the might of Hitler's bombers.'

With a cheery goodbye wave he walked down the stone steps leading from Kate's front door to her pathway, still musing over the poetic heroism of the RAF. 'Reminiscent of Agincourt,' Kate heard him say to himself as he walked towards the gate. 'Quite awe-inspiring. Utterly British. I shall take it as my theme for Sunday's sermon.'

Kate thankfully closed the door on him and returned to her interrupted task. Her toilet things were packed but she hadn't yet packed a nightdress. All the ones she possessed were on the sofa waiting for her to make her choice. She looked at them in something approaching despair. None of them were spectacularly pretty. Her newest, made of serviceably warm winceyette, wasn't even remotely pretty.

Decisively she scooped them up in her arms and went back upstairs with them, pushing them away in one of her dressing-table drawers. She would buy herself a new nightdress in the morning, before leaving for Hornchurch, and the nightdress she bought wouldn't be sensible or made of winceyette. It would be the prettiest and the most frivolous that clothing coupons could buy.

Sitting in the train next day as it pulled out of Liverpool Street Station, two thoughts occurred to her almost simultaneously. The first, the fact that Toby's RAF camp would, in all likelihood, be a considerable distance from the centre of Hornchurch and that she might find difficulty in reaching it on public transport; the second, that she hadn't seen Carrie since she had made her momentous decision to spend Toby's leave with him in Essex and that Carrie would have no idea where she was.

From the train window she looked out on to suburban gardens, all scarred by the tell-tale hump of half-buried, Anderson shelters. Finding Toby's RAF camp would not be such a difficult task and if Carrie knocked for her over the weekend she wouldn't worry overmuch at receiving no reply. Knowing Carrie, she might even guess the reason for the house being empty.

Her excitement at the thought of her coming reunion with Toby intensified as the train chugged its way via Ilford towards Hornchurch. With the war news where Belgium, Holland and France were concerned worsening every hour, it was a miracle he was being granted any leave at all and she was well aware that if France fell and Hitler turned his full might against Britain, it might be many months before they would be able to share another such weekend leave.

The train was packed with young airmen returning to camp and she remembered Mr Giles's remarks of the previous evening. The excitement she had been feeling spiralled into cold terror. It was a terror all too familiar; a terror she always experienced whenever she thought of Toby, strapped into the cockpit of his Hurricane, engaging high above the clouds in personal and deadly battle with a German fighter plane or launching an attack on an enemy bomber.

'Hornchurch!' a guard called out loudly. 'Hornchurch!'

Picking up her overnight bag and wishing it didn't look so obviously what it was, she squeezed her way with other alighting passengers onto the platform. A newspaper placard was displayed prominently bearing the headlines '*Paris raided!*' '*Brussels bombed*' '*Many killed in Lyon*'. As she made her way to the barrier she prayed that Toby's leave hadn't been cancelled and that he wasn't, right at that very moment, at the controls of his plane, searching out the enemy over France or the Low Countries.

'Kate! *Kate!*'

At the sound of his voice her relief was so great that she almost stumbled.

'*Kate!*' he shouted again, vaulting the ticket barrier to the disconcertion of the ticket collector and striding towards her, magnificent in his RAF uniform, his flight lieutenant's stripes prominently emblazoned on his jacket sleeves.

Seconds later she was safe within the circle of his arms, crushed against the comforting broadness of his chest and then, as she turned her radiant face up to his, he lowered his head to hers, kissing her long and lingeringly, utterly uncaring of the crowd of arriving and departing passengers seething around them.

When at last he reluctantly lifted his mouth from hers

she said breathlessly, 'I've just seen the news head-lines and I was terrified your leave would have been cancelled!'

He grinned down at her, his shock of fair hair bleached almost wheat-colour by the sun, 'It very nearly was and I'm going to have to stay pretty close to camp.' With his arm firmly around her waist he began to walk with her towards the irate ticket-collector. 'It isn't going to spoil our time together though. My Group Captain rents a house a quarter of a mile or so away from camp and as his wife has had to scoot up to Yorkshire to tend an ailing parent he's living on base and the house is temporarily up for grabs.' His grin widened. 'We're the lucky twosome who have temporarily grabbed it.'

With her arm hugging his, her head resting comfortably against his shoulder, they walked out of the station and into the street.

'Have things been tough for you since your father was interned?' he asked gently as he led the way towards his parked MG.

She thought of the hostile crowd that had gathered to see her father being led away and the ugly, verbally expressed desire of a member of that crowd and said, 'Not in relation to what thousands of other people are suffering, but it's been disillusioning.'

'Your neighbours?'

She nodded. 'Not Miss Godfrey or Carrie, of course. And not Charlie. But people I never dreamed would ever turn against my father have done so. Leastways, they didn't speak out in his defence when they should have spoken out.'

'War does strange things to people,' he said wryly, able to imagine all too easily the kind of confrontation that had taken place when Carl Voigt had been removed from his home. 'In Norway people are being divided into two camps, those prepared to kowtow to the invaders of their country and those determined to continue resisting.

And those who opt for continued resistance will have a harsh lesson finding out who they can trust.'

Kate remained silent, knowing only too well the truth of his words. If Britain was invaded, her neighbours in Magnolia Square would no doubt divide into two similar camps. And the unexpected resistance heroes would be people like Miss Pierce and Miss Godfrey and Charlie Robson.

Sensing the darkness of her thoughts his arm tightened around her waist. 'I've told you the good news about the weekend,' he said, his voice full of teasing amusement, 'but not the bad.'

'The bad?' Apprehension seized her. 'What's the bad news? What . . .'

'We won't be alone together at the cottage,' he said, keeping his face straight with difficulty. 'We shall be sharing it with a friend of mine, Hector.'

Her eyes widened in dismayed disbelief. 'But I'd thought . . . I'd hoped . . .'

'He's waiting for us in the car. I don't think you'll find his presence a problem this weekend. In fact, I think you're going to rather like him.'

Her dismay deepened into embarrassed despair. The significance of her joining him at Hornchurch had been lost on him. He hadn't understood.

'Toby, I . . .' she began awkwardly and then stopped. The MG was parked prominently in the High Street and sitting in it was an impatient-looking, very large, very black, dog.

Laughter and relief surged through her.

'He's a Labrador,' Toby said as they neared the car and the dog stood up, his powerful tail wagging in joyous welcome. 'He belonged to a chum of mine who was shot down over Maastricht. I promised Rory that if he bought it I'd look after Hector for him. He's rather magnificent, isn't he?'

'Yes,' she said, glad that in fussing and petting Hector she was able to disguise the new set of feelings sweeping over her. 'Bought it'. Was that how Toby and his friends described a fiery and horrendous death? Was that the way they coped with the ever-present nightmare each and every one of them lived with? By coining a slang and trivializing expression for it?'

'We've become pretty inseparable these last few weeks,' Toby said as he opened the car door for her. 'I explained to him that I had an important visitor coming this weekend and that we wanted some privacy but he refused to take the hint.'

He walked around to the far side of the MG and slid into the driving seat beside her, shooting her a down-slanting, heart-stopping smile, the expression in his eyes making her damp with longing. 'And I've told him that if he expects to be taken for a long walk he can forget it. Once that cottage door closes behind us we're not emerging again for anyone. Not even him. This next forty-eight hours are going to be spent in one place and one place only. Bed!'

The cottage stood by itself at the end of a long, winding lane. It was a small, traditional two-up and two-down, set amidst a garden crammed with hollyhocks, delphiniums and Canterbury bells. Inside, in the wood-beamed living-room, was a shabby leather sofa and winged chair and a large, purposeful-looking desk. On it stood a blue pottery jug filled with flowers. She didn't have to ask him if he had picked the flowers himself. She knew he had. And his motivation had been the same as hers when she had shopped for her broderie anglaise trimmed nightdress. Even though they weren't yet married he regarded the time they were now spending together as being their honeymoon, and despite all the difficult circumstances, he wanted it to be as romantic and as perfect as possible.

With her heart banging against her ribs and Hector pushing and shoving at her heels, she followed Toby up the narrow, uneven staircase to the bedrooms.

'What used to be the small bedroom has mercifully been converted into a bathroom,' Toby said, leading the way into a sun-filled, lemon and white decorated bedroom. He dropped her overnight case onto a chintz upholstered button-backed chair. 'You can also see the airfield from here. If Ops want me they'll ring. I'm praying to God they won't.'

'Ops?' she asked, suddenly nervous, playing for time.

'The Operations Room.' There was an edge of tautness in his voice which she knew had nothing to do with their personal situation. 'Disaster is staring France in the face at the moment. The entire base is on stand-by.'

She hadn't walked as far into the room as he had and now, as their eyes held, he made no move towards her. Sensing her apprehension, loving her so much it was a physical pain, he said gently, 'If you've changed your mind, Kate, I'll understand. I know how low and lonely you must have felt when you wrote to me. I know how ghastly it must be for you living at home without your father, but I also know how you've always felt about sex before marriage and . . .'

'It is lonely at home,' she said huskily. 'And I was low and in need of comfort when I wrote to you. But that isn't the reason I decided to come down here this weekend.'

The bed lay between them, its white jacquard bedspread and plump, white, cotton-cased pillows spotlessly bridal.

'I came because I realized how foolish I'd been in clinging to a romantic notion that has nothing whatsoever to do with the life we're now living,' she said, apprehensive no longer, utterly sure of the commitment she was about to give. 'The values I was trying to cling to belong to a world that doesn't exist any longer.'

She thought of Rory, and of Toby facing the same risks, and the very idea of denying herself and Toby the joy and comfort of lovemaking in order that she could walk down the aisle a virgin seemed no longer only anachronistic, but obscene.

A small smile touched the corners of her mouth. 'I came down here this weekend because I love you,' she said, well aware that he had asked her if she was having second thoughts only because his love for her was completely unselfish; because her happiness, mental as well as emotional, mattered to him far more than his own and that if she had changed her mind he would, out of love for her, have contained his savage disappointment.

The excitement that had spiralled within her on the train journey from London was now roaring through every vein and nerve in her body. 'And because I want us to be lovers,' she said simply.

She saw relief swamp his eyes and then they darkened with passion and he closed the distance between them in swift strides. As he took her in his arms she upturned her face radiantly to his, adding softly with a wantonness she had never known she possessed, 'And I want to go to bed with you.'

Later, with the curtains drawn and the room bathed in muted, golden light, they lay naked on the rumpled sheets, their arms wrapped closely around each other.

Kate's nightdress, pristine and unworn, lay draped over the back of the chintz upholstered chair and Toby said in loving amusement, 'I hope you didn't waste precious clothing coupons on that piece of decorative nonsense.'

She moved slightly, pushing herself up on one elbow, the hair he had unbraided cascading heavily and silkily down her back, way past her waist. 'I used up every clothing coupon I possess to buy it, but none of them were wasted.' Her fingers moved slowly across his chest and down towards his stomach. 'It's symbolic,' she said, her voice thickening, 'and I shall treasure it life-long.'

As her fingers moved lower desire flared in him again. 'God, but I love you,' he whispered, pulling her once more down beside him, covering her body with his.

Her legs parted willingly, her arms encircling him. 'Always?' she asked, her lips close against the muscular smoothness of his flesh, knowing the answer but wanting to hear it yet again.

The breath caught in his throat as he re-entered the soft pillar of her flesh. 'Always,' he panted hoarsely, penetrating her deeper and deeper until she cried out beneath him, almost senseless with pleasure. 'Always and for ever!'

The telephone call came at dawn the next morning. He leapt from the bed to answer it almost before she was aware of what it was that had woken them. Praying it would prove to be a wrong number she pushed herself up against the pillows.

The telephone conversation was brief, but not brief enough to be a wrong number. 'Yes,' she heard Toby say abruptly. 'Right away, sir. Ten minutes at the most.'

As she heard him replace the receiver and then begin to take the stairs towards the bedroom two at a time she swung her legs from the bed, reaching for her underslip.

'It was Ops, wasn't it?' she asked unnecessarily.

He nodded, already scrambling into his uniform. 'I haven't time to drop you off in Hornchurch. Phone for a taxi. The number is on the desk.'

'And Hector?' she asked, as Hector bounded into the room, certain he was about to be taken for an early morning walk. 'What about Hector?'

'I'll take him with me back to base.'

He grabbed his jacket and his cap. 'Sorry about this, sweetheart. What a bloody way to have to part! I'll drop you a postcard the minute this show is over.'

She didn't have time to ask him what the 'show' was. One minute he was in the room with her, kissing her a fierce goodbye, the next he was gone.

She ran to the window, yanking back the curtains. By the time she had pushed the window open he had vaulted into the MG and was revving the engine into life.

'*I love you!*' she called out as Hector leapt into the passenger-seat.

With a squeal of tyres the MG swerved away from the front of the cottage and rocked into the lane.

'*Goodbye!*' she shouted, a sob in her throat. '*Goodbye and good luck!*'

The sports car sped down the lane, an incongruous slash of scarlet in the still, green landscape. She stayed at the window not knowing whether he had heard her or not, and she was still at the window when the first of the Hurricanes and Spitfires careered down the airfield and then took flight, winging their way towards France.

The news-stands she passed on her journey back to London left her in little doubt of the seriousness of the situation. 'BELGIUM AND HOLLAND SURRENDER TO NAZIS!' was the first headline to greet her as she entered Hornchurch station. At Liverpool Street the news headlines were, if possible, even more dire. 'BOULOGNE CAPTURED' 'CALAIS SURROUNDED' 'BRITISH TROOPS ENCIRCLED ON FRENCH COAST'.

She bought every newspaper possible, reading as she travelled on the underground from Liverpool Street Station to Charing Cross Station, reading all the way home on the train from Charing Cross to Blackheath.

'The bloody army's collapsed,' a woman she had never set eyes on before said to her as she got out of the train at Blackheath. 'The God-damned Germans are driving us into the sea!'

As she walked across the Heath she met up with a very morose-looking Charlie. 'I suppose you've heard the news,' he said without preamble. 'The British Expeditionary Force is being evacuated from France. 'ettie and Daniel are in a terrible state worryin' about young Danny. They're down at the Jennings' now, waitin' for news on the wireless. If you're goin' down there, tell 'em to keep cheerful.'

'I will,' Kate lied, unable to face the task of explaining to Charlie that as she was unwelcome at the Jennings' home she wouldn't be able to pass his message on for him.

Once home she switched on her own wireless, fiercely anxious to know what part the RAF were playing in the evacuation. The news was all about shipping. Hundreds upon hundreds of privately owned vessels, anything of thirty feet and upwards, were congregating at Ramsgate in order to form part of an evacuation fleet.

When she returned to work on Monday morning Mr Muff's conversation was about nothing else. 'Dunkirk!' he said to her before she had even taken her jacket off. 'It's the greatest evacuation the world has ever seen! Hitler thought he'd got us cornered but he's misjudged us yet again! The RAF will be giving the *Luftwaffe* a terrible pasting. If I had a Union Jack in the office I'd hang it from the window! This evacuation isn't a defeat. It's a triumph!'

Miss Pierce, too, thought the ongoing evacuation of the British Expeditionary Force, a victory. 'The latest news is that troops are already being landed at south coast ports and being put aboard trains for barracks or home,' she said as they sat together at lunch-time. 'It's all a terrible setback, of course, but however terrible the death toll, it isn't total annihilation. The small ships have seen to that. Did you know that even the Thames pleasure cruisers have gone to the aid of the troops?'

The first detailed newspaper account of the evacuation was published on 4 June under the heading 'Operation Dynamo, the great evacuation of Dunkirk, is complete.'

Kate read the report as she ate her breakfast, her relief that RAF planes would in all probability no longer be engaging the *Luftwaffe* in battle above the French beaches, vast. It was a relief that was compounded when Carrie burst into the house, her face radiant.

'Danny's telephoned Mr Giles!' she said as Kate put down her mug of tea and rose from the table to greet her. 'He was lifted off Dunkirk yesterday by a fishing trawler and he's now back at his barracks! Isn't it wonderful news? Isn't it absolutely bloody fantastic?'

'There's some bad news afoot,' Mr Muff said to her unhappily when she elatedly entered the office half an hour later. 'We've all been asked to assemble in the canteen where an announcement is to be made. I rather suspect it means Mr Harvey has passed away. I always did suspect his heart attack was far more serious than we were led to believe.'

Kate stared at him aghast. If his assumption was correct it meant that by suggesting to Toby that they spend his last leave together at Hornchurch, she had unwittingly denied him his last opportunity to see his grandfather.

'It doesn't look very good,' Miss Pierce said to her gravely as they walked down the corridor together towards the canteen. 'It certainly can't be any news to do with the war. If Hitler had invaded we'd hardly be asked to assemble in the canteen in order to be appraised of the fact! I rather think Mr Harvey must have suffered another, and this time fatal, heart attack.'

As they entered the canteen the buzz of speculative conversation from members of staff already assembled, concurred with her assessment of the situation.

'It certainly isn't news of a pay rise,' Kate heard someone say dryly.

'Perhaps we're to be turned into a munitions factory,' someone else said doubtfully.

There were calls for silence and Mr Tutley of Planning and Design took up an authoritative stance facing his co-employees and cleared his throat. 'I have a very unwelcome task to perform,' he said, and Kate saw that he was wearing a black armband.

Cold ice slithered down her spine. Toby had been wrong in thinking his grandfather on the way to full recovery from his heart attack. Mr Harvey was dead and she was responsible for the fact that Toby had not visited him on his last, all too short, leave.

'Though he was only among us for a short time at Harvey Construction Ltd, everyone who came into contact with him will remember him . . .'

The blood began to drum in Kate's ears. What was Mr Tutley saying? Mr Harvey *was* Harvey Construction Ltd.

'A young man . . . cut down in his prime . . . fighting valorously against the powers of darkness above the beaches of Dunkirk . . .'

Kate felt herself sway. It wasn't Toby's grandfather who had died. It was Toby. He was never going to come back to her. She was never going to see him again.

'Risking his life selflessly in order that others might live . . .'

Kate didn't hear any more. Her legs buckled and she slid senselessly to the floor at Mr Tutley's feet.

Chapter Ten

'She's going to have to have a bit more stamina than this if she's going to survive a war,' Kate heard Mr Tutley say dryly to someone. 'It's not as if Toby Harvey was a relative of hers, or a friend.'

'Maybe not,' Mr Muff responded with unusual acerbity, 'but the latest war news is enough to affect anyone's nerves and I'd appreciate a little more sympathy on your part, Mr Tutley. And a little help, too. If you could dismiss everyone and help me assist Miss Voigt to the sick-room . . .'

'She's coming round,' Kate heard Miss Pierce say, vast relief in her voice. 'Stand back gentlemen, please. What she needs is a little air.'

'What she needs is a good cup of tea,' a cleaning-lady said practically. 'The urn's on. How many sugars have I to put in her cup? Two or three?'

'Three,' Miss Pierce said decisively.

Dizzily Kate struggled to raise herself up from the floor and in doing so realized that Miss Pierce was kneeling beside her.

'Take your time, Kate,' her brisk, no-nonsense voice advised. 'Lean on me and breathe deeply for a few minutes before you try to stand.'

'As a mark of respect there will be no more work conducted on these premises until the beginning of next week!' Mr Tutley announced to everyone from a few feet away from her. 'When work is recommenced may I advise male members of staff that armbands will be deemed appropriate.'

In a world of nightmare Kate ignored Miss Pierce's

sensible advice and struggled to her feet. She had to get out of the canteen; out of the building.

'I'm all right,' she heard herself say in a voice that seemed to be coming from a million miles away. 'I don't need the rest-room or a cup of tea.'

'Kate, dear, I think it would be wisest if . . .'

Kate didn't wait to hear what it was Miss Pierce thought would be wisest. Aware that she was being stared at curiously by those members of the workforce who hadn't, as yet, acted on Mr Tutley's instruction and made a speedy exit from the canteen, she said in clipped, curt tones. 'I'm all right. I need to go home.'

'I'll come with you . . .'

'No.'

A spasm of incomprehension passed across Miss Pierce's concerned face. Kate was oblivious of it. She had to have privacy. She had to be able to give vent to the cataclysmic emotions inwardly rending her apart. Above all, she had to assimilate the reality of what had happened. Toby was dead. She was never going to see him again. It was a truth so monstrous she could barely grasp it.

'Do you think young Harvey will get a VC?' a young man from Planning and Design was asking an elderly colleague interestedly, 'Knowing his reputation he's bound to have died performing some kind of heroics. I thought I was lucky being deaf and exempt from active service but now I'm not too sure. It would be nice to be seen to be doing one's bit. Do you think the Home Guard would take me? Or the Fire Auxiliary Service?'

Somehow, someway, Kate walked out of the canteen and out of the building. Was it really only a few days since she had been safe and secure in Toby's arms? And now he was dead. The words battered at her ears like storm waves roaring up a beach. Toby was dead and she was alive and would have to live the rest of her life without him.

There came the sound of a small animal whimpering

in pain. A woman pushing a pram turned to stare after her and Kate realized that she herself had made the sound. Tears scalded her cheeks. Where had Mr Tutley said that Toby had died? Above the beaches of Dunkirk? Was that where his body was now? Dunkirk? And if it was, would it be buried there? Would she be unable to see him buried and bid him a last, loving goodbye?

As she neared the Heath the June sun was hot on her shoulders and her back. Beneath the brassy blue bowl of the sky the distant spire of All Saints' Church shimmered insubstantially. She knew that once she was home the emptiness of the house would press in on her like a physical weight and her footsteps faltered. She didn't want to go home. She wanted only to turn the clock back and for everything to be as it had been before the German armies had poured into France, forcing the British Expeditionary Force to retreat to Dunkirk.

Apart from a distant figure walking a dog the Heath was barren of people and with a choked cry she threw herself face down on the parched grass, weeping and weeping, her heart breaking.

Much later, when the sun had lost its afternoon heat and the sky was shot with the apricot light of early evening she was still there, hugging her knees with her arms, bereft beyond all bearing. One phase of her life, rich and rounded and full of love and laughter, was irrevocably over and no amount of fevered wishing could make it otherwise. No-one could help her to face the lonely future. That was a task she would have to accomplish by herself. Her interlocked fingers tightened until her knuckles were white. Beyond any shadow of doubt she knew that Toby would have expected her to face her future with courage. For a precious beat of time his presence by her side was almost palpable.

'I love you,' she whispered into the golden stillness. 'I love you now and for always.'

A bee circled lazily over a clump of clover near her feet and as it did so a measure of comfort pierced her grief. They had, at the end, been truly lovers. She had memories that no-one could ever take away from her; memories she would treasure in her heart for ever.

Dusk had begun to smoke the air and slowly she rose to her feet. It was time for her to return home; time for her to embark on the long, lonely future that lay ahead of her. With her tear-ravaged face ivory pale, she began to walk once again in the direction of Magnolia Square.

Later that evening there was a knock on the front door and passionately hoping that her visitor was Carrie, Kate ran to the door, opening it wide.

Miss Godfrey stood on the doorstep, dressed in a brown tweed suit and sensibly laced brogues. 'I'm sorry to disturb you like this, Katherine,' she said awkwardly, her eyes deeply troubled, 'but Ellen called on me a little while ago and told me the news.'

'Ellen?' Kate said uncomprehendingly, 'I'm sorry I don't know a . . .'

'Ellen Pierce,' Miss Godfrey said, tucking a wayward strand of greying hair back into the neat coil in the nape of her neck. 'She was worried about you but didn't like to call on you herself, uninvited. After what she told me I thought I had better do so.' Her hazel-green eyes were full of compassion. 'I'm so sorry, my dear. So very, very sorry.'

Clumsily Kate gestured her inside. Though Miss Godfrey and Miss Pierce had been friends for a long time now, Kate knew that Miss Godfrey had never allowed Toby's name to pass her lips and that Miss Pierce was completely ignorant of his many visits to Magnolia Square.

Now Miss Godfrey said, deeply distressed, 'I'm afraid I was so shocked when she told me the news, and of the dreadful way in which you heard it, that I quite forgot to be discreet. Ellen will, of course, say nothing to her colleagues at Harvey's and she sends you her very deepest sympathy . . .' She broke off, her voice perilously unsteady.

Kate was having so much difficulty keeping her own emotions under control that she was unable to make a response and seeing her difficulty Miss Godfrey said thickly, 'If there's anything either I or Ellen can possibly do . . .'

Kate shook her head. 'No. There's nothing. I just need to be on my own for a little while.'

Miss Godfrey regarded her steadily and then, realizing that she was speaking the truth, said gently, 'Then I will leave you in privacy Katherine, but only on the understanding that the minute you feel any differently, the minute you need someone to talk to, you will knock for me.'

'I will, I promise,' Kate said, grateful both for Miss Godfrey's kindness and for the fact that she was about to take her leave.

She opened the door for Miss Godfrey and as she did so Miss Godfrey said, 'Don't take time into consideration, Katherine. I don't mind what time of day or night you knock.'

Unexpectedly, and quite unprecedentedly, she gave Kate a quick, compassionate hug. 'Take care,' she said, her voice unsteady again, 'God Bless.'

For a few seconds after she had finally closed the door Kate wondered if she had made an error of judgement. Perhaps it would have been wisest to have asked Miss Godfrey to stay for a while. She stood in the long, narrow hallway, the emptiness of the large house echoing around her like a tomb.

And if Miss Godfrey had stayed? Kate knew very well what would have happened. The older woman's sympathy would have been more than she could have borne and the battle she was fighting against complete emotional disintegration would have been lost.

Despite the stultifying heat of the late evening she

hugged her arms around herself as if mortally cold. She still hadn't written to her father. The very thought of having to set the fact of Toby's death down on paper filled her with bubbling panic. Her father would be devastated. He would worry about her being alone in the house more than ever.

She was just about to force herself to walk into the sitting-room and to sit at her father's desk when there came another tap on the door behind her. This time she knew beyond doubt that it was Carrie.

Spinning round on her heels she flung the door wide, all her hard-won self-control deserting her.

'*Toby's dead!*' she sobbed, throwing herself into Carrie's arms. '*Toby's dead and I don't know how I can live without him!*'

For the next few days, bringing Rose with her, Carrie virtually moved into the Voigt home. Desperate bouts of weeping by Kate were interspersed with long chats of near-normality as Carrie recounted the day-to-day goings-on in the Square. There were times, much to Kate's incredulity, when she even found herself smiling, as when Carrie described the air raid shelter her father had dug into the back-garden.

'Honestly, you should see the state of it. It wouldn't keep out leaflets let alone old Hitler's bombs. Mum said if that was the best he could do she was going to move in with Miss Helliwell. Her shelter was dug in for her by Jack Robson and Mavis says he's dug it so deep it will survive Armaggedon.'

They were sitting in Kate's bedroom in their dressing-gowns, their hands around mugs of milky cocoa.

'Has anyone heard news of Jack lately?' Kate asked curiously.

Carrie's well-defined dark eyebrows rose high. 'Didn't you know he'd been home on leave? Talk about swagger. He looked as if he'd be able to take on Hitler and his armies single-handed. As soon as word spread he was back there were so many girls hanging around the Robson's gate that Charlie swore he'd set Queenie on them if they didn't take themselves elsewhere.'

Kate tilted her head to one side slightly. 'And Mavis? Is she still impressed by Jack's Commando bravura?'

'She's impressed by something, but whether it's bravura or not I wouldn't be knowing,' Carrie said darkly. 'She's even been taking advantage of Ted being away in the forces to go dancing with him. I told her word would get back to Ted but she said Ted had more sense than to get upset about her protecting a friend and neighbour from the rapacious young women of Lewisham and Greenwich.'

'Rapacious?' Kate said, vastly amused. 'Was that actually the word Mavis used?'

Carrie giggled. 'No. The word she used was a bit more down-to-earth but rapacious sums it up more than adequately. Have you seen Miss Godfrey in her ambulance driving togs yet? It's a treat for sore eyes. Tin hat, tweed-suit and pearls.'

At work the following week Miss Pierce squeezed her hand tightly, the compassion in her eyes conveying far more than her awkwardly stilted words of condolence. 'I know you won't want to speak of it here,' she had said as Mr Tutley, still sporting his black armband, passed close by them in the canteen with a cup of tea, 'but you have my very deepest sympathy, Kate.'

The war news grew even grimmer. Within two weeks of the evacuation of troops from the beaches of Dunkirk, German troops marched into Paris. A week later the French officially surrendered.

'And so Britain now stands alone,' Mr Muff said to her sombrely. 'Have you read Mr Churchill's speech to the House of Commons? He said that we must brace ourselves to our duty and so bear ourselves that if the

British Commonwealth lasts a thousand years men will still say "This was their finest hour".'

By the beginning of July, when news came that the Germans had landed forces on the Channel Islands, Kate was in the grip of such fevered hope that all Mr Muff's stirring comments were lost on her. Her menstrual period was most definitely late, and under normal circumstance it was never late.

'Please God let me be pregnant,' she whispered to herself every night before going to bed. 'Please don't let me start my period! Please let me be having Toby's baby!'

As she lay awake in the darkness she tried not to think of the horrendous problems that would follow if her fierce desire was granted. She would have to break the news to her father. She would have to endure endless gossip and speculation about the paternity of her baby. She would have to give up work and would then have no income. And she would have to face the problem of whether or not to inform Toby's grandfather of her condition.

In the long hours of the night the last problem seemed far the most insuperable. Joss Harvey was ignorant of her existence. How could she possibly write to him out of the blue and tell him that she was bearing his beloved dead grandson's child? Yet if she didn't she would, perhaps, be denying him the same kind of joy that she was experiencing. It was a problem she was unable to resolve and she thrust it to the back of her mind. The important thing at the moment was to establish that she *was* pregnant and only a visit to her doctor could do that.

'I'm afraid it's too early for me to confirm absolutely,' Doctor Roberts, who had brought her into the world, said cautiously. 'I think there is a very strong possibility that you *are* pregnant but only in another two or three weeks will I be able to be more certain.' He fiddled unhappily with his stethoscope. 'I've known you all your life, Katherine. I would never have expected . . . never anticipated . . .'

'The father of my baby died at Dunkirk,' Kate said, keeping her voice steady with difficulty. 'He had asked me to marry him and I had accepted his proposal. I *want* to be pregnant. I *want* to be having his baby!'

Doctor Roberts, well-accustomed to the romantic idiocies of many of his younger female patients, sighed heavily. 'You're not being very realistic,' he said gently. 'Your child will be illegitimate – a bastard. And both of you will suffer for the fact.'

Kate rose from the cracked leather chair she had been sitting on. 'If I *am* having a baby, it will be much-loved,' she said tautly, 'and that is what matters. Not the fact that it will be born out of wedlock.'

Doctor Roberts pursed his lips and shook his head in disagreement. 'I wish that were the case, Kate, but I've lived too long to believe it to be so. The minute a whisper of your condition reaches your neighbours you'll find yourself labelled a woman of loose morals – and be ostracized accordingly.'

Kate gave him a small, mirthless smile. 'You're forgetting that I'm half-German, Doctor Roberts. I know all about being ostracized and being ostracized for my morals instead of my ancestry will merely make a refreshing change.'

Before Doctor Roberts could even think of a suitable response she had walked from the room, her heavy bell-rope of flaxen hair swinging gently against her rigidly straight back.

There were times, at work, when she found the casual gossip about Toby's death nearly unendurable.

'Word is that old man Harvey has taken his grandson's death very hard, very hard indeed,' Mr Muff said to her the morning after her visit to Doctor Roberts. 'It's understandable of course, particularly when you remember that his son died in the last war, fighting Germans. The poor man has no close family left at all now.'

'He was piloting a Hurricane,' one of the typists from Planning and Design said to her when she came into Mr Muff's office with a memo. 'My brother is in the RAF and he says Hurricanes are notoriously unstable at low altitude. If I leave this memo on Mr Muff's desk will you make sure he sees it? And I suppose he must have been flying at low altitude if he was flying over a beach. I wonder if he came down on land or in the sea? Either way he wouldn't have stood a chance, would he? Will you tell Mr Muff that when he's read the memo Mr Tutley would like a reply to it straight away?'

That evening, as she walked from the Heath and into Magnolia Square, she felt utterly exhausted, both physically and emotionally.

Hettie Collins, her black hat crammed over her iron-grey curls, was hurrying towards her. The minute she saw Kate she changed direction, crossing the Square abruptly. Kate shrugged her shoulders. If Hettie chose to react to her as if she were a fully paid up member of the Hitler Youth *Mädchen* there was nothing she could do about it.

She continued on her way, wondering how she was going to endure any more conversations of the kind she had endured that day and she was so deep in thought, her eyes to the ground and not in front of her, that she didn't see the open-topped car parked outside her house until she was nearly on top of it.

When it did register on her vision it did so with so much impact that she felt as if an iron hand had been punched into her chest. It was a blue car, not red, but the young man driving it was in RAF uniform and there was a big, black Labrador sitting in the seat next to him.

She came to an abrupt halt, her heart slamming

against her breast-bone, the blood thundering in her ears.

A young man she had never set eyes on before vaulted from the driver's seat. Like Toby he was fair-haired, but his face was more fine-boned than Toby's, almost effeminate.

'Excuse me, are you Miss Voigt?' he asked, walking towards her. 'We haven't met before but you fit Toby's description. I don't imagine there are many girls with a plait of hair like yours.'

She remained motionless, still trying to recover from the wild, wonderful hope that had, just for a split second, engulfed her.

'Yes,' she said hoarsely, coming to terms with the crucifying cruelty of reality. 'I'm Kate Voigt. Is that Hector in the car?'

Before any reply could be made on his behalf Hector answered for himself, leaping down to the pavement and bounding towards her, his powerful tail wagging frenziedly. 'It most certainly is,' the young man said as she bent down to Hector, pressing her face against his silk-soft fur. 'And my name is Lance Merton. I was a pal of Toby's.'

His clipped, plummy pronunciation was most definitely ex-public school.

She stood up straight again, Hector pressed close against her legs, hope of a different kind beginning to stir deep within her. 'Did Toby leave something for me? A letter . . .'

'No,' he said, his smile fading. 'There was no letter. I'm sorry.'

Once again she battled with disappointment. Then she looked down at Hector and comfort surged through her. 'Have you been looking after Hector?' she asked, wondering if it would be hard to persuade Lance to part with him.

'Yes, but it isn't easy. Not on an RAF base.'

'Would you let me have him?'

'Consider the deed done,' Lance Merton said without the slightest hesitation. He cocked his head to one side slightly. Things were going easier than he had hoped. Ever since he had seen her photograph on Toby's locker his complex, introverted personality had been bewitched by her. She didn't look like any other girl. There was nothing ordinary about her. Her long, thick plait of golden hair reminded him of the medieval princesses of his childhood story books. Even in a photograph she had exuded an air of inner serenity, a gentleness which he found profoundly sexually disturbing. Now that there was the added bond of Hector between them as well as Toby, he would be able to call on her again when her grief for Toby had begun to abate. He felt a sense of deep satisfaction. His purpose had been achieved. He had met her in the flesh and the flesh had not been wanting.

'I'm glad you haven't minded my calling on you like this,' he said, marvelling at how dark her eyelashes were for a natural blonde. 'My mother has relatives in Blackheath and I'm being a dutiful son and visiting them for her.'

'How did you know my address?'

'Toby told me you lived in Magnolia Square and the photograph of you on his locker was taken outside your front gate. I recognized your neighbour's magnolia tree.'

For the first time since he had asked if she were Miss Voigt, Kate felt a *frisson* of awkwardness. He had been a friend of Toby's and had taken the trouble to come and see her. If her father had been at home she wouldn't have had the slightest hesitation in asking him into the house for a cup of tea. But her father wasn't home and despite Lance Merton's near-effeminate features, there was nothing effeminate about his personality.

Beyond his uniformed shoulder she could see Miss Helliwell and Miriam Jennings gossiping together outside Miss Helliwell's gate, their eyes not on each other but on her and Lance Merton.

If she invited Lance Merton into the house news of her action would be all over Magonolia Square by supper-time. Ordinarily she would not have wasted a moment of her time worrying about such a prospect, but if she were pregnant she couldn't afford to be so uncaring. She didn't want wild, incorrect rumours circulating about her baby's paternity.

As the awkward silence lengthened Lance put an end to it, saying blandly, 'I'll say goodbye for now and leave you in Hector's good care. Perhaps next time I'm down this way I could call on you again?'

'Yes, of course,' she said, feeling more than a little ashamed at her inhospitality. If Carrie had been in sight she could have asked Carrie to join them. Or even Miss Godfrey. But Carrie and Miss Godfrey were not in sight.

'Goodbye then,' he said, shaking her hand with sudden and disconcerting formality.

'Goodbye,' she said, wishing that she could reverse her decision and perhaps listen to him talk about Toby.

From the depths of Miss Godfrey's magnolia-tree Billy's strident young voice ensured that she didn't do so. 'Hoy, Kate!' he called out cheekily. 'Who's your friend, an' where's 'is plane?'

'He's a beautiful dog,' Carrie said when Kate formerly introduced her to Hector. 'It was kind of Toby's friend to think of bringing him to you.'

'I'm not sure he did so with the intention of leaving him with me,' Kate said doubtfully. 'He said that it wasn't easy looking after a dog on an RAF base and I asked him if I could have him.'

'Too easy,' Carrie said, sitting back on her heels beside Hector and giving him an affectionate pat. 'He came to see you with Hector with the intention of asking you if you wanted to have him. You simply made it easy for him, that's all.'

'Perhaps. It was an odd sort of encounter, over almost

before it began. He barely mentioned Toby, except to say that Toby had told him whereabouts I lived.'

'Perhaps not referring to a friend's death is his way of coming to terms with it,' Carrie said helpfully. 'Danny never says any of his mates have been killed. He always says they've "pegged" it or "snuffed" it'.

Kate, remembering the offhand way Toby had referred to Hector's original owner as having 'bought' it, didn't disagree with her. And she had more important things to think about than her odd encounter with Lance Merton. She still hadn't started her period and that morning she had been violently sick.

'Did you suffer with morning sickness when you were pregnant with Rose?' she asked curiously.

'Not 'alf,' Carrie said cheerily as Hector nuzzled her ear. 'It's the one reason I'm not too keen on having another one. Morning sickness and early mornings down the market don't mix.'

'How soon after you fell pregnant did you start being sick?'

'I'm not sure.' Carrie wrinkled her brow, trying to remember. 'Two or three weeks. Maybe four. Why the sudden interest?' Before Kate could even attempt a reply comprehension dawned. Her cat-green eyes flew wide. 'Good God, Kate! You're not . . . You can't be . . . Are you *pregnant?*'

For the first time since she had heard the news of Toby's death Kate felt laughter fizzing in her throat. 'Yes,' she said, revelling in her sure and certain inner knowledge, her face radiant. 'Yes, Carrie. I am.'

For the next few weeks, with the exception of Carrie, she hugged her knowledge to herself. Apart from suffering from morning sickness she felt perfectly healthy and she was in no particular hurry to visit Doctor Roberts and be preached at. Nor did she see any need to distress her father any sooner than was necessary. Toby's grandfather was, however, another matter. Morally, she was quite certain that she should tell him. Having the nerve to do so was quite different.

'If only Toby had spoken to him about me it would be relatively easy,' she said to Carrie for the hundredth time as they sat in deck-chairs in the back-garden and watched Rose trying to haul herself up on to Hector's back.

'How do you know he didn't?'

'Because he would have told me.'

There was the merest hint of doubt in her voice. She and Toby hadn't discussed his grandfather during the precious hours they had shared together in the cottage at Hornchurch. It was just remotely possible that in one of his last letters to his grandfather Toby *had* told him that he intended marrying, and that he had given his grandfather her name. And if he hadn't? If he hadn't, any kind of meeting between herself and Mr Harvey would be difficult beyond belief.

'Perhaps it would be easiest to wait until the baby is born,' Carrie said, reading her thoughts. 'With luck it will be the dead-spit of Toby and old man Harvey will only have to look at it to know you're speaking the truth and that the baby is his great-grandson.'

'Yes,' Kate said gratefully, rising to her feet in order to lift Rose away from an admirably patient Hector. 'That's what I'll do. I'll wait until the baby is born and then go and see him.'

'Fat-heads!' Mr Muff said a few days later as he walked into the office and slammed the cardboard box containing his gas mask down hard on his desk. 'What fanciful stories will they think of next! My advice to you Kate is to take absolutely no notice. Treat such remarks with the contempt they deserve.'

From behind her typewriter Kate stared at him in bemusement, wondering if the fat-heads were Hitler and his cronies or Mr Tutley and his colleagues.

'I'm sorry,' she said soothingly, keeping affectionate

amusement out of her voice with difficulty, 'but I haven't a clue as to what you're talking about Mr Muff.'

'Really? You haven't heard?' Even though it was a hot sunny day he had still come to work wearing his trilby and he deposited it carefully on top of a convenient filing-cabinet. 'From the way Tutley's secretary was talking I thought the gossip had already reached you.'

Kate wound a fresh piece of notepaper into her typewriter. 'What gossip? Is it local or national?'

'It's personal,' he said, sitting down at his desk and beginning to rifle through his in-tray. 'And the best way of dealing with it is to ignore it.

'Personal?' Kate's amusement faded. With a slight frown she said, 'About me? In what way?'

Mr Muff gave an ungentlemanly snort of derision. 'According to Tutley's secretary you were on romantic terms with Toby Harvey. She's telling everyone who will listen to her that she often saw the two of you in that dangerous-looking sports car he used to drive. I told her she was being extremely silly and that if Toby Harvey had had a girlfriend, and if news of such idiocy reached her, the young lady in question would be greatly distressed by it. Have you read this letter about the Dover contract? What German guns on the French coast pulverize, Harvey's rebuild. By the time this war is over Joss Harvey will be rich as Croesus.'

'It's all over the building, my dear,' Miss Pierce said to her unhappily when they met at lunchtime. Deep lines of concern etched her mouth. 'When I first heard what was being said I was terribly afraid you would think I was the culprit and then that ghastly secretary of Mr Tutley's announced quite unashamedly that she was the perpetrator. Perhaps the best thing for you to do would be to simply admit that the gossip is true and then it will soon die down.'

Kate made no reply and her face was so set and pale that Miss Pierce thought it best to steer the conversation onto lighter matters. 'I had a very nice letter from your father this morning. He and his fellow internees have begun providing their own entertainment by organizing concerts and recreations. It's nice to know they're not letting their situation get them down, isn't it?'

Kate agreed with her, wishing that her own situation was as uncomplicated. Whether she admitted that the gossip was true as Miss Pierce advised, or followed Mr Muff's advice and ignored it, one thing was certain. It wouldn't cease. Not when her pregnancy began to show.

'So what are we going to do now the Phoney War is over and the Germans really mean business?' Carrie asked, her shoulder-length hair bound in a flower-patterned headscarf worn turban fashion. 'Do we use the Anderson shelters when the siren goes off or do we make for a tube station?'

'It's no use making for a tube station if the siren goes off when we're at home,' Kate said practically. 'They're all too far away. The raid would be over before we even got to one.'

They were standing in front of Carrie's market stall in Lewisham High Street and Mavis hove into view, gaudily splendid in a scarlet-trimmed, halter-neck sundress sporting a vivid design of playing-card faces.

As the dizzying array of diamonds, hearts, clubs and spades, swam before her eyes Carrie said graphically, 'Where the heck did you get that from? It's enough to give half of Lewisham migraine!'

'It is pretty eye-catching, ain't it?' Mavis agreed, twirling around on high wedge-heeled sandals so that they could appreciate her finery more fully. 'You won't see another like it.'

'I don't want to,' Carrie responded tartly. 'What did you make it out of? A tablecloth?'

'Curtaining. It came from a club up West. Ever since they had to put black-out curtaining up it's been laying around, doing nothing. So I had a little word, so to speak, and this is the result. There's loads left. I'm going to make a dress for Beryl next. And a couple of shirts for Ted.'

'There's no mistake, Kate,' Mr Muff said, his usually cheery face almost ashen. 'Mr Harvey is in the building and he wants a word with you. Now.' His voice broke so that it was almost a croak. 'In the boardroom.'

As Kate's horrified eyes held his she felt as if the ground were shelving at her feet. There could be only one possible reason why Mr Harvey wished to speak to her. And both of them knew what it was. The rumours about her relationship with Toby had reached his ears and he wished to determine the truth of them.

She took a deep steadying breath. She would have had to face him and tell him about the baby sooner or later. Though the present circumstances were far from perfect at least by seeing him now the ordeal would be over. She wouldn't have to lay awake at night anymore, fretting in dreaded anticipation of it.

'You'd best be on your way,' Mr Muff said unhappily. 'Mr Harvey isn't a man who takes kindly to being kept waiting. Onwards and upwards, Kate. Seize the nettle. Never say die.'

Finding his exhortations more doomladen than cheering she turned away from him and walked out of the office and into the corridor. What garbled account of her relationship with Toby had been told to his grandfather? Was the old man going to be puzzled or distressed by what he had been told, or just plain furious?'

The boardroom was on the far side of the building. It was a room she had previously never had any cause to enter and as she neared it she noted with a flicker of amusement the change in floor covering and decor. Instead of linoleum there was carpeting; instead of being painted cream and brown, the walls of the corridor leading to the boardroom were an almost spring-like soft green.

The brass-knobbed boardroom door was closed. She paused for a moment before knocking, reminding herself that the man she was about to face was her baby's great-grandfather, not an ogre. She gave a business-like, unintimidated knock.

'*Enter.*'

The voice was a dark, deep growl.

She smoothed her navy-blue skirt, checked that her pink and white cotton sriped blouse was neatly imprisoned beneath her waistband, and opened the door.

The room was vast. The largest mahogany table she had ever seen dominated it. At the far end of the table stood a white-haired, powerfully-built figure.

Shock eddied through her. She had lived so long with the knowledge of Mr Harvey's near-fatal heart attack and Toby's concern for him that she had constructed a mental image of a man dangerously frail. There was nothing frail about the figure confronting her. And he didn't look a day over sixty.

As their eyes held she saw something very like a spasm of distaste cross his face and then he rasped, 'Miss Voigt? That's a German name, isn't it? Were you born in Germany?'

'No.' Despite the sick tightening of her stomach muscles her voice was coolly composed. 'I was born in Blackheath.'

'But your parents are German?'

'My father is German.'

He moved slightly, resting one hand on the high-backed chair that headed the table. His double-breasted suit was grey, as was his tie.

'I don't employ Germans,' he said with such harsh brevity it robbed her of breath. 'Not even half-Germans. I want you off my premises immediately. And for good.'

For one uncertain moment she believed both she and Mr Muff had come to a wildly wrong assumption and that Mr Harvey was entirely ignorant of the office-gossip and had only summoned her into his presence because her nationality had come to his notice.

'Especially half-Germans who are lying trollops,' he said succinctly.

She sucked in her breath as if she had been slapped across the face, anger roaring through her. Only by remembering that she had no idea what kind of a story he had been told did she manage to curb it.

'I am neither a liar *nor* a trollop!' she said tightly. 'And even if I were your accusation would be grossly out of place and ill-mannered.'

He drew in his breath sharply, his nostrils whitening. 'Get the hell out of here! I'm not indulging in a conversation with you! I'm giving you your marching orders!'

Her eyes held his steadily. With a stab of gratification she saw disbelief flare through his eyes as, instead of fleeing from the room, she began to walk towards him.

She halted a mere two chairs width away from him. 'I don't know what you've been told about me and my relationship with Toby,' she said tautly, 'but the least you can do is to have the courtesy of allowing me to tell you about it myself.'

At the mention of Toby's name he flinched. It was as if a rock had moved. 'Out!' he hissed again, high colour flooding his cheeks. 'Don't dare sully my grandson's name by linking it with your own!'

For a brief second she hesitated, despair flooding through her. How could Toby, so easy-going and kind and honourable, have been this man's grandson? The temptation to spin on her heel and leave him fuming amidst his prejudices and presumptions was almost overpowering. With difficulty she resisted it. She had a moral obligation to tell him of the child she was carrying. How he reacted to the news was none of her responsibility.

'I loved Toby,' she said, her voice thick with emotion. 'And he loved me. He wanted to marry me . . .'

'Out!' Joss Harvey roared again, slamming his fist down so hard on the table that the entire room seemed to vibrate.

'He was going to tell you as soon as he felt you had recovered sufficiently from your heart attack to be able to cope with the shock of the news.'

Even as she said the words she wondered how Toby could possibly have thought his grandfather dangerously enfeebled. Hard on the heels of her reflection came the realization that it was over two months since Toby's death; two months since he had declared to her that he would, on his very next leave, confront his grandfather with the news of their love for each other.

'He knew it would be a shock to you because of my father's nationality,' she continued, fighting down the thundering wave of grief that threatened to submerge her. 'He was on the verge of telling you when . . .'

'Out!' Joss Harvey hissed, again grasping the back of the leather covered chair at the head of the table, this time quite obviously for support.

For the first time she realized that his aura of vigour was largely veneer. It was the sheer force of his personality that exuded strength and authority, not physical well-being. Knowing that if she remained in the room any longer there was a risk he would work himself up into such a state that he would collapse, she said simply, 'I'm going, Mr Harvey. But before I do, there is one last thing that I'm duty-bound to tell you . . .'

'*Out!* Not another word! Only a Kraut would have your nerve and insolence!'

Sick at heart, knowing beyond any shadow of doubt the impossibilty of establishing even the slightest of civil relations with him, she said starkly, 'I'm carrying Toby's child.'

He grasped hold of the back of the chair with his other hand, the gnarled knuckles white, his eyes blazing. '*You're a slut and a blackmailing liar! I'll have you interned*

*for this! You repeat your foul lie outside this room and I'll
sue you for slander in every court in the land!'*

Unwaveringly her eyes continued to hold his. She still
didn't feel a resurgence of the anger that had initially
flared through her only seconds after entering the room.
She was beyond anger. Beyond any emotion at all, apart
from pity.

'I feel sorry for you, Mr Harvey,' she said quietly.
'You've lost your grandson and you're denying yourself
the comfort of the legacy he has left behind him.'

The colour in his face deepened to a choleric purple.
She didn't wait for him to draw breath and hurl a fresh
torrent of abuse at her. With a tiredness that was
bone-deep she turned on her heel and walked down the
long room, opening the door and closing it behind her
without a backward glance.

Chapter Eleven

As she walked back along the carpeted corridor and then the linoleum floored corridor that led to Mr Muff's office, she felt emotionally and physically numbed. Joss Harvey's reputation, amongst those of his senior employees who had dealings with him, was such that she had long realized he was a bully. And Toby himself had told her that where Germans were concerned, his grandfather was a deeply prejudiced bigot. Knowing such unpleasant facts was, however, far different from experiencing them at first hand.

As she walked unseeingly past the Planning and Design offices she tried for the twentieth time to come to terms with the fact that the rude, ignorant, tyrannical despot still, no doubt, fuming to himself in the boardroom, was not only Toby's grandfather but her own baby's great-grandfather. She pressed a hand instinctively against her still-flat stomach.

'You're not going to grow up like *him*!' she whispered fiercely. 'You're going to grow up kind and courageous and honourable like your father!'

Mr Muff leapt from his chair in agitation the minute she opened his office door.

'Why on earth did he want to see you?' he demanded, hurrying round his desk towards her. 'Was it about those ridiculous rumours? I find it incredible that Mr Harvey would even listen to them, let alone pay attention to them . . .'

Something very like pain squeezed Kate's heart. She had enjoyed working for Mr Muff. Despite his old-maid fussiness he was both courteous and, where she was concerned, caring.

'The rumours were true, Mr Muff,' she said quietly. 'And though Mr Harvey does not believe them to be true, he has ordered me to leave the building immediately.'

'True?' Mr Muff blinked at her uncomprehendingly. 'Leave the building? You're not making any sense, Kate. How could the rumours possibly be true? And what do you mean by saying you have to leave the building? Has there been a bomb alert? Has Mr Tutley been informed?'

He was already hastily reaching for his trilby-hat and Kate said gently, knowing how much he would miss both her efficiency as a secretary and her companionship, 'There hasn't been a bomb alert, Mr Muff. Mr Harvey has dismissed me.'

Mr Muff stared at her, still not understanding, his bewilderment pathetic.

'I've been fired,' she said starkly. 'Sacked.'

'But that's . . . that's *preposterous*!' He put his hat on his head as if he, too, intended walking from the building. 'It's unthinkable! Outrageous!'

Kate walked across to her desk and began opening drawers, taking out personal possessions. 'Mr Harvey now knows that I'm half-German,' she said, putting a small mirror, a nail file and a packet of headache tablets in a neat pile on the desk top. 'And now that he does, even if it hadn't been for my relationship with Toby, he would be insistent that I leave his employment.'

'But you're *my* secretary!' he protested, too nonplussed by the revelation that the rumours about Kate and Toby Harvey were true to even begin coming to terms with it, seizing instead on a fact that was indisputable. 'And I want you to remain my secretary! I shall speak to Mr Harvey myself, this very minute!' He strode purposefully towards the door, his trilby at a rakish angle.

It wasn't an empty gesture, he was in deadly earnest.

Kate, knowing how very nervous he was of Joss Harvey and of how he would go to any lengths to avoid even the slightest contact with him, was deeply moved by the extent of his indignation and the lengths he was prepared to go to in order to preserve their happy working relationship.

'It's no use, Mr Muff,' she said, scooping her possessions into her shoulder-bag. 'Mr Harvey won't change his mind. Even if he did, I couldn't possibly remain working here.'

Halted by her words, Mr Muff stood at the open doorway, his expression one of abject distress. 'But what am I going to do? I don't *want* another secretary. What if they assign Mr Tutley's secretary to me? Who am I going to chat to about the progress of the war? Who am I going to share my little jokes with?'

Kate put the cover on her typewriter for the last time. 'Miss Pierce will make sure that whoever takes my place is pleasant and friendly,' she said, keeping her voice steady with difficulty. 'I've enjoyed working with you, Mr Muff.'

'And I've enjoyed working with you, Kate. I can't quite believe it's ending like this. So suddenly . . . so utterly without warning . . .'

He looked so lost and forlorn that Kate felt a suspicious pricking sensation behind her eyelids. Knowing that it would be utter foolishness to prolong her leave-taking a moment longer she swung her bag and her gas mask canister on to her shoulder and walked towards the door.

'Goodbye,' she said, knowing that she should also stop by Miss Pierce's office and say goodbye to her.

'Goodbye, Kate.' He clasped her hand warmly, his eyes suspiciously bright. 'Take care of yourself. Always look on the bright side. Never say die. Onwards and upwards!'

Too choked to make any response she merely squeezed his hand tight and turned on her heel, walking down the familiar corridor and out of the building, not even pausing to knock on the door of the Personnel Office. One goodbye had been enough to cope with. She would write to Miss Pierce and would, no doubt, see her to talk to when Miss Pierce next visited Miss Godfrey. As always when deeply distressed she needed to be alone; only when she was alone could she get her thoughts into order and see things in perspective.

It was the end of August now and the midday sun was hot. She looked up at the cloudless sky wondering if, somewhere over the fields of Kent or the English Channel, a pitched battle was taking place between the RAF's Spitfires and Hurricanes and the *Luftwaffe*'s Junkers and Messerschmitts. For the last two weeks or so such engagements had been everyday occurrences.

'Hitler's trying to destroy the RAF both on the ground and in the air,' Mr Muff had said to her grimly when the first all-out attack on an RAF airfield had taken place. 'It's an essential part of his invasion strategy. He won't succeed of course. Our pilots will see to that.'

Many Londoners had travelled out by train to the fringes of the city, to Biggin Hill and Caterham and Croydon where the RAF airfields protecting London were sited, in order to have a grandstand view of the life and death battles taking place above their heads. Kate knew that Mavis had done so, taking Billy and Beryl and a thermos flask and sandwiches, with her.

It was the last thing in the world she would have wanted to do. She still had nightmares about Toby's death; envisaging him trapped in the burning cockpit of his plane, and the mere prospect of watching other pilots die in such a hideous fashion made her blood run cold with horror.

As she neared the Heath she saw, in the sky to the south where Biggin Hill aerodrome was located, the tell-tale circular vapour trails that indicated a close-fought battle had recently taken place. Not for the first time she wondered if Lance Merton was still alive or if he, too, had 'bought' it, like Toby and Toby's friend and Hector's initial owner, Rory.

Her gas mask canister bumped uncomfortably against her thigh as she stepped on to the daisy-starred grass of the Heath. In retrospect she now felt she had behaved incredibly stupidly where Lance Merton was concerned. If she had invited him into the house for a cup of tea he would, no doubt, have talked to her about Toby and she desperately wanted the comfort of being able to talk with someone about Toby. There was no-one with whom she could do so. Carrie had barely known him. Miss Godfrey had known him only well enough to exchange an occasional friendly greeting with him. And any hopes that the baby she was expecting would forge a bond between herself and Joss Harvey had been crushed into total annihilation.

She felt a shudder run down her spine as, for the first time since leaving the boardroom, she allowed herself to think back on what had been said between them. Joss Harvey had behaved despicably. As she reflected on his coarseness and crassness the numbness that had enveloped her began to ebb and a positive sensation, almost buoyant, began to replace it.

Without intending to do so, he had simplified her future and her baby's future. She now had no need to take him into account in any way whatsoever.

'It's just going to be the two of us . . . and Dad,' she said, passing her hand once again across her stomach. 'And we're going to manage perfectly, just as Carrie and Rose manage with Danny never at home now.'

'I don't think you're being very practical,' Carrie said frankly as she swept up the rubbish that had accumulated around her market stall. 'Joss Harvey isn't just anyone, Kate. He's rich. Filthy rich. His acknowledging the baby could transform the baby's life.'

'I don't want Joss Harvey's money, thank you very much,' Kate said tartly, shifting her basket of shopping from one hand to the other, Hector sitting patiently on the pavement by her feet. 'And I'm surprised at you even thinking that I would do.'

'Not even to help rear the baby?' Carrie asked, pausing in her task and leaning on the handle of her sweeping-brush. 'Having an illegitimate kid isn't a doddle at the best of times, Kate. Having one in the middle of a war, when your mum isn't alive to give you moral support and your dad is in an internment camp, is going to be a bloomin' nightmare.'

'I have a home,' Kate said stubbornly. 'And I can make use of it. I can take lodgers in. Lots of women in the Auxiliary Territorial Service have been drafted into the munitions factories in Woolwich and they must all be in need of decent lodgings.'

Carrie regarded her exasperatedly, her hands raw from handling boxes and sacks of produce, her fingernails grimy. 'That'd be all well and good if it was a necessity, Kate. But it *isn't* a necessity. Or it shouldn't be.' She pushed a wing of hair away from her face, leaving a dirt smudge on her forehead as she did so. 'Toby was Joss Harvey's only family. If he had lived he would have been his grandfather's only heir. Now that he's dead, all that Joss Harvey possesses should go, eventually, to Toby's child. And if Joss Harvey could be made to believe that the baby you are carrying *is* Toby's child, that is exactly what would happen.'

'Nothing on earth will ever convince Joss Harvey that my baby is Toby's.' Kate's jaw was set stubbornly, her eyes fierce. 'And he's such a nasty, offensive man that I don't *want* him to acknowledge my baby. I don't want him to have anything to do with my baby.'

Carrie shook her head despairingly, recognizing the note of mulish determination that had entered Kate's voice and knowing that nothing on earth would now shift her in her opinion. It had been the same when they had been children. Though she was the quicker-tempered of the two of them, it was Kate who, when her anger was roused or her mind made up about anything, was quietly and utterly implacable.

'I still think you're making a mistake,' she said, returning to her task and sweeping discarded cabbage leaves into the gutter. 'And what's more, when the baby grows up, he or she might very well think so as well!'

'And so Dad's out looking for a new cart,' Carrie said a little while later as they turned off Lewisham High Street into Magnolia Hill. 'If it wasn't for petrol rationing I think he'd have retired Nobby and looked around for a second-hand van. Nobby must be seventeen now and that's getting on a bit for a horse. As it is, he's going to have to make do with whatever he can find. If he's repaired the old cart once he's repaired it a hundred times and it simply fell apart yesterday morning in the Old Kent Road. Apparently there were potatoes and carrots and caulies everywhere and Dad swears he recognized Miss Helliwell, scarpering off with a cabbage under her coat.'

Knowing that Carrie was trying to amuse her, Kate smiled but it was a smile without any real warmth and she didn't pursue the subject of either Albert Jennings' search for a cart or Miss Helliwell's speedy appropriation of one of his accidentally spilled cabbages. Ever since the day her father had been arrested and interned the neighbours who had stood by, watching with tacit approval, had not spoken to her, nor she to them.

Where Miss Helliwell was concerned, Kate felt bleakly regretful. The anguished expression on Miss Helliwell's face, whenever their paths crossed, spoke volumes and Kate was sure that Miss Helliwell was deeply bewildered by the scene that had taken place that morning and the division that had since sprung up between them.

As Hector padded obediently at her heels and Carrie chattered about Rose, she thought back to the long-ago evening when Miss Helliwell had read her palm. Much of what Miss Helliwell had forecast had come true. After the heartache she had experienced when Jerry Robson had been killed, she had found true love and great happiness with Toby.

She thought of the baby growing in her womb and remembered Miss Helliwell telling her that it was a love from which nothing but good would come. She also remembered Miss Helliwell's reluctance to spell out her future to her in detail and knowing now how her palm must have revealed Toby's tragic, early death, she understood that reluctance all too well.

Carrie broke in on her thoughts abruptly.

'What's that outside my house?' she asked in sudden alarm as they entered the Square. 'It looks like a hearse!'

For one stunned moment both of them came to a halt, staring at the unmistakably majestic, horse-drawn funeral hearse standing directly outside Carrie's home and then, her face drained of colour, Carrie broke into a run.

Slightly hampered by her heavy shopping-basket Kate ran in her wake, Hector, delighted by the unexpected change of pace, bounding delightedly by her side.

By the time they raced up to the hearse a group of interested spectators had already collected around it. Hettie Collins, her black hat for once looking remarkably appropriate, was saying in a loud voice: 'But why isn't the horse wearing purple funeral plumes? He should be doing. It's only proper.'

'Where's Mum?' Carrie gasped, pushing her way through the small crowd. 'Where's Dad? What's happened? Who's died?'

Mavis was nearest to the hearse, resplendent in a shiny, tight rayon skirt and teeteringly high wedged-heel shoes. 'No-one yet,' she said with remarkable placidity, 'but stick around. A murder's likely any minute.'

'But who . . .' Carrie began agitatedly.

Mavis grinned, enjoying herself hugely. 'Dad. If Mum doesn't kill him over this, 'e's safe for life.'

Before Carrie could demand an explanation her front

206

door burst open and her father nearly fell on the pathway in his haste to be out of the house, a frying-pan and a saucepan raining down around him.

'*Clear off down The Swan, you great silly bugger!*' Miriam shrieked from behind him, handicapped by having nothing else near at hand to throw in the general direction of his head. '*If you think I'm ridin' up the Old Kent Road in a bloomin' 'earse every mornin' you've got another bloody think comin'!*'

'This,' Mavis said to a vastly relieved Carrie and indicating the hearse behind her, 'is Dad's new cart. He says he'll be able to get twice as much fruit and veg in it than he could in a normal horse and cart and he also thinks it's got style. Mum,' she added unnecessarily as Miriam hurled a further torrent of abuse after Albert, her arms folded across her heaving chest and every metal curler in her hair bristling with indignation, 'doesn't agree with him.'

'I wouldn't want to tangle with your mam when she's in a takin',' said Charlie Robson to Mavis, wisely keeping his voice low so that Miriam shouldn't overhear him, 'but your dad's got a point. Not only will he be able to cram more in the 'earse than an ordinary 'orsecart, but all the other traffic on the road will give way to 'im. They always do for funeral 'earses. It's traditional.'

'Charlie's right,' Daniel Collins said, admiration in his voice for Charlie's unusual show of perception and for Albert's imaginative astuteness. 'Even army vehicles give way for a hearse. Albert will be up and back from Covent Garden every morning quicker than it takes to spit.'

'I 'eard that, Daniel Collins!' Miriam said furiously, rounding on him so suddenly that one of her metal hair curlers went flying into the street. 'And if you think 'avin' a 'earse is such a good idea I'll tell Albert to stick it outside *your* 'ouse and then we'll see how you like it!'

'I fink we'd better go dahn The Swan, Daniel' Charlie said nervously. 'I fink things are gettin' a bit 'ot 'ere.'

'I think I'll come with you,' Mavis said, rightly judging

that most of the fun was now over and that her father would be in need of all the family support he could get. 'Are you comin' with us, Carrie?'

'No. I haven't even stepped inside the house yet and I've Rose to bath and put to bed.'

Ever since Ted had marched away to training camp Mavis had taken to calling in for a drink at The Swan more and more often and it was a habit Carrie strongly disapproved of.

She said now, impatience replacing relief in her voice, 'Shouldn't you be making Billy and Beryl's supper? Where are they? Or don't you know?'

'They've taken Bonzo up the 'eath,' Mavis said, well aware of Carrie's disapproval and totally uncaring of it. 'Billy will be racin' down the banks of the gravel pit near Black'eath Village, crankin' his arms and screechin' at the top of his voice and pretendin' to be a Stuka dive-bomber and Beryl and Bonzo will be the poor little sods dived upon. When they come 'ome they'll know where I am and come down for me and I'll give them some money for some chips. OK?'

'Not with me,' Carrie said shortly. 'And it wouldn't be OK with Ted, either.'

'What Ted doesn't know 'e can't grieve over,' Mavis said philosophically, 'and I'm not carryin' on this argument any longer. Mum's given enough of a free show for one day without you and me givin' another.'

It was a statement Carrie couldn't disagree with and as Mavis began to saunter off towards Magnolia Hill and The Swan, accompanied by Charlie and Daniel, she turned to Kate, saying wearily, 'I'll pop up and see you later. After I've bathed Rose.'

Kate nodded and, as she walked away from the cluster of neighbours still gathered around the Jennings' gateway, she heard Hettie saying insistently, 'I don't care what anyone says. If that horse is pulling a hearse it should have purple plumes on its head!'

*　　*　　*

'I've never been so shocked by anything in my life,' Miss Pierce said to her half an hour later as she sat at Kate's kitchen table after popping in on her from Miss Godfrey's. 'When Mr Muff told me you had been dismissed I thought he'd taken leave of his senses. "She can't have been dismissed," I said to him. "I'm the Personnel Officer. No-one is dismissed without my being informed of the decision beforehand." Then he told me of your interview with Mr Harvey.'

Kate had made her a cup of tea and her fingers tightened on the handle of her teacup. 'I realized then that the gossip flying around the offices had come to Mr Harvey's ears and that, disbelieving it, he *had* dismissed you.'

Her pleasant, plain face was deeply concerned. 'Harriet thinks I should request an interview with Mr Harvey and that I should tell him that I know, beyond any shadow of doubt, that the gossip about yourself and his grandson *is* true and that . . .'

'No!' Kate pushed her chair away from the table and stood up so suddenly that tea slopped into her cup's saucer. 'Mr Harvey wasn't only abusive to me because he thought I was lying about my relationship with Toby, he was also abusive to me because of my German blood. He's a horrid, hideous old man and I don't want to have anything to do with him ever again!'

Miss Pierce regarded her with an appalled expression. 'But don't you think . . .' She began. It was a sentence that remained unfinished. A sound neither of them had ever heard before impinged on their consciousness. It was a dull, heavy roar. A roar that was becoming ever louder.

'Planes!' Miss Pierce said, pushing her chair away from the table and rising unsteadily to her feet. 'Hundreds of them! Are they ours or are they German?'

It was still daylight and Kate rushed towards the back door, flinging it open. Eastwards, over the Thames, the sky was dark with approaching bombers.

'*They're German!*' she shouted to Miss Pierce as air raid sirens screamed into life. '*Run into the shelter! I'll be with you the minute I've got Hector!*'

From where she was standing she could see Mr Nibbs sprinting down the length of his garden towards his Anderson shelter, his braces down and his trouser flies open, indicating that the Germans had caught him at a very inconvenient moment. Dimly, over the cacophony of wailing sirens and the increasingly deafening roar of the fast approaching planes Charlie could be heard shouting frantically for Queenie.

'*Harriet!*' Miss Pierce said urgently. '*What about Harriet? We can't leave her on her own at a moment like this!*'

Hector had already bolted to Kate's side, terrified by the din. Kate grabbed hold of his collar and thrust him towards Miss Pierce. '*Take Hector and get into the shelter!*' she shouted at her. '*I'll go for Miss Godfrey!*'

As she wrenched the door open, she saw Bob Giles on the far side of the square, sprinting hell for leather towards the vicarage.

Over nearby Woolwich and the Arsenal and ammunition factories, bombs were already falling. Knowing that at any second similar deathly cargoes would be plummeting down over Lewisham, Catford and Blackheath, she hurtled up Miss Godfrey's path and steps, praying to God that the front door would be off the latch. For the first time in her life she burst into Miss Godfrey's home without knocking.

'Miss Godfrey! *Miss Godfrey!*' she shouted, racing through the house towards the kitchen. 'Miss Pierce is already in my garden shelter! Come on! There isn't a second to lose!'

Miss Godfrey strode to meet her, tweed-suited as always. A tin hat emblazoned with the letter 'A' for ambulance was strapped firmly beneath her chin. Her gas mask canister was over her shoulder and her arms were full of blankets.

'Go back and join Miss Pierce immediately, Katherine,' she said authoritatively. 'As a voluntary ambulance driver it is my duty to report immediately to my ARP Centre.'

Kate stared at her aghast and then, knowing instantly that it would be useless to argue with her, she spun on her heel and, with Miss Godfrey close behind her, ran towards the still open door.

The thunder of aircraft and the force of exploding bombs blasted their eardrums. The sky above Woolwich and all points east along the Thames was an inferno of flames and billowing smoke.

For one brief instant Miss Godfrey halted, barely able to comprehend the sight that met her eyes. *'Dear God in heaven!'* she whispered. *'They're razing the East End to the ground!'*

Kate couldn't hear her, but she could read her lips. She thought of the crowded tenements in Poplar and Canning Town and East Ham and knew that at last, after the long period of the 'Phoney War' when Hitler's attention had been focussed upon the Netherlands and Belgium and France and the previous few weeks, when the war had been fought out between RAF and *Luftwaffe* fighter pilots, what everyone had always dreaded was finally happening. The war had come to London and people were being crushed and blasted and burnt to death in their homes.

The bulk of the bombers were nearly directly overhead and as Miss Godfrey began to sprint out of the Square in the direction of the ARP Centre only three other figures were visible. One of them was Daniel Collins in his Auxiliary Fire Service uniform, quite clearly as courageously intent on the same destination as Miss Godfrey. The other two were Billy and Beryl.

Billy was staring up at the planes in rapt wonderment. Beryl, a hair-ribbon adrift and hanging loosely down over her right ear, was standing beside him, her hand trustingly in his.

Bombs were beginning to fall much nearer now. Shrapnel was dancing down the far pavement and as Kate raced across to them she was aware of a great feeling of suction and compression pulling and pushing her.

'*Come with me!*' she shouted to Billy, seizing hold of Beryl and tucking her bodily beneath one arm as acrid smoke billowed around them, almost robbing her of breath. '*For the love of God, Billy!* RUN!'

Billy didn't want to run. He wanted to watch the bombers and the massive explosions destroying the docks, and the fires in Woolwich leaping hundreds of feet high.

With a strength she hadn't known she possessed Kate hauled him protestingly after her; off the street and into her front garden; up the short pathway and then the flight of steps leading to her front door. Everything around them, even the ground beneath their feet, seemed to be lifting and falling. In the house pictures were tumbling off the walls and as they sped through the kitchen Kate saw that the cup Miss Pierce had so recently been drinking out of and which she had left on the kitchen table, lay in shattered smithereens on the floor.

'Faster!' she gasped again to Billy who had blessedly begun to co-operate with her. '*Run faster, Billy!*'

Together they ran down the back-garden path and the steps leading to the Anderson shelter, tumbling into it on top of a distraught Miss Pierce and a terrified Hector.

'Thank God!' Miss Pierce said devoutly and then, as Miss Godfrey failed to follow them, she said urgently. 'But where is Harriet? Why isn't Harriet with you?'

Kate pressed a hand against her heaving side. 'She . . . insisted . . . on going to the . . . ARP Centre,' she gasped with difficulty. 'She's a . . . volunteer . . . ambulance driver.'

Miss Pierce closed her eyes momentarily and then said tautly, 'Yes. Of course. I forgot.'

She was sitting on one of the two long, low benches with which Carl Voigt had furnished the shelter and as she took Beryl from Kate's arms she said, 'Do you think this is it? Do you think the invasion has begun?'

Hector was whimpering in distress and Kate sat close to him, stroking him reassuringly, 'I don't know,' she said as a terrific rushing noise indicated a stick of bombs falling perilously close by. 'It may be that Hitler is just trying to destroy the docks and Woolwich Arsenal before invading.'

The blast of an explosion rocked the corrugated steel protecting them. 'That wasn't the docks or Woolwich,' Miss Pierce said ashen-faced, 'That was only streets away.'

'I want my mum,' Beryl said, her lip quivering. 'I don't like these big bangs. Bonzo didn't neither and he ran home.'

In the wake of the last, terrifyingly near explosion, there came another sound. The long, echoing rumble of falling bricks and masonry.

Mindful of Beryl and Billy's listening ears neither Kate nor Miss Pierce said a word but over the top of Beryl's head their eyes held and both knew what the other was thinking. Had the destroyed building been occupied? Had it been a house in Magnolia Square? Had it perhaps been the home of someone they knew?

'This is a real adventure Miss, ain't it?' Billy said to Miss Pierce with relish, hugging his knees to his chin as he sat on the wooden planking which was the floor of the shelter. 'Can you hear the guns? They're our guns. I bet it's the destroyer moored at Greenwich that's firing 'em. I bet we ain't 'alf giving them bombers 'ell.'

'I sincerely hope your assumption is correct, young man,' Miss Pierce said, greatly cheered by the idea that part of the mayhem was being occasioned by Royal Navy guns.

'Want my mum,' Beryl said again, beginning to cry. 'Don't like it in 'ere. I want my mum to stop the noise.'

Before Kate could make a comforting retort Billy said cheerily, 'If anyone could stop this shindig, our mum could. She ain't 'alf a tartar when she's roused. Grandad says she'd scare old 'itler 'alf to death and that if Churchill 'ad any sense 'e'd use 'er as a secret weapon.'

Despite the gravity of the situation Miss Pierce's lips twitched in a spasm of amusement. Kate was too anxious about the mental agony Mavis was bound to be enduring, not knowing where her children were, to be similarly entertained.

'The minute there's a lull we'll run down to your house,' she promised Beryl, hugging her close.

Another thought struck her and she said to Billy, 'Has your mum got an Anderson of her own or will she be in with your gran and grandad and Carrie and Rose?'

'She'll be in with Carrie and Rose and Gran and Grandad,' Billy said confidently, 'and with our Great-Gran and Christina and Bonzo.'

'Great heavens!' Miss Pierce said, diverted as always by tales of the Lomax's and Jennings' goings-on. 'So many people in a shelter this size? They'll be like sardines in a tin.'

'It was a bit of a tight squeeze when we did it for practice,' Billy admitted, 'but it was cosy. Grandad's fitted it up with all sorts of knick-knacks. A rug and blankets and a pack of playing-cards. He's even got a guzzunder dahn there for Beryl.'

'A guzzunder?' Miss Pierce asked, mystified, aware that the drone of aircraft was rapidly receding and that the brunt of the attack was over. 'What is a guzzunder?'

Billy stared at her, not able to believe her ignorance. 'A chamber-pot,' he said with as much patience as he could muster. 'One wot guzzunder the bed.'

As Miss Pierce tried to stop herself from chuckling, Kate's entire attention was taken up by the need to reunite Beryl and Billy with Mavis at the soonest possible moment. 'It's stopped,' she said abruptly. 'I'm going to make a run for it with the children. You stay here with Hector, Miss Pierce. I shan't be long.'

'But the all-clear siren hasn't sounded yet! The planes may come back! There may even be unexploded bombs in the street!'

'It's only a matter of a few hundred yards and the sooner I put Mavis's mind at rest the happier I'll be.' Kate took hold of Beryl's hand. 'Are you ready, Beryl? Are you going to run as fast as you can?'

Beryl nodded. She'd been able to run fast ever since she could remember. If she didn't, there was always the danger Billy would leave her behind.

'Come on then,' Kate said, praying to God that her judgement was correct and that the attack was either over or in abeyance, 'Let's go!'

Chapter Twelve

Though there was no sound of planes now, or of air raid sirens or anti-aircraft guns, other sounds, those of ambulance and fire-engine bells, filled the acrid air. As Kate hurried Billy and Beryl down the glass-littered pavement she was grimly aware that much of the noise was emanating from nearby Point Hill Road. Was that where the bomb that had rocked their shelter had fallen? Were people laying there now amidst the ruin of their homes, dead and dying?'

'Cor, it ain't 'alf a mess, ain't it?' Billy said as the all-clear sounded and he surveyed Magnolia Square's many blown out windows. 'Grandad criss-crossed our winders with adhesive tape. I bet our winders 'aven't been blown out.'

Kate, too, had prudently criss-crossed her windows with adhesive tape as everyone had been advised to do months and months ago when black-out restrictions had first come into force. The problem was, in the year since the war had begun, the air raid sirens had never sounded for a full-scale attack. People had grown complacent, becoming accustomed to the fact that the war was taking place on other fronts, France and Belgium and in the air over Kent and the Channel.

The dust of the freshly fallen masonry in Point Hill Road was thick in the air and as Kate breathed it in she reflected grimly that people would be complacent no longer. Now that Hitler had directed his attention against London there was no telling how frequent or how intense future air attacks would be.

'There's my mum,' Billy said unnecessarily as Mavis's

unmistakably exotic figure hurried towards them as fast as her skin-hugging skirt and high wedged-heel shoes would permit.

'Where the bloody 'ell 'ave you two been?' she demanded the minute they were within speaking distance, her voice cracking with what sounded suspiciously like a sob of relief. 'The bloody dog 'ad the sense to come 'ome! Why the bloody 'ell didn't you?'

As Beryl hurtled into her arms Billy said in a voice of sweet reason, 'Cos it was fun! We were on the 'eath and we could see the bombers, 'undreds and 'undreds of 'em, and there was flames shooting sky-'igh from Woolwich and the docks and . . .'

Mavis, who for all her free and easy manner where Billy and Beryl were concerned, loved them fiercely and had suffered torments as to their safety during what had seemed the eternity of the air raid, adjusted Beryl more securely in one arm and with her free hand gave Billy a vigorous clip on the ear. 'Fun? With your Gran terrified to death and Bonzo still cowering in a corner of the 'anderson? I'll give you fun!'

'We was in an 'anderson too!' Billy protested before his mother could give him a clip on his other ear. 'We was with Kate and 'ector and . . .'

Mavis wasn't interested in who his other companions had been. With heartfelt gratitude she said to Kate, 'Thanks a million, Kate. If I'd known they were with you I wouldn't 'ave worried, but as it was . . .'

'There just wasn't time to get them down to you, Mavis. By the time I came across them the raid was in full swing. Where are all the ambulances and fire-engines going? Point Hill Road?'

Mavis nodded. 'Dad's round there now, 'elping to search for survivors. If it wasn't for not knowing where the 'ell Billy and Beryl were I'd 'ave gone with 'im. If we're going to 'ave many more of these raids I'd much rather be out and about 'elping people than sitting in a shelter like a rabbit in a bloomin' 'utch.' She looked

217

eastwards in the direction of Woolwich and the fires raging there. 'Dad doesn't think the raid is over yet. He thinks it's just a lull. I better get going with these two before the buggers pay us a return visit.'

Kate nodded. She, too, thought another raid highly likely. As Mavis herded her offspring down to her parents' house Kate began to walk back home. She hesitated when she reached her gate. Despite the distant wail of ambulance and fire-engine bells no air-raid sirens were wailing. Instead of turning in and hurrying up the path she walked on, quickening her pace, heading out of Magnolia Square and towards the Heath. The north-west corner of the Heath was one of the highest points in south London and from it she would have an un-restricted view over the Thames and the docks and Woolwich.

Mr Nibbs was hurrying ahead of her, no longer in a state of partial undress but wearing his Air Raid Warden jacket and with a tin hat firmly on his head. A few other brave souls were also emerging from wherever they had been sheltering, some of them covered with the dust of fallen ceiling plaster, all of them with the same intention as Kate: to take advantage of the grandstand view offered by the Heath and to see for themselves the extent of the bomb damage inflicted on London's docklands.

It was still not dark, but the billowing clouds of smoke rising from either bank of the Thames as it looped its way around the Isle of Dogs and coiled between the East India Dock, Royal Victoria Dock, King George Dock and Woolwich Arsenal, made it seem as if it was. At first sight it seemed to Kate that the entire city was in flames. Blazing warehouses filled the air with the stench of their burning contents; pepper and rum, sugar and wood, paint and rubber, the conflagration staining the sky a dull, magenta-red.

Rows upon rows of terraced houses in the densely populated dockland areas of Bermondsey, Poplar, Limehouse, Canning Town, East Ham and West Ham, were a shambles of fiery destruction.

'Poor devils,' a woman Kate had never seen before, said to her. 'There's not many of those houses have gardens and if you haven't a garden how can you have an Anderson shelter? I hope to God they all made it to public shelters but I bet they didn't. There wasn't enough warning. Let's hope to God there's more warning next time.'

As if on cue, and before Kate could even begin to make a response to her, air-raid sirens over the entire south-east of the city wailed into life.

'Hell's bells, here they come again,' the woman said, her face paling. 'Bye, dear. It looks like it's going to be a heavy evening!'

Yet again Kate broke into a run, this time mercifully unencumbered by Beryl and Billy. Though most of the fires she had just witnessed had been on the far side of the river there was no telling what area this second attack might be concentrated on. Between Blackheath and the river there was nothing but the green open vistas of Greenwich Park and beyond the Park, on the river-bank, lay the Royal Naval College, an Electric Power Station and countless numbers of wharves.

'Where on earth have you been?' Miss Pierce asked agitatedly as Kate scrambled down the beaten-earth steps leading into the shelter. 'I could hear the ambulance and fire-engine bells and they sounded so near I was frightened it might have been the Lomax's house or the Jennings' house that had been hit.'

Kate shook her head, sitting down on the bench beside her, saying breathlessly, 'No. According to Mavis the house hit was in Point Hill Road.'

The heavy drone of innumerable aeroplanes could again be heard and Kate felt her stomach muscles tighten. 'I went up onto the Heath,' she said, slipping her arm comfortingly around Hector's neck. 'The docks are alight. All of them.'

'Then it will be worse this time,' Miss Pierce prophesied grimly. 'The fires will serve as target-lights.' She patted a basket at her side. 'I thought they'd be back and I'm afraid I've taken rather a liberty. I've been in the house and collected some articles I thought we might need.'

Kate eyed the Thermos-flask peeping out of the top of her shopping-basket with deep gratitude. 'You didn't take a liberty. You're a life-saver. Is there Bovril in that flask, or tea?'

'Tea. I've made some sandwiches as well. And I scooped up a magazine and a book that was on one of the armchairs.'

The sickening, now familiar sound of the deafening roar of exploding bombs nearly drowned out her words.

'They're targeting the East End again,' Kate said tautly as Miss Pierce retrieved a copy of *Picture Post* and an Everyman edition of Jane Austen's *Emma* and laid them on the bench opposite. 'It must be hell on earth down there. The fires looked to be completely out of control.'

Miss Pierce looked at her wristwatch. 'The last raid started at approximately five o'clock and ended at six-thirty. If that kind of timing is going to be a precedent, we've an hour and a half before there's going to be a respite. Would you like a cup of tea now? And would Hector like one? His drinking-bowl is in the basket.'

The respite, when it came, was brutally brief. All night, until the early hours of the morning, wave after wave of Heinkel 111K bombers rained death and destruction down upon London, the dockland communities taking the worst brunt of the attacks.

'Thank God it's downhill from here to Greenwich and the river,' Miss Pierce said more than once. 'It's the hill that's affording us some protection. The trouble with the north side of the river is that the ground is all flat.

I don't think there's one hill in the East End, there's certainly not one as steep as the hill leading up from Greenwich to Blackheath.'

In the bleak light of early dawn, as the all-clear sirens finally shrilled into life, Kate and Miss Pierce stepped apprehensively out of the shelter, not knowing what sights they would see.

'At least the house is still standing,' Kate said, seeing with relief that the houses on either side of her own house, for as far as she could see, were also still standing. She thought of the burning shambles of the areas close to the docks. 'I'm going to the ARP Centre,' she said as, with a very subdued Hector at her heels, she stepped into her kitchen. 'The voluntary services are going to need every extra pair of hands possible today.'

'Don't go until you've had some breakfast,' Miss Pierce said in a voice that brooked no argument. 'It will only take five minutes and it will be five minutes well spent.' She held the kettle under the tap and began filling it with water. 'Do you mind if I stay here until Harriet returns? It's just that I'm anxious about her and . . .'

'You can stay here for as long as you want, Miss Pierce. You'll be company for Hector and, when I get back, for me as well.'

Miss Pierce carried the kettle across to the gas stove and put it on the hob. 'Thank God the water and gas mains haven't been destroyed,' she said as she put a match to the gas and a small circle of blue flames sprang into life. 'And you really can't go on calling me by my surname, Kate. Not after the experience we've just endured together and particularly not when your father long ago began addressing me in his letters as "Dear Ellen." '

'Does he?' For a brief moment, as they waited for the kettle to boil, Kate was momentarily diverted from grim thoughts to thoughts of a very different nature. 'How often do the two of you write to each other?' she asked curiously, wondering for the first time if a middle-aged, pen-pal romance was in progress.

Miss Pierce flushed slightly and put three caddy-spoonfuls of tea into the teapot. 'Every week,' she said, deepening Kate's suspicions. 'Your father isn't *lonely* in the camp. As you know, he's helped to form an entertainment committee and he's organized a library, but life in the camp is very isolating for him and he's kind enough to say that he appreciates my letters.'

As Miss Pierce was very carefully avoiding looking at her as she was speaking, Kate sensitively didn't pursue the subject. But she found it interesting. To the best of her knowledge her widowed father had never had a lady-friend. That he might now be beginning to view Miss Pierce in that light was a quite startling thought. What if, when the war was over and he was released from the internment camp, the relationship continued to flourish? What if they eventually married?

'I'll take Hector for a short walk over the Heath,' Miss Pierce said as the kettle began to steam. 'I won't go too far in case the Germans decide to bless us with a daytime raid, just far enough to stretch his legs a little.'

Ten minutes later, warmed by tea and toast and with her gas mask canister slung over her shoulder, Kate set off towards the ARP Centre, reflecting that life was full of the most remarkable surprises. She also reflected that under the circumstances she most certainly couldn't continue addressing Miss Pierce as Miss Pierce. From now on she would have to address her as Ellen. As her father did.

'It's bloody chaos across the river,' Albert said to her wearily a little later as they sat nursing tin mugs of strong tea. 'Daniel says that it's taking the fire services all their time to keep exit routes open so that people can get out of the area.'

'Where will they go?' Kate asked, forgetting that

222

Albert was one of the many neighbours she no longer spoke to and who no longer spoke to her. Albert, equally oblivious, said, 'Another half hour and I reckon we'll see them streaming out of the Blackwall Tunnel and across the Heath, pushing prams and handcarts in the direction of Kent and the hopfields.'

He pushed his tin hat towards the back of his head, sipping at his tea. It was the first mug of tea he had had in twelve exhausting hours and it tasted like nectar. 'You've heard about the house in Point Hill Road?' he asked, a big map of Blackheath and Lewisham pinned to the wall behind him, a box of marking flags nearby.

Kate nodded and Albert said heavily, 'Of all the bloody times for her to be making a parochial visit she has to be making one at five o'clock on a Saturday!'

Kate felt a nauseous sensation in the pit of her stomach. 'Who are you talking about, Albert? Are you talking about Mrs Giles? Was Mrs Giles at the Point Hill Road house when it was hit?'

Albert put his mug of tea down unsteadily. 'Aye,' he said thickly. 'Me and Nibbo helped pull her out about an hour ago. And the others. There were four others.'

'All dead?' Kate's voice was a whisper. It had been obvious to her long hours ago, when she had been sitting with Miss Pierce in the shelter, that hundreds upon hundreds of people must have been killed during the night. Her relief at finding Magnolia Square still standing had, however, fooled her into believing that no-one she knew personally had died or been injured.

Now she said, stunned. 'I saw the vicar just as the raid was starting, he was running towards the vicarage.'

'No doubt he thought he'd find his missus at home,' Albert said, picking up his mug of tea again, his knuckles white. 'As it is, the poor bugger is never going to find her at home again. Bloody Germans. They all need bloody annihilating.'

A man Kate only knew by sight, his Home Guard uniform grey with the dust of fallen masonry, came into the Centre, saying disbelievingly, 'I thought I'd seen everything this last few hours but now I've seen the bloomin' lot.'

'What is it, Fred?' Albert asked, bracing himself for the worst.

'A bloomin' Bentley, that's what it is! A blinkin' army of poor devils from the East End pushing their worldly goods across the Heath and that rich bastard Joss Harvey is sitting in his parked Bentley in Magnolia Square as though it's Derby Day!'

'Whereabouts in Magnolia Square?' Kate asked, knowing the answer already.

'The top end,' her informant said, rummaging in a haversack hung on a hook on the wall. 'Near the Heath. Have you got any chalk, Albert? I want to chalk out a no-go area around the house in Point Hill Road. Until we can raze it completely it's going to be a danger to anyone walking too near it. And we don't want any looters rummaging in it neither. There's reports of some shameful looting going on in Poplar and Bow.'

Kate didn't wait to hear any more. She spun on her heel, hurrying out of the ARP Centre, wondering why on earth Joss Harvey was visiting her; wondering what in the world he could possibly have to say to her.

'I want to know why you didn't insist on telling me the truth,' he said to her pugnaciously as they faced each other yards apart, Kate with her back to her front-garden gate, Joss Harvey with his back against his Bentley. 'Lance Merton visited me early yesterday afternoon. He was a close friend of Toby's and he has relatives hereabouts.' He paused, as if unsure how to phrase his next words.

Kate remained silent, not remotely disposed to be helpful. Further down her side of the Square she could see Miss Helliwell sweeping up the glass that had been blasted from her windows. On the bottom side of the Square Leah Singer was discernible, energetically applying adhesive-tape to windows still miraculously intact. On its island St Mark's church doors were wide open, whether intentionally or because they had been blasted from their hinges, Kate couldn't tell.

Joss Harvey sucked in his breath, his Savile Row, double-breasted, grey silk suit looking bizarrely out of place in a world where Home Guard and Air Raid Warden and Fire Auxiliary uniforms had become the order of the day.

'He assumed we were acquainted and asked after you,' Joss Harvey finally continued, his heavy-jowled face revealing how hard he was finding it to repeat his and Lance Merton's conversation. 'He referred to you as "Toby's fiancée". Naturally I asked him if you had had the impertinence to contact him, claiming such a relationship.' He paused again, hardly able to bring himself to continue.

Again, Kate didn't attempt to make his difficulty any easier for him. Hettie Collins was coming out of the church, a bunch of fake violets drooping from the crown of her black hat. Kate could see that Hettie's eyes were red from weeping. She remembered Hettie's self-imposed weekly task of supplying the church with fresh flowers. Hettie would have been on more than mere neighbourly terms with Mrs Giles, and Mrs Giles' death would have hit her hard.

'He said that though he had called on you some weeks ago, the last time he had leave and was in the neighbourhood, he had done so only because he knew from Toby that the two of you were affianced and intended marrying in the very near future.'

He paused yet again, waiting for her response.

Kate didn't make one. She was still waiting for an apology for the inexcusable names he had called her when they had previously faced each other in his boardroom.

'So why,' he demanded aggressively, 'didn't you state your case with a little more stubbornness and make me aware of the relationship that existed between yourself and my grandson?'

There was nothing remotely conciliatory in his tone.

Along the main road separating Magnolia Terrace from the Heath, a long line of hastily commandeered lorries could be glimpsed, conveying refugees from the burning infernos raging out of control on either side of the river. From Albert's comments, Kate assumed that Daniel Collins was one of the Auxiliary Firemen battling the massive conflagration.

As Joss Harvey cleared his throat with impatience Kate returned her attention to him. He was quite obviously not going to proffer an apology and she hadn't the remotest intention of allowing the conversation to continue as though no apology on his part was necessary.

'When I informed you of my relationship with Toby you not only called me a liar, Mr Harvey,' she said, her tone no more conciliatory than his own had been, 'you called me a half-German trollop, a Kraut, a slut and a blackmailer. You also threatened to have me interned and, if I breathed my "foul lie" outside your boardroom, threatened to sue me for slander in every court in the land.'

He sucked in his breath again harshly. The smell of smoke from the dockland fires wafted towards them on a faint breeze. 'You *are* half-German,' he said unrepentantly, 'and even if you aren't a full-blooded Kraut, your father most certainly is!'

'And you ask me why I didn't state my case with more stubbornness?' Kate's gentian-blue eyes were hard as ice. 'It's a question you've just answered for yourself! I've nothing further to say to you, Mr Harvey. And I don't wish ever to speak with you again.'

Turning her back on him she opened her front gate.

'Stop!' There was a throb of real urgency in his voice as he covered the distance between them in swift strides. 'You said you were pregnant. That you were carrying Toby's child. Is that true?'

She turned, only the gate separating them. His narrowed eyes were fiercely demanding. For one long, long moment she was tempted to say it wasn't true. But that would have been to become what he had accused her of being: a liar. 'Yes,' she said curtly. 'It's true.'

Without waiting for his reaction, she again turned her back on him, walking up the path towards the short flight of steps that led to her front door.

'That child is my great-grandchild!' he said harshly, his hands gripping tightly onto the gate. 'You can't bring up a child on your own! Not in wartime!'

She had reached the foot of the steps and she paused for a moment, certain that now he had accepted that she was carrying his great-grandchild, an apology and reasonableness on his part would follow. She was just about to turn and face him in anticipation of accepting his proffered olive-branch, when he said flatly: 'I want the child. I want to adopt it.'

It was as if a fist had been slammed into the centre of her back robbing her of all breath. Very slowly she walked up the steps, fighting for control. At the top she turned and looked down at him.

'*Never!*' she vowed. '*Not even over my dead body! Never! Never! Never!*'

For a hate-filled moment that seemed as long as eternity his glittering eyes held hers and then, his lips white, his nostrils flaring, he swung abruptly away from the gate, striding towards his Bentley, yanking the door open.

Kate didn't wait to watch him drive away. Trembling from head to foot she turned her back on him for the last time, fumbling with the door-knob in her haste to open the door.

Ellen Pierce opened it for her from the inside.

'Dear God!' she said, taking one look at Kate's shock-contorted face. 'What's happened? Are the Germans sailing up the Thames? Have the Houses of Parliament been captured?'

'How dare he even *suggest* such a thing?' Kate demanded as Ellen pressed a mug of tea into her hand. 'How could he even *imagine* I would part with my baby?'

Ellen Pierce's face was etched with concern. A baby! Until Kate's revelation only minutes earlier she hadn't even remotely suspected that Kate might be pregnant. As she thought of what the stigma of illegitimacy would mean for the child and for Kate, she said tentatively, 'Perhaps Mr Harvey made the suggestion because, not knowing you and how strong a person you are, he thought it was one that you might find welcome and . . .'

Once again, whatever else she had been going to say was lost as the stomach-churning wail of air raid sirens surged into life.

Kate, remembering the hard discomfort of the benches inside the Anderson, scooped two cushions up from the settee.

'There's no time to fill a Thermos,' she said as she hurried with Ellen into the kitchen and saw Ellen's eyes fly longingly in the direction of the kettle. 'Take these cushions while I drag Hector from under the table. You'd think a dog that had lived on an RAF airbase would be indifferent to the noise of sirens, wouldn't you?'

Hector wasn't indifferent, nor were Queenie and Bonzo and the thousands of other animals who uncomprehendingly endured the hell of the next weeks. Every night, and nearly as often through the day, the raids came. No-one, not even the most loonily optimistic, doubted that Britain was fighting for her very survival.

'Barges for the invasion lie in wait across the Channel,' the Prime Minister announced ringingly in a broadcast to the nation four days after the first air raid had given Londoners a foretaste of what was to come. 'And we must regard the next week or so as a very important period in our history. It ranks with the days when the Spanish Armada was approaching the Channel, and Drake was finishing his game of bowls; or when Nelson stood between us and Napoleon's Grand Army at Boulogne. We have read all about this in the history books; but what is happening now is on a far greater scale and of far more consequence to the life and future of the world and its civilization than those brave old days.'

Ellen Pierce, back home in her Edwardian terraced house in Greenwich, shivered at the enormity of Winston Churchill's words. Kate, hurrying between raids to Deptford and the canteen for fire-fighters where she had begun working as a volunteer, wondered if her father and his fellow internees had been allowed to listen to the Prime Minister's speech. Carrie, making Rose an omelette out of powdered egg, wondered if Danny, now fighting the Italians in far-away Egypt, would also somehow hear the broadcast or read a report of it.

'If even Winnie thinks we're up against it, things must be grim,' Mavis said to Kate, trousered legs astride Ted's motor bike. 'How do you like my ATS uniform? Do you think I look like Marlene Dietrich?'

'You might do if it wasn't for the cycle-helmet and goggles,' Kate said, giggling. 'Why have you plumped for despatch-riding? I thought you wanted to drive an ambulance?'

'They wouldn't let me,' Mavis said with a sniff of disgust. 'Said I wasn't qualified as a driver. The ATS weren't so fussy. Not where motor cycles are concerned anyway. Ted taught me to ride this when we were courtin'. Bet he never thought I'd be ridin' it through a bloody blitz though!'

For the rest of September and all through October the murderous onslaught by *Luftwaffe* bombers continued.

Miss Helliwell, unable to manipulate her handicapped sister out into the garden and into the Anderson shelter, had a new-fangled indoor Morrison shelter installed.

'It resembles a reinforced table,' she said to Leah Singer. 'It's much pleasanter than a horrid, damp Anderson shelter. I keep blankets and pillows in it and your son-in-law assures me that it's just as safe as an Anderson or a public shelter.'

Leah had never held an overly high opinion of her costermonger son-in-law's capabilities and found it difficult to reconcile herself to the respect he now commanded amongst their neighbours as Captain of the local Home Guard.

'Are you sure Albert knows what he's talking about?' she asked dubiously. 'Are you sure you and Esther haven't been palmed off with a *chazzerai* ping-pong table?'

'Absolutely not!' Miss Helliwell protested, outraged at the very thought. 'Captain Jennings recommended a Morrison shelter *personally*.'

'He's only Captain of the local Home Guard, *bubee*,' Leah retorted, becoming increasingly annoyed by the esteem Albert was beginning to be so obviously held in. 'He ain't exactly a four-star General!'

'You stay in the Anderson if you want to, Mum,' Miriam said defiantly to Leah. 'I'm off down the public shelter next time the bleedin' sirens go. At least there'll be more company there and we can have a bit of a sing-song. I wish to God we lived near a tube station. The Underground *has* to be safe. Stands to reason when it's so bloody deep down.'

Miriam was wrong in thinking the Underground system a hundred per cent safe. On the night of 15 October bombs pulverized Balham Tube Station, breaking through to the platform far below. A mountain of ballast, sand, sludge and slime cascaded down, burying alive sixty-four of those taking shelter there, nearly all of them women and children. On that one night alone over nine hundred fires raged across the city and when dawn finally broke four hundred Londoners had been killed and nearly a thousand seriously injured.

It was a hell everyone coped with in their own way. As a captain in the Home Guard, Albert Jennings diligently instructed all and sundry, even Miss Helliwell and Hettie, in the art of grenade-throwing, determined that in the event of invasion every single inhabitant of Magnolia Square would make a valiant last stand.

Miss Helliwell was an exceedingly nervous pupil, preferring to aid the war effort by means only she regarded as rational.

'I'm holding seances and trying to contact both Sir Francis Drake and Lord Nelson,' she told Carrie as they stood patiently in a long queue outside the butcher's in Blackheath Village. 'I'm sure that any advice they can give will be invaluable to Mr Churchill.'

'Maybe,' Carrie said, not wanting to give her too much encouragement but not wanting to ridicule her either. 'Problem is, what happens if you do make contact with them and they do give advice? How are you going to pass it on to the Prime Minister? You're not exactly on nodding terms with him, are you?'

As the local Air Raid Warden, Mr Nibbs displayed a resolute determination to do his duty. Only the first raid had taken him by surprise and sent him flying down to his Anderson shelter, his trouser braces dangling wildly. Since then, during night raids, he had toured his district diligently, reporting all incidents, calling up the appropriate rescue services and, if he was first on the scene, doing his best to rescue the trapped and provide first aid for the injured. During the day, like thousands of other exhausted civilians, he had resumed his daytime occupation, opening his shop no matter what the circumstances.

Daniel Collins was also fast becoming a local hero. As an Auxiliary Fireman his voluntary job was, perhaps, the most horrendous of all. Day after day and night after night he battled with his professional and amateur companions against the flames, often not resting for twenty-four or thirty-six hours at a stretch. The danger they faced from collapsing walls and falling brickwork and poisonous fumes was made worse by the fact that the bulk of their work was undertaken while bombing raids were in progress.

'The bombers always aim for the fires,' Hettie would say, squeezed into the public shelter next to Miriam, so fearful for her husband's safety that her knitting needles would clatter against each other. 'Bloody Hitler! May he die from a lingering tumour!'

Mavis, too, risked life and limb daily, delivering messages in and out of heavily bombed areas, much to her son's admiration and envy.

On the night of 3 November, for the first night since 7 September, there was no German air raid over London.

'I couldn't believe it,' one of the middle-aged women who worked in the canteen said to Kate. 'I slept right through! It's done me the world of good. I feel sixteen this morning!'

Though Kate was equally grateful for the undisturbed night, she didn't feel sixteen. She was now five months pregnant and there were times, after long hours dispensing tea and hot soup, that her ankles puffed up and her back ached. And it wasn't only physical discomforts that were dispiriting her.

For many weeks, when she had first begun working at the canteen, she had been known only by her first name. Unlike her neighbours in Blackheath, no-one in Deptford knew that her father was German and her long plait of flaxen hair was no give-away because, like all the other women in the canteen, she wore her hair coiled up beneath a headscarf tied turban-fashion.

When her pregnancy had begun to show, however, salacious gossip had soon followed. Though Doctor Roberts, whom she now had begun to visit for regular check-ups, and Ellen, had warned her of the kind of comments she would meet with when it became known that she was pregnant, she had been unprepared for just how coarse and hurtful some of the comments would be. And then her surname had become known and only one or two of her fellow workers were still speaking civilly to her.

'You'll have to take your ration book elsewhere,' Mr Nibbs said to her brusquely a few days later when, after queueing for an interminable length of time, she finally reached his grocery counter.

It was an ultimatum that Kate had long anticipated. She had registered her ration book with him before the hideousness of her father's internment and, as ration books couldn't be switched arbitrarily from one shop-keeper to another, it was a situation she had resigned herself to.

She said now, tight-lipped, 'You are my designated grocer, Mr Nibbs. I would like a packet of tea and my weekly sugar and margarine allowance, please.'

Mr Nibbs placed her ration book squarely on the wooden counter between them. 'You'll get nothing from me. Your Jerry friends have blitzed Coventry. Going on for a thousand people have been killed. You want tea and sugar and margarine, you go somewhere else for it.'

'Jerry-lover,' a woman somewhere in the queue behind her said viciously. 'And she's pregnant and I don't see a wedding-ring.'

'She's German,' another voice said authoritatively. 'Her father's an internee. I don't know why she isn't. I thought all Germans had been interned.'

Knowing that it would be useless to argue with Mr Nibbs; knowing that at any moment the verbal abuse she was being subjected to might turn to physical abuse, Kate picked up her ration book.

'I don't have any German friends,' she said to Mr Nibbs through lips she could barely move. 'I'm as loyal a citizen of this country as you are,' and turning her back on him she walked out of the shop, past the long queue of muttering women, the words, 'Shameful hussy' and 'No wonder she's a slut if she's German', echoing in her ears.

The first sight she saw as she stepped out on to the pavement was Carrie, walking down the hill that led from the Heath to the centre of Blackheath Village, Rose toddling along beside her in leading-reins.

Kate's first reaction was one of intense thankfulness. At least now she would be able to give vent to her feelings with someone who would be unconditionally supportive. Then she saw the expression on Carrie's unusually cheery face.

'Carrie! Carrie, what on earth has happened? What's wrong?'

For an unnerving second Carrie didn't even seem to recognize her. Her eyes, red-rimmed from weeping, were curiously blank.

Rose, a hand-knitted beret pulled low over her ears to protect them from the bitter November cold, her blue, velvet-collared coat buttoned tightly to her throat, said, not understanding the import of her words, 'Daddy's something called a POW and Mummy doesn't like it.'

'Dear God!' Kate immediately forgot all about her fury with Mr Nibbs and the anger and frustration she had felt towards the women in the queue behind her, anger and frustration commonsense had prevented her from giving vent to. 'Is it true, Carrie?' she demanded, feeling physically sick. 'Has Danny been taken prisoner by the Italians?'

Carrie nodded, expression seeping back into her eyes. 'Yes,' she said, her mental and emotional pain now naked. 'This arrived an hour or so ago.'

With a gauntletted-gloved hand she withdrew a crumpled telegram from her coat pocket.

Kate took it from her silently, her eyes skimming over the block typed words. REGRET TO INFORM YOU . . . YOUR

HUSBAND SERGEANT DANIEL COLLINS . . . REPORTED CAPTURED . . . ENQUIRIES BEING MADE THROUGH INTERNATIONAL RED CROSS . . . ANY FURTHER INFORMATION WILL BE IMMEDIATELY COMMUNICATED TO YOU . . . LETTER CONFIRMING THIS TELEGRAM FOLLOWS.

With the telegram still in her hand she put her arms around Carrie, hugging her tight. 'I'm sorry, Carrie,' she said, her voice choked with emotion. 'I'm so sorry!'

'Those bloody Eye-ties,' Carrie said indistinctly, tears once again beginning to course down her face. 'What will they do with him, Kate? He was in Egypt, for Christ's sake! Will they keep him there or will they ship him off to Italy? What will they *do* with him?'

It was a question Kate couldn't even begin to answer. She said, trying to be as comforting as possible, 'The telegram mentions the Red Cross, Carrie. There are rules for the treatment of prisoners of war. Articles laid down in the Geneva Convention. The Italians will have to treat him decently and once the Red Cross establishes contact with Danny you'll be able to communicate with him through them. You'll be able to send him letters, maybe even food parcels.'

Carrie stepped out of the circle of Kate's arms. 'Maybe,' she said, a note in her voice so odd that Kate couldn't tell what the emotion was that lay behind it. 'But the Geneva Convention and the Red Cross haven't done much for the Jews Hitler is rounding up and slaughtering in Poland and Czechoslovakia and Belgium and Holland, have they? And the Italians are Germany's ally. If the Germans don't give a hang about the Geneva Convention you can bet your sweet life that neither will the Eye-ties.'

There was an expression in Carrie's sea-green eyes that Kate had never seen before; an expression that filled her with stupefied disbelief. It was as if Carrie was regarding her as a stranger; as if she had withdrawn from her utterly.

'Christina's right,' Carrie said bleakly, confirming all

Kate's worst fears. 'Italians, Germans, they're all the same. They're all Fascists. It's in their blood.' And giving Rose a gentle tug on the leading-reins she turned her back and walked away.

Chapter Thirteen

Kate couldn't move. She was paralysed by horror; suffocating in it; drowning in it. Carrie had turned against her. What Christina's first-hand accounts of Jewish suffering at the hands of the Nazis had failed to do, Danny's capture by the Italians had succeeded in doing. Just like Mr Nibbs, Miss Helliwell, Hettie, Miriam, Leah and a host of others, Carrie now regarded her as a creature set apart; a person to be avoided; a person symbolic of Germany and, as such, symbolic of the cause of all their suffering.

'Carrie!' she called out after her, her voice strangling in her throat. '*Carrie!*'

Only Rose turned her head, her little face beneath her knitted beret bewildered by both the events that had taken place a little earlier, when the man had knocked at the door with the piece of paper her Grandad had referred to as a telegram, and the frightening tension she now sensed and couldn't understand.

Carrie's back remained resolutely set against Kate as she continued to walk swiftly up Tranquil Vale, Rose struggling to keep up with her.

With every fibre of her being Kate wanted to run after Carrie; to seize hold of her; to make her see the needless dreadfulness of what would now happen between them. She couldn't do so. Every line of Carrie's back was so rigid and hostile that she knew the kind of response she would receive if she ran after her. It was a response she couldn't face. A response she wouldn't be able to bear to live with.

As she stood transfixed, scarcely able to believe that

what had happened hadn't been hallucination or nightmare, Charlie Robson heaved himself out of the Three
Tuns public house and on to the broad tree-lined
pavement only a few yards away from her.

'You'll catch your death of cold standin' about in this
weather, petal' he said, hiccupping as he did so.

Queenie bounded down the steps of the pub behind
him and made a bee-line for Kate, nearly knocking her
off her feet in the exuberance of her greeting.

Kate buried her hand in Queenie's fur, her throat
tight, her eyes overly bright.

Charlie, never excessively observant at the best of
times, merely said, 'Are you goin' over the 'eath, petal?
Because if you are, I'll come with you. I could do with
a bit o' company. I never see 'arriet now she's racketing
around in that tin bus she calls an ambulance. Gawd
knows what the injured think when they find 'arriet
tendin' 'em in her tweed-suit and pearls. They must
think it's Queen Elizabeth doin' her bit for the nation!'

With Queenie's cold nose nuzzling at her hand Kate
nodded assent to Charlie's suggestion. Carrie was no
longer in sight and a faint sprinkling of snow had begun
to fall.

'It'll look a treat at Christmas if the snow stays,'
Charlie said as he weaved a little unsteadily at her side
and they breasted the hill, looking out from the top
corner of Tranquil Vale across to the chocolate-box
prettiness of All Saint's Church and the frosted expanse
of the Heath beyond it. 'I always like a bit o' snow at
Christmas. It makes it more festive like.'

'I don't think anyone is going to feel very festive this
year, Charlie,' Kate said, not even wanting to think
about Christmas or how she would be spending it. 'Half
of the East End have been bombed out of their homes
and the other half are living without water or gas or
electricity. How can you make a Christmas dinner if
you've no gas or electric to cook with?

'How can you make a Christmas puddin' with food

shortages and no dried fruit?' Charlie asked glumly. ''arriet says Lord Woolton 'as told 'ousewives to use carrots instead.' He snorted in derision. 'Carrots! Who the 'ell wants carrots in their Christmas puddin'?'

Kate, well aware of the·Minister of Food's many suggestions for combatting the increasing food shortages said not very convincingly, 'It might not be too bad, Charlie. His "Woolton Pie" is just about bearable. Or at least it is if you like potatoes.'

'I don't,' Charlie said as he bent down and picked up a twig, throwing it for Queenie to run after. 'Leastways, I don't like 'em when there's nothing else with 'em. I like steak and kidney puddin' and bacon and eggs and liver and dumplin's. And,' he added darkly, 'I like Christmas puddin' stuffed with currants and raisins and brandy and candied peel.'

'Then you're out of luck,' Kate said starkly, looking across the barren Heath and wondering where Carrie and Rose had disappeared to. 'All you're likely to get plenty of, out of that little lot, are dumplings!'

Even when they reached the far side of the Heath, and Kate looked back towards the Village, she could see no sign of Carrie or Rose.

Heavy-hearted she walked with Charlie into the Square. When they reached her gate he said with unusual perception, ''ope you don't mind me saying so, petal. But you look a bit down in the dumps. I'd have a snifter of the old medicinal if I was you. 'ave you got some in? 'Cos if you 'aven't, I could let you have a drop out of my store cupboard.'

Not remotely surprised that Charlie had a plentiful supply of whisky secreted away, Kate shook her head. 'No thanks, Charlie. Though I appreciate the offer.'

Charlie looked relieved. 'Then make yourself a cup of char,' he said kindly. 'A cup of char is a wonderful pick-me-up. 'arriet swears by 'em.'

Promising she would do so she let herself into the house, deeply grateful for Hector's storm of welcoming barking as he rushed to meet her. With Hector in the house, the house wasn't as ringingly empty as it had been in the first few weeks after her father had been interned.

'Have you missed me?' she asked unnecessarily as she bent down to him, fondling his ears as he licked her face in a frenzy of delight.

Ellen had told her that she would catch germs from Hector if she allowed him to demonstrate his affection in such a manner. She had been uncaring. Now, knowing herself robbed of Carrie's friendship, she was even less caring about germs. What she needed was affection and Hector gave it.

'Come on,' she said to him, standing upright again. 'I've cajoled some tripe out of the butcher for you.'

As she walked into the kitchen, Hector charging enthusiastically ahead of her, she reflected that apart from Charlie, and possibly Mavis, the only friends she now had were Ellen Pierce and Harriet Godfrey.

She began cutting the tripe into small pieces. Ellen Pierce was in her late forties and couldn't be described as being anything other than middle-aged and the Lord alone knew how old Harriet Godfrey was. Despite her derring-do as a voluntary ambulance driver she had long been retired and had to be nearer to seventy than she was to fifty.

She scooped the tripe into Hector's bowl and set it down on the floor. Her relationship with Carrie had always been as close as if they had been sisters. Tears glittered on her eyelashes. Ever since she could remember she had always thought of Carrie as *being* her sister. Friendship had never seemed a strong enough word for the bond there had been between them ever since they had met at nursery school. And now, though Carrie had not said so specifically, Kate knew that deep, committed friendship on Carrie's part had been withdrawn.

Snow had begun to fall quite heavily against the kitchen window and she walked desultorily into the sitting-room, wondering if she dare deplete her small stock of coal by lighting a fire.

On the mantelpiece, in the silver frame she had so carefully shopped for, Toby smiled across at her from her favourite photograph of him. It had been taken only a few weeks before he had died. He was leaning against the wing of his Hurricane, his hands casually in his pockets, one foot nonchalantly crossing the other at the ankle, just as he had stood at the door of her office the first time she had set eyes on him. He was in uniform, his sheep-lined flying jacket unzipped, his thick tumble of fair hair falling low across his forehead. And he was looking directly into the camera, his eyes full of laughter, his smile so dear and familiar that for a heart-stopping moment it was as if he were in the room with her.

Icy fingers tightened on her heart. He wasn't in the room with her. He would never be in the room with her again. Grief, so raw and deep it was beyond containment, convulsed her. She began to weep and as the snow-laden sky outside the window darkened into dusk, she continued to weep, her heart breaking, hugging her breast as though holding herself together against an inner disintegration.

She was proved right in her assumption that when Carrie had turned her back on her and walked away from her in Tranquil Vale, she had been turning her back on all the years of friendship that had previously bonded them so closely.

November gave way to December and Carrie didn't knock on her door. Occasionally Kate would see her from a distance with Rose, and sometimes with Bonzo as well. Always, another figure was with them, companionably linking arms with Carrie. Always, that person was Christina Frank.

As Christmas drew nearer the air raids, which had once seemed as if they might be slackening off, increased yet again in intensity. They also differed from the earlier raids in their tactics. Incendiary bombs began to be dropped in far greater numbers than previously, sometimes as many as three thousand in a single raid. Fires raged throughout London and there were times when Kate could hardly remember what it was like to breathe in air unpolluted by smoke and the fumes of sulphur.

Harriet Godfrey was on almost constant call and, far from the long hours and harrowing nature of her work proving to be too much for her, thrived on the danger, driving with panache through blacked-out, hazardously cratered streets strewn with glass and rubble, often doing so when a raid was in progress and bombs were falling.

'I shall be on duty on Christmas Day, Katherine,' she said to Kate a few days before Christmas. 'So many of the other volunteer ambulance drivers have families and it seems only fair that, if possible, that day should be covered by those of us who live alone.'

Kate envied her her busyness. She, too, would much have preferred driving an ambulance or a fire-engine or helping to man the phones at an ARP centre. She had, over the last few weeks, volunteered her services everywhere possible and had been turned down as a driver due to her now obvious pregnancy and been rejected at the ARP centre due to the stigma of her surname.

'And Ellen won't be spending Christmas Day with us,' she said to Hector as she surveyed the fake Christmas tree she had unearthed from the small spare bedroom where suitcases and other miscellaneous items were kept. 'She's looking after too many stray and frightened bombed-out animals to be able to leave them and spend the day with us.'

She opened the ancient cardboard box that her father had kept the tree's decorations in for as long as she could remember. 'So we shall be on our own,' she said, beginning to unwrap a bauble from the sheet of newspaper her father had carefully wrapped it in. 'It's going to be just you and me Hector.'

Though her inner strength of character and defiant attitude towards life had enabled her to cope with her ostracism by neighbours and former friends, the prospect of a Christmas spent without human companionship was agonizingly dispiriting. Christmas was a time for families. She should have been spending it with her father, but her father had now been moved to an internment camp on the Isle of Wight. And she should have been spending it, mentally if not physically, with Toby. If he had still been alive they would now be married and even though the war situation would have ensured that their chances of spending Christmas Day together would have been remote, at least she would have known that, wherever he was, he would have been thinking of her.

She hung the bauble on the tree and then, as always when longing and grief for Toby threatened to overpower her, she folded her arms over the comforting mound of her stomach. She had the baby to look forward to. Doctor Roberts had told her that, in his judgement, she would give birth during the last week of February or the first week of March.

'Fortunately first babies give plenty of warning that they are on their way,' he had said to her reassuringly. 'I had to drive through a hail of incendiary bombs to one young mother last week. It was her third baby and didn't have the manners to await my arrival. By the time I got there it was to find I'd risked life and limb for nothing. The baby was wrapped in a shawl in his mother's arms looking, if I may so, extremely smug.'

Unwrapping another Christmas tree decoration, Kate wondered what the circumstances of her own confinement would be. Whenever an air raid caught her out at home, and not at the canteen, she sat it out in the Anderson shelter with Hector, the loneliness of such hours exacerbated by the knowledge that no-one else in Magnolia Square was enduring the aerial bombardment in such isolation.

In their Morrison shelter, Miss Helliwell and her sister had each other for company. Leah Singer and Christina Frank and Billy and Beryl and Bonzo, all crammed communally in the Jennings' Anderson shelter. Hettie had begun accompanying Miriam to the public shelter at the bottom of Magnolia Hill, where a rowdy crush and a sing-song were guaranteed comforters through the agonizing hours until the all-clear siren sounded. Charlie Robson remained in his own bed during the nights when raids were bad.

'I'm as safe there as anywhere, petal,' he had said fatalistically to Kate. 'If a bomb 'as your number on it, it'll find you wherever you are. And if one of the buggers 'as my number on it I might as well die in the comfort of my own bed as in a perishin' cold Anderson shelter or crammed next to Miriam and 'ettie and their perishin' knittin'-needles.'

If she hadn't been pregnant and had the baby's safety to think of, Kate might have emulated him. When she was at the canteen, and when the raids were at their height, she had used a public shelter along with the canteen's other voluntary workers. Now, however, she no longer made the difficult trip into Deptford.

Ever since her surname had become public knowledge at the canteen she had been made to feel unwelcome. The cratered streets she had to negotiate to reach Deptford had also begun to deter her. Ordinarily she wouldn't have given them a thought, but she was now nearly seven months pregnant and she didn't want to risk a heavy fall and a miscarriage.

She adjusted the decorations on the Christmas tree, surveying them critically, wondering if she was foolish in not ending the loneliness of the hours spent in the Anderson shelter by joining other local people in the public shelter.

A small, glittering, silver bell was making the decorations on the left side of the tree unequal to those on the right-hand side and she hung it more centrally. If she went into the public shelter she risked meeting with the same kind of abuse she had suffered in Mr Nibbs' shop. Miriam and Hettie certainly wouldn't make her welcome and, as she had already painfully discovered, it was possible to be far more lonely in a hostile crowd than on her own.

'I'll stick to the Anderson, Hector,' she said as she draped tinsel over the tree. 'And I'll keep my fingers crossed that the baby doesn't decide to make its arrival when there's a raid on!'

On Christmas Eve, returning from a visit to her new grocer in Lewisham, Kate saw Carrie and Christina ahead of her. They were obviously deep in conversation and occasionally Kate heard the faint, familiar sound of Carrie's infectious laughter.

A pang, almost of physical pain, knifed through her. Though Carrie was no doubt still worrying frantically about Danny's whereabouts and welfare, she had family and friends to comfort her and offer a companionship that took her mind, however intermittently and temporarily, off her anxieties.

Her own footsteps slowed. She had had to queue a long time at the grocer's for her weekly rations and an even longer period of time at the butcher's. Her back ached and the baby in her womb felt as heavy as lead. It was bitterly cold and as she hadn't enough clothing coupons to buy a new winter coat, one that would wrap over the lump that was the baby, she had had to keep moving the buttons on her existing coat. In the early months of her pregnancy this ploy had been satisfactory, but was so no longer. A heavy, knee-length, hand-knitted scarf filled in the gap where her coat no longer met and fastened, but it wasn't an ideal solution and she was not only tired, but cold.

The distance between herself and Carrie and Christina lengthened. They turned off Lewisham High Street into Magnolia Hill, companionably arm in arm, and Kate's footsteps became even slower. Christmas Eve. Even though last Christmas had been the first Christmas of the war, it had been heaven in comparison. Last Christmas her father had been at home. Last Christmas Toby had been alive. It began to sleet and within minutes she could feel the damp seeping through her headscarf. Hector looked up at her miserably, not understanding why she didn't stride out vigorously for the shelter of home, or even break into a sensible run.

'Sorry, Hector,' she said, reading his thoughts and transferring her wicker shopping-basket from one hand to the other. 'but I don't want to catch Carrie and Christina up and don't think I could, even if I tried. I'm tired and my back aches.'

With the wind blowing the sleet stingingly against her face she turned the corner into Magnolia Hill. A middle-aged woman she knew only by sight nearly walked into her, coming from the other direction. Taken by surprise, Kate smiled apologetically as she side-stepped her bulk out of the woman's way. 'Sorry,' she said to her. 'It's miserable weather isn't it?' and then, remembering that it was Christmas Eve, she added, 'Merry Christmas.'

The woman paused for a moment before walking on, staring at Kate hard. No answering smile touched her mouth. 'I don't speak to Krauts,' she said through gritted teeth. 'And I hope you have a piss-miserable Christmas!'

Shock, as fresh as if the insult had been the very first she had received, almost robbed Kate of breath. She had been born in Magnolia Square. Her mother, and her mother's parents, and her mother's grandparents and goodness knew how many other generations on her mother's side of her family, had all been born and bred in South London. How could her neighbours be so unreasonable as to treat her as though she were a German-born, German spy? She'd never even *been* to Germany. She didn't know a word of the language apart from the words of endearment her father sometimes used when speaking to her.

The woman was already yards away, heading towards Lewisham, her cuban-heeled shoes click-clacking on the pavement.

Kate resisted the urge to hurry after the woman and seize hold of her and try to hammer some reason into her head. She knew from past experience she would be wasting her time and Hector was miserably wet, his tail hanging unhappily between his legs. 'Come on, Hector,' she said as the baby gave her a hefty kick, 'Let's get home and get dry and, as it's Christmas, I'll put a decent amount of coal on the fire and leave worrying about running out of it until another day.'

She had just turned into the Square when she first became aware of the sailor. Living so near to the river and the docks and Greenwich Naval College the sight of both Royal Navy officers and sailors and Merchant Seamen, often with kit-bags over their shoulder as this seaman had, was a common sight. What wasn't quite so common was seeing one injured and the young man now walking up the Jennings' pathway was doing so with the aid of a crutch. Even less common, at least in Magnolia Square, was a sailor who was black.

Carrie and Christina had long since disappeared into the house and Kate's first reaction, on seeing the young man knock at the Jennings' front door, was to hope fiercely that it wouldn't be Carrie who opened the door to him. She was too near to the Jennings' house now for the person who opened the door to be able to pretend that they hadn't seen her. And to be cut by Carrie, on Christmas Eve, would be a hurt too deep to be even imagined.

With blessed relief she saw Miriam's ample figure open the door. She also saw the expression of startled surprise on her face. Whoever the Jennings' visitor was, he quite obviously wasn't expected.

'No, I haven't!' she heard Miriam say, indignation in her voice. 'I don't know who gave you your information, but they were wrong.'

Even before the young man had turned, doing so awkwardly as he balanced his kit-bag on one shoulder with one hand and manipulated his crutch with the other, the Jennings' front door was slammed shut.

He reached the bottom of the short, sleet-covered pathway, just as Kate was passing the gate.

'Excuse me,' he said in a voice so rich and dark that Kate found herself wondering what his singing voice would be like. 'My billeting officer told me Mrs Jennings took in lodgers but it appears he was misinformed. You don't know of anyone around here who does take in lodgers, do you?'

Despite his need of a crutch, the misery of the weather and his obvious homelessness, there was nothing remotely dejected about him. He had a jaunty manner and the smile lines running from nose to mouth indicated he was a young man who laughed easily and often. He wasn't laughing now though. Despite his lack of dejection a slightly concerned frown had begun to crease his brow. Considering that it was already late afternoon on Christmas Eve, it was a concern Kate could well understand.

Regretfully she shook her head. 'No. There are rumours that all householders will soon be answerable to civil billeting officers and everyone in Magnolia Square has been notified that if they have spare rooms they will be expected to offer accommodation to families bombed-out of their homes, but the scheme isn't up and running yet, at least not in this area, and I don't know of anyone who takes in boarders. I'm sorry.'

He shrugged philosophically. 'Not to worry. I'll find somewhere. It would be nice if this sleet turned to proper snow, wouldn't it?'

'Yes,' she said, his cheery good humour making her forget how low-spirited she had been feeling. A thought occurred to her and she said, 'I think Mrs Collins took lodgers in at one time. She and her husband live on the other side of Magnolia Square at number thirty-six.'

He shot her a wide grin, his teeth brilliantly white against his dark skin. 'Thanks,' he said, shifting his kit-bag a little more comfortably on his shoulder. 'I'll give her a try. Cheerio.'

'Cheerio.'

As he set off towards the far side of the Square Kate shrugged off the unhappy encounter of a few moments ago. Not everyone was viciously unpleasant. Even if the young man, whose innate good humour had so raised her spirits, had known of her father's nationality, she doubted if his reaction would have been one of jingoistic prejudice.

'Merry Christmas!' he called after her as an afterthought, over his shoulder.

For the first time in a long time her generously full mouth broke into a wide smile. 'Merry Christmas!' she called back, barely aware now of the cold and damp.

As she continued on her way up her own side of Magnolia Square she reflected that if her father had been at home, she would have had no hesitation at all in suggesting to the young sailor that he board with them. Under her present circumstances, however, such a suggestion was impossible. Her illegitimate pregnancy had already ensured that her moral reputation was next to non-existent. If she took in a sailor it would be reduced to zero and she would find herself regarded as the local whore.

Yet again she shifted her shopping-basket from one hand to the other. She had long given up worrying what her neighbours and former friends thought of her, but she couldn't be so cavalier where the coming baby was concerned. Her child would have enough coarse and cruel remarks to contend with without being burdened with even more.

She was still several yards or so from her gate when Leah Singer and Miss Helliwell turned the top corner of the Square. As they approached her Kate could clearly hear their remarks.

'I told him, if he thought someone in Magnolia Square took in lodgers he should speak with his billeting officer and get a proper address,' Miss Helliwell was saying in the same tone of indignation that had been in Miriam's voice a little while earlier. 'Though how a billeting officer could be so insensitive as to give a Magnolia Square address to a black man, I really don't know. There must be plenty of his own kind down near the docks. Why doesn't he try there?'

'He'll have to,' Leah responded dryly. 'Can you imagine what husbands away fighting would say if they knew a black man had taken up board and lodging in their homes? There'd be a right old *shlemozzel*.'

Both of them had become aware of her; neither of them greeted her.

'He didn't speak like a black man,' Miss Helliwell was saying reflectively as Kate opened her gate and they passed within feet of her. 'He spoke quite good English. In fact he sounded very like Sir Richard Grenville.'

'And who is he?' Leah said, keeping her head carefully averted from Kate.

Kate thought of all the happy times she had spent in the Jennings' home; of Leah barrelling to the front door to meet and greet her, her hands and arms dusted with flour; of the oven-warm bagels and blintz's she had pressed on her; the way Leah had always affectionately bantered and teased her.

'He was one of England's most illustrious naval commanders,' Miss Helliwell said, her voice warming with enthusiasm as it always did when the conversation veered round to her contact with the dear departed. 'He was captain of *The Revenge* which, when England was at war with Spain, fought alone against the Spanish fleet. Tennyson wrote a beautiful poem about it. I contacted him in order to ask him if he had any advice for dear Mr Churchill.'

What Leah's reaction was Kate didn't hear. She was already climbing ·the steps that led towards her front door, her fleeting feeling of good cheer entirely dissipated.

The young sailor they were so sure would never find board and lodgings in Magnolia Square had been recently injured. It was an injury he had almost certainly received whilst on active service and yet Leah and Miss Helliwell were speaking of him as though he were not a member of Britain's armed forces, but an outsider. He was being shamefully ostracized, just as she was being ostracized.

When she reached the top step she turned and, much to Hector's impatience, instead of unlocking the door and stepping into the comparative warmth beyond, looked out across the Square.

Dark was falling rapidly but she could still see Leah and Miss Helliwell, talking nineteen to the dozen. She could also see the sailor. He was walking back down Hettie's front path towards the gate and she knew instinctively by the set of his shoulders that he had met with the same kind of refusal from Hettie as he had from Miriam.

As she watched he closed the gate behind him with difficulty, hampered by his kit-bag and crutch, and then he set off towards the bottom end of the Square and Magnolia Hill.

Hector whined and pawed at her coat.

'Just a minute, Hector,' she said, putting her shopping-basket down on the sleet-covered ground.

From the direction of the church she could hear the choir singing carols and knew that they would be doing so with tin hats and gas canisters within hands' reach, ready for a quick dash to the public shelter if an air raid siren should sound.

With Hector barking protestingly behind her she retraced her steps to her front gate and leaned over it, staring down the Park, straining her eyes in the deepening darkness, wondering what course of action to take. It was Christmas Eve. The young sailor was obviously far from home and just as obviously had only recently been discharged from hospital. Whatever his injury, it was a pretty safe bet that he had sustained it under enemy fire. And because of his skin colour he was being treated as a social outcast.

'I'm going to let you in the house,' she said to the sleek-soaked Hector as she turned around and walked back up the steps to the front door, 'but I'm not coming in with you. Not just yet.'

She turned the key in the latch and as Hector bounded gratefully towards the kitchen and his snug blanket-lined box she lifted her shopping-basket inside the hall. Then she stepped outside again, closing the door behind her, and as the church choir launched into *O Little Town of Bethlehem* she began to hurriedly re-trace her footsteps towards Magnolia Hill.

Chapter Fourteen

Ahead of her, in the deepening gloom, she could see the distinctive white of his kit-bag as it bobbed on his shoulder. When he reached the bottom end of Magnolia Hill and The Swan he hesitated for a moment and then entered the saloon-bar. Minutes later Kate followed him.

Despite her father having once been a regular visitor to The Swan she had only stepped over the threshold a couple of times before, usually when it was a Sunday and her father had become so engrossed in Cricket Club matters or a game of darts that he had forgotten the time and the roast dinner awaiting him at home. Then she had had to walk down to The Swan to break the news to him that if he didn't return home soon his dinner would be ruined.

A dozen pair of masculine eyes turned in her direction in disbelief. Albert, resplendent in his cobbled-together Home Guard uniform, was sitting at a table with Daniel Collins. Both men had pint glasses of beer in their hands. At the sight of Kate, Albert was so startled that he slopped a good measure of the precious substance on to the coarse cloth of his trousers.

Nibbo, who only ever fraternized with his coster-monger rival when, as an Air Raid Warden, his duties demanded he do so, was standing at the bar with Charlie. 'What the bloody hell . . .' he began in stunned disbelief.

'What are you doing in 'ere, petal?' Charlie asked, before Nibbo became blatantly abusive. 'You've taken the wrong door, though it's a mistake anyone could make in this perishin' black-out.'

The sailor was also standing at the bar and was also

regarding her with surprise. Considering the advanced state of her pregnancy, Kate didn't blame him. She hardly cut the figure of a young woman out on her own, hoping to pick up some masculine company and have a good time.

'It's all right, Charlie,' she said, walking towards the bar. 'I haven't made a mistake.'

Once at the beer-stained bar she turned towards the bemused sailor. 'I take it Mrs Collins wasn't able to offer you accommodation?' she asked, as The Swan's landlord said loudly and unnecessarily, 'I don't serve ladies in here!'

'No.' In the light of the pub she saw that he wasn't as black as she had first thought. His good-natured face was more dusky chocolate-brown than ebony.

'You can board with me,' she said, seeing no sense in not coming to the point straight away.

On the other side of her the pint glass in Nibbo's hand clattered down heavily onto the bar. Uncharitably she hoped half its contents had been spilled.

'You're a landlady?' the sailor asked, his eyebrows rising in surprise. 'I hadn't realized. I thought you said . . .'

'She ain't a landlady,' Charlie interrupted, perturbed. 'She's a respectable young lady who doesn't want to be doin' with sailors.'

'It's all right, Charlie,' Kate said again, grateful for his concern but having no need of it. 'I've got plenty of spare rooms at home and if I don't fill them soon, the council billeting officer will fill them for me.'

Returning her attention to the sailor she said again, 'If you want a room, I have one.'

''ang on a minute, petal,' Charlie's craggy face was still profoundly unhappy. 'It ain't as if your Dad's still at 'ome . . .'

'I'd never have believed it,' Kate could hear Daniel Collins saying to Albert. 'She might have been brought up by a Jerry, but she was well brought up.'

'It doesn't matter how you bring them up,' Albert responded dourly, thinking of his eldest daughter. 'In wartime women go haywire. Mavis is giving Miriam more grey hair than Hitler's entire bloody air force.'

'I want a room,' the sailor said to Kate, answering her question and ignoring the comments being made around them. He pushed his half-empty glass to one side. 'If you're ready to lead the way, I'm ready to follow.'

For the second time in the short time since he had first spoken to her Kate's mouth curved in a wide smile. There was such innate good humour in his brown, gold-flecked eyes that it was impossible to be in his company and not feel similarly good-humoured. Also, she was well aware that the conversation now taking place between the two of them would be being recounted and embellished the length and breadth of Magnolia Square before morning. And the vastly amused expression in the sailor's eyes told her it was a fact he was equally well aware of. And that he knew exactly what the main subject of the gossip would be.

As their eyes met Kate was aware that he could read her thoughts just as clearly as she could read his. It was the same friendly sensation of empathy that had once existed between herself and Carrie. And it was a sensation she had thought she would never enjoy again.

'Come on,' she said to him, turning away from the bar, her long braid of hair glistening with sleet. 'My dog is on his own at home and it isn't a situation he enjoys.'

'Bloody hell,' she heard Albert say as they stepped into the darkness outside, the sailor negotiating the step adroitly with his crutch. 'If that don't beat the band. Wait till I tell them at home that Kate Voigt's taken in a darky as a lodger!'

Once outside Kate was grateful to discover that the sleet had stopped and that the pavement, barely discernible in the blacked-out darkness, was already beginning to dry.

'If you're going to be my landlady I'd better introduce

myself properly,' her companion said as they began to walk back up Magnolia Hill. 'My name is Leon. Leon Emmerson.'

'Mine's Kate,' Kate said as the faint strains of *Away in a Manger* emanated from St Mark's Church. 'Kate Voigt. My father is German. He's in an internment camp on the Isle of Wight.'

'That must be tough for you,' he said sympathetically, his response very similar to Toby's response when she had first broken the news to him of her father's nationality.

At the memory pain shafted through her. The sunlit afternoon before the war, when she and Toby had sat overlooking the Thames at Greenwich and he had asked her if he could write to her seemed now to belong not only to another world, but to another century.

'Where do you come from?' she asked as they turned into the Square, walking past the waxy cream petals of Miss Helliwell's head-high wintersweet.

His white teeth flashed in the darkness. 'Everyone asks me that and no-one believes me when I tell them the answer.' He adjusted the kit-bag one-handedly with difficulty. 'I'm from Chatham.'

'Your parents weren't born in Chatham though, surely?' Kate asked, bemused.

'My mother was. My father was born in Bridgetown, Barbados. He was an able seaman in Queen Victoria's navy and he met my mother when his ship was laid-up in Chatham Dockyard.'

'And your injury?' she asked, not feeling at all as if she was being intrusive; feeling as if she had known him for years.

'Norway,' he said succinctly. 'I was a member of the gun-crew on the aircraft carrier HMS *Glorious*. We'd been evacuating Allied troops from Narvik and were on our way home when we were caught unawares by two German battle cruisers. They opened fire at a range of about twenty-eight thousand yards and an hour and a half later *Glorious* turned over and sank.' His voice was off-handedly factual but she could tell how difficult he was finding it to keep it so.

'Out of a ship's company of more than one thousand two hundred, only forty-three of us survived,' he continued, and despite all his efforts naked emotion had now entered his rich deep voice. 'Forty-seven airmen were lost as well, including the crews of eight Gladiators and ten Hurricanes who had flown on board rather than abandon their aircraft in Norway.'

Kate remained silent, thinking again of Toby, knowing from harsh experience how trivial even the most well-meaning of words could sound.

'I was one of the few lucky ones,' he said as they approached her gate, and from the rawness in his voice she knew the guilt he felt at having lived when so many of his shipmates had died. 'Four days and nights in a damaged lifeboat and we were plucked from the sea by the RAF.' A glimmer of humour entered his voice again as she opened her front gate. 'I've never been so glad to see air-force blue in all my life.'

As she put her key in the lock Hector could be heard charging down the hall to greet her, barking furiously.

'You'd better take care,' she said dryly. 'He nearly knocks me off my feet when he greets me and he's quite likely to do the same to you.'

He flashed her his ready, easy smile. 'Thanks for the warning. What is he? An alsatian?'

'A Labrador. Charlie, the gentleman who was standing nearby you in the pub, has an alsatian. Her name is Queenie and she has the same disconcerting habit.'

The curiosity he already felt about her, deepened. He remembered the man drinking nearby him in the pub and by no stretch of the imagination could he imagine anyone else referring to him as 'a gentleman'. He had been disreputably dressed with a large beer gut hanging over the broad leather belt holding up his trousers and there had been at least a three days growth of grizzly stubble on his chin and jowls.

Hector leaped up at her and as he watched her lovingly fuss and pat the dog his initial feeling of liking for her, and the heartfelt gratitude he felt towards her for offering him lodgings, increased. She was an oddity, no doubt about that. He had sensed it from the tension she had aroused from the inmates of the saloon-bar the instant she had set foot across the threshold. It had been a tension far over and above that which normally arose when a woman invaded a masculine sanctum. It had been a tension he was all too painfully familiar with. The tension that arose when people were confronted with someone they regarded as being not of their own kind.

'I'll put the kettle on,' she said, giving Hector a last, loving pat. 'I was on my way home from Lewisham when you asked me about lodgings and I'm frozen to the marrow. Leave your kit-bag in the hall for now. I'll show you your room, or rather you can take your choice of room because I've got three that are spare, when we've had a warming drink.'

She began to walk down the long hallway towards the kitchen, pausing just long enough to say over her shoulder, 'The sitting-room is the first door on the left. There's no fire on but I'll light one after I've made the tea.'

Even without the heat of a fire the house had a warm feel to it. A colourful homemade rag rug lay on the linoleum of the hallway. There were pictures on the walls. A reproduction of something that looked both primitive and Italian; a professionally painted water-colour of the pretty church that sat on the Heath just above Blackheath Village; a crayoned picture of a tree with a doll at its foot, obviously executed by a child and framed by proud parents.

As he obeyed her instructions and lowered his kit-bag with relief to the floor, he wondered if she had been the child who, long ago, had proudly brought the picture home from school. He knew that her father wasn't living at home because Charlie had made that clear when they were in the pub and she had since told him the reason for her father's absence and his present whereabouts. Her husband and the father of the child she was obviously expecting was, presumably, serving in the Army or the RAF. If, like himself, he was in the Navy she would surely have mentioned the fact.

As he walked into the sitting-room, Hector sniffing suspiciously at his heels, he wondered if her mother was still alive. There was no sign of there being anyone else in the house. He looked around the room and, though it was a little cheerless without the benefit of a fire in the grate, he liked what he saw.

There was a slightly shabby but exceedingly comfortable looking settee and two matching easy-chairs. The alcoves on either side of the fire-breast were lined with shelves, every one of them heavy with books. A standard-lamp stood behind one of the chairs, strategically placed to give added light for reading. A wireless sat on a low table. On another low table lay a half-opened book, face down.

He picked it up, being careful not to lose the reader's page. His eyebrows rose slightly. It wasn't a light-weight love novel. It was Ernest Hemingway's *For Whom the Bell Tolls*.

As he put it back down on the table he could hear the welcoming sound of tap-water gushing into a kettle. He turned towards the wood-surrounded, tiled fireplace. On one side stood a polished brass coal scuttle and on the other stood an equally gleaming tongs, shovel and brush stand. On the mantelpiece were three photographs in silver frames, two on the left-hand side, and one on the right-hand side.

He walked over to the fireplace in order to see them more clearly. Of the two photographs near together, one was much larger than the other. It was a head and shoulders shot of a bespectacled middle-aged man. It looked as if it had been taken in a garden and as if he had just turned round to face the camera and had been caught unawares.

It was a pleasant face, if not particularly arresting. His hair was thinning; his cheekbones high. There was an abstracted expression in his eyes as if, despite his surprise at being so unexpectedly photographed, his thoughts had not entirely returned from whatever subject they had been dwelling on. It was, Leon mused, the face of an intellectual; of a man far more at ease with academia than the practical world. It was also, quite obviously, Kate Voigt's father.

The smaller photograph was a sepia studio photograph of a young woman dressed in the fashion of nearly twenty years ago. Her mouth was Kate Voigt's mouth, full and well-shaped and generously laughing. Her delicately boned features were that of a perfectly carved cameo. As were her daughter's. Leon felt a pang of sadness on Kate Voigt's behalf. From the age of the photograph it was safe to assume that her mother was dead and had been dead for several years. From personal experience he knew how hard a blow the loss of a mother in early childhood could be.

With an added feeling of empathy towards his new landlady he turned towards the photograph standing alone on the left-hand side of the mantelpiece. It was of an airman. He was wearing a flying-jacket and no cap and it was impossible to tell his rank, but from his proprietorial stance beside his aircraft it was obvious to Leon that he was a pilot and an officer.

He regarded the photograph with interest. So this was Kate Voigt's husband. He wondered why she hadn't mentioned that her husband was an RAF pilot when he had told her of the RAF losses aboard *Glorious* and then cursed himself immediately for a fool. She hadn't told him because she couldn't bear to contemplate a similar fate befalling her husband; because the entire subject of the enormous losses being sustained by air crew was one too horrific for her to be able to talk about.

His eyes held those of the young man in the photograph. Just as Kate Voigt's father's photograph had, in some indefinable way, proclaimed him to be a quiet, self-effacing intellectual, so this photograph indefinably proclaimed public-school education and the confidence, often bordering on arrogance, that accompanied such an education.

His lips crooked at the corners. Kate Voigt's husband was his antithesis in other ways, apart from education and class. Whereas he was five-foot-nine-inches tall, with the broad-shouldered build of a useful middle-weight boxer, the young man in the photograph was easily over six foot tall and possessed a lean, whippy quality as opposed to mere muscle. He was also fair-haired to the point of being almost Nordic.

Wryly he raised a hand to his hair. Tight, coarse curls sprang against his palm. He wondered what the public school educated Mr Voigt would say when he discovered that his heavily pregnant wife had impulsively offered board and lodging to a man his Magnolia Square neighbours had had no hesitation in describing as 'a darky'. His eyes continued to hold those of the young man in the photograph. There was good-humour there; and tolerance. Perhaps he wouldn't mind. Perhaps, on his half-German wife's behalf, he had come face to face with prejudice and was too aware of its ugliness and hurtfulness to ever give vent to it himself.

He surveyed the fire-grate. Apart from coal it was laid ready for lighting. Sheets of newspaper, rolled and then knotted, lay beneath a scattering of precious wood chippings. He bent down, took the tongs from their holder and began laying coal.

By the time Kate entered the room the fire had taken hold and the flicker of the flames was already beginning to cast a cheery glow.

'Thanks,' she said gratefully, setting down a tray

bearing a teapot, a small milk-jug, sugar-bowl and two mugs, on one of the low tables. 'It doesn't matter how carefully I lay a fire, it doesn't always catch hold first time for me. When Dad was at home, he always saw to the fires.'

She began to pour the tea into mugs. 'I thought you'd prefer a mug to a cup,' she said as she did so. 'Dad always does. He says cups are too finicky for men.'

From his position in front of the fireplace he regarded her with intrigued curiosity. She was behaving as though he were a family friend or a formal house-guest, not a lodger. He said, more bemused by her than ever, 'You've never taken a lodger in before, have you, Mrs Voigt?'

She stood perfectly still for a moment, her back and her incredibly long swing of plaited hair towards him, the teapot still in her hand. Then, very slowly, she set the teapot back on the tray. Even more slowly she turned to face him.

Gentian-blue eyes met his.

'It's Miss Voigt,' she said steadily, the huge mound of her belly even more apparent now that she had taken off her coat. 'I'm not married and I never have been.'

It took a lot to disconcert Leon but stunned surprise did so now. Kate Voigt looked a lot of things; beautiful, warm-hearted, unconventional. But she didn't look the kind of young woman to find herself in what was, for women, the oldest kind of trouble possible. His thoughts immediately went to the photograph on the mantelpiece.

As if reading them she said, and this time her voice was not quite so steady, 'My fiancé was killed at Dunkirk. He was a fighter pilot. His name was Toby. Toby Harvey.'

'I'm sorry,' he said, hating the total inadequacy of his words.

She gave a slight, almost infinitesimal shrug of her shoulders. He knew that she was not dismissing his sympathy. She was simply refusing to descend to the level of a trite, conventional response; a response that

262

would be as totally inadequate as his words of sympathy had been.

A chill went through him as, for the first time, he realized just how alone she was. She hadn't said so but he was certain that her mother was dead, her father was in an internment camp and the father of her expected child was buried in a makeshift grave on the other side of the English Channel. No wonder her friend, Charlie, had been so concerned at the thought of her taking into her home a war-injured sailor she knew absolutely nothing about.

As she handed him his mug of tea he said awkwardly, 'I appreciate you helping me out of a tight spot with lodgings over Christmas, Miss Voigt, but perhaps . . . under the circumstances . . . it might be best if I looked for somewhere else to board once Christmas is over.'

She picked her mug of tea up from off the tray and sat down in one of the comfortable-looking armchairs. She was wearing a navy-blue maternity dress, the material obviously salvaged from some other garment in order that her precious clothing coupons could be set aside for baby clothing. The material was warm and serviceable and that was all that could be said in its favour. It should have looked dowdy, but it didn't. She had embroidered small crimson rosebuds on the collar and the dark colour of the dress merely emphasised the pale goldness of her hair and the stunning blueness of her black-lashed eyes.

'Are you being protective of my reputation?' she asked, and the bitterness in her soft, husky voice was so unexpected that it sent a fresh shock vibrating through him. 'If so, it's very thoughtful of you, but you're wasting your time. I don't have a reputation to protect.'

Without being able to stop himself his eyes moved down from her face to the ripe roundness of her belly.

'And it's not only because of the baby,' she said, putting his thoughts into words for him. 'The vast majority of my neighbours have had nothing to do with

263

me since my father was interned. They seem to have taken his internment as proof that he was a German spy or fifth columnist.'

The pain in her voice was so raw he felt his scalp tingle. 'My having an illegitimate baby is merely the icing on the cake. If you're worried about loss of reputation, *I* should be warning *you*. Once it's known you're lodging here, you'll be treated by my neighbours as if you've moved into the *Reichstag*.'

'I think that's a slander I can cope with,' he said equably.

Something in the easy tone of his voice banished all her remembered slights and hurts. She had come to terms with them all long ago. There was no point in reliving them now, especially on Christmas Eve.

Her mouth tugged into a self-deprecating smile. 'Sorry. I didn't mean to sound quite so burningly resentful. It's just that for twenty years my father believed himself to be part and parcel of the local community. And then, almost overnight, he became an outcast. Instead of being Carl Voigt or Mr Voigt, he became a Jerry; a Kraut; a Boche. As I have. And though common-sense tells me I should shrug off the name-calling, it's not so easy to do. It's too hurtful. It's too . . .' she sought for the word that summed up all the loneliness the name-calling had caused her. 'It's too isolating.'

He was still standing, looking down at her, deep understanding in his dark brown eyes. 'I know,' he said simply.

Her eyes held his, the most peculiar sensation surging through her. He wasn't just being politely sympathetic. He really did know.

She remembered the conversation she had overheard between Miss Helliwell and Miriam. 'Though how a billeting officer could be so insensitive as to give a Magnolia Square address to a black man, I really don't know,' Miss Helliwell had said, genuine bewilderment in her voice. 'There must be plenty of his own kind down near the docks. Why doesn't he try there?' And in The Swan, as the two of them had left together, Albert had said disbelievingly, 'If that don't beat the band. Wait till I tell them at home that Kate Voigt's taken a darky in as a lodger.'

The isolating phrase 'his own kind' and the word 'darky', were expressions he was quite obviously all too familiar with. And no doubt he was familiar with other, even more derogatory expressions; 'a touch of the tar brush', 'half-caste' and 'half-breed.'

It was a strange realization, knowing that she was in the company of someone who quite genuinely knew the depth of hurt and isolation such prejudiced and insulting name-calling occasioned. Harriet Godfrey and Ellen Pierce were sincere in their deep outrage whenever they heard either herself or her father referred to in disparagingly racialist terms, but no matter how genuine their indignation and sympathy, they didn't *know* how it felt to be at the receiving end of such abuse. The young man now standing on her hearthrug and looking down at her with empathy in his gold-flecked eyes most certainly did know.

'Does one ever get used to it?' she asked quietly, knowing that he was well aware of the realization she had come to; that she knew how he suffered in a similar, though far worse, way.

'No, Miss Voigt' he said candidly, his eyes continuing to hold hers. 'You learn how to cope with it, but you never get used to it.'

It was odd to hear someone she felt she already knew so well, addressing her so formally. 'Please call me Kate,' she said, knowing instinctively that, even if she hadn't been so heavily pregnant, he wouldn't mistake her friendliness for forwardness and take it as licence to make a sexual pass at her. 'Being referred to as Miss Voigt makes me feel as middle-aged as a couple of friends of mine, Harriet and Ellen. Because they are so much older than I am it was years before I began calling

Harriet anything other than Miss Godfrey and it was months before I began using Ellen's christian name.'

He grinned, his crutch still propped under one arm, the mug in his free hand. 'I don't think the same situation applies here, does it? I'm twenty-six and I'm pretty sure I must be at least four or five years older than you.'

A smile quirked the corners of her mouth. 'I'm twenty-three. Are you going to stand there all night, or are you going to sit down? Or do you want to see the rooms and choose one before you sit down?'

'If it's all right with you, I think I'd like to see the rooms. It's a long time since I sat down in comfort in front of a fire and when I do, I don't think I'm going to want to move again in a hurry. Not unless we're unlucky enough to have a raid.'

Kate put her mug of tea back down on the tray and, hampered by the bulk that was the baby, rose a little lumberingly to her feet. 'I'll show you the rooms and when we come back downstairs I'll put the wireless on. It's a better warning than the sirens of an approaching raid. As soon as enemy aircraft cross the Kent coastline the volume reduces to next to nothing.'

'And what do you do then?' he asked as, Hector still at his heels, he began to follow her from the room.

'I make a Thermos of tea, grab a blanket, cushion, book, gas-canister and tin helmet and sit it out in the Anderson.'

'Alone?' he asked, as they reached the hall and he picked up his kit-bag.

'No.' She flashed him a sunny grin. 'With Hector. When it comes to air raids he's the biggest coward going. He's always first in and last out!'

Chuckling, he followed her up the stairs, negotiating them with admirable dexterity considering his handicaps of a heavy kit-bag and crutch.

'This is my father's room,' she said opening a door to reveal a bed fully made-up, snowy linen sheets turned back over a crisp, white bedspread. There was a bedside

266

table with a bookstand and books on it, an alarm-clock and lamp. The wardrobe, tallboy and dressing-table were walnut; the carpet was imitation Persian, patterned in deep wines and sea blues. It was a room polished and dusted as if its occupant had only just vacated it and was due to return at any moment. Knowing how long it had been since her father had last slept in it, knowing that she had no idea of how long it would be before he returned, he found the housewifely care she still lavished on the room deeply moving.

'I think I'd be happiest not moving into your dad's room,' he said, wondering what it would be like to have a daughter or a wife or a mother who cared so much for him that she would keep his room in such a constant state of readiness for his homecoming. 'You said you had another two rooms free. Either of them would suit.'

'One is used as a lumber-room,' Kate said, moving further down the pleasantly wide landing. 'Though I don't suppose that will cut much ice with the council billeting officer when he comes to call!'

Moving past a bathroom she opened another door. 'This is the other spare room. It isn't quite as comfortably furnished as Dad's room but you can see the Heath from the window.'

Leon, accustomed since early childhood to the barrack-like dormitory of an orphanage and then in later years, before he joined the Navy, to a string of soulless, cheerless lodging-rooms, thought it looked exceedingly comfortably furnished. In fact, he thought it looked like a little corner of paradise.

There was a larger than average-sized single bed covered with a plump blue eiderdown. There was a comfortable-looking armchair near the window. There was a wickerwork bedside table and a table-lamp with a sunflower-yellow shade. There were colourful rag rugs scattered on the floor. A white-painted wardrobe stood against one wall, a matching dressing-table against another. There were shelves in an alcove laden with books and a bowl of pot-pourri on the window-ledge.

'I'm afraid it's a little spartan,' Kate said doubtfully. 'There isn't a heater in here and there's not much drawer-room.'

'I'm a sailor,' he reminded her with his easy, infectious grin, vastly amused by her concept of spartan. 'I'm used to keeping all my belongings ship-shape and tidy in less space than a mouse could turn in. This is the most drawer-space I've had in years.'

He swung his kit-bag to the floor. 'I don't know how long I'll be here,' he said, aware that she hadn't thought to ask. 'As soon as I'm declared fit for active service I'll be off. It might be two months. It might be longer.'

'Two months?' Her eyes widened. 'How can you possibly imagine you'll be fit for active service in two months? You can only walk with the help of a crutch!'

'I can only walk *now* with the help of a crutch,' he said, a note of steel-hard determination entering his voice. 'Give me another two weeks and I'll have thrown it on the wood-pile. And another few weeks after that and I'll be almost as good as new.'

Without knowing exactly how he had been injured Kate could hardly contradict him but she privately thought he was being highly optimistic. She was also suddenly aware of how closely they were standing together; of how small the bedroom was.

'I'll go back downstairs and put the wireless on,' she said, not wanting him to think she was being deliberately provocative; not wanting anything to spoil the easy friendliness that had sprung up so naturally and quickly between them. 'As it's Christmas Eve I might be able to tune in to a Carol Service.'

As if, again, sensing her thoughts he took a step or two further into the bedroom, increasing the distance between them. 'I'll be stowing my gear away,' he said with an easiness that robbed the moment of even the slightest hint of tension. 'I have some rum if you want to add it to your Christmas pudding.' His wide smile once again split his dusky face. 'Or, as it's Christmas, you can pour a tot into your next cup of tea!'

Instead of being the loneliest Christmas of her life, it turned out to be a Christmas full of teasing and laughter. Pretending to be appalled that she hadn't troubled to put up any Christmas decorations Leon rectified the situation by borrowing a pair of her father's secateurs and, aided by his crutch, disappeared into the night. When he returned he did so with his free arm hugging several branches of red-berried holly.

'I noticed your neighbour's holly-tree earlier on,' he said, laying his bounty on the table in high satisfaction. 'I thought at the time your neighbour was a fool for not having taken advantage of it. It would have sold for threepence a branch in Lewisham High Street.'

'Which neighbour?' Kate asked, giggles rising in her throat. 'Left-hand side or right-hand side?'

'Left-hand side. If it's someone you're particularly friendly with they won't mind and if it isn't, it doesn't matter very much, does it?'

Her neighbour next door down was Mr Nibbs. 'It doesn't matter very much,' she said, giving vent to her giggles. 'Where shall we put the holly? Over the picture frames?'

'And the mirrors. And don't forget the Christmas pudding. You'll need a tiny piece for the top of that.' A look of alarm flashed across his good-natured face. 'You have got a Christmas pudding, haven't you?'

'Yes. I made one because I thought the two friends I spoke to you about earlier might be spending Christmas with me. As it is, Harriet has volunteered to stay on call as an ambulance-driver and Ellen has taken too many bombed-out animals into her care to be able to leave them.'

His relief was so vast she couldn't help saying, fresh laughter thick in her voice, 'I hope you won't be disappointed. There are no raisins and currants in it. Only ersatz dried fruit.'

'And what,' he asked, dreading the answer, 'is ersatz dried fruit?'

Her laughter was husky and unchained. 'Grated carrot.'

He closed his eyes in mock despair and then, opening them again, said, 'Then you'll just have to be extra generous when you pour the rum over it!'

Later on in the evening he brought a pack of playing-cards down from his room and taught her how to play brag. Later still they listened to a Midnight Carol Service on the wireless. The volume stayed steady and no sirens sounded.

'I think we're going to be lucky tonight,' Kate said as she made two bedtime drinks.

Leon knew that she was referring to the blessedly *Luftwaffe*-free night sky but he said, suddenly serious instead of teasing, 'I already think myself pretty lucky. If you hadn't come down to The Swan and offered me a room I'd be in an overcrowded hostel tonight.'

She flushed slightly, not wanting his gratitude, only the uncomplicated comfort of his friendship. 'And I would have sat on my own all evening,' she said, handing him one of the mugs of milky Ovaltine, 'apart from Hector, of course.'

'Of course,' he said, and because he sensed the discomfort his seriousness had aroused in her, his voice was light and easy again. 'And now I'm off to bed,' he said, before even the least shadow of awkwardness could fall between them. 'Goodnight, Kate. And Merry Christmas.'

'Merry Christmas, Leon.'

She stood alone in the kitchen, listening as his crutch tapped its way up the stairs; until his bedroom door had opened and then closed. A few minutes later there came a dull clatter. A smile touched her mouth. He had dropped his crutch to the floor, no doubt heartily wishing he was doing so for good.

She leaned against the solidity of a kitchen dresser that had once belonged to her mother's mother, sipping at her drink. Despite the easy camaraderie that had existed between them almost from the first instant they had spoken to each other, it was an odd feeling having a man other than her father in the house. Especially one who was physically so very different from any other man she knew. And by physically different, she wasn't thinking of his injured leg, but of his skin colour.

She stared thoughtfully across the kitchen to the far wall. Above a calendar a twig of red-berried holly balanced precariously. He was an attractive man and his skin colour was part and parcel of his attractiveness. She liked the way his hair curled as tightly as a ram's fleece. She was fascinated by the paleness of his palms in contrast to the rest of his body. She certainly didn't like him *in spite* of his being black, just as she wouldn't want him to like her *in spite* of her being half-German. She simply liked him as he was. As he, apparently, liked her.

She eased herself away from the dresser and crossed the kitchen towards the sink, turning on the tap and rinsing out her mug. Harriet Godfrey had once gently asked her why she didn't cease wearing her hair in such a pronouncedly Germanic way. 'I could cut it for you,' she had offered. 'You needn't have it too short. A shoulder-length bob would look lovely. And it wouldn't shriek the fact that you are half German.'

'But I'm not *ashamed* of being half German,' she had said to Harriet's deep disconcertion. 'To be ashamed would mean that in some way I was ashamed of my father. And I'm not. He's the kindest, most tolerant person I've ever met. And as he's German, it means there must be other Germans with the same qualities. They can't *all* be rabid Nazis. There must be some Germans, however small a minority, who are as appalled by Hitler as we are and who are vehemently opposed to everything he stands for.'

'Maybe there are,' Harriet Godfrey had said, deeply troubled, 'but it isn't a viewpoint I would express to anyone else if I were you, Katherine. I think what you are saying would be very much misunderstood.'

It was an understatement, and Kate knew it. Yet she didn't think Leon would misunderstand. If an action as simple as a haircut could change the way he was perceived by people, she doubted if he would take it. He would want people to accept him for what he was, not for what they could be led to believe he was.

She turned the tap off and reached for a tea towel. And Leon was half West Indian and she was half German. In their different ways they were both misfits. Misfits who instinctively understood one another.

She put the two dried mugs away in a cupboard and looked around the kitchen, checking that it was neat and tidy to come down to in the morning. A sensation she hadn't experienced for a long, long time, flooded through her. It was one of unalloyed happiness. Her father was safe and well in his internment camp on the Isle of Wight. Her baby was kicking gently, making its presence felt. And it was Christmas morning, the most special morning of the year.

As she walked out of the kitchen and through the darkened house to the foot of the stairs, she knew she had a lot to be grateful for. And high on the list was a man she hadn't met until eight hours ago; a man who was now sleeping beneath her roof in a bedroom only yards from her own; a man she knew, beyond any shadow of doubt, was her friend.

Chapter Fifteen

On Christmas Day afternoon they took Hector for a walk on the Heath. Down beyond Greenwich, on the north side of the Thames, smoke hung heavy in the air.

'The East End,' Kate said bleakly. 'The fires after a raid sometimes last for days. I can't remember the last time I breathed in clean air. There's always a smell of smoke and sulphur.' She shivered, but not from cold, hugging her arms around her coated, distended body. 'How long do you think it's going to go on for, Leon? Is Hitler still planning to invade us as soon as possible or will he wait until the weather is in his favour? Will he wait until spring?'

'God knows,' Leon said, pausing for a moment and leaning on his crutch, his eyes crinkling at the corners as he looked over the Heath in the direction of the river. 'He's likely to do anything, isn't he? No-one was prepared for him invading Norway. The Norwegians hadn't even mobilized. And if he can launch invasion forces, in April, against a country with Norway's terrain, a bit of English Channel snow and ice won't deter him.'

'So we can expect anything?' Kate said as Hector raced in circles around them, impatient for the walk to continue.

Leon's laughter-lined face was grim. 'Where Hitler's concerned, we can expect the worst,' he said starkly, having too much respect for her to tell her anything but what he believed to be the truth.

She was silent for a moment and then she gave herself both a mental and a physical, shake. 'Have you ever been to Barbados?' she asked, changing the subject completely.

He grinned, the crinkles at the corners of his eyes deepening. 'No, though I expect if I stay in the Navy long enough, I will. Have you ever been to Germany?'

She shook her head, her mane of plaited hair swinging gently against her back. 'No.'

There was no need for either of them to say anymore. Unsaid but understood was the knowledge that their non-English heredity was equally alien to them; that though they didn't fit smoothly into the social fabric of the country of their birth, they would feel even less at home in Barbados or Germany.

Leon crooked his lips wryly. However unfamiliar Barbados might be to him, when he eventually visited it he would assimilate a damn sight more quickly than Kate ever would if she were to find herself in Nazi Germany. His wry amusement deepened. For once in his life he had met someone with a far more grave social disability than his own. If it came to a choice between being half West Indian or half German, he'd plump for being half West Indian every time!

'Come on,' he said, throwing a stick for Hector. 'Let's walk into Greenwich Park and get a proper view of the river and the City from General Wolfe's statue. At least St Paul's is still standing. That's something to be grateful for.'

'And Big Ben,' she said, falling into step beside him. 'Though you can't see it as clearly from the Park as you can St Paul's. You'd think two such landmarks would be prime targets, wouldn't you?'

'I imagine they are,' Leon said dryly, looking eastwards into the winter-grey sky, wondering when the *Luftwaffe* would next appear; wondering how much more punishment the battered city could take. 'I imagine all that's spared them so far is luck.'

* * *

Three nights later it seemed to both of them as if all luck for London had run out. It was late evening when the radio went off without warning.

'They're on their way,' Kate said, rolling her knitting up and sticking her knitting needles firmly into her ball of wool. 'I think there'll be time to make a Thermos of tea, there usually is. Will you take Hector into the shelter for me while I put the kettle on?'

'No,' Leon said, closing the atlas he had been studying and rising to his feet. 'I won't.'

Her eyes widened.

He held his hand out to her, helping her to her feet. 'I won't do it, because that's what you're going to do. *I'm* the one who's going to stay behind and make a Thermos of tea. Take your knitting with you.' The rising wail of sirens nearly drowned his voice. 'And my atlas.'

Though his voice was quiet there was utter authority in it. Kate didn't trouble to argue against it. There wasn't enough time and the issue wasn't important enough.

She tucked her knitting under one arm, picked up the Atlas and said to Hector, 'Come on, Hector. Shelter time again. Lead the way.'

Hector's heavy black tail hung miserably between his legs. He didn't like the sirens and he didn't like the word 'shelter'. He knew what it meant. Hours of sitting in a half-buried tin hut in the back garden enduring unspeakable roaring and whooshing sounds.

'Be careful out there in the dark!' Leon shouted after Kate as she stepped out of the kitchen door on to the narrow path leading down to the shelter.

Kate felt almost light-hearted as she made her way cautiously towards the Anderson, Hector pressing close against her. Always, previously, this was a nightmare she and Hector had endured by themselves. Tonight they wouldn't be doing so. Tonight they would have Leon to keep them company.

The few steps leading down into the Anderson were damp and slippery and she descended them with very great care. She was nearly eight months pregnant and she didn't want any accidents.

Hector whined and nuzzled her hand with his head. She patted him lovingly. 'It's all right, Hector,' she said as she stepped inside the pitch-black shelter. 'And we're going to be snug tonight. Leon has put a paraffin heater in here and a storm lantern.' She fumbled in her pocket for the matches that went everywhere with her. 'We'll wait till Leon joins us before lighting up,' she said, talking to him as if he were a person, as she always did. 'It will save him having to fight with the black-out curtaining in order to get inside.'

She sat down, her hand lovingly on the silky-smooth fur of his neck. 'It may only be a hit and run raid. It may even be a false alarm.'

Moments later, as Leon limped down the steps and into the shelter, she knew that her optimism was unfounded. Eastwards, in the distance, came the approaching *zhoorzh, zhoorzh, zhoorzh* sound of hundreds of unsynchronized German engines.

'Have you got the matches?' Leon asked, handing her the Thermos flask. 'And if your next door neighbour is an Air-Raid Warden, why the hell didn't he check on you before haring off to the ARP post? To the best of my knowledge he doesn't know I've moved in here as a lodger. For all he knows you're on your own.'

'We don't speak,' Kate said succinctly. 'We haven't spoken ever since he supported the Cricket Club Committee's decision to relieve my father of his captaincy of the team.'

Leon lit the storm lantern and turned his attention to the Aladdin paraffin heater.

'Mr Nibbs is scrupulous where duty is concerned,' Kate continued, aware that for the first time she was talking about Mr Nibbs without bitterness or rancour in her voice. 'It must worry him, his not knocking to check on me.'

'Then he should stop worrying and do it.' Leon's voice

was blunt. He had no time for a man so unchivalrous.

'He can't,' amusement was thick in her voice, 'because he's even more stubborn than he's scrupulous. In fact, when I think of his dilemma, I feel quite sorry for him.'

'I don't.' There was no amusement in Leon's voice. 'He knows you're pregnant and on your own. He should be checking on your safety whenever there's a raid.'

The sound of the ack-ack guns on the Heath blasting into life made further conversation impossible. Kate removed her ball of wool from her knitting needles. She was knitting a matinee-coat for the baby. Leon picked up the atlas he had been studying earlier and opened it up again at North Africa, trying to work out just where British and Australian soldiers were engaging with the Italians.

The *whoosh* Kate had come to recognize as being the sound of dropping incendiary bombs, filled the air. She looked across the lamp-lit shelter towards Leon. His concentration seemed to be entirely on the map he was studying. A slight frown knitted his eyebrows. They were extremely nice eyebrows; well-shaped and attractively winged.

Sensing her eyes on him he raised his head slightly and looked across at her. 'Don't worry,' he said comfortingly, 'for the moment everything is falling on the City.'

'The City? Not the East End? How can you tell?'

'I'm a sailor,' he said with the easy, friendly smile she had grown so accustomed to. 'I can judge distances by sound.'

She believed him. She believed everything he told her because it was impossible to even imagine him telling an untruth.

He returned his attention to the map and outwardly she returned hers to her knitting. Inwardly she was praying that St Paul's wouldn't be hit; that when she and Leon looked out over the City in the morning they would still see Sir Christopher Wren's masterpiece and not a burning pyre.

Leon's attention, too, drifted. Instead of concentrating on what the British army's next move would be in North Africa and what part the navy might play when Libya's coastal strong-points were attacked, he found himself staring across at Kate.

Her head was bent over her knitting, the needles flashing like quick-silver between her long, supple fingers. He thought her very beautiful; the most beautiful woman he had ever seen. There was strength as well as delicacy in her features. It showed in the stubborn set of her chin and in the pure line of her jaw. Once she had made her mind up about anything, he suspected it would be the very devil to get her to change it. Yet she was also heartachingly loving and gentle. Not towards him, of course. Towards him she was friendly and generous and he had the commonsense to know that that was the most he could ask for. It was the way she treated Hector that revealed the innate loving gentleness that so attracted him, as well as the way she talked about the coming baby.

The atlas lay forgotten on his knee. From perilously near, Woolwich or Greenwich, there came the sickening crump and blast of falling bombs. The tin walls of the Anderson vibrated. The ack-ack guns on the Heath pounded deafeningly. Hector whined and crept even closer to Kate's feet. She broke off from her knitting to put a hand down to him, comforting him.

Watching her, Leon felt a lump form in his throat. Once, long, long ago, a woman with the same gentleness in her eyes and the same kind of inner strength, had also broken off from her knitting and stretched a hand down comfortingly. He couldn't have been more than three years old, for when he was four years old she had died in the street of a heart-attack, a loaf of fresh bread and a bunch of flowers in her arms.

He shut off that memory, as he had shut it off for twenty-three years. It was too painful; too traumatic for him to dare to dwell on it. Instead he remembered the warmth and comfort of sitting at her feet while she knitted or sewed, telling him stories and nursery-rhymes.

In memory he could almost feel the flickering yellow flames of the fire and see again the pictures she had helped him to find in the red-hot coals. He never remembered her as being anything other than soft-spoken and loving, yet she had been strong, too. She had had to be, marrying a West Indian sailor fifteen years her senior in pre-First World War Britain. If mixed marriages were regarded as unpleasant oddities now, in 1940, they were regarded as being little more than obscene violations of nature in 1912. She had been a school teacher from a conventional, middle-class home and not for the first time he wondered how she had endured the insulting and salacious remarks he knew she must have met with.

The noise of plane engines and explosions was horrendous, nearly as deafening as a bombardment at sea. He noticed that though Kate was still knitting, her face was ashen. He touched her lightly on the knee.

'It's all right,' he shouted across to her. 'Everything is falling on the City. There won't be many lives lost. All the businessmen will be safely at home in their Andersons.'

She smiled, a touch of embarrassed colour flaring in her cheeks, ashamed that she hadn't been thinking of the businessmen who worked in the City but only of the survival of St Paul's.

He mistook the colour in her cheeks for discomfort at the way he had touched her to attract her attention. Cursing himself for an idiot he once more outwardly returned his attention to the atlas. After all the care he had taken ever since he had moved in with her, not to say or do anything that might raise the awkward spectre of sex and make her feel uncomfortable, why had he tapped her on the knee and not on her arm? It was an action taken without thought, but he knew now how she would react to any increase of familiarity between them and was appalled at how fiercely disappointed he felt.

Once again he began to think of his father and mother and what an odd couple they must have made. His father had been born in 1864, a year before slavery was officially abolished in the United States of America. He had been very black and defiantly proud of his blackness.

A smile tugged at the corner of Leon's mouth. His mother had always insisted that he attend Sunday School and even after her death and up until his father's death, when he was eight years old, he had done so. It was in a book given out at Sunday School that he had first seen pictures of African tribal chieftains: naked, with war-paint on and standing amongst spears, they had looked magnificent.

They had also looked, apart from their nakedness and splendidly barbaric finery, just like his father. It was then that it had occurred to him that there was something exciting and special in being black. His father was certainly special. It had been quite a revelation and from that moment on any racial insult hurled at him in the school playground or worse, the classroom, was robbed of any power to hurt. The ones who hurled the insults were the losers and the ones to be pitied. They weren't special. They didn't have a special dad who could, if he wanted to, easily look like a magnificent warrior.

There was a lull in the nightmare bombardment. 'Do you think it's over?' Kate asked, breaking in on his thoughts of the past. 'Could we take a look outside?'

He didn't think it was over for one minute, but he knew how claustrophobic many people found it, hiding semi-underground and not being able to see what was taking place around them.

'I think we could get a little air,' he said, more than happy to have a look-see himself. If it hadn't been for ensuring her safety, he wouldn't for one minute have even entered the Anderson. Despite the handicap of his injured leg, he would have been volunteering his services at the nearest ARP post.

Mindful of her discomfort when he had touched her knee he didn't offer her his arm as she stepped outside into the night, but he watched her feet with hawk-like concern, ready to steady her instantly if she stumbled.

'Dear Lord,' she whispered devoutly as she reached the top of the shallow flight of steps and stood on the overgrown grass of the garden. 'Look at the sky, Leon! It looks as if it's full of blood!'

Everywhere was red. Even though they couldn't see across the city and the river from where they were standing, it was obvious that the worst fires of the war were raging. The smell of burning hung in the air like fog. Kate felt a dusting of ashes sweep her cheek. Tears stung her lashes.

'Could we go up on to the Heath and take a look across the city?' she asked a little unsteadily. 'Though you can see best from the Park, you can also get a good view from the north-west corner of the Heath.'

Giant searchlights swept and re-swept the stained sky. 'No,' he said, knowing what it was she wanted to see and knowing that it would have to wait until morning. 'This little lot isn't over yet, Kate.'

Even as he finished speaking there came the roar of a fresh wave of approaching aeroplanes and the nearby ack-ack gun opened up, blasting upwards to no very good effect but making those who could hear it feel that at least some kind of retaliation was taking place.

'We'd better take shelter again,' he said, fearful for her safety. 'We'll go up to the Heath the minute the all-clear sounds.'

She nodded, her fingers crossed, thinking of St Paul's and wishing as hard as she was able.

'The City has been pulverized,' Harriet Godfrey said to her six hours later as Kate made her a cup of tea. 'It's been the worst night of the war. Indescribable. Unbelievable.'

'We've seen the damage for ourselves, from a

281

distance,' Leon said quietly. 'It looks like a raging hell down there.'

'It is,' Harriet Godfrey said, her voice thick with weariness. She had been on duty all the way through the nightmare of the raid and was utterly exhausted. 'God knows when the fires will be brought under control. The fire services are doing their best but the water mains were hit and the back-up service from distant pipes failed.'

'What about the Thames?' Kate asked, hugging the knowledge of the miraculous escape of St Paul's Cathedral to herself like a comforting blanket. 'Couldn't the firemen take water from the Thames?'

'It was low-tide last night,' Leon said, answering the question for her. 'I don't suppose the water could be reached.'

'It couldn't.' Harriet Godfrey accepted the cup of tea Kate proffered her and reached with an unsteady hand for the sugar-spoon. 'The tide has turned now but the damage has been done. Huge swathes of the City have been reduced to charred rubble. I felt as if I were living through the Great Fire of London in 1666. The streets in the City are still as narrow as they were then and fire just leaps from one building to another.'

'But they didn't hit St Paul's,' Kate said, unable to refrain from putting her heartfelt feelings into words.

'Incendiaries certainly did hit St Paul's,' Harriet said, not wanting Kate to be under illusions. 'That the Cathedral isn't a smouldering shell this morning is due entirely to the vigilance of its fire-watchers and their swift, preventative action. The trouble in the streets around it was that the buildings, being all banks and offices, were not only locked but double-locked. No-one was fire-watching in them. No-one was able to smother an incendiary the instant it landed.'

'They will in future,' Leon said dryly. 'You can bet your life there'll be laws brought in immediately to ensure that no property is left unguarded.

'I'm sure you're right, Mr Emmerson,' Harriet Godfrey said, rising wearily to her feet. 'But any such laws will be too late for the Barbican and Moorgate areas of the City. Almost every single building is ruined.' She turned to Kate. 'Thank you for the tea, Katherine. It was much appreciated. I'm going to bed now before I fall asleep on my feet.'

During the next forty-eight hours, as firemen and volunteers continued to fight the raging fires, Leon set about making the Anderson even more comfortable for Kate. He removed one of the school-benches and replaced it with a narrow single bed. Though he hadn't referred to it, he had been appalled by the discomfort she had endured, heavily pregnant and all night in the Anderson without being able to even sit comfortably, let alone lie down. He assumed her father, when he had furnished the shelter, had had little idea of the length of time raids would last. And he could have had no idea that his unmarried daughter would become pregnant.

'It looks like Buckingham Palace,' Kate said in grateful amusement when he showed her the results of his labours. 'You'll never guess who I've just seen in Magnolia Square. Jack Robson, Charlie's son. He's in the Commandoes but is home on a forty-eight hour pass.'

'He's a good bloke,' Leon said, referring to Jack as Kate put a plate of sausage and mash in front of him. 'He's converted the Misses Helliwells' Morrison shelter into a table tennis table and he and Mavis have been having a rare old time showing off their table tennis skills to Emily and Esther.'

'Emily and Esther?' Remembering the way she had overheard Emily Helliwell speak of Leon to Miriam Jennings, Kate's eyebrows rose. 'Are you referring to Miss Emily Helliwell, Magnolia Square's famed clairvoyant and palm-reader, and her sister, Miss Esther

Helliwell? And if you are, since when did you get on first name terms with them?'

'Since the day I rescued their cat from the clutches of a rather vicious bull-terrier.'

'Was Faust wearing his gas-mask at the time?' Kate asked, amused. 'He was almost the first Magnolia Square inhabitant to be kitted out with one.'

It was Leon's turn to be amused. 'No,' he said, chuckling as he speared a sausage. 'And he didn't have it in a canister around his neck, either.'

The laughter died from Kate's eyes. 'How is Esther?' she asked, dispirited by the knowledge that there had been a time when she would have known; a time before her father's internment; a time when she had called in to have a cheery word with the wheelchair-bound Esther almost as often as she had called in at the Jennings'. 'The raids must be horrendous for her,' she said, wondering how on earth the two old ladies managed through an air raid on their own. 'Is she suffering terribly?'

Leon speared another sausage with his fork and chuckled. 'Suffering? You're joking. Esther doesn't suffer through a raid. She enjoys them!'

Kate's jaw dropped and her mouth fell open.

Leon's chuckles increased. 'Esther's exact words when I asked her how she coped with the stress of an air raid were, "Stress? Stress? Bless you for being so concerned young man, but the truth is, I haven't had so much excitement for years!" '

As a bitterly cold January edged into a freezingly cold February, Leon was able to dispense with his crutch not only in the house, but outside of it too. Acting as an unofficial fire-watcher for Magnolia Square, his fund of anecdotes about the Square's inhabitants, increased. He told Kate of how the Jennings' had found an unexploded bomb in their rear garden and of how Miriam had strapped it firmly to Billy's back and sent him off on his

284

bicycle with instructions to deliver his cargo to Shooters Hill Police Station.

'Apparently the officer in charge took one look at him and what he was loaded with and told him he was in the wrong place and that he should take his present to the ARP post. When he got there Mr Nibbs was on duty and apparently only relieved him of his burden with the greatest reluctance.'

And it was via Leon that she learned that Ted Lomax had been recommended for a medal after courageously saving the lives of wounded comrades when under heavy fire. He also told her of how Miriam was now not only looking after Beryl and Billy while Mavis braved the Blitz as a motor cycle despatch-rider, but that she was also caring for a little girl Beryl's age, whose family had been bombed out of their Catford home.

'Her name is Jenny,' Leon said to her as they sat out another night of bombing in the Anderson. 'She's a pretty little thing, but quiet.'

'So Billy has two female acolytes now, not just one,' Kate said, laughing despite the sickening *crump, crump, crump* of shells spattering into Magnolia Square. 'That young man is going to finish up with a harem!'

In the second week of February, on the same day, Kate received a postcard from Lance Merton and Leon attended his long-awaited medical and was declared once again fit for active service.

'But you're not fit!' Kate protested, hardly able to believe what he was telling her. 'You still limp badly!'

'What's a limp between friends?' Leon said humorously, hiding his real feelings with difficulty. 'There's a fellow flying in the RAF who has two tin legs.'

Ordinarily, he would have been over the moon at having persuaded the medical officer that he was fit enough to return to duty. He had never enjoyed long spells ashore, even in peace time. But that had been because time spent ashore was always time spent in cheerless lodgings. He had never had a home to return to. He had never, since his father had died, known anything approaching a home. Until now.

They were in the kitchen and it was early evening. A pot-bellied wood-burning stove gave out cosy heat; soup simmered on one of the gas hobs; there was a batch of freshly baked bread on a wire cooling tray on the table. Though he didn't know how it had happened, and he couldn't even tell her that it *had* happened, Kate Voigt's home had become his. Unintentionally, by her generosity and gentleness and gaiety, she had made it so. Reluctance to leave such a haven, knowing that he was in all likelihood leaving it for ever, was not the only reason for the tumult raging behind his false show of humour.

The baby was due in a few weeks time. Though the subject had never been mentioned between them, he knew that she was depending on him still lodging with her when her time came. For if he wasn't there, who else would look after her? Who else would queue endlessly at the shops for groceries and vegetables? Who else would make sure there was enough wood in the house to eke out her small supply of coal? And if she went into labour suddenly, without warning, who else would notify the doctor?

At the thought of her struggling on her own, his heart felt as if it was being squeezed by icy fingers. Harriet Godfrey would give her all the help she could, as would her other middle-aged friend, Ellen Pierce. It wouldn't be easy for them though. Harriet Godfrey was wholeheartedly committed to her ambulance-driving work and Ellen Pierce lived a fair distance away and had her large collection of bombed-out and abandoned animals to care for.

Not for the first time his thoughts turned to Carrie Collins. When Kate had told him how close she and Carrie had once been, and the cause of the rift that now divided them, he had been appalled. He wondered what Carrie's response would be if he were to approach her with the aim of effecting a reconciliation between them.

'When will you be leaving?' Kate asked him, breaking in on his thoughts, her voice sounding as if it were being strangled in her throat.

The prospect of life without him was nearly intolerable. He cheered and comforted her and even through the heaviest bombardments by the *Luftwaffe* his presence made her feel safe and secure. She had imagined he would be with her all through the spring and possibly all through the summer too. She wasn't mentally prepared for him leaving so abruptly; she wasn't prepared for the loneliness that would follow; for the sense of loss she knew she would feel.

'I'm not sure. I have to wait to be notified.'

He saw the postcard she was holding and said, still wondering how the hell he could arrange for her to be suitably looked after during her confinement, 'Who is that from? Ellen?'

'No.' Her voice was odd. Thick. She looked down at the postcard in her hand as if seeing it for the first time. 'It's from someone who was friends with Toby, Lance Merton. He was in Toby's squadron and he came to visit me after Toby's death. Hector was with him when he visited me and he was kind enough to leave him with me. Hector was Toby's dog.' she said, wondering if she had told him so previously; wondering how to phrase the question she so desperately wanted to ask.

'He sounds like a decent bloke,' Leon said, sure that whatever kind of bloke Merton was, they would hate each other on sight. 'And a lucky one, too. Not many pilots who fought in the early days of the Battle of Britain are alive to tell the tale.'

'No. He is lucky. I think that's why he drops me the occasional postcard. Just to let me know that he's still alive.'

Leon was damn sure he knew the reason Merton

dropped her the occasional postcard. He was determined to keep in touch with her. And when the opportunity arose, he would visit again. And when he visited her again he would do so in the hope that she had recovered sufficiently from her grief over Toby Harvey's death to be able to consider him as a replacement. His hands clenched into fists.

'I don't suppose you have leave very often in the Navy,' Kate said, wondering how she could frame her question without sounding as if she were taking far too much for granted, 'but when you do have leave . . . if you want to come back here . . .'

'Like a shot,' he said, aware that for the first time since they had met, their conversation was stiltedly awkward and constrained.

She smiled, but it wasn't her usual smile. It was brittle, almost false. The happiness flooding through him was chilled immediately. Had her invitation been prompted by pity? Had she made the offer because she knew he had no family and she felt sorry for him?

Hardly able to contain her relief at his answer, Kate said, her voice still odd, still thick, 'Good. I'm glad. I'll make sure the billeting officer doesn't put anyone else in your room.' So that he shouldn't be aware of the depth of her relief she began busily laying cutlery on the kitchen table, saying as she did so, 'It's a pity you won't be here when the baby is born. It will be months, perhaps, before you know whether it's a girl or a boy.'

'I'll be thinking of you both,' he said gruffly. From the moment they had first met the baby's existence had disconcerted him. He wasn't accustomed to being in the company of a pregnant woman. Not one he knew was pregnant, anyway. Not one so heavily pregnant. It made him feel unsure; uncertain. Should she be walking Hector so energetically on the Heath between bombing raids? Was it wise for her to get down on her hands and knees to clean the kitchen floor? He had offered to do it for her but she had laughed his offer away, saying that she was pregnant, not ill, and that she *enjoyed* cleaning the floor.

Her preparations for the birth, and her unfazed attitude towards it, had disconcerted him even more.

'What is this for?' he had asked one evening as she began putting everything she would need for the birth in a basket, not sure he truly wanted to know the answer. 'The crepe bandaging?' The electricity was down and in the light of emergency-candles her blue eyes looked almost amethyst. 'It's to hold the pad on the baby's tummy in place.'

He must have looked blank for she gave a husky giggle, saying, 'After the umbilical cord has been cut, Doctor Roberts will put a sterilizing pad on what will be the baby's tummy-button.'

'Is that what the safety-pins are for?' he had asked, thankful the bandaging wasn't for a more grisly purpose.

She nodded. 'And the alcohol and string and lint.'

As she was talking she was putting other items into the basket. A pair of strong scissors, Vaseline, antiseptic.

Watching her, he had worried then about how she would manage. Now, knowing that he wouldn't be around to do the heavy tasks in the house and to take care of her safety and the baby's safety during an air raid, he worried even more.

He would have to speak to both Harriet Godfrey and Ellen Pierce. And he would have to speak to Carrie.

Harriet Godfrey and Ellen Pierce both assured him that they would take good care of Kate in his absence. Leon was reassured, but only marginally. It was highly likely that when Kate went into labour, Harriet Godfrey would be miles away, driving her ambulance through streets strewn with shattered glass and rubble. And Ellen Pierce didn't live near enough. Depending on the activity of the *Luftwaffe* it might be days after the baby's birth before Kate could even get a message to her. Which left Carrie.

'She ain't at 'ome and she ain't dahn the market,' Billy

said to him helpfully when he knocked on the Jennings' door and asked for her. 'She's doing war-work. Can I give 'er a message?'

Leon shook his head. He knew he was on exceedingly dangerous ground in speaking to Carrie about Kate and he didn't want the situation made even more volatile by any message Billy might mutilate.

'No,' he said. 'I'll catch up with her later.'

'She's workin' as a clippie on the buses,' Billy said, staring at Leon with undisguised fascination. 'If I touch yer, will any o' that black rub off?'

It was a sincerely asked question, not meant to be rude or insulting.

'No,' Leon said equably, knowing that Billy could have no idea of the echoes his question had raised in him. The chant by the orphanage bully when he had first arrived there, nearly insensible with shock after his father's perfunctory burial: '*Your father was a nigger!*' The demand to know if he could swing from tree to tree like a monkey; if his hair was real hair, or wire.

'Are you joining your ship soon?' Billy asked, wanting to keep Leon on the doorstep for as long as possible, hoping some of his mates would see the two of them deep in conversation. 'My mum says you're a bloody fool for playin' fit when you could swing it for a bit longer. She says my dad was a bloody fool as well, riskin' 'is neck when 'e 'ad no need. My dad's goin' to get a medal. I don't know anyone else whose dad is goin' to get a medal. 'ave you got a medal?'

'No. Sorry to be a disappointment, Billy.'

''S' all right,' Billy said magnanimously. 'Not everyone's a 'ero.' His gap-fronted teeth flashed in a smile of blinding brilliance. 'My dad is though!'

'This came for you while you were out,' Kate said, handing him an official-looking buff envelope. For once there was no smile of welcome for him on her face. She knew what the envelope contained. She knew that soon, within hours maybe, he would be leaving the house with his kit-bag over his shoulder.

He slit the envelope open and read the brief notification within. 'I'm to report for duty in twenty-four hours time. My ship is HMS *Viking*. It doesn't say so, but I imagine we'll be sailing to the Mediterranean to give back-up to the troops in North Africa.'

She winced, shock flaring through her eyes.

'Steady on,' he said, concerned. 'The Med isn't bad news, Kate. It's a cinch compared to convoy duty in the Atlantic.'

'It's not that . . .' She took tight hold of the back of the nearest chair. 'It's the baby.' There was incredulity in her voice. 'I'm having a contraction, Leon! The baby's on its way!'

Chapter Sixteen

'*Jesus Christ!*' It was the first time he had ever blasphemed in front of her but he could no more have contained his reaction than flown to the moon. How long did babies take to come? How long was it before he had to be aboard ship? If she was beginning labour now, in the early afternoon, did it mean the baby would be born sometime during the night when, in all likelihood, there would be an air raid at its height?

'Are you sure?' he demanded as her tense fingers began to relax their hold of the chair-back. 'I thought you weren't due for another two weeks or so?'

She took a deep, steadying breath, her body slowly once again relaxing. 'I'm sure.' There was excitement in her voice. And apprehension. 'Doctor Roberts told me first babies take their time. He said I wouldn't need to send word to him until the contractions are coming regularly.'

Leon stared at her. 'Regularly? What's regularly? Every five minutes? Every fifteen minutes? Every half an hour?'

His alarm was so obvious that she began to giggle. 'Every fifteen minutes probably. I don't remember him saying.'

'Jesus Christ, Kate!' For the first time he felt utterly exasperated with her. 'Do you mean you didn't ask him? Do you mean you don't *know*?'

'I'll be able to tell when it's time to send for him,' she said confidently. 'Will you help me get things ready? I need to strip the bed and put newspapers on the mattress. And then I need to fold some flannel sheets into thick pads and . . .'

'Sit down. *Sit down.* I'll do it.' He ran a hand through his short, crinkly hair. 'Where do you keep the sheets?' he asked, wondering if he should try and get a message to Ellen Pierce; if he should contact Harrriet Godfrey.

'In the airing-cupboard on the landing. And there's no need for me to sit down. The more I walk around, the sooner the baby is likely to put in an appearance.'

He didn't even attempt to argue with her. Instead he turned on his heel, heading for the stairs. He had twenty-four hours before he had to be aboard his ship. Would the baby be born within twenty-four hours? Despite her insistence that it wasn't necessary, wouldn't the most sensible course of action be for him to contact Doctor Roberts?

He opened the airing-cupboard. The flannel sheets were folded neatly on a slatted-shelf next to a pile of cotton sheets and pillowcase covers. He scooped them up into his arms. God Almighty, but it was worse than being under fire! How could she possibly be so serene about it all? Was it because no-one had told her of the difficulties that could be involved? It certainly didn't sound as if Roberts had troubled to explain much to her.

When he went into her bedroom with his cargo it was to find her already stripping the bed of its blankets and sheets. She turned her head as he entered the room, a smile on her face. Then she gasped, sucking in her breath, her hand shooting out to grasp the brass knob of her bed-head.

'*What is it?*' He crossed the room swiftly towards her, tumbling the sheets on to the bed as he did so. 'Is it another one? How long is that since the last one? Should they be coming so quick, so soon?'

Her voice, when she finally answered him, was not quite as confident as it had been. 'I don't know. Carrie would know . . .'

She very rarely spoke of Carrie because to speak of

Carrie was to open herself up to more hurt and pain than she could bear.

He said, knowing the sense of loss she was feeling; knowing that it was Carrie she needed with her at a time like this, not a ham-handed male, 'Go back downstairs and make yourself a cup of tea. I'll see to the bed. And when I've seen to the bed, I'll go round and have a word with Doctor Roberts.'

This time she didn't suggest that it wasn't yet necessary. With a hand to the drumming throb in the middle of her back, she said, 'Would you like a cup, too? And a sandwich?' Husky laughter entered her voice. 'You'd better take me up on that last offer. It might be quite some time before I'm able to offer again!'

Even before she had lumberingly made her way to the foot of the stairs he had completed her interrupted task of stripping the bed. Newspapers. Where were the newspapers? He looked around the room and saw them, neeatly stacked and tied with string by the side of her dressing-table.

With ship-shape neatness he spread them deeply and evenly over the mattress, then he folded the flannel sheets into thick pads and laid them over the top of the newsprint. Though she hadn't specifically told him to do so he then tucked a spotlessly clean cotton sheet over the protected mattress. The result looked intimidatingly surgical but he doubted if she wanted a top sheet putting back on the bed and he had the common-sense to realize that she certainly wouldn't want dust-harbouring blankets putting back on it.

He ran a hand through his tight-knit hair again. His cup of tea and sandwich could wait. He was going straight to Doctor Roberts' surgery. Kate's pains were coming too close together for him to be able to rely on the old adage that first babies took their time. This one might very well not be doing. It might, instead, be just about to give him the most spectacular send-off to sea he'd ever experienced.

'Miss Voigt?' Mrs Roberts stressed the 'Miss'. 'It's a first baby, isn't it? I'll tell my husband, when he returns. I don't anticipate that being until late afternoon but if Miss Voigt has only just gone into labour it will be plenty soon enough.'

She began to close the door and Leon strategically placed a foot so that she couldn't do so. 'Kate's pains are coming quite close together. And they seem to be fairly strong. Strong enough to take her breath away. I'd like to have Doctor Roberts' opinion. If you could tell me whereabouts to find him . . .'

'There's a war on!' Mrs Roberts' face had now become openly hostile. 'Or perhaps, not being British, you hadn't noticed? When my husband returns from his rounds I will tell him that Miss Voigt's baby is on its way. He certainly won't want disturbing with the news sooner than is absolutely necessary.'

Leon's face was as expressionless as a mask. He should have realized the kind of reaction he might meet with. No doubt Mrs Roberts believed him to be the baby's father. The distaste in her eyes certainly indicated that she did so. Breathing in deeply through his nose he turned his back on her, not lowering himself to state that he was as British as she was. He knew the Mrs Robertses of this world and he knew that remaining to argue with her wouldn't do him, or Kate, the slightest good. It would only make her even more intransigent. As the local Air Raid Warden, Mr Nibbs would no doubt be aware of Doctor Roberts' whereabouts. He'd have a word with him. After he had first gone back home to check on Kate.

She was sitting on one of the kitchen chairs, her hands gripping the seat, her back arched, her eyes closed, Hector whimpering at her feet.

'Kate!' He crossed the kitchen in swift strides and squatted down in front of her. 'Are you all right?' he asked, his voice harsh with urgency. 'Is there anything I can do?'

She shook her head, her eyes still closed. 'No,' she managed at last, her voice a gasp. 'Poor Hector can't understand what's wrong. Where is Doctor Roberts? Is he on his way?'

'He's on his rounds. His wife refused to say whereabouts. The men at the ARP post will know.' He had never felt more helpless or inadequate in his life. 'I'm going up there now, Kate. I'll be back with him as fast as is humanly possible. Do you want me to help you upstairs before I go? Have you banged on the wall to try and attract Harriet Godfrey's attention?'

She let out a long, shuddering sigh as the pain eased. Opening her eyes she said tautly, 'Harriet's not in. She's on duty. She was leaving her house when the postman delivered your letter.'

There were beads of sweat on her forehead and he felt his stomach turn a sickening somersault. If the contractions she was experiencing were merely early warning contractions, then he was a Dutchman. This baby wasn't going to take a long, leisurely time over being born. It was going to make its appearance in the world in the least possible time.

'Could you help me upstairs, Leon?' There was a look of apology in her eyes. 'I'm going to have to lean on you pretty heavily.'

His throat tightened. He wanted to tell her that she could lean on him for as long and as heavily as she wanted; that she could lean on him for the rest of her life. He said instead, 'I'm going to need to put my arm round your waist. Is that OK? I won't be hurting the baby, will I?'

She giggled and the knowledge that she still felt capable of giggling infinitely reassured him. It meant that despite the pain of the contractions, she wasn't afraid. And he didn't want her to be afraid. Not ever.

'What waist?' she asked, heaving herself to her feet to

Hector's vast relief. 'I haven't had a waist since last summer. And no, you won't hurt the baby.'

He slid his arm around her and she leaned against him. It was the closest physical contact there had ever been between them. He only wished to God it was taking place under different circumstances.

'No,' she said when they reached the top of the stairs and he began to lead her towards her bedroom, Hector bounding ahead of them. 'I need the bathroom, Leon. I need to take a bath.'

He sucked in his breath, appalled at how little he had realized the necessity of her having a woman with her. He couldn't help her in and out of the bath and she damn sure wasn't in any state to manage on her own.

She said gently, reading his thoughts as clearly as if he had spoken them out loud, 'I can manage, Leon. Try and find Doctor Roberts. I think I'm going to need him quite soon.'

He'd never been more reluctant to leave anyone in all his life. 'Don't lock the bathroom door,' he said tautly. 'Just to be on the safe side. Don't try and get in or out of the bath if you feel a contraction coming on. Don't . . .'

'Go,' she said as the pain in her back intensified and she felt another contraction beginning to gather up steam.

He took one look at her face and the urgency in her eyes. 'I'm going,' he said, turning on his heel, praying to God that the leg he had injured would be strong enough to stand up to a desperate run.

Kate turned on the geyser over the bath thankful that, unlike in the East End, Magnolia Square's gas mains were still intact. As the contraction took hold and as the blessedly hot water began to run into the bath she sank to her knees, leaning her weight on the edge of the bath, breathing deeply. How long were the contractions lasting for? She wasn't wearing a watch and she didn't know.

She dropped her head down over the steaming water. She mustn't fight the pain. To fight the pain would be to brace her muscles against it and that would be to hinder what her body was trying to achieve. Hector pressed up close against her, disturbed and distressed. She sucked in another lungful of air and then let her breath out in a harsh pant. She should have asked Leon to time one of the contractions. Leon. Without Leon where on earth would she be? The answer came immediately. *Frightened.* She would be frightened. But it was impossible to be frightened when Leon was with her. '*Hurry!*' she said aloud as the contraction began to ebb and she forced herself again to her feet in order to turn off the geyser. '*Hurry, Leon! Hurry and get back to me!*'

Leon was hurrying. Despite having been declared fit enough to return to active service he still had a slight limp and he cursed it heartily as, hampered by it, he sprinted as fast as he was able for the Heath.

Giant silver barrage balloons were tethered near to the ARP post. It was a breezy, damp day and instead of riding high in the sky in their efforts to keep enemy aircraft at a high altitude, the balloons were floating nose to wind a mere few hundred feet up, surging restlessly in the rushing air, their stabilizing fins flapping furiously.

'What's the rush?' Mr Nibbs asked authoritatively as Leon burst in on him.

Leon had no intention of launching into a long explanation. 'I need to get hold of Doctor Roberts,' he gasped, panting for breath. 'Fast. Do you know whereabouts he is?'

'Down Point Hill. A bomb-damaged house has collapsed and a woman and child have been injured.'

Leon sucked a deep breath of air into his lungs and spun on his heel.

'*He won't want distracting from what he's doing down there,*' Mr Nibbs called out after him and then, as Leon showed no intention of respecting his authority, he added bad-temperedly beneath his breath, 'Especially by a bloomin' darky!'

At least Point Hill wasn't far. Leon pounded over the grass of the Heath and then over pavement, grateful for all the effort he had put into strengthening his leg. The minute the ruin of what had once been a family house came into view, his heart sank. The front wall had cascaded down across the pavement and into the road. Brick-dust and plaster-dust hung heavily in the air. Air Raid Wardens helped by members of the Home Guard had formed a human chain and were dismantling the wreckage brick by brick. A small group were squatted precariously on the highest point of the collapsed building, peering down into a chasm, indicating that at least one person was still trapped in the ruins.

'Stay away, if you please!' a policeman called out to him, confirming his worst fears.

'I'm looking for Doctor Roberts!' Leon shouted back, taking no notice of him. 'Is he here? I need a word with him, urgently!'

'He's here but he's in no position to indulge in small talk,' the policeman said grimly. 'We've a young mother and child trapped beneath this little lot. The kiddie's hurt badly and Roberts is giving what aid he can.'

'I still need to speak to him!' Leon's heart, already slamming after his long run, began to slam even faster. Roberts wasn't going to be able to leave until the woman and child had been extricated and taken to hospital. It was a task that could take minutes . . . or hours. He was going to have to get the name and address of a midwife off Roberts or, failing that, he was going to have to get Kate to the nearest hospital.

'One of Doctor Roberts' patients is in labour,' he said tersely. 'It's her first baby.'

The policeman snorted, not unsympathetically. 'Women! I've never known one yet that had a proper sense of timing. You'd best ask Roberts what he wants you to do. Only don't offer my services. Things are bad enough as it is without my turning my hand to mid-wifery!' With a nod of his head he indicated the group of rescue-workers squatting high on the rubble.

'Careful, mate!' one of the men shouted as Leon began to make his way carefully towards them. 'They're trapped in what was the kitchen. The nipper was playing house apparently and her mum had come to tell her she shouldn't be playing in a bombed-out building when the whole ruddy lot went.' He eyed Leon's navy cable-knitted sweater short-sightedly. 'Are you fire-service or ambulance?'

'Neither,' Leon said, treading very, very carefully in order not to cause a fresh tumble of rubble and make a dire situation catastrophic, 'But I need an urgent word with Doctor Roberts.'

'You'll have to shout your urgent word,' an Air Raid Warden who had been listening to the conversation, said tersely. 'We've lowered Roberts into the kitchen and he's giving first aid to the kiddie. She's trapped,' he added unnecessarily as Leon clambered to his side, 'and we aren't going to be able to get her out till this little lot,' he indicated the devastation around them with a jerk of his thumb, 'is carted away.'

Beneath a criss-cross of shattered wooden beams Leon looked down through what had once been the first floor of the house and into a chaotic shambles of fallen masonry and wrenched-off doors. A pair of trouser legs were visible, their owner obviously stretched out full length, belly down.

'The kid's pinned under the table,' the Air Raid Warden said helpfully. 'Her mother's with her and that table is all that's keeping an avalanche of bricks and mortar from tumbling down on top of them, and on Roberts as well.'

Leon inhaled a lungful of dust-laden air. '*Can you hear me, Doctor Roberts?*' he shouted into the pit. '*My name is Leon Emmerson. I'm Kate Voigt's lodger. Her baby's on the way and her pains are coming quick and heavy.*'

The trousered legs moved slightly and then a muffled voice shouted back, 'She'll be all right for hours yet . . . the minute I'm out from under this little lot I'll be right with her!'

'*She's not all right!*' Leon shouted back, wondering how, with no previous experience of childbirth he could be so utterly sure, '*Have you the address of a midwife I could call? Or another doctor?*'

The reply was so muffled, Leon could barely hear it. 'It's a first baby! You're panicking unnecessarily! Now get the hell out of here! All this shouting could bring whatever's still standing down on top of us!'

'He's right,' the Air Raid Warden said grimly. 'Vibrations are funny things. Sometimes it only takes a whisper to bring hundreds of tons crashing down.'

Leon swore. From the minute he had seen the pulverized building he had known there wasn't a hope in hell of his returning to Magnolia Square with Doctor Roberts in tow. Somehow he would have to get Kate to hospital.

He made his way carefully past the human chain passing bricks from hand to hand. Unless more efficient help arrived it would be a long time before the entombed mother and child would be free and even when they were free he doubted if Doctor Roberts would be in any condition to bring a child into the world. He would very likely be in need of medical treatment himself.

He slipped beneath the cordon that had been erected around the collapsed house and broke once again into a run. He had to get Kate to hospital. If Harriet Godfrey had been home it wouldn't have been the slightest problem. Harriet could have run the two of them to hospital in her ambulance. But Harriet wasn't at home. He pounded up to the top of Point Hill Road. Who else in Magnolia Square had transport? Albert Jennings had a hearse, but it was always full to the gunnels with either full crates of fruit and vegetables, or empty crates.

Beneath his running feet paving-stones gave way to grass. He would have to telephone for an ambulance and he didn't know anyone in Magnolia Square who was on the telephone. The ARP post. Relief surged through him. He would be able to summon an ambulance from the ARP post. First, though, he had to get back to the house. He needed to reassure Kate. He sprinted as fast as he was able across the road edging the Heath. And he needed to reassure himself that Kate hadn't fallen when getting in or out of the bath; that she hadn't hurt herself or, in falling, hurt the baby.

The second he was in the house he heard her groan. It wasn't the groan of someone weary or in discomfort. It was the deep, deep groan of someone rapidly slipping to the point where dignified containment of pain was impossible.

His stomach lurched. 'Kate!' he shouted as Hector stormed towards him. 'I'm back. *Kate!*'

With an agitated Hector at his heels he tore up the stairs, his hands clammy with sweat on the bannister rail. His first thought was that she had fallen getting in or getting out of the bath. Dear God in heaven, why had he allowed her to take a bath when there was no-one in the house to help her if she got into difficulties? He should have run down to the Lomax's and seen if Mavis was in. Christ! He should have dragged someone in off the street if necessary!

'Leon!' Her voice was a gasp and it was coming from the bedroom, not the bathroom.

Without slowing momentum he grasped hold of the knob on her bedroom door and pushed it open, hurtling into the room, dreading what he might see.

She was on the bed, lying flat, her hands above her head gripping tight onto the brass bars of the bed-head.

'Leon!' The relief in her eyes was vast. It vanished the instant her eyes went past him to the empty doorway. 'Where's Doctor Roberts?' she asked hoarsely. 'The baby is coming, Leon! *Where's Doctor Roberts?*'

He crossed the room towards her in swift strides,

aware of several things simultaneously. She had obviously succeeded in having a bath. Her dark-blue maternity dress was nowhere to be seen. Instead she was wearing a white cotton nightdress, high at the throat, the long sleeves demurely ruffled at the wrist. The wicker shopping-basket containing all that was necessary for the birth was on the floor near the bed.

On her dressing-table was a pile of baby things. A tiny wrap-around vest; a winceyette nightie; a soft, hand-knitted matinee-coat; bootees; muslin inner napkins and terry napkins; a shawl. And when she said the baby was coming, she wasn't exaggerating. He could tell from the barely suppressed hysteria in her voice that she was *in extremis*. If her fear got the upper hand now, it would be almost impossible for him to help her. He needed her co-operation. He needed her to help him bring her baby into the world.

He said in a voice of quiet calm, a calm he was very far from feeling, 'Doctor Roberts is tending an emergency. An injured child. He'll be with us just as soon as he can.'

'*But I can't hold back the baby, Leon!*' Her voice, usually so soft and husky, was hoarse. '*The pains have changed! I'm having to push!*'

As if to prove the truth of her words her fingers tightened on the bars of the brass bed-head, her back arching off the mattress in a spasm of agony.

Any last doubts he might have had about the possibility of leaving her for the length of time it would take him to reach the ARP post and phone for an ambulance, vanished. He was going to have to deliver the baby himself and he was going to have to break the news to her the minute her violently strong contraction was over.

It lasted a full sixty seconds and it was the longest sixty seconds of his life. When it was over her face was bathed in sweat and her eyes were dazed. Comfortingly he took hold of her hand and squeezed it tightly. 'Listen to me, Kate,' he said thickly. 'Listen to me very carefully.

There isn't time to get you to a hospital or to get anyone here to see to you. I'm going to have to look after you, do you understand?'

She nodded, her fingers tightening on his. 'Yes . . . there's another pushing pain coming, Leon! There's hardly any time between them now . . .'

She stopped speaking abruptly, her nails digging into his hand till he thought she would draw blood, her eyes closing as she battled with the pain; battled for consciousness and self-control.

The second it began to ebb he said urgently, 'I'm going to go in the bathroom to scrub my hands. And I'm going to take Hector with me and leave him in there. Having a dog in a room where a baby is being born can't be hygienic.'

She nodded, releasing her hold of him, drawing deep, panting breaths. It was going to be all right. Leon would make sure everything was all right. As long as Leon was with her she could cope. And soon her baby would be born. Soon Toby's child would be kicking and crying and hungry in her arms.

She heard the gush of the hot water geyser and as another overriding pushing pain contorted her body, she drew her knees up, her feet splayed wide and planted firmly on the mattress. In this position she could push easier. In this position she could hook her hands under her thighs and work with the pains convulsing her. It wasn't ladylike and it wasn't modest but she was beyond such considerations. She was beyond caring about anything but pushing her child from her womb.

She never even heard Leon re-enter the bedroom. One minute she was bearing down, panting with agony and effort, the next Leon was saying with tender reassurance, 'You're doing fine, Kate. There was a glimpse of the baby's head at the height of the last contraction. Another couple of pains and it will be over.'

There had been a moment when he had re-entered the room and seen her on the bed, her nightdress up around her knees, her hands hooked under her sweat-sheened thighs, her knees raised, when his courage had nearly failed him. The moment had been occasioned only by his concern for her feelings; for his concern for her modesty. It vanished the second he realized she was beyond any such considerations.

As she grasped that he was with her she said, a sob of need in her voice, 'Leon? Oh thank God you're here, Leon! The minute the baby's head appears make sure it can breath. Make sure its mouth and nose are clear . . .'

She broke off with a ragged cry. This time her contraction brought the baby's head to the mouth of her vagina. It remained there just long enough for her to summon her last reserves of strength and just long enough for Leon to spread his hands out ready to ease and support the baby's head when the next contraction came.

Though only the crown of the baby's head was visible Leon could see the one thing that mattered most. A pulse beating beneath a matt of dark-gold, sticky hair. The baby was alive. His lips moved in silent prayer. Let it stay alive. Let there be nothing wrong with it. Please God let it cry the minute it was born.

Kate gave a cry that was only a fraction from being a scream and then, so suddenly that it took his breath away, the dark-gold head burst from her body, face-down and mewling.

He could hear Kate gasping over and over again, '*Oh God! Oh God! Oh dear God!*' and then Toby Harvey's child slithered, streaked with mucus and blood, into his large, capable, welcoming hands.

It was a boy. Never, ever, had he felt such turbulent emotion; never, ever, had he felt such a deep need to protect and to cherish. 'It's a boy, Kate,' he said unsteadily, barely trusting himself to speak. 'It's a boy and he's perfect!'

Tears of exhaustion and happiness streamed down

Kate's cheeks. 'Let me see!' she begged, her eyes radiant. 'Oh, please let me see! Shouldn't he be crying louder! Are you sure he's all right? Has he got all his fingers? All his toes? Oh, isn't he *beautiful*, Leon! Isn't he *beautiful?*'

Very gently, with all the love in the world, Leon lifted the slippery little body and laid it on Kate's belly. 'He's magnificent,' he said, knowing the moment was one he would never forget, not even if he lived to be a hundred. 'Absolutely magnificent.'

She reached a hand down to touch the baby's wrinkled, red skin. 'When can I hold him?' she asked longingly. 'When will you be able to cut the cord?'

'When the after-birth comes away,' he said, trying to remember all he had ever heard about umbilical cords. It was precious little.

'You'll have to tell me how to do it,' he said, already deciding that if she didn't know he would leave the cord well alone until Doctor Roberts finally arrived.

'It's easy,' she said with quiet confidence, her attention on the baby, stroking his sticky hair with feather-light strokes. 'You need scissors and string and antiseptic and one of the little pads I've made. I've sterilized the scissors and they're in a pan of cooled boiled water in the bathroom.'

The baby stopped mewling and began to cry, his arms and legs flailing angrily.

'He's hungry,' Leon said with a grin. 'Let me put a towel over him so he doesn't get a chill.'

As he did so she drew in a sharp breath and then said, 'I think the after-birth is on its way. Can you spread some newspaper beneath me, Leon?'

He nodded and as he set about his task she said, awed by everything he had done for her and the manner in which he had done it, 'I don't know how to begin to thank you, Leon. Even Doctor Roberts couldn't have been as calm and reassuring.'

His grin deepened. 'That remark shows just how

much attention you were paying to everything! I felt about as calm as an earthquake!'

She began to giggle and he said in mock rebuke, terrified of allowing her to see how deeply moved he was; how very much he cared, 'Don't giggle. You'll rock your son. And speaking of your son, have you decided yet what you're going to call him?'

'Matthew Toby Leon Carl. Matthew, because it's a name I've always liked. Toby after his father. Leon after yourself. And Carl because Carl is my father's name.'

His throat tightened. 'That's quite a handful for such a little person,' he said, not allowing his eyes to meet hers for fear of the emotions he might reveal.

'He'll grow into them.' Her husky voice was laden with love and then she sucked in her breath sharply again. 'It's the after-birth,' she said as alarm flared in his eyes. 'It's coming!'

'Then push,' he said, anxiety seizing hold of him. Dear God, it wasn't over yet. She might begin to haemorrhage and then what would he do?

She didn't haemorrhage. She lay back against the pillows he had eased beneath her head and shoulders, feasting her eyes on the warmly-covered mound that was her son, touching the top of his head ever so gently with her fingertips as Leon speedily and efficiently dealt with the after-birth and then tied off the cord and cut it.

'It's a pity the Navy doesn't have a call for midwives,' she said, watching him with tender amusement. 'You'd make a first-class midwife.'

He dropped the scissors and string into the wicker shopping basket and grinned back at her. 'Maybe I'll take it up if I ever return to civvy street. Your son is badly in need of a bath. Do you have a bowl handy?'

'In the bathroom.'

'I'll bring it in here and bath him in here,' he said, knowing how loath she would be to have Matthew taken from her sight even for a few minutes and more nervous than he cared to admit as to how to go about bathing a tiny, slippery, crying baby. He needed her to be able to tell him what to do. His heart seemed to lurch within his chest. He needed her, period. He needed her to bring warmth and laughter into his life. He needed her in order to feel whole and happy. He needed her because he loved her.

Abruptly he turned away from the bed and walked out of the room and across the landing to the bathroom. Hector, tired of waiting for the attention due him, had fallen asleep. As he stepped over the dog he wondered if there was a hope in hell of his ever achieving with Kate the kind of relationship he longed for.

She had left an enamel washing basin out in readiness and as he began to half fill it, first with cold water and then with warm, his heart seemed to physically hurt. Even allowing himself to speculate on such a possibility was crass stupidity. Middle-class girls like Kate didn't marry half-caste sailors. He turned off the geyser. That wasn't a hundred per cent true. His mother had married his father and despite the many difficulties they must have encountered it had been a triumphantly happy marriage.

He tested the temperature of the water in the enamel bowl and added a little more cold water, deep in thought. His parents had married nearly thirty years ago when a black face in Britain was a rare sight. It was a rare sight no longer, at least not in and around ports such as London and Cardiff and Portsmouth.

He stared down into the water like a seer. When the war was over he doubted if black faces would be a rare sight anywhere in Britain. With luck America would eventually come into the war and black GIs would become a common sight. And after the war, when Britain finally floored Nazi Germany, a massive influx of labour would be needed to rebuild the country and set it on its feet again and it would only be commonsense if the bulk of that labour came from Britain's Empire, from countries such as Jamaica and Trinidad and Barbados.

If and when such a situation arose, marriages such as his parents' marriage would be anomalies no longer. The widely held belief that a girl was scraping the bottom of the barrel if she went out with someone racially different would have to be drastically revised. He remembered Mrs Roberts' reaction earlier in the day when she had suspected he might be the father of Kate's baby and his jawline hardened. Where the Mrs Robertses of the world were concerned, such a change of attitude couldn't come a minute too soon.

He turned away from the bath, the bowl of water in his hands, and stepped carefully once more over Hector. He was worrying over a problem that, where he and Kate were concerned, was really no problem at all. If Kate were in love with him she wouldn't allow any gibes or taunts to discomfit her; she would simply dismiss them as being beneath contempt. It wasn't his West Indian blood that was a bar to their friendship developing into a love affair; it was the love she still felt for Toby Harvey. A love her son's birth had doubtless fiercely reinforced.

Kate, too, was thinking of Toby. As Leon came back into the bedroom with the bowl of warm water and placed it on the convenient height of her dressing-table, she thought of how proud he would have been of his son. Tears stung her eyes, tears far different to the tears of joy and exhaustion still drying on her cheeks.

'Come on, little fella,' Leon said, turning towards the bed and gently lifting Matthew Toby Leon Carl into his arms. 'Time for your first bath . . . and do you need it!'

'The water isn't too hot, is it?' she asked anxiously. 'Have you tested it by dipping your elbow into it?'

'As if I've been doing it all my life,' he said, removing the towel that had been serving as Matthew's temporary shawl. 'Now what do I do? Just lay him in the water?'

She pushed herself up against her pillows in order to supervise the operation. 'You'll have to keep a firm but gentle hold of him. Can you support his head and shoulders with one hand and soap and rinse him with the other?'

'I can try and I could do it a lot easier if he'd stop kicking.'

'He's a very good kicker.' Her voice was thick with amusement again. 'He used to keep me awake with his kicking night after night.'

With intense concentration and with more care than he could remember taking over anything, Leon slid Matthew into the gently warm water. The instant he did so Matthew screwed his eyes up tight and opened his mouth wide, crying lustily.

'He's all right,' Kate said as she saw the appalled look on Leon's face. 'Soap him all over as quickly as possible, especially between his fingers and toes and all his little creases. Then, when you've rinsed him, wrap him in his towel and wash his hair.'

'How?' Leon asked, terrified Matthew was going to slip from his grasp; terrified that he was in some way hurting him.

'Don't worry. I'll tell you. Try to keep the bandage around his tummy-button from becoming too wet, won't you?'

Leon tried. He also tried not to get soap into Matthew's eyes, not to lose hold of him, not to become too disconcerted by his kicking and crying. It was worse than trying to sail a destroyer single-handed.

'Now pat him dry,' Kate said, as serene as if he was making a competent job of his task. 'Then wrap the towel firmly around him so that he feels secure and tuck him under your arm as you would a newspaper only with your hand supporting his neck and head. Then hold him over the bowl. That way you can easily wash his hair with your free hand.'

To his amazement he found she was right. And to his relief, Matthew's sobs subsided into intermittent mewls of protest.

'How do you know all this?' he asked as he scooped up water and let it trickle through Matthew's sudsed hair.

'I watched Carrie bathing Rose when she was new-born and sometimes Carrie allowed me to bathe Rose myself.'

Watching Leon as he handled her son with infinite care she felt a bond of closeness to him that she had never experienced before. Not with anyone. Not even with Toby. Her heart almost ceased to beat. Where on earth had that last thought come from? It certainly wasn't true. It couldn't be.

She waited for a sense of affirmation that it wasn't true. None came. Instead, the certainty that she had never been as close to anyone as she now was to Leon, persisted.

She drew in a deep, steadying breath. What in the world was the matter with her? She had been utterly, hopelessly and irrevocably in love with Toby. They had been as close as it was possible for two people to be. Of *course* she had been closer to Toby than she was to Leon. Hadn't she?

No, an inner voice said to her implacably. *Although you loved Toby, and he loved you, you never* lived *with Toby. You never spent time with him, day in and day out as you have over the last couple of months with Leon. You didn't know Toby as you know Leon.*

It was a breathtaking realization. And it begged a question of dizzying enormity. If she felt closer to Leon than she had to Toby, was she in love with Leon? And did she no longer love Toby?

The answer to her second question came instantly. Of course she still loved Toby. She would always love him. He had become a part of her and he would remain a part of her until the day she died. Until a split second ago she had believed that loving Toby precluded her from ever falling in love with anyone else, ever again. Now, in a flash of stunning maturity, she knew that

311

love didn't operate like that. No matter how deeply she might love in the future, her love for Toby would never be diminished. Love wasn't finite. Though she loved Matthew Toby Leon Carl with all her heart it didn't mean she would never love a second child, or a third or a fourth, just as wholeheartedly. And if the day ever came when she had more children, her love for Matthew Toby Leon Carl wouldn't be diminished one iota.

As she watched Leon gently but awkwardly manoeuvering Matthew's chubby little arms into the arm-holes of the tie-around vest she felt so much gratitude welling up inside her that she thought she would burst with it. He had brought her child into the world and he had done so in a manner that hadn't caused her the slightest pang of embarrassment. He never had embarrassed her, or made her feel sexually uncomfortable. Except once. And that had not been intentional.

He had been shaving in the bathroom and she had accidentally walked in on him. He had been facing the mirror, his back towards her, and had been wearing only trousers. The deep breadth of his dusky-toned chest would have done credit to a middle-weight boxer and there had been dimples in his strongly muscled shoulders. Though she had apologized and left the bathroom immediately it had been a sight she had never forgotten. And she had never forgotten it because it had been so pleasing.

Even at the time she had found the incident deeply disconcerting, though until now she had never admitted to herself *why* it had been so disconcerting. Now, however, she knew. Now, watching him as, with a look of intense concentration on his face, he struggled to figure out the best way of fitting her crying and kicking son into a muslin nappy, she knew it had been because he had aroused feelings in her she had thought suppressed forever.

'Come on, little fella,' he said comfortingly as

Matthew's cries turned to hiccupping sobs of genuine distress. 'Let me just wrap this shawl around you and then you can go to your Ma.'

'Leon . . .' Tentatively, she stretched a hand out towards him.

He turned towards her, his dark, laughter-lined face splitting in a wide, easy smile. 'I'm sorry it's taken me so long, Kate. I never realized baby clothes were fastened with so many ribbons before.'

'Leon . . .' her heart had begun to drum in loud, throbbing strokes. He had never made the slightest sexual overture to her. What if he hadn't done so not out of respect for her but because he wasn't remotely sexually attracted to her? What if, by saying what was in her heart, she destroyed a friendship that had become central to her very being. 'Leon . . .' she said again, knowing that such a moment, as he lifted her shawl-wrapped son from the bed and turned towards her with him, would never come again, 'Leon . . . I . . .'

'*Kate!*' a female voice shouted in stark anxiety from the foot of the stairs. '*Kate! Are you in? Are you all right? Is that a baby crying?*'

Leon had turned towards her, about to lay Matthew in her arms. Now he hesitated and Kate could see a reflection of her own crushing disappointment in his amber-brown eyes. The wonderful sense of closeness and privacy that had been generated between them was about to be shattered. Panic suffused her. Once it was shattered she knew she might never again have the courage to put all that was in her heart into words.

'Leon . . .' she said again with desperate urgency. 'Leon I . . .'

It was too late. Harriet was already hurrying in great concern up the stairs saying, 'It *is* a baby! Katherine! For the love of God, is anyone with you? *Are you all right?*'

A second later she stood in the bedroom doorway

staring around in vain for a doctor or midwife her eyes coming back in stupified disbelief to Leon standing by the side of the bed, his jersey sleeves pushed up to his elbows, Kate's newborn son lying snugly in the crook of his arm.

Chapter Seventeen

Stray wisps of hair escaped from the normally immaculately tidy bun in the nape of Harriet's neck as she said in a stunned voice, 'Where is Doctor Roberts? Has he left already? Why . . .'

'He hasn't been here,' Kate said, enjoying the moment hugely despite her exhaustion and her longing to put her son to her breast. 'Leon went for him when I began labour but there's been a nasty accident in Point Hill Road and Doctor Roberts was needed there and couldn't leave.'

As she was talking Leon lowered Matthew into her arms. For a brief precious moment their eyes met and Kate's enjoyment at disconcerting Harriet so profoundly vanished to be replaced by a far deeper emotion. This was the moment when, if they had been alone, she could have told Leon everything that was in her heart. Her throat tightened and unshed tears glittered on her eyelashes as she gently cradled her child. It was a moment she wanted to share with Leon, and Leon alone; a moment so precious she knew it would never come again.

'Then who delivered the baby?' Harriet demanded hoarsely, so fearful of the answer that she had to hold on to the doorjamb for support.

'I did,' Leon was barely able to keep his massive disappointment from showing in his voice. Why had Harriet Godfrey chosen this moment of all moments to call on Kate? Why couldn't he and Kate and Matthew have been left alone for just a little longer? There was so much he wanted to say to her and it would have been so easy to say it now.

He wanted to tell her that he loved her. He wanted to tell her that even if he'd been Matthew's father it would be impossible for him to feel any closer a bond to Matthew. He had delivered, bathed and tended him and the wonderment and tenderness that had filled his heart as he had done so was one that had rocked him to the very centre of his being. He wanted to cherish and protect Matthew not only now, but through all the years of his childhood. And he wanted to cherish and protect Kate as long as he had breath in his body.

In the doorway of the room Harriet Godfrey braced herself. It was no use being overcome with shock. There was a war on and Kate's naval lodger had acted with commendable practicality. She took in a deep breath, smoothed the palms of her hands down the rough tweed of her sensible gored skirt and stepped towards the bed decisively.

'I'll take over now, Mr Emmerson,' she said, as both Kate and Leon had known she would. 'I think the best thing for you to do would be to contact Millie Bready, the local midwife, and ask her if she will make a visit as soon as possible. Doctor Roberts doesn't make as much use of her as other local doctors, preferring to deliver his patients' babies himself, but in the present circumstances I'm certain he would want us to contact her. She lives at number ninety-four St John's Park.'

Leon was well aware that it was sensible advice but he wished that Harriet had volunteered to run the necessary errand herself, leaving him alone for a little longer with Kate and Matthew.

'And I would very much appreciate it if you could get a message to Ellen Pierce,' Harriet added as she adjusted Matthew's shawl, allowing Kate to put him to her breast with more ease. 'Between Ellen and myself we should be able to look after Kate until she's on her feet again. And with luck Ellen will be able to find someone to look after her animals for a few days and not have to bring them with her.'

316

Leon pulled down the still damp sleeves of his jersey. He had to be aboard ship within a few short hours and Ellen Pierce would very likely have complicated arrangements to make before she could return with him to Magnolia Square. Panic was something alien to his nature but he felt something akin to it as he realized how very little time there was before he would have to say goodbye to Kate.

Reading his thoughts, sharing his sense of despair at the rapidly diminishing amount of time left to them, Kate lifted her eyes from the downy blond head at her breast, her eyes meeting his.

'There's no need to wait for Ellen if she has arrangements to make,' she said, wondering how long it would take him to go first to the midwife's and then to the far side of Greenwich; wondering when he would have to leave to report to his ship.

'Returning without Ellen wouldn't be very gallant,' Harriet said forthrightly, busily putting scissors and cord and lint and bandages back into the wicker shopping-basket. 'If I bring a bowl of warm water and soap in from the bathroom do you think you can manage to wash with it, Katherine? Or would you prefer to wait for Millie?'

'I think I can manage to wash myself,' Kate said, her voice thick with defeat, knowing that there was now not even the faintest chance of recapturing the joyous intimacy she and Leon had shared such a short while earlier.

'Then I'll go and fill a bowl with warm water.' She turned her attention to Leon saying briskly, 'There's no time to waste, Mr Emmerson. Millie Bready may very well be attending another confinement and may take some tracking down. And just in case Doctor Roberts doesn't come straight here after leaving Point Hill Road, but returns to his surgery, a message should be left for him at the surgery informing him that Katherine's baby has been born.'

Well aware that if he delayed for even a second longer Harriet Godfrey would think of yet another task for him to accomplish en route to Greenwich, Leon gave one last look towards Kate and left the room, frustration raging within him.

Millie Bready was a large, cheery, heavy-bosomed lady with a face as round as a currant-bun. 'Dear Lord,' she said, when Leon explained the situation to her as briefly as possible, 'so you delivered the baby, did you?' She eyed his naval jersey, a twinkle in her eyes. 'It's come to something when sailors are delivering babies as well as begetting them! I hope you didn't tie the umbilical cord in a reef knot, young man!'

Mrs Roberts was too concerned about her husband's welfare to waste her breath being offensive. 'I'll pass the message on,' she said brusquely, 'when I see him.'

She shut the door in his face and a little woman with curlers in her hair, scouring the surgery steps, said, 'She's got a lot on 'er mind. There's been a right to-do dahn Point Hill Road. A woman an' a kiddie trapped in a collapsed building. The doctor' 'ad 'imself lowered dahn to 'em 'ours ago an' 'e's still with 'em. I 'ope e's all right. 'e's a nice man but 'e's a lot to put up with, if you catch my meanin'.'

'The baby's here? Already?' Ellen Pierce ushered him into her pin-neat sitting-room. 'Of course I'll come, but I'll have to bring Macbeth and Hotspur and Coriolanus with me. My neighbour will put food out for the cats but the dogs can't possibly look after themselves. Do you think Harriet will mind?

Leon was certain that Harriet Godfrey would mind but he had no intention of saying so. He wanted to get back to Magnolia Square as speedily as possible, not spend precious time finding temporary dog-sitters for Ellen Pierce's little band of strays.

'Why the Shakespearean names?' he asked as he followed her into the kitchen.

'Because I thought they deserved *proper* names,' Ellen said as three dogs of assorted sizes leapt up from the comfy, blanket-lined baskets they had been snoozing in, joyfully expectant of a walk, 'not silly names such as Rover and Patch and Fido.'

A black Scottie threw itself yappingly at Leon's legs and as he bent down and tickled it under its chin he said, 'I presume this is Macbeth?'

'That's very perceptive of you, Mr Emmerson,' Ellen said, wondering why it was she always felt so comfortable in Leon Emmerson's company. 'And though Hotspur is a mongrel he's a mongrel with a lot of Welsh terrier in him. And Coriolanus is . . . well . . . shall we say a little *combative?*'

Coriolanus didn't look very combative to Leon. Large and ungainly and betraying no sign of even a particle of pedigree, he lolloped over and, with one ear erect and the other flopping over, he nuzzled lovingly against Ellen Pierce's lisle-stockinged legs.

'They were all abandoned and terrified when I took them in,' Ellen said, threading stout lengths of garden twine through their collars to serve as leads. 'I found Macbeth running loose during the dreadful night of the raid on the City. Hotspur was trapped in a bombed house for two days before firemen found him with his dead owners. It was my local Air Raid Warden who brought Coriolanus to me. The poor animal had been a guard-dog in a river-front factory and been left there all alone during weeks and weeks of bombing raids. How he wasn't blasted or burnt to death I'll never know.'

As they walked through Greenwich and then up the hill that ran past Harvey's and led to the Heath, Ellen continued to talk about her dogs. Leon didn't try to turn the conversation to other subjects. He knew that behind her rather forbidding exterior was a shy woman who, until Kate had entered her life and introduced her to

Harriet Godfrey, had enjoyed few close friendships. The dogs she had taken into her home had obviously filled an emotional void in her life and provided her with the subject matter to chat with ease to a near stranger.

Though he made encouraging remarks every now and then his thoughts were far from the dogs padding at his heels. Kate. Even from the very first she had been far more than a landlady. He remembered how, soaked with rain and heavily pregnant, she had defiantly entered The Swan and, in front of neighbours already hostile to her, had offered him a room.

Even if she hadn't already been ostracized by the majority of the other inhabitants of Magnolia Square, she would have been ostracized after that action. As Charlie had said to him, not unkindly, 'Darkies don't usually room in Black'eath. People 'spect 'em to room in Bermondsey or Deptford. 'aving a darky in Magnolia Square takes a bit o' gettin' used to.'

Though Charlie had quickly got used to it and was amiably friendly, the majority of his neighbours still showed no signs of getting used to it and Leon could well imagine their reaction if he and Kate were to marry.

He was holding Coriolanus on his makeshift lead with one hand and he dug his free hand deep into his trouser pocket. If that day ever dawned he wouldn't give a damn what anyone thought.

'And does the baby have a name?' Ellen asked him as they crossed the Heath beneath the shadow of the elephant-like silver barrage balloons. 'Is she going to name him after her father?'

When they arrived back at the house Harriet Godfrey took one look at the dogs crowding around their heels and winced.

'Really, Ellen! Couldn't you have found someone to look after them for a few days? It's difficult enough having Hector in the house. No-one told me he was in the bathroom and he nearly knocked me off my feet when I went in there to fill a bowl with warm water.'

'There may not be room for them here, with Hector and a new baby, but there's plenty of room in your house and rear garden,' Ellen said, refusing to allow her friend to intimidate her. 'They'll stay in the kitchen, of course, as they do when they are at home.'

Harriet Godfrey blanched. Leon grinned. He had enormous respect for Kate's elderly friend but she could be annoyingly high-handed and it made a refreshing change to see someone getting the better of her.

'Then take them round there now,' Harriet said crossly. 'And take them in the back way. I don't want paw-prints all over my hall carpet. It was my mother's and it's Turkish.'

Leon had begun to walk towards the bottom of the stairs and she turned towards him, saying, 'The midwife is with Katherine at the moment, Mr Emmerson. Could you bring me some coal in, or do you have to leave now for your ship?'

'I'll bring some coal in,' Leon said tightly, knowing that she wasn't being intentionally cutting; knowing that it had never occurred to her that anything other than a formal landlady/lodger relationship existed between himself and Kate and that it certainly hadn't occurred to her that they might want time alone together before he left for his ship.

He walked tensely past the bottom of the stairs and his packed kit-bag and through the kitchen into the back garden, yanking the door of the coal bunker open with angry frustration. How on earth was he going to get any private time with Kate now? Harriet and Ellen certainly wouldn't be leaving the house before he had to report to his ship and it wasn't beyond the realms of possibility that Millie Bready wouldn't be leaving it either.

He shovelled a precious amount of Kate's small stock of coal into a bucket. For all he knew, Kate was as oblivious as Harriet Godfrey of his need to talk with her in private. He tipped a second shovelful of coal into the bucket. If she was, then speaking to her would very likely jeopardize their entire relationship for once she knew his feelings for her were not platonic, but deeply sexual, she could hardly invite him to return as a lodger when he next had leave.

He dropped the shovel to the ground and picked up the bucket. His tending her while she had been giving birth had certainly forged a bond between them but was it, on her part, merely a bond of gratitude? If Harriet Godfrey hadn't arrived when she had, he would have known. A pulse began to beat at the corner of his jawline. Harriet had not only arrived, she showed no intention of leaving. And he had to leave first thing in the morning, probably before Kate even awoke.

'She's sleeping,' Ellen said to him when he announced his attention of saying his goodbyes. 'Harriet's pacing the bedroom floor with Matthew in her arms trying to encourage him to sleep as well. I'll tell them both you said goodbye.'

Leon stared past her and up the stairs. If he barged up there, waking Kate in order to say goodbye to her, they would only have an outraged Harriet as an audience. The thought chilled him. It was better to leave without any goodbyes, secure in the knowledge that she wanted him to return; that she had promised to keep his room ready for him.

He swung his kit-bag on his shoulder. All his life he had looked forward to the moment when leave came to an end and real life, life at sea, began. But that had been when his leaves had been spent in cheerless lodgings; before Kate; before he had been given a taste of what a home could be like.

'Bye Ellen,' he said, surprising and pleasing her by giving her an affectionate kiss on the cheek. 'Take care.'

'I will,' Ellen said, her plain face flushing rosily. 'Goodbye, God bless.'

He turned and walked out of the house, still limping

slightly. One day, God willing, he would be back. One day he might be able to truly call Magnolia Square his home.

'He left just before eight o'clock,' Ellen said, settling a late breakfast tray down on the bed. 'He asked me to pass on his goodbyes to yourself and Harriet. There's been a message from Doctor Roberts. He's calling round sometime this morning and . . .'

Kate was no longer listening to her. He'd gone. Although she had told him she would keep his room ready for him she had no way of knowing if he would ever return; no way of knowing if he would even write to her. Beneath the bedcovers her fingers curled tightly into her palms. She was going to miss him. She was going to miss him so much she didn't know how she was going to bear it.

'. . . poor Doctor Roberts had a truly terrible time yesterday,' Ellen said, busily collecting talcum powder and vaseline and soap and towels ready for Matthew's morning bath. 'Apparently it was late evening before the rescue services managed to free the little girl and Doctor Roberts stayed with her, comforting her, right until the moment Albert Jennings lifted her clear of the wreckage.'

'What about her mother?' Kate asked, forcing her thoughts away from Leon until she had the privacy to indulge them, certain that when she did so she would give way to tears.

Ellen hesitated. She hadn't realized that Kate knew so much about the situation in Point Hill Road and hadn't intended telling her of the fate of the little girl's mother. Chiding herself for her carelessness she said regretfully, 'I'm afraid she died, Kate.'

'So Albert and Miriam 'ave taken the kiddie in,' Charlie said to her, his bulk perched incongruously on her dressing-table stool. 'With 'er mum dead the poor little sod didn't 'ave any family, 'er dad died fighting the

Eye-ties and her gran and grandad lived next door to New Cross tram depot and copped it when the depot received a direct 'it last Christmas.'

'She does nowt but cry,' her second visitor said, enlarging on the subject, 'and she goes to school in Lewisham. It's gran that's goin' to 'ave to take 'er to school an' she says when Beryl starts school at Easter she'll 'ave to go to Lewisham as well 'cos she 'ain't trooping to two flippin' schools every day.'

Having relieved himself of the duty of a visitor by imparting up-to-the-minute gossip Billy turned his attention to the present he had brought for the baby. 'It's liquorice-water,' he said, referring to the grubby bottle he had placed on Kate's dressing-table. 'Me an' Beryl made it ourselves. There's two sticks of liquorice in it an' it 'ain't 'alf strong.' He eyed the bottle, obviously reluctant to part with it. 'Do yer think it might be a bit too strong for the baby?' he asked hopefully. 'Me an' Beryl could allus make another one for when 'e's older.'

Kate hid a smile with difficulty, 'Matthew *is* a little young for liquorice-water,' she said, enjoying Billy's expression of vast relief. 'Would you mind very much taking this one back and making another one for him when he's a little older?'

'Nah,' Billy said, trying to sound regretful and failing utterly. 'Liquorice-water doesn't save so me an' Beryl'll just 'ave to drink this ourselves. It don't 'alf make your teeth go black,' he added confidingly, 'though that doesn't matter for babies, does it, 'cos they don't 'ave any!'

'Miss Helliwell gave me a card to give to you,' Harriet said a day or two later, returning from a shopping trip that had entailed a thirty minute queue for a loaf of fresh bread and an hour long queue for a dubious piece of brisket. She put her basket down on Kate's kitchen table.

'I think she'd like to come and see the baby but is a bit unsure as to whether she would be welcome.'

Kate had long since forgiven Miss Helliwell for being one of the bystanders when her father had been escorted away to his internment camp. 'I'd like to see her,' she said, continuing with her task of lifting nappies from the pail in which they had been put to soak and dropping them into a wash-tub of steaming soapy water. 'Did you know that she and Leon are friends? They have been ever since he rescued Faust from the jaws of a bull-terrier.'

Harriet Godfrey had not known. In twin-set, tweed suit, brogues and pearls she negotiated a way between the wash-tub and the mangle in order to reach the rocking-chair. 'There are far too many dogs in Magnolia Square,' she said grimly, sitting down with relief. 'And their numbers haven't been helped by Ellen's strays adding to them. Coriolanus leapt the garden fence and was on the loose for the whole of yesterday afternoon. It was Charlie who brought him back.'

Kate wiped her hands dry on a towel and opened Miss Helliwell's card. It was homemade and gaudily decorated with moons and stars and astrological symbols.

'I also managed to get some fruit at the Jennings' market stall,' Harriet continued, 'Caroline was there, filling in time before her bus shift started. I told her you had had the baby.'

Kate stood very still, her stomach muscles tightening. 'What did Carrie say?' she asked at last as Harriet proffered no further information.

Harriet, well aware of the estrangement between Kate and Carrie and having a good idea as to its cause, said, 'She didn't say very much because Christina Frank was with her. She did ask me to give you her best wishes though.'

Kate's face whitened. Best wishes. Even near strangers offered best wishes when a baby was born. She remembered her own euphoria when Rose had been born; how she had been round at Carrie's house the instant she heard the news; how she and Carrie had kissed and hugged and shared the joy of Rose's birth.

Harriet saw the stricken look on her face and said with unaccustomed gentleness, 'I think Caroline is as unhappy about your broken friendship as you are, Katherine. Perhaps when you first take Matthew out in his pram it would be a good idea to walk down to the Jennings'. Everyone likes to see a newborn baby and babies make it very easy for people who have grown apart to become close again.'

At the beginning of the following week, when Ellen had returned to her home in Greenwich and Harriet had returned to her full-time ambulance-driving duties, Kate laid a warmly dressed Matthew in his pram. She would call on Miss Helliwell and her sister and she would call at Carrie's.

It was a typically cold, blowy March day and there was a hint of rain in the air as, hampered by Hector, she manoeuvred the pram inexpertly down the short flight of stone steps to the front pathway.

She was concentrating so hard on her task that she was oblivious of the chauffeur-driven Bentley parked at the far side of the road, opposite her gate.

With the cumbersome pram safely on the level, she leaned forward and pulled its hood up. Heavy masculine footsteps crossed the road towards her and Hector began to bark. She raised her head, a smile on her face, expecting to see Charlie or perhaps even a mellowed Albert Jennings or Daniel Collins or Mr Nibbs.

'I'd like to see my great-grandchild,' Joss Harvey said unequivocally, the astrakhan collar of his overcoat pulled high against the inclement weather.

She gripped the pram handle tightly, too taken by surprise to make any immediate reply. Why on earth hadn't she realized Joss Harvey would seek her out when his great-grandchild was born? Why hadn't she been expecting this confrontation and been prepared for it?

'Is it a boy or a girl?' Joss asked, ignoring Hector and walking closer to the pram.

'It's a boy.' Reluctantly she put on the pram's brake and leaned forward, lowering the hood in order that he could see his great-grandchild more clearly. 'I've named him Matthew. Matthew Tobias Leon Carl.'

Joss Harvey made a snorting sound, presumably at the un-Englishness of his great-grandson's last two names and the non-inclusion of his own name.

He stood for a long moment staring down at the shawl-wrapped, blanketed baby. 'Is he healthy?' he asked gruffly.

She nodded, tensing herself in case he again brought up the subject of adoption.

He didn't do so. He bent over the pram and with a leather-gloved forefinger pulled the shawl clear of Matthew's face so that he could see him even more clearly. 'You can't keep him in London,' he said at last, still feasting his eyes on him. 'It isn't safe. February may have been a light month for raids but the reprieve won't last much longer. He needs moving with a nanny to Somerset or Dorset. I can make all the necessary arrangements . . .'

'No!' It took all Kate's willpower not to snatch Matthew from the pram and hug him to her breast. 'You're only making that suggestion because you want Matthew for yourself! You want him as a replacement for Toby!'

He straightened up, turning towards her, saying harshly, 'I'm making the suggestion because I don't want my great-grandson blasted to kingdom-come in a Jerry bombing raid! I lost my son to the bastards in 1918. I've lost my grandson to them and I'll be damned to hell before I lose my great-grandson to them!'

The passion and truth in his voice almost undid her. What if in the next air raid Magnolia Square was obliterated just as street after street in the East End and Deptford had been obliterated? What if Matthew died and she survived? How would she be able to live with herself, knowing that her selfishness had kept him in London when he could have been safe in Somerset or Dorset?

'No,' she said again, her voice strangled in her throat. 'Other women are keeping their babies with them in London . . .'

'Not if they've any choice they're not!' Joss said as Hector growled menacingly at him. 'It's about time you started thinking of what Toby would have wanted for his son, and what he would have wanted would be for his son to be safe!'

She released the handbrake on the pram. She couldn't stay and talk to him a second longer. He was so forceful and aggressive that if she did anything might happen.

'I have an appointment,' she lied stiffly. 'Goodbye.'

Joss snorted derisively. 'I don't believe you, young woman. You're frightened of me because I'm telling you home truths you don't want to hear. For as long as the Blitz on London lasts I can give Matthew a safe home. Think about it. And think about what the consequences may be if you come to the wrong decision.'

She pushed the pram past him, down the path and out through the open gateway, consumed by fear and doubt. Joss Harvey *was* Matthew's great-grandfather. He was entitled to visit Matthew and take an interest in his welfare. And remembering how devoted he had been to Toby, his interest was sincere, of that she was sure.

Behind her, Hector was making rushing little darts towards Joss, barking noisily. Kate didn't turn her head. Hector might threaten but he wouldn't bite and eventually Joss Harvey would tire of staring fumingly after her and would return to his chauffeur-driven car.

Knowing that she had a very big decision to make she walked in a turmoil of emotion towards Miss Helliwell's. She was almost there before Hector finally caught up with her. Dimly, behind her, she heard the sound of the Bentley heading out of the Square and down Magnolia Terrace.

'It took you a long time to shoo him away,' she said chidingly as Hector bounded around the pram, eager to be praised. 'What was the matter? Did you know he was family?'

Family. Incongruous as it seemed, where her son was concerned, Joss Harvey *was* family. And he was obviously going to ensure that Matthew grew up knowing it.

'Oh, my dear, isn't he just the most wonderful thing!' Esther Helliwell cooed, sitting in her wheelchair in a room almost completely taken up by a Morrison shelter, holding Matthew in her arms with utmost care.

'He's a treasure, an absolute treasure,' her sister said, her eyes suspiciously bright. 'I must work out his astrological chart straight away. I'm sure it will be auspicious. I can feel in my bones that he's a little chap destined for great things. Perhaps he will be a musician or a poet or even an explorer!'

Later, as Kate was leaving the house, Emily said awkwardly, 'We've missed you calling in, dear. You will call again, won't you? Your lodger kept us in touch with how you were keeping. Such a nice young man. He'll come home safe to you. I've read it in the stars and the stars never lie.'

Once out in the Square again, Kate hugged Miss Helliwell's words to her. Miss Helliwell had been right about so many things in the past. She had forecast Carrie and Danny's marriage and she had quite obviously foreseen Toby's death. That was why, when she had read her palm all those years ago, she had said that great heartache lay in store for her.

She began to push the pram towards Carrie's. Miss Helliwell had also said that after the heartache would come great happiness. Was Leon going to be the cause of that great happiness? With his companionship and sunny, easy-going nature he had already brought more happiness into her life than she had believed possible a few short months ago. Her hands tightened on the pram handle. She missed him terribly and the empty sensation wasn't eased, as yet, by letters. But he would write to her. She knew he would. And when he next had leave in England he would return to Magnolia Square.

'*You're a bloody whore!*' a tortured masculine voice shouted, making her jump nearly out of her skin. '*Bloody Commandoes! They all think they're bloody Errol Flynn!*'

The Lomax's battered front door had burst open and Ted Lomax, in army uniform and with his kit-bag over his shoulder, was striding down the path at a near run, his face contorted by rage and grief.

Kate came to an abrupt halt. If she'd continued walking she would have run into him.

From the open doorway came the sound of near-hysterical sobbing and then Billy shot out of the house, his face pinched and white. '*Dad! Dad! Come back!*' he cried, tearing down the path and into the street. '*Come back, Dad! Please come back!*'

Ted Lomax showed not the slightest sign of coming back. As startled neighbours came out on to their door-steps, Ted stormed into Magnolia Hill, Billy desperately running in his wake.

Kate's eyes flew back to the doorway. There was no sign of Mavis, though her sobs were so loud they could probably have been heard in Lewisham High Street. Beryl was there, though. With her knickers hanging below the hem of her dress, her eyes frightened and bewildered, she was a pathetic little figure and Kate instinctively turned the pram in at the gate and put the brake on.

'*I haven't seen him for nearly a year and he comes home and says he's leaving me!*' Mavis sobbed as Kate walked into the house, holding Beryl's hand. '*And he hit me! Ted! My lovely, gentle Ted! He hit me!*'

She was sitting at the kitchen table, tears pouring down her face, a sodden handkerchief held tightly in one hand.

'*How could he be so stupid?*' she continued between shuddering gasps for breath. '*I've always been friends with Jack. The whole bloody street knows I've always been friends with Jack!*'

Deciding that her best course of action was to make a restorative cup of tea Kate began filling a kettle with water. Carrie had forecast long ago that trouble would come of Mavis's friendship with Jack Robson. As she put the kettle on the gas hob she wondered who in Magnolia Square had been busybody enough to write to Ted informing him of the time Mavis and Jack spent together whenever Jack was home on leave.

'And there's never been anything in it,' Mavis continued, her sobs subsiding, the ring of truth naked in her voice. 'Jack's in love with Christina Frank. He's been in love with her for years.'

She wiped mascara-smeared tears from her face with the backs of her hands. 'Why the hell can't men have *brains*,' she demanded passionately. 'If I'd wanted to have an affair with Jack I'd have had one years ago! I wouldn't have waited till there was a bloody war on!'

'Ted will be back,' Kate said comfortingly, hoping to God her prediction would prove correct.

'What's the matter, *bubbelah*?' Leah Singer's voice enquired anxiously as she stepped into the house. 'What's the *tummel*?'

As her grandmother walked down the hallway towards the kitchen Mavis straightened her shoulders and wiped her nose on her handkerchief. 'Now for the inquisition and the "I told you so's." Thank God Carrie's bus shift doesn't finish till eight tonight. If she'd been home I'd never have heard the end of it.'

Miriam came into the house hard on Leah's heels and Kate didn't stay. Knowing now that Carrie was not at home or down the market, she didn't bother knocking at the Jennings' or walking into Lewisham. Instead, much to Hector's delight, she pushed the pram up on to the Heath and walked across it and into Greenwich Park.

Early that evening, just after seven o clock, the volume on the radio crackled and faded. Seconds later the air-raid sirens moaned into life. It was the first time there had been an air raid since Matthew had been born and it was the first time, for a long time, that she had had to endure one without Leon for company.

Wishing fervently that Harriet was home, or even that Mr Nibbs would call on her, Kate scooped up Matthew from his cot. 'We're just going to have to sit it out together, my darling,' she said as he opened his eyes, his little fists flailing.

The Anderson was far more comfortable than it had originally been. Leon had put a camp bed in it for her and an oil heater and a hurricane-lamp. With Hector whining in dread at her heels and with distant anti-aircraft guns already opening up at the enemy, she hurried down the dark path and down the roughly hewn steps into the shelter.

It was a long, horrendous night. Occasionally she lifted back the heavy black-out curtain over the shelter's open doorway and each time she did so it was to see a smoke-filled sky criss-crossed with beams of hundreds of searchlights, pin-pointing the attacking planes for the benefit of the anti-aircraft guns. From what she could see and hear it was obvious that this time the German planes were not directing their attack solely on the City and the docks. From the direction of Eltham, even further away from the river than Blackheath, loud explosions sent flames murderously across the night sky.

Kate rocked Matthew tightly in her arms, knowing that family homes were being bombed. Their occupiers would presumably be in Anderson or Morrison or public shelters but no shelter was immune from a direct hit. A bomb dropped perilously close, far closer than Eltham, and the ground shuddered beneath her feet. For the first time ever she knew real fear. Not fear for herself, but for Matthew. If anything happened to him she would never forgive herself. Never. Never. Never.

When the all-clear at last sounded and she stumbled out into the pale light of early dawn she did so exhausted. Matthew had cried almost incessantly the entire time they had been in the shelter. Hector had alternately whined and howled. She had been unable to sleep and the night had seemed endless.

She was sitting in her father's old-fashioned rocking-chair in the kitchen, breast-feeding Matthew, when Harriet tapped on the front door and walked into the house.

At the sight of her elderly friend's obvious weariness Kate's heart contracted. 'Were casualties very high, Harriet?' she asked quietly.

Very slowly Harriet unstrapped her tin hat and laid it on the kitchen table. 'Horrendous,' she said bleakly. 'Eltham, Bromley, Orpington. I've never known so many private homes be hit so far south of the river.'

Wearily she sat down. 'A three year old girl and a canary were the only survivors in one house that was hit. Arrangements will be made for the child, of course, but the authorities are so over-stretched that the local Home Guard officer asked me if I would take her in temporarily.'

'And are you going to?' Kate asked, deeply disturbed at the thought of the child's plight.

Harriet tucked a tendril of dishevelled grey hair back into her bun. 'How can I? It would mean my giving up my ambulance-driving duties. I don't want to sound immodest, Kate, but I'm now one of the depot's most experienced drivers and they can't afford to lose me.'

Kate believed her. Harriet's commonsense and implacable calm were exactly the qualities needed when a bombing raid was at its height.

'I did wonder about having a word with Hettie Collins. Despite all her ridiculous prejudices where you and your father are concerned, she's basically kind-hearted.' She rubbed her eyes wearily. 'I would have approached Miriam, but Miriam has already taken one orphaned child into her home and she certainly couldn't take in another one. I don't know where everyone who lives in that house, sleeps. Presumably Caroline shares a room with Rose and the child they've given a home to and . . .'

'I'll take her in,' Kate said decisively, moving Matthew from her right breast to her left breast. 'I've plenty of room here and the local billeting officer never makes any use of it.' There was no need for her to add the reason. Harriet was as aware as she was herself that it was because of her German surname.

Harriet's ramrod straight shoulders sagged with visible relief. 'Will you, Kate? It will only be temporary, of course, but I'm sure the poor little thing will be better off with you than being passed from pillar to post by the authorities.'

With one mission for the day successfully accomplished she perked up visibly. 'Gossip reached me that Mr Harvey has been seen in Magnolia Square again,' she said, unable to keep her voice completely free of curiosity. 'I presume he came in order to see Matthew?'

Kate hesitated. She hadn't intended telling anyone of the true purpose of Joss Harvey's visit, but Harriet Godfrey's advice to her had always been sound, if at times unwelcome.

'He came in order to see Matthew and to suggest that I allow him to be evacuated to Devon or Somerset with a nanny.'

Harriet's heavy, straight eyebrows rose. 'With a nanny? Not yourself?'

Kate shook her head, her long plait of hair swinging gently against the back of the rocking-chair. 'No. He

334

would never ask me to accompany Matthew. He wants Matthew to himself.'

'It's only natural that he wants time with him,' Harriet said reasonably. 'He's an old man and he must be aware that he may not have very much time left in which to form a relationship with Matthew.'

Kate remained silent and Harriet said promptingly, 'From what you yourself have told me, he was a devoted grandfather to Toby. And Toby was devoted to him, was he not?'

Kate nodded. It was the mutual devotion that had existed between Toby and his grandfather that was causing her so much mental anguish. If Toby had been alive she knew beyond any shadow of doubt that he would have wanted his son to spend time with his grandfather. And she knew also that he would not have wanted his son to remain in a city being blitzed by the *Luftwaffe*.

Harriet's eyes were compassionate. 'I know it must be a hard decision for you to make, Katherine. It can't be easy facing the prospect of being separated from a two-week-old baby, but the separation may not be for very long. And Matthew would be safe. Or as safe as is humanly possible.'

Kate bit her lip, tears glittering on her eyelashes as she looked down at her now contentedly sleeping son. In her heart of hearts she knew that Harriet's advice was sound. It was what Toby would have wanted her to do and it was what commonsense told her to do. It was going to be hard, though; it was going to be the hardest thing she had ever done in her life.

Chapter Eighteen

When Joss Harvey took Matthew from the house it seemed to Kate like a bizarre rerun of the day the police escorted her father from the house. True, this time the force wasn't the legal force of the law, but Kate felt as if it was. From the moment Harriet had given it as her opinion that, while the heavy bombing on London continued, Toby would have wanted Matthew removed to the countryside in the care of his great-grandfather, she had known she had no option.

'It's a disgrace, of course, that Mr Harvey is not offering to evacuate you as well,' Harriet had said, privately thinking it deeply shocking, 'but if he had, I can't imagine he would have agreed to you taking Hector with you and you couldn't possibly have taken Daisy.'

On hearing her name, the little girl standing beside Kate had taken hold of her hand. Kate had given it a comforting squeeze. Even though Daisy had only been with her a couple of weeks she certainly wouldn't have wanted her to have been handed back to the authorities and put into an orphanage. And Matthew would be well cared for. In a surprising act of courtesy Joss Harvey had introduced her to the young woman he had engaged as a nanny.

Ruth Fairbairn was only a year or two older than Kate and there had been instant, unspoken empathy between them. Sensing Kate's anguish she had given her a reprieve of another two weeks by saying to Joss Harvey, 'I can't accept responsibility for Matthew until he's been weaned from breast milk to dried milk, Mr Harvey.

It would cause all sorts of emotional and digestive complications.'

Just as when the policeman had escorted her father from the house and into internment a large number of her neighbours were out in force to witness the event and gossip about it amongst themselves. The car, itself, had been an object of great speculation.

'I thought King George had come visiting,' Hettie Collins said, her coat buttoned tightly to the throat, her battered black straw hat rakishly decorated with a bunch of imitation cherries.

'More likely old Hitler,' some wit replied, mindful of Kate's surname.

'Blimey, 'e's not the father, is 'e?' a joker asked.

'Don't be daft! The old git coming down the steps must be the father.'

As Joss Harvey's white-haired, portly figure descended the steps to the pathway, followed by Ruth Fairbairn in her distinctive nanny's uniform, Miriam Jennings said knowledgeably, 'That's old man 'arvey of 'arvey Construction Ltd and he ain't the father, he's the great-grandad. Kate was keepin' company with 'is grandson.'

'The one wot was killed at Dunkirk?' her questioner asked, impressed. 'Is 'e the father then? I thought someone said it was a darky baby. She 'ad a darky livin' with 'er. I know 'cos Nibbo told me.'

Kate was only a few steps behind Matthew's nanny, Matthew in her arms, and she heard all the comments clearly. They didn't surprise her. In the months since Matthew's birth she had overheard lots of similar remarks.

Joss Harvey's chauffeur was standing beside the car, holding the nearside rear door open. As Ruth reached him she turned to take Matthew from Kate's arms.

'I'll take very great care of Matthew, Miss Voigt,' she promised, her eyes compassionate.

Kate nodded, unable to speak. This was it. This was

the moment she had dreaded. This was the moment when she had to hand her son into the care of a near stranger. He was sleeping and she resisted the almost overpowering temptation to wake him in order to see him smile and gurgle up at her one last time before parting with him. Very tenderly she kissed him on his forehead. 'Goodbye, my precious,' she whispered softly, tears glittering on her eyelashes. 'It won't be for long, I promise.'

Then, feeling as if her heart was going to break, she laid him in Ruth Fairbairn's arms. Ruth stepped into the car. With dreadful finality the chauffeur closed the door.

'Six weeks,' Joss Harvey said to her as the chauffeur opened the front passenger-seat door for him. 'I'll send you a train ticket in six weeks, and every six weeks after that, so that you can visit him.'

'I shall bring Daisy with me,' she said thickly, knowing that Joss Harvey hadn't given Daisy a thought.

Joss Harvey opened his mouth to say she would do no such thing and then became aware of their unwanted audience. Curtly he nodded unwilling acquiescence and stepped into the car.

Small footsteps hurtled down the pathway behind Kate. Daisy had been told to stay in the house with Harriet and Hector until Kate returned but she had been terrified that Kate might never return. Now she tugged at Kate's hand, saying in distress, '*Why have you given the baby to that lady, Auntie Kate? Where is that man taking them?*'

Kate slipped her arm around Daisy's shoulders. It's all right, Daisy,' she said, fighting back tears, determined not to give way to them in public. 'We'll see Matthew again soon, I promise.'

The chauffeur opened the driver's door and slid behind the wheel, closing the door after him. Through the Bentley's back window Kate could see Matthew's little fingers stretching and then clenching into tiny fists.

'Please don't wake!' she said to herself fearfully.

'Please don't wake and start to cry! I couldn't bear it!'

Ruth Fairbairn adjusted his white lacy shawl slightly, and began to rock him. The chauffeur turned the ignition and put his foot down on the clutch. Seconds later the Bentley was pulling away from the curb, heading out of Magnolia Square towards Magnolia Hill and Lewisham.

'Her dad may be a Jerry but you've got to feel sorry for her,' the woman standing next to Hettie said as Kate turned abruptly on her heel and, holding Daisy by the hand, walked swiftly back up her garden path. 'I wouldn't want to have been separated from my little nipper when he was so small.'

'And she can't be all bad if she's taking the little girl in,' someone else said charitably. 'And the kiddie's happy with her, that's obvious.'

This time Kate didn't hear a word of the remarks being made about her. All she wanted was privacy in which to give vent to her crucifying sense of loss.

The next few weeks would have been unbearable if it hadn't been for Daisy and Hector's companionship and the letters she received from her father and from Leon. Her father, as always, encouraged her to look on the bright side.

At least you have the comfort of knowing that Matthew is in a safe part of the country and that he is being well-cared for, Liebling, he wrote at the beginning of April. *Thousands of mothers whose children have been evacuated by the government can only hope for the best where the welfare of their children is concerned . . .*

Kate remembered Billy and Beryl's dreadful experience and was suitably grateful. At least Joss Harvey had had the courtesy to introduce her to Matthew's nanny and she knew that Ruth Fairbairn would be caring and diligent. If she wasn't, Joss Harvey would sack her on the spot.

Leon's letter she read over and over again. His ship

was no longer in the Mediterranean but had been detailed to Atlantic convoy duties. Which of the three main convoy routes between Britain and Canada his ship was sailing he didn't say and, familiar with the censorship even her father's letters suffered from, she knew she couldn't expect such information. It was public knowledge, however, that one of the routes from Scotland to Canada went via Iceland. She thought of the harsh North Atlantic seas and the German U-boats that infested them and shivered with apprehension. *Give Matthew a cuddle for me*, he had written in large, clear handwriting. *I miss you. I even miss Hector!*

She had smiled and then her smile had faded. She had been hoping for something far more personal. There was a restraint in his letter that unnerved her. Had he begun to feel embarrassed at having tended her so intimately when Matthew was born? Had she been foolish in thinking there could ever be anything more than friendship between them? Certainly she couldn't now write back to him in the manner she longed to do. She couldn't tell him she loved him. She couldn't tell him she was looking forward to him returning to Magnolia Square just as fiercely as she was looking forward to Matthew's return.

Daisy kept her from brooding. She was a sunny-natured little girl and her resilience in recovering from the loss of her parents and grandparents led Kate to believe that the home she had lost had not been a happy home. The canary that had accompanied her when Harriet had first brought her to the house held pride of place in his cage in the living-room, much to Hector's agitation. Because of Daisy, Kate found herself baking gingerbread men, with raisins for eyes, and reading nursery rhymes and bedtime stories.

Billy, who had inbuilt radar where home-baking was concerned, soon began calling in for a gingerbread man, bringing Beryl with him.

Beryl was now five and going to school with Jenny, the little girl who had also lost her family in a bombing raid and who had become part and parcel of the Jennings' family.

'Will you read me a story as well?' she asked shyly one evening as Kate was putting Daisy to bed.

Kate had willingly obliged and Beryl had sat on her knee, a mug of cocoa in her hand as Kate began to read to her from her own much-loved copy of J M Barrie's *Peter Pan*.

At the end of the month she had another, far different, visitor.

'I was in the neighbourhood and thought I'd call,' Lance Merton said as he stood on her doorstep, resplendent in his uniform, looking down at her from his rangy six-foot-two-inches.

'I'm glad you did,' she said, surprised and pleased. 'Have you time for a cup of tea?'

He nodded and she led the way along the hallway to the kitchen, the days when she had been too conscious of the gossip such a visitor would arouse, long gone. Ever since Joss Harvey had so ostentatiously taken Matthew away, Matthew's father's identity had been common knowledge. No-one would now imagine Lance Merton was the father of her child and if they thought his visit indicated promiscuousness on her part, then it was just too bad. She didn't give a damn anymore what people thought about her and she hadn't ever since she had realized she was in love with Leon.

'I see you're a Group Captain now,' she said, noting his signal flashes.

'For my sins,' he said wryly as Hector bounded welcomingly up to him. His eyes widened as he saw Daisy, standing on a stool in order to be able to reach the baking board, playing with left-over gingerbread mixture.

'This is Daisy,' Kate said, seeing his bewilderment and being amused by it.

Daisy turned towards him, surveying him critically, a dusting of flour on her nose. 'Hello,' she said, a slight frown creasing her forehead. 'Have you brought our baby back?'

Realizing that Daisy had confused Lance Merton's RAF uniform with the uniform Joss Harvey's chauffeur wore, Kate said gently, 'Our baby isn't coming home just yet, Daisy. We're going on a train ride to visit him next weekend.'

Mollified and losing immediate interest in their visitor, Daisy returned her attention to her gingerbread mixture, squeezing and patting it and enjoying the sensation as it squelched between her fingers.

Remembering that Lance Merton knew nothing about Matthew and thinking that he would be bewildered, Kate said, 'I was pregnant when Toby was killed. I had a little boy.'

'I know,' he said, not asking where Matthew was and looking slightly uncomfortable. 'Mr Harvey told me.'

Kate's eyebrows rose slightly. Wondering what else Joss Harvey had told Lance Merton about her and wondering also what Lance's motives were for calling on her, she turned on the tap, filling the kettle.

Had Lance called to see her again because he was attracted to her? If such a possibility had occurred to her the last time he had called on her, when she had still been so devastated by Toby's death, she would have been outraged. It was evidence of how far she had travelled in coming to terms with that grief that she now felt nothing approaching outrage. It was Leon, of course, who had achieved what she had once thought impossible and eased her grief. Though Toby would always hold a place in her heart, and though she would always remember him, she would never again do so feeling that part of her had been wrenched away and the scar left wincing with the cold.

'Is Daisy your niece?' Lance asked curiously.

'No.' Kate put the kettle on the hob. 'She was bombed

out of her home a couple of months ago and has been with me ever since.'

Lance looked relieved and with a flash of amusement Kate wondered if he had thought that Toby's child wasn't her first illegitimate child.

'And the baby?' Lance asked. 'What did you call him?'

A deep smile curved her mouth. 'Matthew Tobias Leon Carl.'

'Carl?' He looked startled. 'That's very German . . .'

The joy went out of her smile and her stomach muscles tightened. 'Carl is my father's name,' she said, crossing to the kitchen-dresser and taking down two cups and two saucers.

'I see,' he said, still looking troubled. 'I can understand you wanting to name the baby after your father, but wouldn't it make sense if your father changed his name? Especially his surname. There's no need to go through life handicapped by having a German name. You could quite easily have Voigt changed to Verity or Vincent.'

She took a deep, steadying breath. He wasn't meaning to be offensive. Lots of people would think his suggestion eminently sensible. It was what the Royal family had done during the First World War and what lots of other families of German descent had done.

She put a milk jug and sugar bowl on the table, knowing that she could never explain to him the complexity of her feelings where her father's nationality was concerned. Instead, changing the subject, she said chattily, 'Are you still stationed at Hornchurch?'

He shook his head. He had taken his RAF cap off and his hair was short and straight and almost as blond as Toby's had been. 'No, I'm at Debden. It's still reasonably near to London, thank God.'

She wondered if the gratitude was because London was where his family were or if it was London's nightlife he was grateful for.

As if reading her thoughts he said, 'I'm a veteran now

where piloting fighters is concerned. There's not many of us left from pre-Dunkirk days.'

Kate's heart went out to him. He had been a war-time pilot for over a year. A year of dicing with death nearly every minute he was airborne; a year of seeing friends taxi off the runway with him and never return; a year of living constantly on his nerves. No wonder he was tense and no wonder he took advantage of London's nightlife every opportunity he got.

As she put the teapot on the table he said tentatively, 'I don't have to be back at Debden until tomorrow night. I'd thought of going to the West End tonight. Having a meal and a spot of dancing, that sort of thing. Would you come with me?'

'I . . .' Kate sought for words in which to say no without hurting his feelings. He had been Toby's friend and he had given her Hector and she didn't want to seem to be giving him the brush-off. Neither, however, did she want to go wining and dining with him in the West End. To be once again in such close proximity to an RAF uniform would bring back heartaching memories of Toby. And if Lance were attracted to her, she didn't want to encourage him. Her own heart had already been given elsewhere.

'I can't,' she said, pouring tea and avoiding his eyes. 'I've never left Daisy with a babysitter. I don't even know of anyone who would babysit for me.'

He looked startled and she realized that mundane necessities such as baby-sitting had never occurred to him. She also realized that he had not, as yet, asked her where Matthew was.

'Surely a neighbour . . .'

She shook her head. 'The one neighbour who would babysit for me is on night duty as a volunteer ambulance-woman. Would you like a biscuit with your tea? I have some homemade ginger biscuits.'

He took a ginger biscuit from the tin she proffered him and then said, 'What about tomorrow, through the

344

day? We could drive down to Brighton with a picnic. I'm sure Hector and Doris would enjoy that.'

'Her name is Daisy, not Doris,' Kate corrected, in a quandary.

Daisy had heard the word 'picnic' and was looking towards her, round-eyed. Even Hector was looking hopeful.

'It would do me the world of good,' Lance said frankly. 'I need to be able to forget about the war for a few hours and a joy-ride to the coast would be just the trick.'

Under the circumstances it was a small enough request and looking at his drawn face Kate didn't see how she could possibly refuse.

'That would be lovely,' she said, wishing his public-school accent wasn't so like Toby's; knowing that every minute they were in the car together, his uniformed arm brushing hers, she would be thinking of the times she and Toby had driven out into the countryside blissfully happy and carefree and with no intimation of how little time they had left together.

'Are we really going on a picnic, Auntie Kate?' Daisy was asking, stepping down from her stool, a toy rolling-pin held in her chubby hand, 'A proper picnic with sandwiches and cake and lemonade?'

Kate nodded, scooping her up on to her knee. Though it was still only late April and not yet sun-bathing weather Daisy would enjoy playing on the beach at Brighton. Or she would if the beach hadn't been barbed-wired to deter German troops from landing on it.

There was barbed-wire, but not all the way along the beach. They picnicked with their backs resting against a recently erected pillbox and Daisy paddled and Hector raced over the sand at the tide-line until he was exhausted.

'I think I've done it,' Lance said, raising his face to the weak sun as seagulls circled above them, 'I think I've managed to forget about the war.'

She smiled, knowing he didn't mean it for a moment. The war was impossible to forget. Where ice-cream huts once stood, observation posts now stood. Instead of deck-chair repositories there were concrete bunkers. And Toby was dead and Leon was somewhere in the vast Atlantic, his ship prey to German U-boats and battleships.

Lance closed his eyes, his blunt eyelashes blond-tipped. She looked across at him, marvelling at how similar he was in physical looks to Toby and how dissimilar in personality. Where Toby had possessed an air of easy self-assurance, there was something permanently taut about Lance. Toby had constantly teased and joked with her. Lance rarely smiled. She picked up a handful of small pebbles, letting them trickle through her fingers. He had very little to smile about, of course, harrying German bombers month in and month out, but she couldn't imagine him being light-hearted even in peace time.

When he dropped her and a tired Daisy and Hector off in Magnolia Square early in the evening, she knew that he wanted to kiss her goodbye. Feeling slightly ashamed of herself she lifted Daisy into her arms, making any such attempt impossible.

'Goodbye,' she said, opening the door of his sports car with her free hand, her voice friendly and nothing more. 'Thank you for a lovely time, Lance.'

As she stood on the pavement, Daisy still in her arms, she saw his face tighten with disappointment and felt even more ashamed.

'Goodbye,' he said. 'Take care.'

'Goodbye.' This time there was far more warmth in her voice, 'Good luck.'

As he gunned his sports car into life and it roared out of Magnolia Square towards the Heath, she knew that he had read her unspoken message of sexual uninterest very clearly. Certain that he would never call on her again she began to carry Daisy up the front path, Hector plodding wearily at her heels, sad that he had been unable to settle for the friendship she would willingly have given.

Half an hour later there was a knock at the door and she wondered if he had had second thoughts and had come back in the hope of finally parting from her on terms she would have found acceptable. Instead, when she opened the door, she found herself facing Carrie.

'I hope you don't mind . . . I know it's a bit of a cheek when I haven't spoken to you for so long . . . but I wondered how the baby was and why Mr Harvey had taken him away,' Carrie said awkwardly.

'Oh Carrie! Please come in!' Kate's voice was thick with relief and joy. Since the day she had set off with the intention of calling on Carrie and found herself instead at Mavis's, she hadn't stopped debating with herself as to whether or not she should make another attempt. Her difficulty had been that she no longer had Matthew with her and without Matthew she had no excuse for knocking on the door of a house she had been asked never to visit again.

Feeling almost sick with thankfulness that the dreadful silence between them had at last been broken, she said as she led the way into the kitchen, 'Would you like a cup of tea, Carrie?'

Carrie, still in her bus conductress's uniform after a long work-shift, said, 'A cup of tea would be smashing. And have you one of those gingerbread men Billy and Beryl are so fond of?'

'I'm afraid you're out of luck,' Kate said as Hector barked a greeting from his basket beneath the kitchen table. 'We've just come back from a picnic at Brighton and eaten every last one.'

Carrie sat down in the rocking-chair, her awkwardness ebbing. Kate was making things easy for her. There had been no bitterness in her voice when she had greeted her; no resentment.

'Who's we?' she asked, as the long months of estrangement began to slip away as if they had never been.

Kate put the kettle on, 'Daisy and Hector and Lance Merton, an RAF chum of Toby's. It was a bit chilly down there but it made a nice change and Daisy loved it.'

'Is Daisy the little girl you've taken in? The little girl who was bombed out?' Carrie asked, looking round for a sign of her.

'Yes. She's in bed now. She was asleep even before I got her in the house.'

'How old is she?' Carrie unpinned her hated bus conductress's cap from her hair and rammed it in her pocket. 'Mum's seen her when the two of you have been out shopping and she says she can't be much younger than Rose. Rose could do with a playmate. Beryl and Jenny are at school all day now and besides, being five-year-olds, they think Rose is still a baby and haven't the patience to play with her.'

'Daisy is three and she'd love to have a friend.' As Kate sat down at the kitchen table an emotional thought struck her. 'She and Rose are just the age we were when we first made friends.'

A spasm almost of pain crossed Carrie's square-jawed face. 'So they are,' she said, her voice as thick as Kate's had been when she had welcomed her into the house. She linked her fingers together tightly in her lap. 'I've hated this last year, Kate,' she said with typical frankness. 'I never intended to stop speaking to you. It just . . . happened. I was so upset about Danny being taken prisoner . . . and Christina's stories of what Jews are suffering in Germany and Eastern Europe were so terrible . . . I just couldn't think straight.'

Kate stretched out her hand, taking hold of one of Carrie's hands. 'I always understood, Carrie. I always knew how difficult it was for you . . . and I always knew that one day everything would be all right again between us.'

Carrie's hand tightened on hers and then both she and Kate were on their feet, hugging each other, tears spilling down their cheeks.

'Oh God, Kate! I've been so miserable not seeing you! I wanted to come up when the baby was born but I was scared that after the way I'd behaved you wouldn't want anything to do with me!'

'And I was scared of bringing Matthew down to see you, not knowing how you'd react!'

They began to laugh through their tears. 'And what about the intriguingly attractive stranger who was lodging with you?' Carrie asked, the old familiar teasing humour back in her voice. 'Mum nearly had ten fits when Dad told her about him. Apparently he'd called on her, asking if she took in lodgers and she'd turned him down flat. According to Miss Helliwell, it was a very big mistake on Mum's part. I must say I'm in agreement with Miss Helliwell. From what I saw of him he looked extremely fanciable.'

Kate wiped the tears from her cheeks, smiling radiantly. 'He is.' There was going to be lots of time to talk to Carrie about Leon. Meanwhile she wanted to know how Danny was and what the situation now was between Mavis and Ted.

'Tell me about Danny,' she said, beginning to pour freshly brewed tea into two mugs. 'Do you hear from him regularly via the Red Cross? Do your letters reach him? And what's the latest on Mavis and Ted? Has she heard from him since he stormed off after accusing her of having an affair with Jack Lomax?'

The next few hours were just like old times. With their hands comfortingly around hot mugs of tea, sweetened with Nestlé's milk, they caught up on months and months of gossip; Danny, Leon, Rose and Jenny and Matthew, Carrie's war work on the buses, Kate's decision to allow Joss Harvey to take Matthew to Somerset. It was only as Carrie was finally taking her leave that an edge of awkwardness again entered her voice.

'I'd love to ask you to start calling at the house again,' she said as she lingered on the doorstep, 'only Mum still thinks that as your dad is German you must be a member of Hitler's Youth Movement.'

Kate shrugged. She didn't care too much what Miriam thought of her. All that mattered to her was that she and Carrie were friends again. 'It doesn't matter,' she said philosophically. 'She'll think differently I expect when the war is over and our lives get back to normal again.'

Carrie's thick dark hair swung loosely forward around her face. 'Do you think that's the way it will end?' she asked tautly. 'Do you think we will grind Hitler into the dust?'

Kate's eyebrows rose in startled surprise. 'Well of course I do. Don't you?'

In the late night air Carrie shivered. 'I don't know. Sometimes, during a raid, I get so frightened. Dad thinks that now it's spring Hitler will be preparing for a do-or-die attempt at invasion. He thinks I should have Rose evacuated but when I think of what happened to Beryl and Billy I can't bring myself to do it.'

Her green eyes flashed fire. 'God, but I hate this war!' she said with sudden passion. 'I hate what it's done to us all. Danny in some God-awful prison-camp and Rose not even remembering him; your dad locked up as if he were a spy; Toby dead at twenty-six; Jenny and Daisy's families blown to smithereens in their own homes; Ted brooding on what Mavis might be up to while he's away, fighting. If I knew which way it was all going to end I could cope with it.'

She grinned suddenly, recovering her sense of humour. 'Or I could if I knew it was going to end the way you think it's going to end! At least the bloody *Luftwaffe* haven't visited us yet tonight. With a bit of luck we might be able to sleep the night through instead of having to scurry down to the blasted shelter in our nighties!'

For the rest of the week, despite the fact that there were heavy raids on both Tuesday night and Thursday night, Kate felt as if she were walking on air. She and Carrie were friends again. Rose and Daisy had declared themselves to be 'sisters'. Hettie Collins had stopped her in the street to ask after Matthew. And she was going to be with Matthew from Friday evening to Sunday afternoon.

'I could always look after Daisy for you,' Ellen said when Kate left Hector with her. 'She wouldn't be any trouble and . . .'

'I appreciate the offer, Ellen, but Daisy is looking forward to seeing Matthew again nearly as much as I am. And she'll be company for me on the train.'

She didn't add that Daisy might also prove to be company for her once she reached her destination. As she left Ellen's elegant terraced house in West Greenwich she wondered, not for the first time, exactly what sort of situation would greet her at her journey's end. Would she be treated as a guest or as an unwelcome intruder? Would Joss Harvey treat her with curt politeness or would he be cantankerously rude to her? Would Joss Harvey even be there or would it only be Ruth Fairbairn?

'Will there be a seaside like there was at Brighton?' Daisy asked, wriggling into a comfortable position on the rough moquette of the train seat, her little legs sticking out in front of her.

'No.' Kate swung their overnight bag and gas-mask canisters on to the rack above Daisy's head. 'Matthew's living in the country, Daisy. There'll be fields and cows and sheep and maybe horses.'

As she sat down next to Daisy she hoped she wasn't

misleading her. All she had was the address. Tumblers, East Monkton, Taunton. It sounded comfortable and 'cottagey' but remembering the large and dignified Harvey home in Blackheath Kate doubted if Joss Harvey's temporary country residence would be as unpretentious as its name.

At Taunton station they were met by Joss Harvey's chauffeured Bentley. Kate's heart sank. If the Bentley was in Somerset, then so was Joss Harvey.

Daisy scampered eagerly onto the backseat. 'Does the King have a car like this?' she asked, round-eyed. 'Are we going to a palace, Auntie Kate?'

Kate didn't answer her, she merely squeezed her hand. This kind of life-style was the life-style Toby had grown up with. It was a fact she had always known but it was a fact which, until now, she had never really comprehended.

As the Bentley eased its way into Taunton's main street she realized for the first time how little she had known about the circumstances in which Toby had been brought up. The knowledge carried with it a pang of heartache. Had he really, in some ways, been a stranger to her?

For the first time another thought occurred to her, chilling her to the bone. Joss Harvey had made his intentions of maintaining contact with Matthew abundantly clear. Which meant that on visits to his great-grandfather Matthew, too, would become accustomed to a life far different to the modest one enjoyed in Magnolia Square. Would he one day become dissatisfied with what she could offer? She knew enough of Joss Harvey to know that if there was even the faintest chance of such a thing happening he would exploit it to the full.

As the Bentley purred through Taunton's mellowed stone suburbs her stomach muscles tightened. The battle between herself and Joss Harvey, where Matthew was concerned, had not been won when she had adamantly refused his demand that he adopt Matthew. That incident had only been an opening skirmish. The real battle lay ahead and would probably be ongoing for years.

'The dried milk and bottles are kept in this cupboard here,' Ruth said to her as she showed her round a large, airy nursery. 'You quite obviously don't want me around for the next twenty-four hours and so Mr Harvey has agreed to my having this evening and tomorrow off. I'm going to visit my parents in Yeovil, public transport permitting.'

Kate felt a rush of warmth towards her, grateful for her sensitivity. 'Is Mr Harvey in the house?' she asked, hugging Matthew close to her breast, unable to take her eyes from the perfection of his little face.

'Yes, he spends every weekend here. He's not a very courteous man,' she added wryly, 'I wouldn't take offence at the fact that he didn't trouble to greet you when you arrived.'

Kate hadn't taken offence. She had been vastly relieved. Later, when Ruth had left for Yeovil and when Matthew had fallen contentedly to sleep in her arms, she had carried him down the stairs to the hall and laid him in his quite magnificent pram.

'Are we going for a walk?' Daisy had asked hopefully. 'Are we going to see cows and sheep and horses?'

'We most certainly are.' During the car ride to the house Kate had been relieved to see that her promise to Daisy, that she would see fields and sheep and cows and even horses, was going to be easy to keep.

Tumblers was set deep in the countryside, so deep that if the chauffeured car hadn't been waiting for her and Daisy at the station, Kate knew they would never have been able to reach it.

As she tucked a fine wool blanket around Matthew a door opened and a young girl in a maid's uniform walked out of what appeared to be a sitting-room. She kept her

353

eyes carefully averted from Kate, not speaking.

'Good afternoon,' Kate said, refusing to be treated as if she didn't exist. 'It's lovely weather, isn't it?'

The girl flushed scarlet, still not speaking.

Kate shrugged. It had been obvious from the moment Ruth Fairbairn had greeted her that the household staff knew who she was and that they also knew her status as a guest was ambiguous.

Wryly, Kate wondered where she and Daisy were to eat. She hadn't thought to ask Ruth and it was too late to do so now. Presumably they would eat in the nursery, off trays. That would solve Joss Harvey's problem admirably.

As she pushed the pram out onto the gravelled drive she thought of how different it would have been if Toby had lived only a few weeks longer and they had married. She would then have been Mrs Harvey and her status at Tumblers couldn't possibly have been ambiguous.

'It's very quiet, isn't it?' Daisy said a little nervously, breaking in on her thoughts. 'Is it always so quiet in the country?'

Kate paused. They had reached the narrow road at the bottom of the short drive and on either side of them fields, interspersed by occasional copses of trees, stretched out as far as the eye could see.

'It is quiet,' Kate agreed, discovering to her surprise that, like Daisy, she found the stillness unnerving. 'I suppose the cows and sheep wouldn't like it if there were milk-carts and coal-carts and bicycles everywhere.'

'There's nowhere to go for a cup of tea, is there?' Daisy said a little while later as they stood by a dry-stone wall, regarding a flock of morose-looking sheep. 'And there's no sweet shops or fish and chip shops or pie and mash shops.' She tucked her hand into Kate's. 'I don't think I like the countryside,' she said confidingly. 'There's too much of it and it's too empty.'

Kate, too, found herself hankering after the familiar sight of a Lyons tearoom. She wondered how on earth city-bred mothers, who had been evacuated with their young families, coped. No wonder so many of them had returned home, preferring to brave Hitler's bombs rather than the strangeness of a way of life totally alien to them. Smiling wryly to herself she turned the pram and began to walk back to the house. Living so near to the gorse-covered expanse of Blackheath it had never previously occurred to her that she was just as much a city-girl as if she had been brought up in Bermondsey or Deptford. It was quite a revelation. Almost as much of a revelation as the realization of how different Toby's lifestyle had been from her own.

'If Mr Matthew is settled for the night, Mr Harvey would appreciate you coming downstairs to have a few words with him,' the maid who had earlier scurried past her in the hall without speaking said, standing in the nursery doorway to deliver the message.

Kate's stomach muscles tightened. She had begun to optimistically think her visit was going to pass without such a summons being issued.

'Thank you,' she said politely, wondering where on earth in the large house Joss Harvey would be waiting for her. The sitting-room? The dining-room? A study? She didn't ask the maid. Such a show of ignorance would only have emphasized how out of her depth she felt. Why on earth did Joss Harvey insist on his household staff being uniformed? And how could anyone seriously preface a three-month-old baby's name with the prefix 'Mr'?

'I have to go downstairs for a little while to speak with Matthew's great-grandad,' she said to Daisy as she tucked her into the camp-bed that had been put in the pleasantly furnished bedroom adjoining the nursery. 'I don't think I'll be very long.'

Daisy had nodded sleepily, trusting her completely. She didn't like the countryside but she liked the pretty bedroom and Matthew's nursery. There was a rose-pink nightlight and pictures of Humpty Dumpty and Little Bo Peep and Tom, the Piper's Son, on the walls. She had had an egg for her tea and chocolate blancmange. Her eyes closed. It had been a real egg, not a make-pretend egg made out of powder. Maybe she would be able to have another one in the morning, for her breakfast. Maybe she would even be able to take one home with her for Rose.

Kate coiled her heavy braid of hair into a discreet roll in the nape of her neck. She had worn a neat olive-green two-piece to travel to Somerset in. The colour wasn't one she would normally have chosen but clothing coupons and shortages meant there was only 'utility' material available. When she had bought the olive-green serge she had suspected it had originally been woven for some type of uniform. She lifted the collar of her white blouse out over the collar of the nip-waisted jacket in an attempt to make it look a little more chic. It still looked suspiciously like a uniform. Reflecting wryly that she looked almost like a member of Joss Harvey's staff she made her way down the wide staircase, wondering what the 'few words' were he wished to have with her.

'Mr Harvey's in the drawing-room, Miss . . . Mrs . . .' indicating the room Kate had seen her coming out of earlier in the day, the maid tailed off in embarrassment.

Kate felt sympathy for her. It couldn't be easy knowing how to address the mother of your employer's illegitimate great-grandchild.

'Thank you,' she said and then, remembering her only previous formal interview with Joss Harvey, she raised her head high and set her chin, determined not to be bullied.

The moment she stepped into the room shock vibrated through her. It was a large room, high-ceilinged with a deep bay of heavily curtained windows. Two deep sofas flanked a marble fireplace; other chairs, some winged, some button-backed, proliferated. There was a low, large, glass-topped, Chinese-lion-legged table between the two sofas and other occasional tables dotted the room. One had a chess-set on it. Another was thick with silver-framed photographs.

In that moment, as the atmosphere of the room impinged on her senses, Kate knew that Tumblers was no casually rented house. It hadn't been appropriated after she had made her decision to allow Matthew to be given a home far from bomb-torn London. The room she was now in was a family room that had taken on its character over a long period of time. It was a room she knew with utter certainty Toby had been familiar with. It was Joss Harvey's country home and there had never been any question of his taking Matthew to 'somewhere in the country, perhaps Somerset or Dorset'. Joss Harvey had known all along where he was going to bring Matthew and that was to the house his father and grandfather had lived in before him.

She wanted to be able to think out the reasons why Joss Harvey should have thought such deviousness necessary but the realization that Tumblers was no casually rented property was not the only cause of the shock-waves vibrating through her. Joss Harvey was standing full-square in front of the fireplace and standing nearby him, a glass of whisky in one hand, was Lance Merton.

'Good. I'm glad you felt able to join us,' Joss Harvey said with a show of such unexpected civility that she had to restrain herself from turning around to see if someone had entered the room behind her. 'I believe you know Group Captain Merton. He used to come here with Toby in the old days and has visited regularly since Toby's death What would you like to drink? A sherry? I have a *Serciel*. I bought it in Madeira in the spring of '39. If I'd known how soon we were going to be at war I'd have bought an extra crate.'

'I'll have a whisky, please,' Kate said, certain that he would disapprove, and uncaring.

With great difficulty Joss Harvey restrained himself from saying she would have no such thing and instead crossed the room to a generously-laden drinks table.

'I didn't know you would be here,' Lance said as she moved towards the welcoming glow of the fire. 'When Mr Harvey told me you were visiting I don't know who was the most surprised, me at realizing your son had been evacuated here or Mr Harvey at realizing the two of us knew each other.'

'And so the two of you enjoyed a jaunt to Brighton the other week, did you?' Joss Harvey asked her rhetorically, crossing the room towards her and handing her a cut-glass tumbler containing a surprisingly generous measure of whisky. 'When he was small, Toby used to enjoy trips to Brighton. Of course, most holidays he spent down here, in Somerset, and then we went for seaside day trips to places such as Minehead and Burnham-on-Sea.'

As the conversation moved from the attractions of various English seaside resorts to the attractions of the more exotic holiday destinations Joss Harvey had been to, Kate felt quite unpleasantly disorientated. Joss Harvey being openly hostile to her she could cope with. His apparent friendliness she found decidedly sinister. What was he trying to do? Had he decided that, as threats had failed to persuade her to allow him to adopt Matthew, a friendlier approach might succeed? Or was his change in attitude due to the fact that he had discovered she was on friendly terms with Lance Merton? And if it was, why did the fact matter to him?

It wasn't until the next afternoon, as she was about to step into the chauffeured Bentley with Daisy, that the answer came.

'Britain can be proud of young men like Group Captain Merton,' Joss Harvey said, standing on the gravelled drive. 'It's thanks to them that Britain is still free and not enslaved under the Nazi jackboot. He went to the same public school as Toby, did you know that?'

Kate, too anguished at having had to part from Matthew again to give much thought to Lance Merton, shook her head.

'His father owns a large amount of land in West Somerset,' Joss Harvey continued as Daisy scrambled onto the Bentley's rear seat. 'They're a very old, very well-respected family.'

Kate stepped into the car. Nothing he was telling her remotely surprised her. The hint of arrogance in Lance Merton's tense personality was the kind of arrogance that stemmed from the power of having money and of having had the kind of education that money buys.

Joss Harvey stood at the open car door, looking down at her. 'I don't know what it is about you, young woman, but you appear to have a profound effect on young men. It's my belief Lance Merton is as bewitched by you as my grandson apparently was.'

The chauffeur approached, about to close the car door, and Joss Harvey frowned him away. Taking hold of the car door's handle himself he said, 'If I'm right, our little dilemma will be very neatly solved.'

He closed the door and through the open window Kate's eyes held his, tension shooting through her. She had been right in thinking that her acquaintanceship with Lance Merton was somehow responsible for Joss Harvey's change of attitude towards her. And now she was about to find out why.

'Lance Merton would make an ideal stepfather for Matthew,' Joss Harvey said as if it was the most reasonable remark in the world.

Kate sucked in her breath. The chauffeur fired the engine into life and Joss Harvey's eyes flicked across to Daisy. 'You'd have to make alternative arrangements for her, of course,' he said, raising his voice and stepping back from the car as it began to move away from him. 'You can't expect an eligible bachelor to saddle himself with a bombed-out slum child as well as with a young stepson!'

Kate grasped hold of the handle, about to hurl herself out of the car and give vent to her red-hot rage. It was too late. The chauffeur's foot was pressed hard on the accelerator and she knew that he would refuse any demand that he bring the car to a halt. Defeated, knowing that asking the chauffeur to stop would be futile, she sank back against the leather upholstery, her fists clenched, the knuckles white.

Chapter Nineteen

How dare he make such an outrageous suggestion to her? And how dare he refer to Daisy as a slum child? She didn't know which of his disgraceful remarks she was maddest about. Slum child, indeed! No wonder he'd waited until his chauffeur had had the Bentley in gear before he'd expressed his opinions. And his idea that Lance Merton would make an ideal stepfather for Matthew was preposterous. Lance Merton wasn't remotely interested in Matthew. When he had visited her, he hadn't even troubled to ask where Matthew was.

She was still simmering with anger when their train, crowded with soldiers, eased out of Taunton station. Joss Harvey was trouble. She had known it the moment she had met him and she had certainly been right to be suspicious of his sudden show of civility towards her. It wasn't genuine civility. If Lance hadn't visited and betrayed how interested in her he was, Joss Harvey wouldn't have conceived his crackbrained idea and she wouldn't have been invited down to the drawing-room for a 'few words'.

The mere thought of Joss Harvey's rudeness and deviousness made her feel mad enough to spit and she made an exasperated clicking noise with her tongue.

One of the soldiers crammed into the carriage looked across at her with interest. She was a beauty all right. He'd never seen a girl with hair such a rich shade of barley-gold. Not naturally, at any rate. Though it was wound in a heavy coil in the nape of her neck he could tell that it was uncommonly long. There was a prim neatness about her olive-green two-piece and white blouse that was at odds with the flash of fire in her eyes. He grinned to himself. She was certainly mad as hell at something or someone. He wondered if the kiddie with her was hers. His eyes flicked to the fourth finger of her left hand. There was no wedding-ring there. Maybe if he played his cards right he'd be in with a chance!

Kate was too immersed in her own thoughts to be aware of the young soldier's interest in her. She didn't like Matthew remaining in Joss Harvey's care. The longer he was with Joss, the more reluctant Joss would be to return Matthew to her.

The train had pulled into a station and as even more soldiers, cumbered by kit-bags, squeezed onto the train she saw the headline 500-POUND BOMB HITS LONDON SUBURBAN DANCE HALL!' emblazoned across a newsstand. Her thoughts of perhaps bringing Matthew back to London vanished. London was too dangerous. However much she distrusted Joss Harvey, at least she knew that Matthew was safe and well cared for with him. And when the time came to bring Matthew home, she would do so. Joss Harvey wouldn't be able to stop her. An entire army wouldn't be able to stop her!

By the time she and Daisy arrived home she'd also given a lot of thought to her relationship with Lance Merton. Cross as she was with him for having betrayed to Joss Harvey that he was romantically interested in her, she didn't want to cease being on friendly terms with him. He had been Toby's friend and for that reason, if for no other, she wanted to remain in contact with him. And there was no reason why she shouldn't. Joss Harvey could think what he liked.

Some of her anger began to ebb. If, in thinking that she might marry Lance Merton, Joss Harvey continued treating her with civility, then her visits to Tumblers would be a lot less stressful and she would have the added satisfaction of knowing she was making a monkey out of him. She felt a surge of wicked pleasure. She would enjoy making a monkey out of Joss Harvey. She would enjoy it enormously.

'The East Enders copped a packet while you were away,' Carrie said when she brought Rose to the house to play with Daisy. 'There were so many enemy aircraft overhead the house walls were shaking. I took Rose to Miss Helliwell's and sat it out with her and Esther and Faust in the Morrison. Or should that be under the Morrison? It's just like a glorified table with protective wire around the sides but Miss Helliwell has deep faith in it.'

'Well, as she can presumably read her own future as well as other people's, she should know whether it's safe or not,' Kate said wryly. 'Harriet tells me the elderly couple who lived next to Daniel and Hettie have moved out and gone to live with their daughter in Berkshire.'

Carrie nodded, looking regretfully towards the kettle. She was in her bus conductress's uniform and on her way to work and didn't have time to stay for a cup of tea.

'That's right. The last couple of raids broke their nerve. A bombed-out East End woman has already moved into the house. She seems a good sort but she's got shockingly ulcerated legs and moves at a snail's pace. God only knows how she manages to reach a shelter when there's a raid on.'

'I don't,' Nellie Miller said breezily to Kate. 'When the Jerries are overhead I just stay in bed and curse the buggers.'

She was sitting on a dining-chair in her handkerchief-sized front garden enjoying the warmth of the May weather. 'I can't sit in a deck-chair,' she said to Kate, shifting her heavy weight a little more comfortably on the hard wooden chair. 'If I sit in a deck-chair it takes nine strong men to haul me out of it again!'

A fly landed on one of her elephantine-like, grossly disfigured legs. She swatted it away. 'Nasty creatures.

Anything suppurating attracts 'em. My legs should be bandaged, by rights, but I can't manage it meself. It takes me all my time to put me shoes on let alone bend over long enough to put bandages on.'

'Then how do you bathe them?' Kate asked, concerned.

'With bloomin' great difficulty,' Nellie said darkly.

Kate transferred her wicker shopping-basket from her right hand to her left hand. She'd never done any nursing but she knew that ulcerated legs should be bathed regularly and then kept scrupulously dry and clean.

'I'll do them for you, if you like. Shall I come down and do them later this afternoon, about four?'

Nellie's heavy jowls trembled emotionally. 'Bless you, dear. Would you really? It's not a favour I've ever liked to ask of anyone because they're not a very nice sight. In fact, they're a bloomin' 'orrible sight and they often stink to 'igh 'eaven, but if you're sure you don't mind . . .'

'I don't mind,' Kate said as Hector, who had been waiting impatiently for her to continue with their walk down to Lewisham High Street, finally ran out of patience and began running in circles around her. 'Is there anything you want from the market? Any fruit or veg?'

'I wouldn't say no to a couple of nice apples. And I could do with some potatoes bringing in. Thank Gawd there's some things that aren't bloomin' rationed. What I wouldn't give for a nice piece of fruit cake stuffed with sugar and butter and eggs and currants and raisins and candied-peel!'

As May progressed fears that Hitler was on the brink of launching an invasion force increased. On the tenth, London suffered the worst air raid of the war. In brilliant moonlight over five hundred German planes dropped hundreds of high explosive bombs on the city and over 100,000 incendiary bombs. The Houses of Parliament were hit and the chamber of the House of Commons was reduced to rubble. The twelfth century roof of Westminster Hall was set ablaze and the square tower of Westminster Abbey caved in. Big Ben was scarred, though the clock itself cheered Londoners by continuing to keep perfect time.

'Dear old Big Ben,' Esther Helliwell said as her sister and Carrie lifted her gently back into her wheelchair after a long, harrowing night in the Morrison shelter. 'The Germans haven't silenced *him*, have they? And they won't silence our dear Mr Churchill either!'

London wasn't the only city to have its heart nearly torn out of it. Portsmouth, Coventry, Liverpool, Belfast, Southampton, Hull, Plymouth, were all pulverized, with fires raging for days. And then suddenly the night skies were empty. No sirens screamed into life. No ack-ack guns opened up.

'It's a bit bloody eerie, ain't it?' Albert Jennings said uneasily to Mr Nibbs. 'What do you think it means, Nibbo? What do you think old Hitler's up to now?'

Nibbo didn't know and neither did anyone else. Every night Londoners expected the *Luftwaffe* to return. Night after night they didn't do so. Then, on 22 June, all was explained.

'German forces have this morning invaded Russia,' a BBC newscaster announced portentously. 'Hitler's armies are believed to be sweeping towards Moscow.'

'What an extraordinary move for Hitler to have made,' Harriet Godfrey said to Charlie Robson as they walked companionably across the Heath together. 'Another couple of raids like the raids of May the tenth and I don't believe Britain could have held out for much longer. Now, just at the moment when he should have seized his chance and attempted an invasion, he's turned his armies and his attention towards Russia.'

'Well, while he's doin' that, 'e's leavin' us alone,' Charlie said reasonably. 'Do you fancy a quick drink in The Princess of Wales, 'arriet? Me throat's parched.'

★ ★ ★

All through the summer a spirit of optimism reigned. Though the Germans were making substantial advances through Russian territory, they were meeting fierce and courageous resistance.

'The Russkies are proving to be pretty tenacious fighters,' Daniel Collins said to Albert as they walked down Magnolia Hill together, Albert in his well-worn Home Guard uniform and Daniel in his Auxiliary Fireman's uniform. 'With them as allies we might just win the day, Albert.'

Harriet also thought that Britain and her Allies might win the day. 'Or at least we will if the Germans fail to capture Moscow before the Russian winter sets in,' she said to Kate. 'Remember Napoleon? He was defeated by the Russian winter. Pray God Hitler is as well!'

Kate listened as tensely as anyone else to the news broadcasts charting the fierce fighting taking place in Russia, but her real interest wasn't in what was happening in Russia, but what was happening on the high seas of the Atlantic.

On one of her kitchen cupboards she had pinned up a map cut from a newspaper. It showed the various convoy routes across the Atlantic and also the routes German battleships and U-boats could be expected to take and the air range of German aircraft. In imagination she tried to be with Leon aboard his battleship but it was an impossible task. His letters to her were constantly cheerful and totally uninformative of what his day to day life was like.

Over the weeks and months she did glean some information, however. She learned that a convoy could comprise of as many as sixty ships and that it was the slowest ship that set the pace. She also learned that escort ships such as Leon's took the convoys out to a given point and then sent them on their way, returning as escort for incoming convoys. Other information was far more important to her. In every letter he told her that he missed her; that he couldn't wait to be striding into Magnolia Square again, past the Jennings' and the Lomax's and Miss Helliwell's, towards her front gate.

Her visits to Somerset took on a regular rhythm. Sometimes Joss Harvey was there, sometimes he was not.

'You'd think Mr Harvey would be too old to be the active boss of a company as big as Harvey's, wouldn't you?' Ruth Fairbairn said to her as she put clean laundry away in a chest of drawers decorated with nursery-rhyme characters and Kate dangled a gurgling Matthew on her knee, 'but he's up in London part of every week supervising what he says are colossal rebuilding programmes.'

Lance Merton also visited her with regular frequency. Sometimes he took her and Daisy and Hector into Kent for a picnic, sometimes they simply went for a walk in Greenwich Park or across the Heath. On one occasion he told her he was in love with her. She had crushed his hopes as gently as possible and, believing she had done so only because she was still grieving for Toby, Lance had accepted the rejection with good grace. Unknown to Kate it was not, however, a rejection he regarded as being final.

In October the submarine war in the Atlantic claimed the lives of more than seventy American sailors when a U-boat attacked a US battleship on convoy duty west of Iceland.

'I didn't know the Yanks were helping us out in the Atlantic,' Charlie Robson said to Kate, his collarless shirt stuffed any-old-how into the broad leather belt holding up his trousers.

If there was one aspect of the war that Kate was knowledgeable about it was the war in the Atlantic.

'They've been helping out for a while now, Charlie,' she said, giving Queenie a friendly pat. 'Or as much as they can without coming into the war themselves.'

'And why the 'ell don't they?' Charlie asked, mystified. 'Why the 'ell don't they get properly pitched in and stop shilly-shallying?'

Two months later all shilly-shallying was over. On 7 December the world woke to the news that the Japanese had bombed Pearl Harbour. Four days later Mavis was once again acting as the local town-crier by leaning out of her bedroom window and shouting at the top of her voice, *'Now I know Hitler's bloody mad! He's just declared war on America!'*

'The Yanks will soon sort the Jerries out,' Nellie said confidently as Kate knelt at her feet and dusted her ulcerated legs with antiseptic powder. 'I'm rather partial to a Yank meself. Or I am if they all look like Clark Gable!' She stretched her left leg out so that Kate could begin bandaging it. 'That boy of Charlie Robson's looks a lot like Clark Gable, doesn't 'e? Christina showed me a photograph of 'im in 'is Commando gear. Very tasty, I thought. She said 'is brother was killed in Spain. Did you know 'im, dear?'

'Yes,' Kate said, thinking of the teddy bear that sat on her dressing-table and of a sunny, carefree, laughter-filled day on the Heath. A day that now seemed to belong to another lifetime.

'She's a nice girl, that Christina,' Nellie said as Kate fastened the bandage at her knee with a safety-pin. 'A bit quiet o' course. She doesn't 'ave the go about 'er South London girls 'ave. Still, she's 'ad a lot to put up with, losing 'er family in those terrible camps.'

She paused, looking down at the top of Kate's head and her long braid of sun-gold hair. 'I take it you and she ain't exactly on friendly terms, dear?' she said at last, her kindly eyes troubled. 'It's silly, ain't it? You're not a bloody Nazi an' I don't suppose your dad is either. Life's too short to 'old grudges against people who don't deserve to 'ave grudges 'eld against 'em an' I told 'er so. Would you like a nice cup o' tea when you've finished bandagin' me up? Me legs are so much better since you started lookin' after 'em you'd never believe it. Angel's 'ands you 'ave, an' I told Christina so.'

'*I'm going to be home for Christmas,*' Leon wrote in his plain, firm handwriting. '*Then I'll be off the Atlantic route and on another ship on the Arctic route to Murmansk and Archangel.*'

She knew that convoys had been ferrying precious supplies to the beleaguered Russians ever since September. And she knew that the dangers they faced, being within German air striking distance for much of the way, were even more perilous than the dangers facing them on the Atlantic.

She hugged his letter to her breast. She would worry about the Arctic run to Murmansk and Archangel later. He had written that he was coming home for Christmas! Home! Was that truly how he thought of herself and Magnolia Square? And if it was, did it mean that guardedness in his letters was merely because he unsure of what her response might be if he was to more frank? Was he nervous of saying what was in his heart in case he didn't meet with a like response, just as she had been nervous in the hours after Matthew was born?

'Oh, but we're going to have a *wonderful* Christmas,' she said to Daisy, knowing that where she and Leon were concerned, the time for nervousness and caution was at an end. 'Leon's coming home and you're both going to love each other on sight and we're going to have the best Christmas ever!'

Part of that best Christmas was the *Luftwaffe*'s continued absence from London. It meant that Matthew need no longer stay in Somerset. He could come home.

'I don't agree with you, young lady,' Joss Harvey said brusquely. 'The war is far from over and London is far from being out of danger. Matthew is settled here. Disturbing his routine and returning him to London is not in his best interests.'

'I'm the one who knows what my son's best interests are,' Kate retorted, noting with interest that he was now referring to her as 'young lady' not 'young woman'. 'Our agreement was that Matthew would stay in Somerset until it was safe for him to return to London. At the moment it is safe. And he's coming home with me.'

Joss Harvey sucked in his breath, his face purpling. For a few seconds he didn't speak, his inner battle obvious, then he said tightly, 'If that is your considered decision then of course I can't overrule it. I would suggest, however, that you wait until after Christmas before taking Matthew back to London. It would be typical of the Germans to make a surprise attack on Christmas Day when they would imagine we would be least prepared for it. And I would appreciate one Christmas at least with my great-grandson.'

It was disconcertingly near to a plea and Kate hesitated. There was a glimmer of sense in what he was saying. It *was* quite possible that the *Luftwaffe* would pay London a Christmas visit. And despite all his forcefulness and apparent good health Joss Harvey was an old man. The Christmas coming might be the last Christmas he would be able to spend with Matthew.

'All right,' she agreed, knowing that she could afford to be generous. 'As long as it's quite understood that when I visit in February I take Matthew home with me.'

'Absolutely,' he said, unable to conceal the depth of his relief. 'Would you like a whisky? Have you seen anything of Lance, lately?'

When Christmas Eve dawned Leon had still not walked into Magnolia Square, his kit-bag on his shoulder. Kate refused to panic. He had said he would be home for Christmas and he was a man who kept his promises.

'Let's go down to the market,' she said to Daisy, wrapping her up warmly in a coat and Fair Isle beret and scarf. 'If we're lucky Mr Jennings might have some nice apples on his stall.'

With Hector at their heels they set off, walking down towards the bottom end of the Square and Magnolia Hill. As they reached Miss Helliwell's magnolia tree Kate's tummy muscles tensed. Miriam Jennings was walking towards them, Rose and Jenny at either side of her, holding her hands. And with them was Christina.

''lo, Auntie Kate!' Rose called out, letting go of her grandmother's hand and running towards Kate. 'It's Christmas tomorrow and Santa Claus is bringing me a doll's house!'

Kate's eyebrows rose. A doll's house! How on earth had Carrie managed to buy a doll's house?

'It ain't really a doll's house,' Miriam said as Rose scampered off to introduce Jenny to Hector. 'It's a birdcage Albert found when Cambridge Gardens was bombed in May. Gawd knows what happened to the bird, I don't. Albert said the cage would come in useful, an' it 'as. 'e's covered the sides in cardboard and put a bit of old lino on top as a roof. Me an' Christina dug out bits an' pieces to furnish it. We found bits of old wallpaper for the walls and dyed a bit of hessian for a carpet an' fringed it. It looks a fair treat.'

'I bet it does,' Kate said warmly. It was the first time in eighteen months that Miriam had spoken to her and she had no intention of being childish and snubbing her. If Miriam was prepared to build fences, then so was she.

'If you're 'oping to find any fruit dahn the market, you'd best be quick,' Miriam said, catching hold of Rose's hand again. 'Albert 'ad a fair supply in first thing but it'll soon go. 'ave a nice Christmas. Ta-ra.'

'Ta-ra,' Kate said as Miriam began to walk away from her.

'Bye,' Christina said, falling into step beside Miriam.

Kate swung her head round, hardly able to believe her ears, but Christina already had her back towards her. She stared after her, wondering if she had been imagining things. A friendly goodbye? From Christina Frank? It almost beggared belief.

'If Rose is getting a doll's house from Santa Claus do you think she'll let me play with it?' Daisy asked as they walked past the Lomax's and the Jennings'.

'Of course she will,' Kate said confidently, looking forward to the expression on Daisy's face when she found a doll in her Christmas stocking. It was one she herself had been given when she was four years old and she had made it a magnificent new set of clothes out of an old rose-pink silk blouse.

'Why is that big army lorry parked there,' Daisy asked curiously as they turned the corner into Magnolia Hill.

The lorry in question was parked at the very top end of Magnolia Hill, as near to the Square as it was possible for it to get. 'I don't know,' Kate said, wondering if perhaps it was something to do with Ted and if he was home on Christmas leave, and if his rift with Mavis was at an end.

'Billy shouldn't be playing in it, should he?' Daisy said with a three-year-old's self-importance. 'I've just seen him climbing into it. I 'spect he's pretending to drive it. Little boys can't drive big lorries, can they?'

Mr Nibbs was walking up the far side of the street, deep in conversation with Daniel Collins. Kate grinned to herself. If Nibbo spoke to her today it would be a hat trick!

Hettie Collins was walking towards them, her well-worn black coat buttoned high to the throat, her black hat decorated with a seasonal sprig of holly, a shopping-basket over her arm.

At the bottom end of Magnolia Hill, where The Swan dipped steeply into the busy High Street, Queenie could be glimpsed, sitting patiently on the pavement waiting for Charlie.

'There's probably someone in the lorry with him,' Kate said, and then three things happened at once.

Leon swung into Magnolia Hill at the corner opposite to The Swan. The lorry began to move, edging silently forwards. Mavis suddenly appeared, her peroxide-blonde hair in pin-curls, slippers on her feet, shouting, '*Put the bloody brake on, Billy!*'

Billy didn't put the brake on, presumably because he couldn't reach it. The lorry began to gain momentum. Hettie Collins screamed and dropped her shopping-basket. Mr Nibbs shouted, '*What the bloody hell . . .*' Daniel Collins sprinted into the middle of the road and began racing after the lorry, trying to catch it up. Mavis began to scream.

Instinctively Kate also began to run. The lorry was thundering loudly over Magnolia Hill's cobbles now, hurtling suicidally down towards the busy junction with the High Street.

As she ran she saw Charlie and a half a dozen other men tumble out of The Swan. She heard Nibbo shout, '*Get someone to stop the traffic in the High Street for Christ's sake!*' She saw Hettie Collins begin to cross herself time and time and time again. And she saw Leon sling his kit-bag to the ground and, as the lorry rocketed towards him, she saw him tense himself and spring.

Her own screams now merged with Mavis's. For a brief second she saw his uniformed figure cling to the lorry's nearside door and then he threw himself bodily through the open window.

'*Jesus, Mary and Joseph, they'll both be killed!*' Hettie sobbed as Kate raced past her, Daisy sobbing in her wake, vainly trying to catch up with her.

There were only yards now between the careening lorry and the buses and vans and horse-drawn carts unsuspectingly plying up and down the High Street.

Suddenly the lorry swerved, heading diagonally across the road towards The Swan, tyres screeching as it did so.

'*He's got the brakes on!*' Daniel panted to Kate, still running, '*He's going to crash it into The Swan rather than let it crash in the High Street!*'

Charlie and his mates had already realized the same thing and heavy boots were scattering left and right at high speed.

Kate was in the road now, the cobbles hard beneath her feet. If Leon crashed the lorry into The Swan lives would no doubt be saved in the High Street but what would happen to him and Billy?

'*It's slowing down!*' Daniel shouted from behind her. '*He's going to make it, thank God!*'

The lorry shuddered and lurched on to the pavement and then, a hair's breadth from the pub's walls, it rocked to a halt.

From everywhere people began running towards it. Ted Lomax, wearing only a pair of hastily donned trousers, his hair and chest still wet from the bath he had been having, raced like a man demented past Daniel. Bob Giles, his distinctive clerical collar showing above a husky jumper, was running down Magnolia Hill from the direction of the vicarage. Even Hettie was running, her basket of shopping forgotten, tears of relief staining her cheeks.

As Leon flung the driver's seat door of the lorry's cab open Mavis was the first on the scene. '*You stupid little bleeder!*' she sobbed at Billy as Leon handed him down to her. '*I'll bloomin' kill yer when I get yer 'ome!*'

Kate didn't hear Billy's reply. As Leon sprang agilely down from the cab to the pavement she rocketed towards him, throwing herself into his arms.

If anyone was surprised by her action, they didn't say so.

'That was a bloody brave thing to do, mate,' Daniel Collins was saying as Leon's arms closed around Kate.

'If you'd misjudged that leap you'd have likely killed yourself.'

'You deserve a medal,' Hettie was saying, one hand pressed against her still palpitating heart, her sprig of holly hanging half off her hat after the exertion of her run. 'Doesn't 'e deserve a medal, Nibbo? If it wasn't for 'im little Billy would most likely be dead now.'

'And so, very likely, would a lot of other people,' Nibbo said, thinking of the carnage that could have been caused if the lorry had careered into a two-decker bus.

Leon wasn't listening to him, or to the other words of admiration flooding over him. Kate was in his arms, where he had always wanted her to be, and he hadn't the slightest intention of letting her go.

'Oh God, I thought you were going to be killed!' she was saying, her voice breaking with emotion.

Her head was against his chest and she was hugging him so tightly he could hardly breathe. He looked down at the shining gold of her hair, knowing that from now on there would be no barriers of shyness or uncertainty between them.

'Who? Me?' he asked quizzically, his amber-brown eyes full of love. 'When I'm about to spend a second Christmas Day with you and Hector? I wouldn't be so careless.'

'And Daisy,' she said thickly, raising her head to his, her eyes shining with happiness. 'You haven't met Daisy yet.'

'No,' Leon said, looking across the top of her head to where a small figure was running towards them as fast as her little legs would carry her. 'But I think I'm about to.'

Ted Lomax had been hugging Billy. Now he came across to Leon and held out his hand to him. 'We haven't met, but I'm Billy's dad,' he said as Leon reluctantly released hold of Kate with one arm in order to accept his proffered handshake. 'I can't thank you enough for what you just did. If you hadn't been there . . .' he

375

shuddered, and not just because he was half-naked and it was the middle of winter.

'I only did what anyone would have done if they'd been where I was,' Leon said, beginning to feel slightly embarrassed by the fuss that was being made.

'Not many people would have leapt on a lorry going that speed,' Ted said frankly, 'I just want you to know that I appreciate it. And that I won't forget it.'

'You both need a strong hot cup of tea down you,' Hettie said practically. 'Come on, let's get back to the Square and I'll put the kettle on. Are you comin' with us Nibbo? Charlie?'

'I don't think so, 'ettie,' Charlie said, eyeing the still open door of The Swan. 'I rather fancy a drop o' somethin' a bit stronger.'

'I dare say Daniel does as well, but he ain't going to have any,' Hettie said tartly before her husband should get any similar ideas. 'Come on, Daniel. And give Ted a lend of your jacket. He must be freezing.'

Daisy had come to a stop a few feet from Kate and Leon. Kate had told her a lot about Leon and she had been fiercely looking forward to meeting him. Now, however, she felt suddenly shy. He looked so different from anyone she had ever seen before, with his dusky skin and crinkly black hair. And he had his arm around her Auntie Kate's shoulders in a way she wasn't sure she liked. She was *her* Auntie Kate, after all, and though she didn't mind sharing her with baby Matthew she wasn't sure she wanted to share her with anyone else.

Leon, seeing the doubts and uncertainties flashing across her face, slid his arm from around Kate's waist and squatted down on his haunches so that he and Daisy were on eye-level.

'Hello,' he said with a friendly grin. 'I'm Leon. Are you Daisy? I've heard a lot about you.'

'And I've heard a lot about you, too,' Daisy said, slightly reassured.

'I hope we're going to be friends. I've got some

oranges and bananas in my kit-bag. Shall we go home and put them in a fruit bowl?'

'A banana?' Daisy's eyes were like saucers. She had heard about bananas but she'd never seen one, much less eaten one. 'A real banana? Not a pretend one?'

'A real banana,' Leon said solemnly. He stretched his hand out to hers. 'Come on, let's have a cup of tea at Mrs Collins' and then you can help me unpack my kit-bag.'

Daisy put her hand willingly into his. Her Auntie Kate had told she would like Leon and, as usual, her Auntie Kate had been right. No-one else she knew would be having bananas for Christmas. And no-one else she knew had a friend who looked so wonderfully different from everyone else.

'I missed you,' Kate said fervently as, her hand clasped in his, they followed the Collinses and Lomaxes and Mr Nibbs into the Square.

His hand tightened on hers. 'And I love you,' he said, his eyes meeting hers as Daisy skipped at her side and Hector bounded ahead of them.

Kate's heart somersaulted. It was as if there were only the two of them in the whole wide world; as if the little throng of neighbours only a few yards ahead of them didn't exist.

'I love you,' she said softly. 'Every time I wrote to you I wanted to tell you. I'm glad now that I didn't, that I'm telling you now, face to face.'

'So am I.' He wanted to kiss her so badly he hurt. 'And I'm glad you're telling me today, in this exact spot.'

Her eyes widened uncomprehendingly and a wide, easy grin split his face. 'We're just about to walk past the Jennings'. Don't you remember what happened here, a year ago almost to the hour?'

Joyous laughter bubbled up in her throat. She certainly did remember. And she owed Miriam Jennings a huge favour. If Miriam had taken him in as a lodger, instead of being rude to him and slamming the door in his face, then he would never have approached a complete stranger to ask if she knew of anyone who took in lodgers. And she owed Hettie a favour, too. For if Hettie hadn't also refused to take him as a lodger the stranger in question would never have impulsively walked down to The Swan and told him that, if he wanted it, she had a room she could let him have.

'It's our anniversary,' she said, hugging his arm. 'What could be more perfect?'

'Nothing,' Leon's heart was full to overflowing. Never again would he feel a loner or an outsider or a misfit. He had a family again. When the war was over, Kate and Matthew and Daisy and Hector would be waiting for him. Years and years of being together and loving each other lay ahead of them, or they did if his ship survived being blasted to eternity by a German U-boat or battleship. As they turned in at Hettie's gate his jaw tightened. He'd survive the war. He wasn't going to let anyone, not the entire German Navy or Air Force, rob him of the happiness he knew lay ahead of him with Kate as his wife.

That he and Kate were now far more to each other than lodger and landlady seemed to be accepted by their neighbours without question.

'You look after that fella of yours,' Hettie said to Kate a little while later as she pressed a mug of tea with condensed milk, into her hand. 'He's a real hero.'

And Mr Nibbs said, 'It's very fortunate your young man is no longer hampered by an injured leg. If he had been he'd never have been able to make such a magnificent jump.'

'I've scored a hat trick,' Kate thought to herself as Ted made Billy apologize to Leon for all the trouble he had caused and Hettie sat down at her piano and began playing *Knees Up Mother Brown* and Mavis began to lead the singing. 'First Miriam speaks to me and then Christina Frank and now Mr Nibbs, all in one day!'

*   *   *

Later, leaving Daisy happily thumping out tunes on Hettie's piano, she walked up her own front path, Leon's arm around her shoulders. 'I think I know how Miss Helliwell feels when she predicts the future,' she said joyously. 'I *know* the tide has turned as far as the war is concerned. I *know* you're going to come home safe.'

They had climbed the short flight of steps to her doorstep and he turned her round to face him. 'And I know I'm going to love you for as long as I live,' he said, and very firmly he drew her into his arms and lowered his mouth to hers.

As her mouth opened lovingly, her tongue slipping willingly past his, she knew with utter certainty that the heartache Miss Helliwell had spoken of so many years ago wasn't Jack Robson's death, but Toby's. She knew also that when Miss Helliwell had predicted she would know long-lasting happiness and deep love, she had been speaking not of Toby, but of Leon.

This time, when they entered the house, she had no need to lead the way up the stairs and to show him which room was his. With his kit-bag hoisted easily on his shoulder and with his limp no longer discernible he led the way up the stairs and at the top, where the doors of the four bedrooms and bathroom led off, he opened the door not of the room with the plump blue eiderdown on the bed and the bedside lamp with a sunflower yellow shade, but of her room, holding it open so that she could walk past him into it.

Flushing rosily, glowing with happiness, she did so. From now on the room would be their room. From now on, whenever they were together, wherever they were, she would always share a room with him, as she would share everything with him, lifelong.

Chapter Twenty

They had thirty-six hours together before he returned to sea. Thirty-six hours of unadulterated happiness; of laughing and loving and feeling completely right together. They went to a midnight Carol Service at the church; they took Daisy and Hector for a walk in Greenwich Park and a walk across the Heath; they visited the Misses Helliwells and used their Morrison shelter as a table tennis table as Mavis and Jack had once done.

When the time for parting came Kate drew comfort from remembering the words Miss Helliwell had spoken to her, so many years ago.

'She told me that after heartache I would know a great and lasting love,' she said, her head resting against the comforting broadness of his chest as he held her close, his kit-bag ready and waiting near the door. 'That means we're going to be in love with each other for years and years and years, Leon. It means you're going to come home safe. It means nothing terrible is ever going to happen to us.'

His arms tightened around her. Fond as he was of Miss Helliwell he didn't share Kate's implicit trust in her psychic powers. The war was far from being over and thousands of tons of Allied shipping had already been torpedoed into oblivion on the winter convoy routes to Murmansk and Archangel.

Keeping his dark thoughts to himself he said huskily, 'I love you. I'll always love you. Never forget it, Kate. Promise?'

She turned her head, looking up into his dear, kind,

compassionate face. 'I'll never forget, Leon,' she said, tears glittering on her eyelashes at the knowledge that it would be months, years even, before she saw him again. 'Whenever you think of me, I'll be thinking of you.'

He lowered his head to hers one last time, kissing her with a passion and a need that almost unstrung her and then he was gone, his footsteps running lightly down the steps outside the front door.

She couldn't bear to go to the door and watch him as he walked away; she was too frightened she would lose self-control and that his last sight of her would be with tears streaming down her face.

Daisy's hand slid into hers. 'It isn't nice people going away, is it?' she said, her voice wobbly. 'You won't go away, will you, Auntie Kate?'

'No, darling.' Kate hugged her tightly. 'And people come home again,' she said, reassuring herself as well as Daisy. 'Matthew will be home soon. And one day Leon will be home again as well.'

'I thought you were going for Matthew this weekend?' Carrie said, dumping her bus conductress's ticket-machine and leather money-bag down on the nearest chair and staring down at Kate, a frown of concern creasing her forehead.

Kate lay on the settee, propped up by cushions and covered by a blanket. 'I've got 'flu,' she said thickly, reaching for one of the many handkerchiefs that were stuffed beaneath the cushions. 'Don't come too near me or you'll get it as well.'

'If you're so bad I'd better take Daisy down to my mother,' Carrie said practically. 'Before I do, shall I make you a hot drink? Have you any rose-hip syrup? A spoonful of that in hot water might make you feel better.'

Two weeks later, Kate still felt foul. She no longer had a temperature and she was no longer alternately shivering and sweating, but she still didn't want to eat and still felt nauseous.

'Perhaps you should pop along and see Doctor Roberts,' Carrie suggested. 'You might have picked up another bug, besides 'flu.'

Doctor Roberts put his stethoscope away and told her to put her blouse back on. Walking to his desk and sitting down at it he eyed her strangely. 'You're certainly run-down,' he said as she sat opposite him, fastening her blouse buttons, 'but that's to be expected after a bad bout of influenza.'

'I've had influenza before and I've never felt sick with it,' Kate said, wanting to be utterly sure she wasn't carrying anything contagious before going to Somerset to collect Matthew.

Doctor Robert chewed the corner of his lip for a moment and then, deciding that nothing was to be gained by beating about the bush, said bluntly, 'You were sick, however, when pregnant, weren't you?'

Kate stared at him.

Doctor Roberts sighed. He wouldn't have thought it possible that a girl as well brought-up as Kate Voigt could fall pregnant a second time while still unmarried, but from the dawning comprehension on her face it obviously *was* possible.

'When did you last menstruate?' he asked, wondering what the world was coming to and blaming everything on the war.

'I'm not sure . . . it's not something I ever think about . . .' Kate's mind raced. It had been before Christmas . . . before she and Leon had become lovers . . . five or six weeks ago, possibly seven.

'I suggest you come back and see me in a month's time,' Doctor Roberts said heavily. 'By then a physical examination might confirm whether or not you are pregnant again.' He clasped his hands on the top of his desk. 'It's not part of my duties to give out contraceptive

382

advice, unasked, to unmarried women, Kate. However, I do sincerely wish you had felt able to come to me and . . .'

'It wasn't necessary, Doctor Roberts.' Happiness was spiralling through her so fiercely she could hardly contain it. 'If I am pregnant, I want this baby just as much as I wanted Matthew. My boyfriend is a sailor. He's going to be over the moon when I write to him with the news.'

Doctor Roberts shuddered. A sailor. The father of her last child had been an airman. No doubt in a year's time she would be back again, pregnant with a child fathered by a soldier.

'I'll see you again in four weeks,' he said, wondering what on earth his wife would say when Kate's condition became obvious and the neighbourhood began talking; wondering what Carl Voigt would say when he heard he was to be grandfather to a second illegitimate child.

'How I'm going to tell my father, I don't know,' Kate said wryly to Carrie. 'It wasn't too bad before. He did at least know Toby and like him and when I finally plucked up the nerve to write to him with the news that I was pregnant he was amazingly understanding.'

'He'll like Leon, too, when he meets him,' Carrie said, rather entertained at the idea of Kate, who everyone had always regarded as being very prim and proper in comparison to herself having a second love child. 'What about Miss Godfrey? What is *she* going to say?'

Miss Godfrey didn't say anything because Kate didn't tell her. There was no need as yet and she had other things on her mind. Joss Harvey had written to her saying that Matthew had a heavy cold and that he thought it inadvisable for him to be moved to London until he had fully recovered.

Kate had brooded over the short and to-the-point

letter for quite a while. Was Matthew unwell or was Joss Harvey simply stalling for time? And if Matthew *was* unwell, shouldn't she be with him? She thought of the hideous influenza she had just recovered from and was uncertain for how long influenza germs hung around. She certainly didn't want to take any germs down to Somerset with her, perhaps making Matthew's condition even worse.

'We're just going to have to be patient,' she said to a disappointed Daisy. 'We're just going to have to wait until Matthew is better before we go and collect him and bring him home.'

On Saint Valentine's Day they had a visitor. 'I can't stay for long,' Lance said, a box of chocolates in his hand. 'I just wanted to wish you a happy Valentine's Day.'

Kate eyed the be-ribboned box in disbelief, feeling nauseous no longer. 'Where on *earth* did that come from, Lance? An American airman or the black market?'

A rare smile touched his mouth. 'Ask no questions and get told no lies.'

Kate smiled sunnily. 'Wherever they came from, they look gorgeous. Daisy won't be able to believe her eyes when she sees them. She's down at the Jennings' at the moment, playing with Rose.'

Lance followed her into the kitchen. It was the heart of her home and he had become accustomed to sitting in it as if it were a drawing-room.

'There's something we have to talk about,' he said, grateful that Daisy wasn't there and that they had a little privacy for once. 'I know how deeply you've grieved for Toby and it's the reason I haven't pushed things. I've wanted to give you time to get used to the idea of a new relationship.'

She turned to face him. This conversation was one they had had before and was one she had hoped wouldn't be raised again.

'Please don't say any more, Lance,' she said gently,

'There's something you don't know, something I have to tell you . . .'

'No,' he said forcefully, taking hold of her by the shoulders. 'I let you avoid the issue once before but I'm not going to do so again. It's been eighteen months since Toby died and you can't grieve for ever. Nor can you continue bringing up a young child single-handedly.'

She opened her mouth to protest and he said, 'Joss Harvey won't allow it, Kate. I know him. I know what he intends. Now will you please listen to me?'

The words she had been about to speak died on her lips. Joss Harvey. What did Lance know about Joss Harvey's intentions where Matthew was concerned? Had she been right in suspecting that Matthew didn't have a cold? Was the lie all part of some terrible plan to separate her from her son for ever?

'I've known Joss Harvey since I was thirteen or fourteen and Toby and I used to spend time together during school vacations,' Lance said, his hands still firm on her shoulders. 'And one thing I know about him is that he always gets what he wants. And what he wants now is something I want also.'

'I'm sorry,' she said, a small frown puckering her forehead. 'I don't know what you mean.'

He was standing so close to her that the buttons on his RAF jacket were brushing her blouse.

'Joss Harvey wants us to marry, Kate,' he said, his eyes hot as they held hers. 'If we marry you'll be an unmarried mother no longer and he will no longer feel ashamed of his great-grandson's illegitimacy. Even more to the point, if we marry he knows he will be ensured future contact with Matthew, something that might not happen if you were to marry anyone else.'

Kate's eyes flashed with remembered indignation. 'Joss Harvey has already informed me of his plans for me and when he did so I told him that my future was none of his concern!'

'And you were quite right to tell him so,' Lance said,

keeping his voice steady with difficulty. Dear God in heaven, what if she turned him down? What if he lost her for ever? 'But can't you see how fortuitous it is that he feels the way he does?'

His voice throbbed with the intensity of his feelings. 'I love you, Kate. I fell in love with you long before I met you, when Toby first talked to me about you and showed me your photograph. That Joss Harvey feels as he does will simply make life easier for us. I was a junior architect when I joined the RAF. Joss has already said that when we marry and when I'm demobbed, there will be a position for me on the board at Harvey's.'

Kate sucked in a deep, unsteady breath. No wonder Joss Harvey had been so certain he could manipulate Lance Merton into marrying her. She wondered what other bait had been proffered. Had Joss Harvey also promised that when he died, and until Matthew reached adulthood, Lance would have total control of Harvey's? Had Joss begun to view Lance as a substitute for the grandson he had lost?

And was it so surprising if he had? Lance had been educated at the same exclusive public school as Toby and they had been school friends. Toby had been tall and blond and loose-limbed and though Lance didn't possess the easy-going nonchalance that Toby had possessed, he was just as tall and just as Nordically fair. Unbidden, another thought came winging into her mind. He was also just as eligible, or so most people would judge.

She looked up into his tense, narrow, high cheekboned face. The wife of Group Captain Lance Merton wouldn't receive slights or snubs from anyone, she would be socially and financially secure, her lifestyle very similar to that which it would have been if she had married Toby. Even more importantly, her relationship with Joss Harvey would be amicable. Matthew wouldn't grow up enduring the misery of knowing he was the cause of battles between them. They would be, to all outward purposes at least, a united family.

It was a tempting prospect. A handsome husband. Social status. Financial security. She put her hands against his chest and said quietly, 'I can't marry you, Lance. I'm not in love with you.'

His jaw tightened. 'You might find out differently if only you stopped grieving . . .'

'I have stopped grieving,' she said starkly, 'or at least I've stopped grieving in the way that you mean.

'Then why . . .' he began, impatience edging his voice.

'I'm in love with someone else.'

For a second his eyes remained blank and then shock flared through them, followed swiftly by disbelief.

'And I'm having a baby,' she said, wanting him to be in no doubt at all as to her full commitment to another man.

There was no mistaking her sincerity and the disbelief in his eyes vanished.

'You're pregnant?' He dropped his hands from her shoulders as if he had been burned. *Pregnant?*

He couldn't have sounded more incredulous if she had said she had leprosy.

'Yes,' she said firmly as he stepped abruptly away from her. 'Leon doesn't know yet, but when he next has leave . . .'

She was about to say that when Leon next had leave they would be getting married but before she was able to Lance said:

'*Leon?* What kind of a name is that, for Christ's sake?'

Kate's eyes held his. She knew instinctively the kind of reaction she would meet with if she told him Leon was part West Indian and she knew also why it was she had never been able to become really close to him.

She said, indifferent to his reaction, 'Leon is a very popular West Indian name.'

'West Indian? *West Indian?*' He looked as if he had been slapped hard across the face. 'Dear Christ! I treat you like the Virgin Mary because I believe you're still grieving for Toby and all the time you're consorting with a . . . a . . .'

He couldn't bring himself to even say the word.

As she saw the revulsion in his eyes she knew they were never going to have a civil conversation again and that it was the end of their always unsatisfactory relationship; never lovers, not even true friends.

'He's a sailor,' she said, knowing that she was making a dire situation worse and not caring, 'And he used to be my lodger . . .'

'Jesus!' He looked as if he were going to be sick. 'You kept me at arm's length and all the time you were laughing behind my back, behaving like a whore with a black seaman! And I wanted to marry you!'

His nostrils were pinched and white, his eyes blazing. 'Did you behave like this behind Toby's back, too? Is Matthew Toby's child or is he the offspring of another so-called lodger? A Ukrainian, perhaps. Or a Pole?'

Oddly, she felt no anger towards him. Only pity.

'Goodbye, Lance,' she said quietly. 'Please take your chocolates with you.'

With something that sounded like a half-strangled sob he snatched the gold-paper-packaged box from the kitchen table and turned on his heel, slamming the door behind him so viciously that it rocked on its hinges.

Only when the front door had also slammed did she realize she was trembling. She sat down in the rocking-chair. In a minute, when she was quite sure his car was no longer in Magnolia Square, she would go down to Miriam's and see if Carrie was home.

'You're out of luck,' Miriam said cheerfully, inviting her in. 'Everyone else is at 'ome, bar Carrie and Albert. 'ave you come to take Daisy 'ome? Because if you 'ave, she won't want to go. She's upstairs with Rose, playing with the doll's 'ouse.'

'I'll leave her here for a little longer then,' Kate said,

still bemused that, thanks to Nellie Miller's propaganda work on her behalf, she was again a welcome guest at the Jennings'.

'Ma's just made some bagels,' Miriam said, and Kate noticed that Miriam's own beefy red arms were dusted with flour. 'Come into the kitchen and 'ave one.'

They had barely moved half a dozen steps down the clutter-filled passage-way when the air raid sirens wailed into life.

'Bugger,' Miriam said graphically, side-stepping a wooden clothes-horse heavy with freshly ironed laundry. 'It's another of them bloomin' "nuisance" raids. Two planes at the most. If it wasn't for the kids I wouldn't bother traipsing down to the shelter.'

Kate sympathized. Though a daylight 'nuisance' raid wasn't as inconvenient as a night one, when it meant deciding whether or not to leave a warm bed for the nearest shelter, it was exceedingly annoying. Most Londoners now took them in their stride, refusing to give the pilots of the planes the satisfaction of being the cause of widespread disruption. Like Miriam, Kate would have liked to have ignored the sirens but, like Miriam, she felt too responsible for the children to be able to do so.

'I'll go upstairs and bring Rose and Daisy down,' she said to Miriam. 'Where have we to go? The Anderson or the public?'

' 'ardly anyone goes to the public any more for a "nuisance". I'll get Ma and Christina to keep us company in the Anderson. We can take some bagels with us.'

Kate ran up the stairs, calling, 'Rose! Daisy! Can't you hear the sirens? Come on, we're going down the shelter!'

'And what about Hector,' Daisy asked anxiously as she and Rose tumbled out of the bedroom Rose shared with Carrie. 'Where's Hector? He doesn't like the sirens, Auntie Kate. He won't be happy on his own. Can we go and get Hector?'

'No,' Kate said firmly, shooing her and Rose

downstairs. 'It will only be one or two planes and they'll have gone away in a few minutes. Hector will be fine. He'll get under the kitchen table and most likely fall asleep.'

'Bonzo never falls asleep,' Rose said as Kate hurried her through the kitchen and out into the back garden. 'And he always wears a tin hat. Grandma bought one 'specially for 'im and Grandad painted 'is name on it in white paint.'

As the two children scampered down the concrete steps into the shelter Kate could hear the approach of planes. She looked up, shielding her eyes against the unusually bright February sun. As Miriam had predicted there were only two of them, their intention not so much to cause damage by bombing as to cause widespread disruption by obliging vast numbers of London factory workers to down tools and head for the nearest shelter. Kate ducked her head down and entered the Anderson. The ack-ack guns on the Heath had already opened up on the invading planes and with a little luck would bring one, or even both of them, down.

'And if they do bring one of the *momzers* down, where will it fall, my life?' Leah Singer was asking practically. 'Better they don't hit one than they fall out of the sky on top of us!'

It was the first time Kate had ever been in the Jennings' shelter. Albert had fitted it out with a couple of bunk-beds, a deck-chair, a large rag-rug and a storm-lantern and there was a beer crate from The Swan with half a dozen bottles in, most of them empty.

'Sit down, *bubbelah*,' Leah said, shifting up a little so that Kate could sit beside her and Christina on the bottom bunk-bed. 'Why do the *shleppers* always fly over our heads? Why can't they fly over the heads of the rich instead?'

'They do, Ma,' Miriam said, pulling a well-worn jacket on over her sleeveless flower-patterned overall. 'In the last proper raid Bromley didn't 'alf cop it.'

'Not like the East End,' Leah persisted, lifting Bonzo on to her knee. 'No-one's copped it like the East Enders.'

The two planes sounded to be heading directly for Magnolia Square.

'I can't understand why the ack-ack guns don't bring 'em down,' Miriam muttered, hugging her arms across her ample chest. 'And will you two stop jumping up and down on that top bunk, Rose and Daisy? You're making so much racket I keep thinking we've been 'it!'

'Will Albert be all right?' Christina asked suddenly. 'You don't think the planes will strafe the High Street, do you?'

There was no way of knowing and no-one replied.

'At least Beryl and Jenny will be in the school shelter,' Miriam shouted as the droning engines above them caused the walls of the shelter to vibrate. 'And so will Billy if he 'asn't scarpered off for the arternoon. The trouble with Billy is that . . .'

It was a sentence she never finished.

There was a screaming, whooshing sound, as if all the air around them was being sucked up into the sky and then a blast so tremendous that none of them thought they would survive it. The earth buckled and ruptured beneath their feet, an avalanche of flying masonry and timber and tiles thundered down on top of the Anderson's steel roof. Kate was plucked from the bunk-bed and thrown bodily into the steel-grooved wall opposite. She could feel blood, hot and sticky, streaming down her face and when she opened her mouth to scream Daisy's name, she choked on smoke and cordite fumes.

'We've been 'it! We've been 'it!' Miriam was screaming unnecessarily, proving that she was at least alive.

There were other screams. Rose's and Daisy's. But they were screams of terror, not pain.

From outside came the roar and crackle of flame. 'The 'ouse is gone,' Miriam was sobbing, picking herself up

391

from where she had been thrown. 'Oh, what am I goin' to tell Albert! What's Albert goin' to say?'

Kate pushed herself away from the still rocking wall of the shelter. Miraculously Rose and Daisy were still on the top bunk-bed, clinging to each other hysterically. '*I'm here, darling. I'm here,*' she shouted reassuringly, reaching up to lift Daisy down to the ground.

As she did so, the earth juddered.

'I've got Rose,' Christina said in a voice of remarkable calm. 'Let's get out of here! Quick!'

'*Oy veh! Oh veh! Oh veh!*' Leah moaned, clutching a half-stunned Bonzo to her chest. 'All through the Blitz he wears his helmet and today, when he needed it, I left it behind!'

As they stumbled out into the fresh air their first reaction was disbelief at finding that Miriam was wrong and that the house was still standing, their second all-engulfing horror at the scene only a few doors away.

The entire two upper storeys had collapsed and flames were shooting up through the right-hand side of the wreckage from the ground floor.

'Oh dear God!' Kate whispered, letting go of Daisy so great was her shock. 'It's the Misses Helliwell's house!'

Without another word she and Christina broke into a run. Somewhere in the distance fire-engine bells were clanging. As she and Christina ran and scrambled over the debris that had once been a neat and tidy pathway Kate was aware of other people running in the same direction, but she and Christina were the first on the scene.

Masonry and exposed wooden joists shivered and settled amid huge clouds of rising dust. The fire was gaining hold, feeding on crushed furniture and doors. Where the Misses Helliwell's sitting-room had been was a cascade of bricks and smashed roof-tiles and, somewhere buried beneath it, the Morrison shelter.

With smoke stinging their eyes Christina and Kate began clawing at the rubble, hurling it away from above where they judged the Morrison to be. The flames were roaring nearer and still the fire-engine had not screeched to a halt.

'I'm with you, girls!' Mr Nibbs panted, seizing the corner of a crushed brass bedstead and dragging it from the debris with almost super-human strength.

The fire was scorching them as they dug and clawed with lacerated hands. Dimly Kate was aware that the fire engine had arrived. She could hear Daniel Collins' voice. Hear the blessed hiss of water.

'*The gas pipes may be leaking!*' a male voice shouted. '*There may be an explosion! Get those girls to a place of safety!*'

There was a spitting sound and as Kate ignored the warning and heaved a jagged corner of ceiling moulding to one side a demented animal, fur on end, sprang from what had very nearly been its tomb and leapt past her shoulders.

'Faust!' Kate gasped to Christina. 'They always took him with them into the Morrison. They must be directly beneath us!'

Male hands had come to their aid, but despite the arrival of the firemen, the fire was still crackling and roaring closer and closer.

'There's a gap here!' Daniel Collins shouted to his fellow auxiliary firemen. 'We need someone thin to worm a way down! The old ladies are elderly and one of them's a cripple, they're not going to be able to scramble out unaided!'

'I'm thinner than any man,' Kate said swiftly, beating out a shower of sparks that had landed on her dress.

'You're not thinner than me,' Christina said, pushing a way past her. 'And I'm not pregnant.'

'Pregnant?' Daniel Collins eyes nearly popped out of his head. 'If you're pregnant, Kate Voigt, you shouldn't be risking life and limb on a bomb site! There could be a gas explosion any minute, either that or the whole bloody lot could cave in!'

'Oh, *helloooo*!' A frail voice called faintly over the din of rescue-workers and the menacing roar and crackle of flames. '*Oh, can anyone hear me? Is anyone there?*'

'Hold on tight, Miss Helliwell!' Daniel shouted down into the ink-black gap between broken joists and brick-work. 'We're going to have you and your sister out in a jiffy.'

'That's if the sister's alive,' a fireman said pessimistically. 'She always looked as if a puff of wind would be enough to finish her off, let alone one of Hitler's ruddy bombs.'

No-one paid him any heed. Despite Kate's protests Christina was squeezing herself down into the narrow gap they had uncovered.

'Does she know the bloody danger?' another of Daniel's colleagues asked him. 'We haven't got the fire under control yet and if she gets trapped down there . . .'

As Christina wriggled down into the debris Kate dropped to her hands and knees at the edge of the opening. Emily, at least, was alive. Surely if Esther had been killed by the blast Emily would have shouted the news up to them?

Reading her thoughts Daniel said, 'They may not have been together when the bomb fell. They may have done what a lot of other people do when it's only a nuisance raid. Ignored it.'

From below their feet came the sound of muffled voices.

'*Have you got her?*' Daniel shouted down to Christina, a coil of sturdy rope in his hands. '*Are we going to be able to lift her out?*'

There was a silence that seemed to last for ever and then Christina's voice shouted back, 'We need to get the other Miss Helliwell out first. She isn't conscious but she's alive.'

'We'll have to get a shift on, Daniel,' Daniel's colleague said to him grim-faced. 'The fire's still alive below the rubble. It could reach them at any moment.'

Daniel didn't reply. Keeping firm hold of one end of

the rope, he threw the coil into the narrow void at his feet. As he did so there was a hiss and a spurt of flame shot through a narrow crack only feet away from him. A fireman immediately doused it with a hose but everyone who saw it knew what it meant.

'You'd best get clear,' Daniel said to Kate. 'There's nothing else you can do now.'

Kate ignored him. At the bottom of a deep dark shaft she could see the tops of two heads, one white-haired and one glossily dark. The glossily dark head turned, looking upwards. 'She's out cold, Kate! I'm going to lift her up as high as I can. If you can reach down and get hold of her . . .'

Laying flat on the rubble Kate stretched down into the pit and as Daniel and another fireman began to haul steadily on the rope looped around Esther's chest and under her arms, did as Christina asked.

As Esther's lolling head began to surface other hands came to her aid.

'Christ! Is she dead?' Someone asked anxiously.

Someone else said, 'She needs fresh air and she needs lying down. Have you got hold of her? Can you carry her somewhere where a doctor can look at her?'

From down below there came the sound of harsh coughing and a wisp of smoke curled into the air. 'Are you ready with the rope?' Christina shouted urgently. 'The fire is on the far side of the Morrison! We're being choked down here!'

Daniel threw the rope down again and Christina looped it swiftly around Miss Helliwell. This time, the operation was easier. Dazed and disorientated Miss Helliwell was hauled inch by excruciating inch to the surface, like an unwieldy bucket from a well.

'Oh, Kate!' she gasped as Kate's hands reached down to her. 'Oh dear, oh dear! I was in contact with one of the dear departed when all of a sudden the world just erupted around me!'

'You were very near to being one of the dear departed

yourself,' Daniel said dryly as he lifted her free of the jagged opening. 'Now let's get Christina out of there before she chokes to death.'

'*I can smell gas!*' one of the firemen shouted urgently. '*Get everyone as far away as possible, Daniel!*'

As the crowd of sightseers that had gathered in the debris-strewn road retreated prudently to St Mark's Church's grassy island, Kate leaned so far over the edge of the opening that unseen strong hands grabbed her legs to prevent her from falling into it head first. Smoke stung her eyes and heat beat up into her face in waves.

'*Can you reach my hands?*' she shouted down to Christina.

She could hear Christina dragging something and then scrambling on top of it and then the pale oval of her face looked up into hers.

'I think so . . .'

Somewhere, something gave. Kate was aware of shouts of alarm. She ignored them, stretching her hands down to Christina's. Their fingers touched and then, with the blood rushing dizzyingly into her head and the smell of gas nearly overcoming her, Kate stretched far enough to be able to grasp hold of Christina's wrists.

'*Pull me back!*' she cried to whoever was holding on to her legs. '*I've got her! Pull me back!*'

Mr Nibbs, now aided by Daniel, pulled. Seconds later Christina was being hauled to safety and Kate was pushing herself up onto torn and bleeding knees.

'*Now let's get the hell away from here!*' one of the firemen shouted. '*There's going to be a God-almighty explosion any minute!*'

The explosion came only seconds later. Kate and Christina had only just reached the comparative safety of St Mark's when the broken debris that had once been the Misses Helliwell's home blasted scores of feet into the sky. Tiles on houses as far away as Miss Godfrey's shattered down into gardens and on to the pavement. Every window in Mavis's house blew out. Flames leapt across to the tree in the Jennings' garden, burning furiously.

'Don't worry,' Bob Giles was saying comfortingly. 'The firemen will soon have it under control. Other emergency services are already on their way.'

'Blimey,' Miriam said as she looked at the yawning gap which had once been the Helliwells' home, 'our Billy's goin' to be sick as a parrot missing this little lot.'

'And what about Mavis's winders?' Leah said, hugging a still whimpering Bonzo protectively to her chest. 'I told her she should have kept the sticky-tape across 'em, but would she listen?'

'Are you all right?' Kate asked a violently trembling Christina.

Christina nodded, 'Yes. And you? Your face is still bleeding.'

'And my hands and my knees,' Kate said with an unsteady laugh, vastly relieved to be suffering from nothing more than cuts and gashes. 'How did you know I was pregnant? Was it just a guess?'

Christina shook her head, a dark wing of hair falling across a soot-smudged cheek. 'No, Carrie told me.'

They looked at each other, realizing for the first time the way they were clinging on to each other. Neither of them released their hold.

'I think I'm becoming very English,' Christina said, a hint of a giggle in her voice. 'I'm in desperate need of a cup of tea!'

'So am I,' Kate said as Albert's horse and hearse clattered into the Square. 'And I think my house is going to be quieter than yours. Come on. We can patch ourselves up with iodine and sticking-plaster while we're waiting for the kettle to boil.'

With their arms still tight around each other's waist they began to walk across the grass.

'God works in mysterious ways,' Nellie Miller said to Bob Giles. 'That fidgety bastard Hitler's done those two quite a good turn if he did but know it!'

Chapter Twenty-one

The following Saturday, leaving Daisy in Carrie's care, Kate travelled by train to Taunton. Although she had written a postcard to Joss Harvey, telling him of the date and time of her arrival, no chauffeured Bentley was waiting for her. She was in too happy a mood at the prospect of being permanently reunited with Matthew to be much put out. The war-time postal service was erratic and Joss Harvey had obviously not yet received her postcard.

She stood on the pavement outside the station in the late February sunshine, her cherry-red coat buttoned up to her throat, her long mane of flaxen hair prudently twisted into a coil in the nape of her neck. She could phone the house, saying that she was at the station, and then no doubt the chauffeur would come and collect her. Or she could get a taxi. She wondered what a taxi would cost.

'Excuse me, Miss,' a young man in a clean butcher's apron said a little nervously, 'You're Mr Harvey's daughter-in-law, aren't you? I've seen you when I've been delivering to Tumblers. Is anything wrong? You look as if you have a problem.'

'I'm just trying to make my mind up about something,' Kate said with a friendly smile, recognizing him as one of Joss Harvey's regular tradesmen. 'And I'm not Mr Harvey's daughter-in-law. I'm Miss Voigt.'

The sandy-haired young man coloured slightly. He was as well aware of her single status as everyone else who worked or had business at Tumblers, but it hardly seemed manners to draw attention to the illegitimacy of Mr Harvey's great-grandchild.

'If I can be of any help . . .' he said hesitantly, eager to remain in her company for a little longer.

'I was just wondering what a taxi would cost to Tumblers.'

'I wouldn't know about the price of taxis,' the young butcher said, 'not ever having any call for them. It's a fair distance, though. Whatever the price, it won't be cheap.'

Kate frowned slightly . . . She hated the thought of telephoning and specifically asking to be collected from the station. It was too much like asking a favour of Joss Harvey. On the other hand, she couldn't afford an expensive taxi journey.

Thinking out loud, she said regretfully, 'I think I'll have to telephone the house.'

'There's no need for that, Miss,' the young butcher said helpfully. 'I'm on my way out there now. That's my van across the street. If you'd like a lift, it would be my pleasure.'

It was a far pleasanter ride than usual. He chatted to her about Toby, referring to him as 'Mr Toby'. 'I'd be about twelve and Mr Toby would be fifteen or sixteen,' he said as they motored gently through the undulating countryside. 'He took me fishing and I caught the biggest trout I've ever seen in my life. It were a grand day. He never had no pretensions, Mr Toby. No pretensions at all.'

The pang of loss she always felt when she thought of Toby swept over her. Her hands clasped a little tighter in her lap. Thank goodness Leon had come into her life. Toby would have liked and approved of Leon. Unlike Lance, Toby had possessed no snobbishness or prejudice where class or creed or colour were concerned. As her present companion had said so succinctly, he had had no pretensions. None at all.

When they reached Tumblers the butcher dropped her off at the front of the house and then motored round to the rear and the tradesmen's entrance.

She pressed the doorbell, fizzing with happiness at the thought that she would never do so again, at least not in order to visit Matthew.

'Mr Harvey would like to see you, Miss Voigt,' the maid who opened the door to her said, avoiding her eyes. 'He's in the drawing-room.'

Kate suppressed a surge of impatience. She didn't want to see Joss Harvey. She wanted to dash up the stairs to the nursery and scoop Matthew into her arms and never let him go.

Briskly she walked across the hall to the drawing-room door and opened it. Joss Harvey had been grudgingly civil to her ever since it had occurred to him that she might one day marry Lance Merton and the last thing she expected was a reenactment of their terrible interview in his boardroom. The minute she saw his face, however, she knew that that was exactly what was going to happen.

'You got here then?' he barked ungraciously.

'Yes.' Her eyes held his unflinchingly. If he wanted to mar the occasion with rudeness and hostility then there was nothing she could do about it, but she certainly wasn't going to allow him to intimidate her.

'And I suppose you think you've come for my great-grandson?'

He was standing in front of the marble fireplace, his legs apart, his hands clasped behind his back.

'I don't think,' she said, stung into waspishness. 'I know.'

'No, you don't.' There was such triumph in his voice that warning bells began ringing in her ears. 'I had a visitor last week,' he continued, 'and my visitor told me a lot of very interesting things about you, Kate Voigt.'

She knew then. Before he said another word, she knew what was about to come. His visitor had been Lance. Lance had told him about Leon and that she was pregnant. And Joss Harvey's attitude towards Leon was quite obviously exactly the same as his informant's.

'I'm going to the nursery,' she said crisply, turning away from him, knowing there was absolutely no point in remaining to talk to him.

'Feel free.' Joss Harvey rocked back comfortably on his heels. 'You won't find anyone or anything in there. If it comes to a court case I have no doubt at all that the law will be on my side. You're nothing but a trollop and totally unfit to have care of a child, certainly not *my* great-grandchild . . .'

She whipped round to face him, hardly able to believe her ears. At the gloating relish in his eyes the blood drained from her face. He wasn't going to give Matthew back to her. He had never had any intention of giving Matthew back to her.

'What have you done with my son?' she whispered hoarsely. '*Where's my baby?*'

'Where you won't find him,' he said succinctly.

Her heart felt as if it had ceased to beat. Without wasting another second in fruitless argument she spun on her heel, running from the room; running across the hall; running up the broad, curving staircase; running along the corridor towards the nursery; running, running, running.

The nursery door rocked open. The room was empty. Not even the chest of drawers that had contained Matthew's clothes remained. Around the lemon painted walls nursery figures jeered down at her. Miss Muffet. Tom, the Piper's Son. Humpty-Dumpty. Wee Willie Winkie.

She spun on her heel, panic bubbling high in her throat. He'd taken Matthew and hidden him but he couldn't get away with it. He *couldn't*!

'I can,' Joss Harvey said with terrible certainty. 'Two illegitimate children in little more than two years? The second one to a black sailor? No judge in his right mind would grant you custody of Matthew when he could grant custody to me. You may have made a fool out of my grandson and a fool out of young Merton, but you haven't made a fool out of Joss Harvey. I knew what you were the first minute I set eyes on you. A scheming, money-grabbing, Kraut-trollop . . .'

She didn't wait to hear any more. Nothing could be gained by staying to argue with him and he certainly wouldn't listen to reason. She needed to get back to London as quickly as she could and she needed advice; professional advice.

She rushed out of the house at such high speed that the butcher, a delivery made and an order taken, almost ran her over.

'Do you want another lift?' he asked unnecessarily, 'Hop in. I'm going straight back to Taunton.'

' 'e's done *what*?' Miriam exclaimed, standing over her steaming copper, drumming the clothes clean with a posser. ''e can't 'ave!'

'You must go to the police!' Christina said urgently, sitting at the kitchen table, Rose on her knee. 'The police will help you. Kidnapping is a crime . . .'

'You need a solicitor.' Carrie had been putting her father's shirts through the mangle, being careful to keep the buttons to the very edge, free of the rollers, so that they wouldn't break.

She let go of the mangle handle. 'I don't know where you'll find one, but Miss Godfrey will know.' With her eyes dark with compassion she crossed the kitchen floor, hugging Kate tightly.

'There's something else you have to know,' she said, her voice cracking. 'Leon's ship has been torpedoed. It was on today's lunchtime news. There are reports that some survivors were picked up by a U-boat, but that losses were heavy. I'm sorry, Kate. Truly sorry.'

The next few days were a nightmare. She wasn't officially Leon's next of kin, although when the naval authorities knew that she was carrying Leon's child they were duly sympathetic. Even so, there was very little they could tell her.

'Some survivors of *The Maiden* were picked up by the U-boat that sank her,' she was told when she enquired. 'How many we still don't know. Eventually the Red Cross may be able to provide us with a list of names of those taken prisoner, but that won't be forthcoming for quite some time. If we have further news we will of course contact you.'

'Kidnapping?' the sergeant at Shooters Hill police station said, scratching the top of his bald head. 'But didn't you say, Miss, that the gentleman in question is the child's grandfather . . .'

'Great-grandfather.'

'And that he's Mr Harvey of Harvey Construction Ltd?'

'Yes.'

'And that the child has been an evacuee with him since last March?'

'Yes.'

'Then I don't rightly see how Mr Harvey, having removed his great-grandchild to a place of safety, can be accused of having kidnapped him. You're worrying unnecessarily, Miss, if you don't mind my saying so. All mothers of children still evacuated feel the same way, it's only natural.'

'But Mr Harvey no longer has Matthew with my consent!' Kate persisted passionately. 'And I don't even know where he is!'

'No-one knows where anyone is, these days,' the sergeant said wryly. 'Take my eldest boy. He's with the Eighth Army in North Africa, but whereabouts in North Africa, God only knows. As for Mr Harvey, he's a very respected and responsible citizen. When those houses in Point Hill Road were bombed it was Mr Harvey who saw to it that temporary accommodation was erected on the site almost immediately.

Believe me, Miss, your little lad couldn't be in better hands.'

'And Mr Joss Harvey is the great-grandfather of the child in question?' the solicitor Miss Godfrey had referred her to asked, taking his spectacles off his narrow nose and placing them on his leather-topped desk.

'Yes.'

'And you were not married, or ever married, to the father of the child, Mr Harvey's grandson, Toby Harvey?'

'No. We were engaged to be married when he was killed at Dunkirk.'

'And Mr Harvey has accepted that the child in question is his grandson's child?'

'Yes,' Kate said, disliking the solicitor's tone intensely.

'And as I understand it, Mr Harvey's objection to returning the child to your care is that you are at present pregnant again?'

'Yes.'

'And still unmarried?'

'Yes.'

The solicitor picked up his glasses and replaced them carefully on his nose. 'I'm sorry, Miss Voigt. Under the circumstances I don't think I can act for you. Mr Harvey's reputation is unimpeachable and . . .'

Kate didn't wait to listen to any more. As she strode out of the stuffy offices into the brisk March air she wondered savagely if she would have been treated in such a cavalier manner if she had been a man and had fathered two children out of wedlock.

'So what are you going to do now?' Carrie asked as they walked across the Heath, Hector and Bonzo bounding ahead of them.

'I don't know,' Kate's hands were plunged deep in her coat pockets, the knuckles clenched. 'But I'll think of something and I'll get Matthew back. *Nothing* is going to stop me getting Matthew back!'

That evening, when she had put Daisy to bed, she sat before the fire, racking her brains for a way of gaining the kind of support that she needed. If only she knew whereabouts Matthew was, it would be a help. The fire crackled and spat. Wherever he was, she had one thing to be thankful for. He was in the care of Ruth Fairbairn and being well looked after.

Her heart seemed to miss a beat. Ruth! Ruth had always been sympathetic towards her. Ruth wouldn't have taken Matthew to another address if she had known that by doing so she was colluding in a virtual kidnapping. If only she could get in touch with Ruth Fairbairn her problem would be solved!

'Try contacting her via the *Lady* magazine,' Harriet suggested helpfully. 'All nannies read it because it's stuffed with adverts for nannying jobs. It's where Mr Harvey probably advertised Ruth's position.'

The notice Kate had inserted in the Personal column was short and to the point. *Would Miss Ruth Fairbairn please contact Miss Kate Voigt, 4 Magnolia Square, Blackheath, London. Urgent.* 'If Ruth sees it, she'll contact me,' Kate said to Carrie, deep circles carved beneath her eyes. 'God, but I can't believe anyone can behave as Joss Harvey is behaving!'

'I can't believe so many people seem to think he's behaving rationally and within his rights,' Carrie said grimly, thinking of the police sergeant and the solicitor. 'Mum always says if she's ever born again she's going to be a man. I'm beginning to understand what she means.'

The week-long wait until the next copy of the *Lady* was published was the longest week of Kate's life. What if Ruth didn't buy the magazine that week? What if none of her friends did either and no-one told her of the notice in the Personal column? Even worse, what if it came to Joss Harvey's attention and he dismissed Ruth and moved Matthew to a different address with a different nanny?

'Cheer up, it might never 'appen!' Billy called out to her cheekily as she set off down to Lewisham market to do some shopping. Clad in a moth-eaten jumper and short trousers and a balaclava helmet and hob-nailed boots he was straddling a branch of Miss Godfrey's magnolia-tree, waving a rusty bayonet high in the air. 'Do you like it?' he shouted down to her. 'I scrounged it from the ammunition dump. I've got loads more at 'ome. If the Jerries ever land I'm goin' to multicrush 'em . . . ! Pulverize 'em!'

Kate continued towards Magnolia Hill, wondering what else Billy had scrounged from the ammunition dump. It would be typically careless of Mavis to have allowed him to amass an arsenal in their back garden. From behind her she could hear him singing lustily:

'Whistle while you work!
Hitler is a twerp!
Goering's barmy
So's his army
Whistle while you work!'

Despite all the worries on her mind, a smile touched the corners of her mouth. Billy, at least, was having a good war.

'I didn't see any sense in simply writing,' Ruth Fairbairn, said to her, standing on the doorstep looking like a vision from heaven, Matthew jumping up and down excitedly in her arms. 'As soon as I read the message I knew that you didn't have a clue where Matthew was and that Mr Harvey had lied to me.'

'Mam . . . Mam . . . Mam . . . Mamma.' Matthew chanted, stretching out chubby arms towards her.

Kate was beyond speech. With a sob of joy and with tears of relief streaming down her face she reached out hungrily for him.

'Mr Harvey told me you were quite happy with the

new arrangements but that you wouldn't be visiting as often because you were having another baby and the travelling was difficult,' Ruth said as Kate hugged Matthew so tightly that he yowled with protest. 'I shall lose my job now, of course, but I don't care. He was never an easy man to work for.'

Between pressing kisses on Matthew's rosy cheeks Kate said, 'Come in, Ruth! Please come in! I've been out of my mind with worry! I was terrified you wouldn't see the message and I didn't know what I would do if you didn't!'

Ruth followed her into the house saying, 'I never did like the set-up down in Somerset. Even though it was awkward, you not having been married to Matthew's father, there was no need for Mr Harvey to have made it *quite* so awkward. The staff didn't even know your name when you first visited.'

Kate wasn't listening to her. She was feasting her eyes on her son's face, saying joyously, 'You're home, Matthew! You're home and you're never going to go away again without me, not ever!

Ruth stayed with her for the rest of the day, accompanying her down to the Jennings' where Daisy was playing with Rose. They were still there, eating jam-filled pancakes that Leah had made for them, when Bob Giles arrived.

'What a nice vicar,' Ruth said later as they eventually made their way home. 'Did you say he was widowed? I like this part of London, Kate. It has all sorts of unexpected attractions. I might try and land a job in Blackheath and if I do I might just start going out to church again!'

'I'm glad you've got the little fella back home with you,' Nellie Miller said to her as Kate bandaged her legs, 'but you don't want to be too complacent. A man like old 'arvey won't take kindly to being bested. What you need is a solicitor . . .'

'No, I don't,' Kate said with feeling. 'I went to a solicitor when I was trying to get Matthew back legally and he was stupifyingly unhelpful.'

'That's because he was a man,' Nellie said dismissively. 'What you need is a lady solicitor and I know just where to find one.' She lifted a bandaged leg out of the way with both hands and submitted the other leg for treatment. 'This will probably come as a surprise to you, and it came as a surprise to my brother as well, but his eldest girl, Ruby, is a qualified solicitor. Gawd knows where she got the learnin' from, but she's sharp as a razor and if anyone can take on old 'arvey, she can.'

'Mr Harvey doesn't have any legal rights whatsoever where Matthew is concerned,' Ruby Miller said breezily, a cigarette crammed into the corner of a carmine-red mouth. 'And in case he thinks he can make a fight of it, in my letter of warning to him I shall point out that he is both a liar and a thief and that he runs the risk of these regrettable qualities coming to public notice.'

'A thief?' Kate said, startled. 'I'm not sure that . . .'

'He stole your child from you,' Ruby said flatly. 'Pillars of the community do not resort to baby-thieving. Nor can they afford to be branded liars and I shall inform him that I am quite prepared to testify against him on both counts. Now to practicalities, I don't suppose you're adverse to Matthew visiting him as long as you can be sure he won't try and pull another fast one on you, are you? It would be daft not to when that little nipper of yours could stand to inherit a tidy sum.'

'If I do agree to Matthew occasionally visiting him, it's not because of mercenary reasons, it's because I know that it is what his father would have wanted,' Kate said, feeling breathless by the speed at which events were now beginning to move.

Ruby grinned and took the cigarette from her mouth. 'I believe you, thousands wouldn't. And I can promise you that from now on Mr Joss Harvey will mind his manners where you and Matthew are concerned because if he doesn't, he's going to find himself languishing in a prison cell at His Majesty's leisure. Would you like a glass of Jack Daniels? I have an American serviceman client who keeps me well supplied.'

'So now your worry is whether Leon was one of the survivors picked up by the Germans when *The Maiden* sank,' Carrie said, her thoughts not only on Leon but Danny.

It was now nearly two years since he had been taken prisoner and though she was able to make contact with him by letters and parcels sent via the Red Cross, the two years felt like twelve.

'I *know* he was one of the survivors,' Kate said fiercely, rolling out pastry for jam-tarts. 'He survived when his ship was sunk off Norway and he'll have survived when *The Maiden* went down. If he was dead I would know. I would be able to *feel* it, in my heart. And he isn't dead, Carrie. He said he would come back to me and one day he will.'

All through the summer she waited for confirmation from the Navy that Leon had been picked up from the sea alive. None came. As the baby within her womb began to move and to kick vigorously she lay awake night after night wondering if, before *The Maiden* had been sunk, he had received her letter telling him that she was pregnant.

In August, when the war news seemed to reach an all time low with twenty-nine merchant ships sunk in the Arctic, two thousand Allied prisoners being taken after the failure of a major commando raid on the French port of Dieppe and the Germans launching a new offensive in North Africa, Miriam said to her bleakly, 'Doesn't look too good, does it? Remember 'ow we thought it would be all over by Christmas when it first began? We were livin' in a fool's bloomin' paradise, weren't we?'

'It just seemed simpler in 1939,' Kate said gently, not wanting to encourage Miriam's doom and gloom.

Miriam sighed. 'Too right, it did. Who'd 'ave thought then we'd 'ave ended up fighting in North Africa and the Far East? I know I didn't.'

She sighed again, this time far more heavily. 'And I never thought when your dad was taken away that it'd be for years and years, Kate. I've never 'ad the bottle to say so before but I'm sorry for what 'appened that day, for watchin' and being pleased about it. Albert's felt bad about it for a long time. I don't know what got into us. It was a bit like 'avin' a fever. Neither of us were really thinkin' straight. All we wanted to do was to 'it back at old 'itler and the only German to 'and was your dad. Silly, really.'

Kate thought of the pain Miriam and Albert's action had occasioned herself and her father. It was a pain she doubted if Miriam would ever be able to understand.

'Yes,' she said quietly, refusing to demean herself by holding grudges, 'Silly, really. Has Christina told you her news about Jack? Has she told you that in his last letter he asked her to marry him and that she's written back saying she will?'

At the end of September she again went into labour. This time, instead of Leon delivering the baby, Doctor Roberts delivered it. She had never missed Leon more.

'It just wasn't the same,' she said to Ruth who now, with a living-in job at Blackheath Village, was a regular visitor to Magnolia Square. 'And when Doctor Roberts saw how olive-skinned Luke was he said he had jaundice and it took me ages to persuade him that he was perfectly healthy and that he was always going to be this colour!'

Christmas, she spent with Harriet at Ellen's house in Greenwich. With Ellen's three dogs and half a dozen stray cats plus Hector, Daisy, Matthew and Luke, it was the noisiest, most boisterous Christmas any of them had ever had.

'And the happiest,' Ellen said to her, cuddling Matthew on her knee. 'What a lot your father has to look forward to when he eventually comes home, Kate. Two beautiful grandsons and a little step-granddaughter.'

'Of course Daisy isn't Dad's step-granddaughter,' Kate said that evening to Harriet. 'Legally, I have no claim to her at all. What do you think I should do to ensure that no-one ever takes her away from me? Do you think I'll be allowed to adopt her?'

'Ask Ruby Miller,' Harriet said sagely. 'If she's managed to keep an ogre like Joss Harvey at bay, she'll be able to arrange an adoption. Do you think this cardigan I'm knitting for Daisy is going to be big enough? She's growing so fast I can hardly keep up with her.'

All through 1943 life continued as near normal as rationing and the absence of menfolk allowed and though there were still air- raids they were nothing like the number or the intensity that had characterized the Blitz.

In September, as she pushed Luke's pram across the Heath, Matthew toddling along beside her and Daisy running ahead with Hector, Charlie called out to her, ' 'ave you 'eard the good news, petal? Italy's surrendered! It looks like young Danny will soon be on his way 'ome!'

Charlie's hopes were unfounded. In October Italy declared herself to be at war with her former ally, and as Italians and Germans fought and as British and American troops attempted to fight their way towards Rome, Italy was plunged into chaos.

★   ★   ★

By Christmas there had still been no news of Danny and Kate still hadn't received news confirming that Leon had survived the sinking of his ship and been taken prisoner. Both she and Carrie lived on hope.

'And so you should dears,' Emily Helliwell said to them. She and Esther had been living with Nellie Miller ever since their home had been bombed and she was busy brushing snow from Nellie's pathway. 'Both your young men are going to come home. My spirit guide has told me so and Moshambo never lies.'

'What I've never understood,' Carrie said as she and Kate continued walking up Magnolia Hill, 'is why Miss Helliwell never knew her house was going to be bombed.'

'Perhaps she never thinks to ask Moshambo about her own future,' Kate said, not wanting to think that Miss Helliwell might be fallible. 'What is he anyway? A Red Indian chief?'

'A Zulu warrior,' Carrie said, a chuckle of laughter in her voice. 'I wonder if he appears before her half-naked like those pictures of Zulus in the National Geographic. If he does it's no wonder she calls him up from the spirit world so bloomin' often!'

In May, as fighting in Italy between the Allies and the Germans intensified and as rumours grew that the long awaited invasion of Europe by the Allies was imminent, Christina rushed into Kate's house, her eyes shining. 'Jack has a twelve hour leave,' she announced in a voice that still held a trace of a German accent, 'and he wants us to celebrate it by getting married!'

'If anyone had told me six years ago, when she spat at my father at the church fête, that Christina Frank would one day ask me to be one of her bridesmaids I would have thought they were stark, staring mad,' Kate said as Carrie knelt at her feet, pinning the hem of the dress that was to be her bridesmaid dress. 'Is your Gran very upset that it's going to be another St Mark's

Church wedding? She must surely have hoped that Christina's wedding would be Jewish.'

'Gran's kept her thoughts to herself this time,' Carrie said dryly. 'I think she's just grateful that Christina is marrying and settling down here, in Magnolia Square, not moving on to America as so many other Jewish refugees are. Anyway, 'ow the heck could it be a Jewish wedding with Jack Robson as the bridegroom?' she asked, putting a final pin into the hem. 'It's a miracle it's even going to be a church wedding. I don't suppose for one moment Jack Robson was ever christened. I can't quite see Charlie seeing to such niceties, can you?'

Kate giggled and stepped away from Carrie so that she could see her reflection in her dressing-table mirror. 'What do you think?' she asked, regarding herself critically. 'Do you think everyone will know it's a dress that's been in my wardrobe since before the war?'

Carrie regarded the ice-coloured blue dress enviously. 'No,' she said, wishing that she could make the same kind of alterations to some of her pre-war clothes. 'How you've stayed so sylph-like after two babies beats me. None of my old clothes will go anywhere near me. I'm going to have to make do with a dress made out of black-market parachute silk!'

On the day of the wedding all Magnolia Park was out in full force. Albert purloined a trap from somewhere so that, with Nobby in the shafts, Christina would have a proper carriage to transport her the few yards to the church.

'He wasn't going to,' Carrie said, her green cat-eyes alight with laughter. 'He was going to use the hearse but Mum nearly flailed him alive when she found out. Poor Christina didn't want a carriage at all. She wanted to walk, but Mum wouldn't have that, either. God knows where the trap came from. Its owner probably doesn't know it's missing yet.'

Beryl, Jenny, Rose and Daisy were bridesmaids.

Where Kate's gleamingly gold chignon was decorated with a single lush white rose, the children all wore circlets of pink rosebuds. Carrie was Matron of Honour, buxomly splendid in pearl-grey parachute silk. Christina was ethereal in the wedding-gown that had once been Carrie's, her long veil held in place by a cluster of gardenias.

It was the groom, however, who attracted the most attention. Tall and broad and dark he had left Magnolia Square a likeable rogue and returned a war hero.

'Doesn't he look *handsome*!' an admiring Hettie said to Miriam. 'There always was an attractive swagger about those Robson boys. Jerry Robson had it in spades. There was a time once when I thought Jerry and . . .'

Miriam never did find out what Hettie had once thought. The bride had reached her place at the bridegroom's side and the entire congregation was rising to its feet to sing, 'O Perfect Love'.

Twenty minutes later, as the bridal party turned away from the altar to make its way back down the aisle, Kate's eyebrows rose high. The bridegroom's father, Charlie Robson was standing in the front right-hand pew, and he was not standing there alone. Harriet was next to him resplendent in a navy blue suit, the collar edged in white, a broad-brimmed navy blue hat shading her eyes. It was the first time Kate had ever seen her in a suit that wasn't made of serviceable tweed and she looked stunningly elegant. It wasn't her elderly friend's elegance that had taken her by surprise, though. It was the way her gloved hand was quite openly resting in Charlie's mammoth paw.

'Did you see?' she asked Carrie the minute they entered the church hall for the reception. 'They were definitely holding hands! In front of all of Magnolia Square!'

'I don't know why you're so surprised,' Carrie said, her parachute silk rustling and crackling with every move she made. 'They've been friends for yonks now. And

414

Charlie looks quite personable when he's had a shave and his shirt is buttoned and he's wearing a tie and a jacket.'

'Charlie looks *alien* in a tie and jacket,' Kate said, unable to get over the wonderment of it. 'I wonder where on earth they came from? Do you think Harriet bought them for him? Do you think there's going to be another wedding very soon?'

Overhearing them, Nellie Miller, stately in royal purple, said dryly, 'Yes, but not the one you have in mind, dear.'

Carrie was immediately all interest. 'Come on then, Nellie,' she said, eager for a bit of titillating gossip, 'Spill the beans. Who is it going to be? You and Clark Gable? Miss Helliwell and Nibbo? My Gran and General Montgomery?'

'The trouble with you, Carrie Collins, is that you're a cheeky hussy,' Nellie said with affection. 'And why the 'ell you need me to point out somethin' that's so flamingly obvious, I don't know. It's right in front of your eyes if you would but look,' and with a knowing nod of her head she indicated the couple standing a few yards behind Kate.

Both Kate and Carrie turned their heads. Ruth Fairbairn and Bob Giles were deep in conversation, oblivious of the wedding guests thronging around them.

Carrie's eyes widened with astonishment. 'Well, I'll be blowed,' she said expressively, 'Especially when you consider where they met!' She began to giggle. 'I must go and tell my Mum. She's going to be tickled to death!'

Within weeks of the wedding there was exhilaration as first Rome was liberated by the Allies and then the long awaited invasion of Europe finally took place.

'They've landed in Normandy!' Mavis announced as she breezed into The Swan. 'No wonder Jack had to bugger off so quickly after the wedding. You can bet he was one of the first ashore and I know my Ted will be there.'

'Are things all right between you and Ted now?' Kate asked her as they walked up Magnolia Hill together after shopping in Lewisham market.

'They've been all right ever since that fella of yours saved Billy from killing 'imself and gawd knows how many others in that bloomin' lorry,' Mavis said, shifting her heavy basket of shopping from one hand to the other. 'Ted said 'e realized then what it would be like to lose Billy and 'e said that if 'e was to divorce me, 'e'd be losing Billy voluntarily.'

She shot Kate a wide, irrepressible smile. 'Course, that ain't the *real* reason 'e's started behaving like a man with some sense. The real reason is 'e realized what an idiot 'e'd been, but 'e's too much pride to admit to it.'

With her free hand she tucked a stray wisp of peroxided blonde hair back into her upswept Betty Grable hairstyle.

'Christina 'elped, of course,' she said as they neared her front garden, a front garden Billy had vandalized so that it looked little different from a bomb-site. 'She told 'im Jack was in love with 'er and that they were goin' to get married and that if there'd been any funny business between the two of us she'd 'ave been the first to be up in arms about it.'

'I'm glad Ted realized how wrong he'd been,' Kate said as they turned into the Square.

Mavis chuckled. 'Now, who says 'e 'ad it wrong?' she said, pausing at her open gateway before walking up her littered pathway. 'And what makes you think I'd be so daft as to let Christina know my business? Credit me with some sense, Kate.'

As Kate's eyes widened Mavis gave her a knowing wink. 'Cheerio,' she said, her grin nearly splitting her face. 'Life ain't 'alf interestin', ain't it?'

*   *   *

July saw a return of the hideous days of the Blitz. This time it wasn't bombs dropped from wave after wave of enemy aircraft that decimated the city; this time it was something even more terrifying.

'Flying bombs,' Mr Nibbs said to her, grim-faced, 'Pilotless planes designed to explode on impact. 'We're in for a heck of a time until the RAF can find the bases they're being launched from and destroy them.'

'Nibbo wasn't exaggerating, was he?' Carrie said to Kate as they sat in the public shelter surrounded by their neighbours. 'What I hate about doodle-bugs is that you often get no warning. At least during the Blitz the sirens always went off in plenty of time and we heard the planes coming.'

'I don't see why the sirens can't always go off in plenty of time for doodle-bugs,' her mother said peevishly, busy peeling an apple.

'They're too small and fast for radar to detect them,' Kate said, lifting Matthew into a more comfortable position on her knee. 'That means there's often no air raid warning or when the warning is sounded it's sounded too late for people to be able to find shelter.'

'Well, they should do something about it,' Miriam said unreasonably, handing a slice of apple to Rose and Daisy. 'At least in the Blitz you knew where you were. With these bloomin' things, no-one knows where they are. One minute you're doing the housework, the next you could be dead.'

In September came even worse horrors. 'I don't know what the 'ell's 'appenin', petal,' Charlie said to Kate as he stopped for a chat at her front gate, 'but I do know that explosion we 'eard this arternoon wasn't caused by a doodle-bug.'

'It was a gas explosion,' Mr Nibbs said authoritatively that evening in The Swan. No-one disputed with him. It had certainly been unlike any previous explosion and as there had been no planes in the air, if it hadn't been a doodle-bug, what else could it have been but a gas explosion?

They were soon to find out. 'Rockets?' Hettie said disbelievingly to Daniel. 'What do you mean, rockets? You've been listening to too many science-fiction programmes on the radio, Daniel. It's turned your head.'

'They must be bloody rockets,' Daniel said to Nibbo. 'Nothing else could arrive from out of nowhere and cause such destruction. I was down New Cross this afternoon and a whole street has been demolished by one of the bloody things. Not just one or two houses, Nibbo. A whole street! There's no fighting back against such weapons. Unless the RAF find where they're being launched from there's going to be nothing left of London.'

Thousands of Londoners were in agreement with him. Evacuation began again on a massive scale. In November, after countless 'gas explosions' in south-west and south-east London, a public statement was issued confirming what had already become general knowledge. After surviving the Blitz and the flying bombs London was now under rocket attack.

Christmas was grim, with many Londoners being reluctant to spend too much time out of deep shelter.

'Not that we 'ave any deep shelters in Black'eath and Lewisham,' Miriam said savagely, worn down by five and a half years of tension and hardship. 'It's all right for those who live near tube stations but what about the rest of us? Andersons and Morrisons and public shelters are no protection against bloody rockets!'

January was even worse, with deep snow and freezing weather conditions adding to the misery.

'But it's goin' to get better, petal,' Charlie said reassuringly as he walked with Kate across the snow-bound Heath. 'The Germans are on the run now and once the RAF bomb the rocket launching bases we'll be 'ome and dry.'

By February Charlie's spirit of optimism was widespread. By March his prediction had come to fruition. The Allied armies crossed the Rhine and everyone knew they were living through the final days of the war.

In April, when the front gardens in Magnolia Square were drowned in a haze of blue Muscari and violet Aubrietia and purple pansies, Kate received her most joyous news for a long, long time.

'My dad's coming home!' she said to Carrie, her face radiant. 'He's going to see the children for the first time! Isn't that wonderful news? Isn't it absolutely marvellous?'

The day her father walked once again into Magnolia Square was one of the happiest of her life. He was a little thinner in the face than he had been, but other than that he looked no different to when he had been taken away.

'Oh Dad! *Dad!*' she cried, throwing her arms around him, tears of happiness streaming down her face. 'It's so good to have you back home!'

'It's good to be back, *Liebling*,' Carl said huskily, his eyes behind his glasses overly bright. 'And now are you going to introduce me to my grandchildren? And to little Daisy?'

The next morning there was a rather hesitant knock on the front door. When Carl opened it he found Albert on the doorstep.

'Our Carrie told us you were home,' he said awkwardly. 'Me and Miriam just wanted to say we were pleased.'

'Thank you, Albert,' Carl said gravely. He had had plenty of time to consider how he would react in such a situation and, like his daughter, he had decided that nothing would be achieved by holding grudges.

At his civil response Albert visibly relaxed. 'Perhaps you'd like to come down The Swan for a pint tonight? Nibbo and Daniel'll be there. What's past is past, isn't it? All water under the bridge. We might even get a cricket team together again now this bloody war is on its last legs.'

Over the next few days and weeks Albert's statement that the war was on its last legs was amply verified. The Allies stormed into Berlin. Hitler committed suicide. Carrie received news that Danny was on his way home to her. Christina received news that Jack had been mentioned in despatches.

'It's all over bar the shouting, *Liebling*,' her father said to her as he sat in his armchair, Matthew on his knee. 'Prisoners are being released the length and breadth of Europe. You'll soon know if Leon is alive. The waiting is nearly at an end now.'

'*It's over!*' Mavis screamed on 7 May, rushing out of the house into the street, the voice of a radio newscaster clearly audible on her radio. '*The Jerries have surrendered! It's over! It's over! It's over!*'

On all sides of Magnolia Square windows slammed up and doors flew open.

'And about bloody time!' Miriam shouted, running out of her house in hair curlers and pinafore and beginning to dance a knees-up in her front garden.

Hettie Collins rushed across the Square to join her.

Miss Helliwell began to hang a Union Jack from her bedroom window.

Nibbo stood on his front doorstep, his braces hanging down, tears streaming down his cheeks.

Miss Godfrey stood holding on to the wrought-iron scrollwork of her front gate, saying, 'Thank God! Oh, thank God!'

Daniel Collins sent his Auxiliary Firemen's helmet skimming across St Mark's Church's grassy island.

Albert fisted the air, shouting, 'Three cheers for Winnie! Three cheers for Mr Churchill! If it hadn't been for him this day would have never dawned!'

Leah Singer seized hold of Bob Giles and, much to the vicar's surprise, began dancing a jig with him.

Charlie emerged with three pots of paint he'd been saving for the occasion and lustily singing 'There'll Always Be an England' began liberally painting his front door red, white and blue.

Nellie Miller lumbered into her garden and bellowed, *'What about a party then? What about the biggest bloomin' party Magnolia Square has ever known!'*

Chapter Twenty-two

It was unanimously decided to hold the party the following Saturday.

'After all, we don't want to miss out on the fun of the celebrations tomorrow, up town, when Churchill announces the end of hostilities officially, do we?' Carrie said sensibly. 'And by Saturday, Danny might be home and Kate might have news of Leon.'

Carl said he didn't feel up to celebrating up town and that he would look after Daisy and Matthew and Luke. Miriam said she was going to do her celebrating in The Swan and that she'd keep an eye on Rose. Mavis said Beryl and Billy were big enough and daft enough to look after themselves and what the 'eck were they waiting for, why didn't they go up town *now*.

The trains into Charing Cross were so packed they had to stand up all the way. It wasn't the slightest hardship. Total strangers were greeting and kissing each other like long-lost friends. A rousing chorus of 'Pack up Your Troubles in Your Old Kit-Bag' was lustily sung by everyone all the way from Blackheath to Lewisham and 'Two Lovely Black Eyes' all the way from Lewisham to New Cross.

' 'ow about "The White Cliffs of Dover?" ' someone shouted as the train began to steam out of New Cross. Carrie didn't need a second prompting. Arm in arm with a soldier she'd never set eyes on before she launched into her favourite song, singing it in a full-throated contralto all the way into Charing Cross station.

'Where to first?' Christina asked as they spilled out of the station into the thronged cobbled forecourt.

'Trafalgar Square,' Mavis answered promptly, her arm around Kate's waist. 'Do you think that airman will give me 'is 'at to wear?'

The airman did give her his hat to wear. Christina bought a bunch of penny Union Jacks. Carrie was kissed by a sailor. Kate was dragged laughingly into a conga line.

In Trafalgar Square the crowds were so vast they could barely move. 'I'm going to ask those soldiers to give us a hoist on to one of the lions!' Mavis yelled, and before Christina or Kate could protest they found themselves swept off their feet into big, beefy arms and then manhandled up onto the back of one of the giant bronze lions.

High above the heads of the rest of the crowd they waved their flags and joined lustily in the communal singing. 'There's a sailor on Nelson's Column doing a strip!' Mavis shouted.

'Roll out the Barrel!' the joyous crowd surging below them sang.

'Give us a kiss, love!' a soldier demanded of Kate and, before she could assent or refuse, clambered up on to the lion, kissing her with commendable thoroughness.

'Oh, you beautiful doll, you great big beautiful doll,' a posse of GI's chorused as Mavis provocatively lifted her skirt and showed a mesmerizing amount of leg.

'They're burning an effigy of Hitler near the fountain!' someone hollered over the din.

The bells of St Margaret's, Westminster, pealed triumphantly. Motor-bus horns blared. The Americans blasted into a raucous rendering of 'Battle Hymn of the Republic.'

'Let's try and make our way towards the Palace!' Christina shouted, her sleek dark hair tumbling over her shoulders nearly as hoydenishly as Carrie's. 'I want to see the King and Queen!'

As young men they had never seen before and would never see again, helped them slither down from the lion and as they battled out of the Square and towards the Mall, Kate felt as if the entire world was intent on seeing King George and Queen Elizabeth.

'Long live the cause of freedom!' someone shouted. 'Long live Winnie! God Save the King!'

'And so you saw the King and Queen *and* Mr Churchill,' her father said to her late that night as he made her a cup of milky cocoa. 'That must have been quite a sight.'

'It was unforgettable,' Kate said, remembering the scene on the Palace balcony as the Prime Minister, flanked by King George and Queen Elizabeth, had stepped forward to acknowledge the frantic cheering of a crowd so vast it seemed to stretch into infinity. 'Everyone was blowing whistles and throwing confetti and the Princesses came out onto the balcony and then, later on, there were fireworks.'

'And you came home and left Carrie and Christina and Mavis enjoying the fun?' her father asked, his voice gently querying.

She nodded, her eyes dark with the anxiety she could no longer hide. 'Everyone was so happy – wild with joy, and I just couldn't bear it any longer. All I could think of was Leon. It's been three years, Dad. Three years without any word from the Navy or the Red Cross . . .' her voice broke and she began to weep, the rigid self-control she had exercised for so long deserting her.

'I've been so *certain* he was taken prisoner,' she said, burying her head against his chest as he put an arm comfortingly around her shoulder, 'but if he had been, surely he would have managed to get word to me by now? Surely by now I would know if he was on his way home to me?'

'If you were his wife and legal next of kin, perhaps you would have heard,' her father said gently. 'But you're not his wife and that may be one explanation why the authorities, despite their promises to the contrary, have failed to contact you. Another thing to take into account is that if Leon *was* taken prisoner, then he was taken prisoner by German forces operating in Arctic waters and he might very well have been despatched to a prison camp in a part of Russia occupied by them. If he has been, then it's not surprising there has been no news. You've been strong for so long, *Liebling*, and you're just going to have to be strong for a little longer.'

'But what if it isn't just for a little longer, Dad?' Her voice cracked with pain. 'What if Leon doesn't come home? What if I'm going to have to live without him for the rest of my life?'

There was no reply he could give her and he didn't attempt one. The next few weeks would bring the answer to her question and when it came, however difficult it might be, he knew that from somewhere she would find the strength to live with it.

On Wednesday, totally unannounced, Danny Collins marched into Magnolia Square, his hair glinting red in the summer sunlight.

'It's Danny!' Billy yelled, slithering down from his perch high in Miss Godfrey's magnolia tree. 'Someone run and tell 'is Mum and Dad! Someone run and tell our Carrie!'

By the time Danny reached the bottom end of the Square he was like the Pied Piper, with Billy leading the way in front of him, banging two hastily purloined dustbin lids together, Beryl skipping at his side, her hand held in his, Daisy and Jenny and Matthew trooping behind him not knowing who he was but knowing he must be someone special, Charlie loping in their wake, Queenie at his heels, and Nibbo trying to catch up with the procession, eager to be one of the first of Danny's neighbours to welcome him back home.

A dark-haired figure walking into the Square from Magnolia Hill stood suddenly stock still. She had been carrying two bags of shopping and as realization dawned and her eyes widened she dropped both bags abruptly onto the pavement, uncaring of the eggs that broke and the fruit that bruised.

'Danny!' she shrieked. 'Oh my good God! *Danny!*'

No-one had ever seen Carrie run so fast. She streaked past her gate and past Mavis's gate, her mass of dark hair tumbling around a face radiant with joy.

Daniel, who had been trimming his garden hedge, dropped his shears.

'It's our Danny!' he said disbelievingly and then, raising his voice, 'Hettie! Hettie! Come quick! Danny's home. Our boy's come home!'

'It was lovely to see them both,' Hettie said later to Miriam, dabbing her eyes dry with the corner of her pinafore. 'He just swept her off her feet and it was as if he'd never been away.'

'Well, let's 'ope Kate's fella comes 'ome soon and sweeps 'er off 'er feet,' Miriam said, not wanting to think of anyone grieving when their two families were so happy. 'It'd be a sin and shame for 'er to 'ave to bring up three kiddies on 'er own, especially when one of 'em's an orphan she took in out of the kindness of 'er 'eart.'

On Saturday morning the weather was glorious. Daniel and Bob Giles hauled trestle tables out of the church hall and set them in a long continuous line down the grass outside the church. Miss Godfrey and Miss Helliwell fixed white sheets of paper to them with drawing-pins to serve as tablecloths. Nibbo was in and out of every house gathering up every wooden chair he could find. Danny and the landlord of The Swan rolled a great barrel of beer out of The Swan's cellars and up Magnolia Hill, placing it strategically outside the rose-covered ruins of what had once been the Misses Helliwell's home.

'Do you think fifteen of these are going to be enough?'

Hettie asked the world at large as she ferried a bowl of quivering multicoloured jelly from her kitchen to the paper covered tables, a Union Jack jauntily pinned to her hat.

'They'll do for me, Hettie,' Nibbo said, depositing his latest haul of chairs beside the top table, 'but I don't know what everyone else is going to have!'

Charlie was trundling Hettie and Albert's piano down their garden path. 'Whereabouts do you fink this should go?' he queried, 'It ain't 'alf 'eavy. Do you think I should just leave it 'ere, near the gate?'

'I need some more teapots!' Nellie Miller bellowed. 'An urn's all right if everyone's filing up to it, but for a do like this I need teapots!'

Leah put a huge plate of almond whirls next to one of Hettie's mammoth bowls of jelly. 'I'm doing some chicken, *gedampt*, just the way Carrie and Danny like it,' she said to Hettie. 'And some blintz's with cream cheese and jam. And bagels.'

Mavis plonked a bottle of lemonade, a bottle of cream soda and a bottle of raspberry fizz down on one of the tables. 'That's our Billy seen to,' she said, crimson painted nails flashing as she dusted her hands together. 'Now why the 'ell couldn't someone have had the sense to invite some Americans? Gawd knows what they might have brought with 'em. They might even have brought some blueberry pie!'

Kate put a huge plateful of bread and butter next to Leah's almond whirls. She had barely slept the night before. For hour after hour she had lain awake thinking of Leon. Had she been foolishly stubborn in clinging so long to the belief that he had survived the sinking of his ship? Ever since they had been children Carrie had told her she was as stubborn as a mule. Had her stubbornness, this time, led her into living in a fool's paradise? Had she been wrong in believing that Leon was still alive? Was he dead, and had he been dead for three long years?

'Let's 'ave some balloons tied to the backs of the chairs and the trees,' Nellie ordered, looking remarkably like Henry VIII as she stood full square on the grass, her hands on her massive hips and her swollen legs straddled. 'And what about a bit o' bunting? We must 'ave a bit o' bunting.'

Emily Helliwell was wheeling Esther out of Nellie's garden and Kate went to help her negotiate the clumsy wheelchair down the kerb and into the road.

'Thank you, my dear,' Esther said sunnily. 'Isn't it a beautiful day? It reminds me of our celebrations for the Relief of Mafeking.'

Kate smiled in response but her heart was aching. How would she get through life without Leon as her lover and her friend? How would she survive if she never saw his crinkly dark hair and dusky face and sunny smile ever again?

'Oh, Leon!' she whispered passionately beneath her breath. 'I *need* you! Come home! Oh, please, *please* come home!'

'It's about time this party got under way,' Albert said, putting boxes of drinking straws at strategic intervals down the length of the tables. 'Let's get the kids sat down before Billy Lomax scavenges all the fairy-cakes. Play a tune on the Joanna, Hettie. What about "Knees Up Mother Brown" for starters?'

Kate stood near the top trestle table, the only one not singing lustily. Ellen Pierce had come over to Magnolia Square for the day to join in the celebrations. She visited often and Kate knew that Ellen came not only to see her, but to see Carl. There were going to be wedding bells there soon, perhaps even sooner than for Bob Giles and Ruth Fairbairn.

Carrie and Danny were standing with their arms around each other's waist, little Rose clinging on to Danny's hand as though she was never, ever, going to let him go.

Charlie was polkaring a pearl-earringed, tweed-garbed

Harriet down the length of the pavement, much to Beryl and Billy's open-mouthed astonishment.

Miriam and Albert were doing one of their famed knees-ups.

It seemed that everywhere she looked people were in happy couples or if, like Mavis and Christina, their menfolks arms weren't yet around their waists, they were radiantly confident that they soon would be.

'I have an announcement to make!' Bob Giles said, satisfied that everyone had a drink of some kind in their hands and taking advantage of a brief pause in Hettie's enthusiastic piano-playing.

' 'e's gettin' married!' Billy shouted through a mouthful of cream cake. 'The vicar's gettin' spliced!'

'No I'm not, Billy.' Bob Giles said easily as Ruth Fairbairn flushed scarlet. 'Though I might very well be doing so in the near future. The banns are going to be called tomorrow, however, for two of our friends and it's fitting that this joyous celebration today should be crowned by the news of their happiness.'

Kate's eyes shot towards her father and Ellen. Surely her father would have told her first? Or had he wanted it to be a happy surprise for her?

'Raise your glasses please,' Bob Giles said, beaming around at his flock, 'To Harriet and Charlie! And may they know years and years of blissful married life together!'

Utter bedlam broke out. Hettie sprinted from her place at one of the tables back to the piano and began thumping out a deafening rendering of 'Here Comes the Bride'. Daniel put his fingers in his mouth and uttered a piercing whistle that had every dog in the vicinity running madly in his direction. Nibbo began whirling his football-rattle. Miriam ran up the length of the tables to where Charlie and Harriet were sitting and to Harriet's astonishment and Charlie's bemusement planted huge kisses on their cheeks.

Kate's eyes met Carrie's. 'I told you so,' Carrie called

across to her laughingly. 'Though I bet it's something Moshambo didn't know!'

Despite the sickening apprehension in her heart Kate laughed back and then her eyes went beyond Carrie, down to the bottom end of the Square, and her laughter faded. An athletic-looking, broad-chested figure had just turned into the Square from Magnolia Hill. Though the sun was in her eyes she could see that he had a kit-bag over his shoulder and that he was in naval uniform.

The blood drummed in her ears. He was dark. Very dark.

'How about giving us a song, Kate,' Nibbo was demanding. 'How about "We'll Meet Again?" '

Kate wasn't listening to him. Her heart was hammering so hard she thought it was going to burst. It was Leon. It had to be Leon. It couldn't possibly be anyone else.

'Let's 'ave somethin' with a bit more oomph to it,' Mavis said, standing up from the table in a cotton leopard-printed skirt so tight it fitted like a second skin and peep-toed sandals so high it was a miracle she could walk in them. 'Lift me on the Joanna, Nibbo, and I'll give you "Boogie-Woogie Bugle Boy." '

'What's the matter, Mummy,' Luke was saying, pulling on her dress. 'Why are you looking so funny? Why won't you sing for Mr Nibbs?'

Very gently she lifted his hand away from her skirt. He'd come home. He'd said he would come home and he had. How could she ever have doubted him? She took a couple of steps forwards, her legs so shaky she was terrified they were going to let her down.

She saw Leon's face split into a wide, joyous smile. She saw him toss his kit-bag over the nearest garden gate and break into a run.

'Leon!' she cried and then, her legs shaky no longer, she was running, running as she had never run in her life before. As he sprinted towards her and the gap

430

between them closed she felt as if her heart was going to burst.

'Oh, Leon! *Leon!*' she gasped, hurtling into his arms. 'You're home! You're *home!*'

As her hands slid up around his neck and he crushed her against him she knew absolute joy. From now on nothing and no-one would ever part them again. From now on they were going to be a family. From now on their love was going to be a refuge and a peace that no hardship or trouble would ever be able to storm.

His mouth was hot and sweet on hers. Their tongues touched and slipped past each other. Dimly, in the distance, she was aware of a storm of cheering and whistling. Somewhere on the Thames tug-boat horns blasted. 'See, the Conquering Hero Comes' was being played loud and hard on the piano.

When at last he raised his head from hers she looked up into his dear, kind, sunny-natured face and said in a voice thick with love, 'We have a baby, Leon! We have a son!'

'I know,' he said, his voice raw with emotion, all the love he felt for her blazing in his amber-brown eyes. 'I received your letter the morning we were torpedoed. It's been in a pocket next to my heart every day and night since.'

He raised his head slightly, looking towards the groaningly-laden tables and the bunting and the balloons, saying with a catch in his throat, 'I think it's time you introduced us.'

'His name is Luke,' she said, as with their arms around each other's waists they began to walk to where their family and neighbours were waiting for them, 'and he was two years old last September.'

As Daisy and Matthew began to run towards them holding on to the hands of a toddler with a mop of unruly dark curls and an instantly recognizable beaming smile, and as Charlie led the throng in the Square in an exuberant rendering of 'For He's A Jolly Good Fellow', neither Kate nor Leon had the slightest shadow of doubt that they were the luckiest and happiest two people in the whole wide world.

THE END